SOL & LUNE

BOOK ONE

KATHRYN MOON

This is a Reverse Harem Paranormal Romance and is not suited for those under the age of 18.

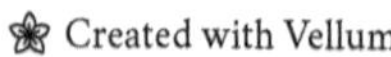 Created with Vellum

Alicia, I knew the second this book began, it belonged to you. You are a source of inspiration and joy and I love you.

CONTENTS

Part IV
THE PRISONER OF OSHAIN

I

THE GENERAL'S BED

Lumen picked the hem of her apron up and wiped the sweat from her brow, smearing the earth from the fields further into her skin. Horse hooves clapped up the road behind her, but the onions were nearly picked and fall could turn to winter any night now. In her experience, a horse running at that pace never carried good news and losing a harvest to a frost wouldn't make that better.

"Lady Fenn!"

She wrestled the last three heads of onion up from the earth, dropping them into the wheelbarrow, and turned to see Oliver Spragg racing up the dusty road that lined the field. She wiped the sweat from her neck and chest and dropped the apron as he tugged on the reins, thighs gripping hard to the tired old ribs of the horse.

"Who won?" she asked him, but the answer was written in the lines at the corners of his eyes, the way his mouth clenched as he stared back at her.

Stalor's army gained more miles of Oshain land in the war. Green hills, dense woods, and rich farmland trampled beneath the boots of soldiers who'd been fighting battles of territory for the past two decades. Her head spun and she thought she might faint, wished she could blame it on a day's worth of harvesting instead of the terror that lurked in her heart.

"Westbrook and his men are nearly arrived," he said. He shifted to dismount and Lumen shook her head, pushing strands of white blonde hair out of her eyes, feeling the fever of being out in the sun too long lingering in her cheeks.

"Go to the tenants, tell them to stay inside. I'll meet the General at the Manor," she said, gathering her breath.

"Lady Fenn," Oliver murmured, but his fist was already tightening around the reins.

"Go," she repeated, keeping her eyes off Oliver's left shoulder, where his sleeve was knotted off before the elbow he'd lost in battle.

He kicked the horse back into motion and Lumen spared herself a second to watch him. Handsome, quiet Oliver, a man she would never have seen or spoken to if not for the war taking her father, her brothers, and all the local men old enough to serve. The setting sun glowed golden over his shoulders, a dark trail of sweat against the spine of his shirt. She caught herself before her staring could be called mooning, not that there was anyone out to spy on her these days, and turned away.

She frowned down at the wheelbarrow full of onions. She didn't like the thought of appearing at the Manor at the same moment as the Stone General and his men, covered in field dust and hefting farm work. But without the onions there would be very little to serve tonight that wouldn't be needed later in the winter months.

The enemy is coming to claim my home and I am worrying over onions, Lumen thought. She wrapped her tired fingers around the handles and heaved, pushing home. Her heart began to thump in her chest, blood rushing in her ears.

Word had come from the Mallen estate in spring. Westbrook and his men were not *kind* to the estates they claimed. Lady Myra Mallen had seen Westbrook eyeing her eldest daughter and, thinking it might curry some favor for the family, sent the young woman into his bedchamber within a week of the army's arrival. From what Lumen could gather from whispers, Imogen Mallen had been passed around Westbrook and his soldiers like a jug of ale before her mother finally took her and her sisters off to the convents.

Lumen could leave for the convent now. Drop the wheelbarrow in the road. Forget the onions. Forget the Manor. The tenants.

Except the only tenants left were too old or infirm to leave on their own. And Oliver Spragg. They'd all end up dead if she left.

She took a shortcut through the field up to the back of the Manor, stomach turning and mind determined. She would stay on the estate as her mother had bid her. The land belonged to her mother's mother and all the women before them. It was alright for her brothers to go and die in the war. Lumen must stay and die on the estate. Preferably on her knees in the chapel.

The Manor house was sprawling and spindling, surrounding a circular courtyard at the heart of the structure and a wing that branched off into a narrow hall, leading to the Lunar chapel at the back of the building. She reached the kitchen doors first, heaving open the hatch to the cellar and dumping the onions in with a grimace. It would have to do for the moment and hopefully the cats were keeping the mice in line.

She left the barrow by the door and dashed inside to the sink, fingers tangling in the knot of her apron. It hadn't kept her clean, the cuffs of her dress were stained with sweat and dirt, as was her hem, but it kept the worst of the mess off the front of her. She pumped water into the sink and grabbed the bristle brush, scrubbing her hands red and raw and digging the bristles under her nails. She splashed cool water over her face and frowned when it ran in muddy rivulets back down into her palms.

Maybe it would be best if she didn't look her finest.

Somewhere, far off, the sound of horse hooves approached. The echo built through the empty Manor until it resembled distant thunder. Lumen had never minded storms, even as a child. It was easier to pretend what was coming was a nice, sturdy raincloud—to whet the crops' thirst and make harvesting a muddy business—than to know it was her doom riding in.

She filled the largest pitcher with fresh water and stacked the most cups she could carry onto a tray before leaving the kitchen. She crossed hallways and passed the corridor to the dining room, taking herself out to the courtyard. There was a mirror hanging in the hall by the doorway and she stopped at the sight of herself. Her nose and cheeks were burnt red from sun after a summer's worth of work, but she'd be nearly moon white again once winter set in. One eyebrow was darkened from floss blonde to brown by mud. She set the pitcher on the table in front of the mirror and rubbed the mud away, skin peeling and stinging.

Her face was featureless in the dark, pale and shadowed, strange gray eyes set too wide apart, blonde hair tangled and dusted with earth. *My silly little moon*, her mother's voice rang in her head.

"Mother Lune, protect me," she whispered at her reflection. Except she was not Mother Lune and she could not grant such wishes.

The horses were arriving, men's voices shouting. Lumen picked up her pitcher and crossed the wide, round courtyard, birds calling warnings from the rooftops. She could see them through the windows as she reached the grand front hall, filling up the drive with horses, carts, men on foot. She left the water and cups on the entry table, men's laughter tearing through the silence of the house as she opened the front doors. Their voices quieted as she stood on the steps.

She knew at once which one was *him*, the General. The uniform might have been enough—that shocking red coat with its black iron and gold plated armor—but it was the way the other men moved out of his way before he had to ask, clearing their horses to the side to make room for him to appear in front of her. His coal stallion kicked stones up her steps as the soldiers' laughter died and he stayed grinning. He had that Stalor skin, tanned and browned, but his hair was inky black, a mane of tangled curls. There was a strangely twisted scar running down his left cheek, still dark, recent.

His eyes ran over the length of her, an amused twitch of his brow as he saw the filthy hem of her skirt.

"Go and fetch your lady," he said to her, and at the sound of his voice—dark and grim—Lumen understood why he was called the Stone General. "We're coming in either way. If she's hiding we'll find her and that won't be any better than greeting us at the door as her station demands."

Go and run out the back and then let them search the house and find no one. Lumen swallowed down the thought. They would ransack the chapel and sell all her family possessions and that would be the *true* end of her family.

"I am the lady of the house," Lumen said, refusing to shrink although her heart punished her with pounding twice as fast.

The men behind Westbrook shifted, exchanged snickers and glances, and anxiety spiked in Lumen's chest. She had contradicted him.

"Lady Fenn was meant to be some daft old Lunar," he answered her, eyes narrowing on the mud splatters on her simple dress. "They told us in Mallen."

Lumen's mouth hung foolishly open for a moment, wondering how to answer that respectfully, to both him and her own mother. "Then you were lied to. Lady Alana Fenn was my mother. She is dead, sir."

"And your staff?"

"Gone." Dead or left.

"Who's been tending your damn fields then?" he asked, leaning forward in his saddle, dark brow tangled together.

"I have. And... those left of the tenants who are able."

He frowned at her. She was already a disappointment and she didn't know if this was a good or bad thing. For a moment, some wild bout of imagination struck her and she thought they might just...leave her be.

Westbrook turned to look at his army and the men in the yard were watching her and not him.

"Well, you have company now," Westbrook said and it was not her imagination that his tone turned darker with the words. "How many can you house?"

Her heart sank to the ground. "A... a dozen, maybe." There were rooms enough but it would stretch the food thin to serve that many.

Westbrook raised an eyebrow at her. "Make it two." He

turned to the men behind him, calling out orders. "Finley, pick your patients. Jones, tell the others to make camp."

"But, sir-" It was an enormous man in the front seat of a cart with a face that looked like it needed immediate attention and hair cut so close and unevenly he might as well have cut it himself with a broadsword.

"Send them to camp, Jones!" Westbrook barked, and then with a swift ease he jumped down from his horse, passing the reins over to a towering man with long fingers paired and wrapped in bandages. The General walked in slow, crooked steps up the stairs until his face was level with hers, lips curling and dark eyes gleaming. "We are *so* grateful for the hospitality, Lady Fenn."

THE CHAPEL WAS LOCKED and Lumen ignored the request for the key, watching as men carried in stretchers of the injured soldiers. She pressed her lips shut as Westbrook plucked a few silver ornaments off the mantle and tossed them to a young boy who chased his heels.

"Sell these for the most you can get for them. Casks of ale... some animals. Ask Healer Brink for his list."

Lumen didn't know the worth of the trinkets, they were old and tarnished, but she held her tongue and kept her chin to her chest until some request was made of her.

"Show me the best of the rooms with eastern light."

It was her room, but that hardly seemed to matter. Within weeks the house likely wouldn't even belong to her. If she was still in it. If she was still alive.

He stood by the foot of the bed, staring out the windows onto the squash patch. Her bed was unmade, the sheepskin kicked back from when she'd woken at dawn. She liked the eastern light too, it was the only thing that dragged her out of bed in the morning. The narrow bed frame pushed to the wall, the red polish of the wood worn away in some places and the canopy caked with dust. He made the small room smell like horses and metal and sweat.

"This is yours," he said, staring at the dent she'd left in the mattress that morning.

"Yes, sir."

"Small for the lady of the house."

"My mother's was grander but it's on the north end."

"You didn't take it?"

Lumen's mouth parted, words dying on her tongue as he stared at her. "It- it was hers."

He grunted and Lumen thought that was the end of it. She spotted her nightdress on a chair by the door and realized she would have to find somewhere else to sleep that night.

"It would have been better if you had family here," he said suddenly, just as she was sneaking to the door. He turned and Lumen froze as his eyes studied her. "Even a little lad of a brother might have been able to speak up for you."

"I was the youngest. As far as I know I'm the only one of my siblings left," she said, tucking her night dress behind her back and hiding it there.

Westbrook frowned at her, deep lines across his forehead. She didn't mean to skid backwards, pressing herself to the door, but he came toward her with such a furious expression on his face that she acted out of instinct, wincing as her head thunked against the wood.

He grasped her face in blood encrusted fingertips and tipped her chin to the side, eyes studying her like a flank of meat. "You have a funny look about you," he said. "You remind me of..." *the moon,* she thought, "...a fish," he concluded with a sneer, hand gesturing up to her wide-set eyes.

Lumen's eyes widened, staring at him out of the corners. He reminded her of some enormous snarling black cat but that didn't have quite the same effect as calling someone a fish so she kept it to herself.

"But you're well-formed and they haven't seen soft flesh in some weeks," he said, finger tapping on her cheek. "Lady Fenn, I'm afraid I have to offer you some choices. You can come to this bed tonight and please me, and you'll only have one man gasping on your neck at night. If that doesn't suit, you can try and run from here. When my men find you what happens next will be none of my concern. Or I suppose you can lock yourself in some cellar, but I don't like your odds there either. Jones is a determined fuck and his mother was a whore so he won't touch them for company. But you? You're just his type."

He pressed in close, the metal plating of armor scraping against her dress, digging into her breasts and soft stomach. He was just tall enough that his lips came to her forehead, not that he set them there. His hands pressed to her belly, fingers splayed out over her ribs and Lumen held her breath, eyes fixed to his chin. Then he reached behind her, snatching the night dress out of her grip and tossing it back to the bed, as if she'd already made up her mind.

"You won't need that."

He left her in the room, skin burning where he'd set his hands. Her cheeks were hot and she couldn't force her eyes to the bed, a distorted vision of them together there racing through her head, details too foggy and nerves too frayed to make sense of how she felt. Only that the heat began to spread beneath her skin, rushing into her veins and turning her muscles weak.

WESTBROOK'S MEN BUILT A BONFIRE IN THE HEART OF THE courtyard, roasting meat over the fire as Lumen served them a thrown together course of onion broth and warm loaves of bread. There wasn't much else she could do for them but pour the ale they'd brought with them. As long as she kept doing that no one complained that the broth was thin and the loaves were coarse.

"Walk slower by me, little spirit," a man, a giant, rasped at her as he sat on a bench by her hip. It was Jones, the one from the yard who'd been sent to turn the army away from the house, who apparently wanted her 'soft flesh.' He grinned, face lit red by firelight, and the stitches in his cheek stretched but he didn't seem to notice. "Haven't smelled anything as fresh as you in months."

"Gideon," Westbrook growled at the man.

Jones just winked a swollen eye at her as she ducked back into the shadows, finding a seat in an archway where she could watch the men from a safe distance. There were only six of them. Westbrook sat in a chair he'd dragged out from her father's study. The tall healer with bandaged fingers, huddled cross-legged in the grass, sopping his soup up with chunks of bread. Gideon Jones, drank and twisted in his seat to watch her. The scrappy boy who ran errands was huddled on the ground, his cloak wrapped tight around him, hood dangling over his face as he snapped discarded bones with surprising strength and sucked the marrow out. The remaining two sat with their backs to Lumen, a pair of average looking men whose dark expressions made her skin crawl, and who she had yet to hear speak a single word.

More men were laid out in the dining room that had been transformed into Healer Brink's makeshift hospital. The man had come into her kitchen while she was making the soup and raided her stores without a word. She considered telling him that her mother's office was better suited to his needs, full of herbs and tinctures, and then remembered that these men were not here to help her. She did not need to help them.

Her eyes scanned the group around the fire, snagging against General Westbrook's stare. Her skin went numb and her stomach flipped as she looked at him. Her head had been full of him for hours, brain skipping over and over again on his offer. Her choices.

Run. Hide. Go to his- her- *his* bed.

"Purest skin I've ever seen," Gideon said and Lumen's eyes fell to her lap. "You ever seen skin that white?"

"Jones, enough," the healer snapped.

"Grant's ass is that white," the boy chirped up. "You seen Grant's ass? Hand to His Light I thought the moon was setting in my damn tent when Grant's ass fell out of bed, buck naked."

The men laughed but when she risked another glance up Westbrook was still staring at her, eyes dark and narrowed on her, flicking to Gideon.

"She looks like a ghost," Gideon murmured, and Lumen made the mistake of meeting his eyes, earning another bruised wink.

She leapt up from the archway, darting into the nearest hall, making her way back to the kitchens. From a window she heard the General snarl.

"If a single one of you so much as gets up to piss an inch farther away than those arches, I'll chop your cock off and cook it over that flame for the dogs to eat."

She washed in the kitchen, wondering how long she had.

How long to decide. Would Westbrook's protection stick if she was caught by one of the men on her way to his bed, or did she have to be there, waiting on the mattress for him to appear?

There are worse things than marital rites. It had been strange talk for a death bed. Lumen had sat there at her mother's side a decade ago, only just having started her courses, and listened to a winding, disjointed explanation of what went on in a marriage bed. Or between lovers. And it had sounded strange at the time, if not completely awful. She understood it better now, had felt flashes of those urges watching Oliver in the fields, back working as he harvested with her.

Except the General is not my husband or my lover, she thought.

Voices echoed in the hall and she froze at the pump, listening and trying to catch what direction they were heading in. To her? To their beds? Would she meet them on her way to...

To the chapel, to lock herself in and hide?

Or to Westbrook?

She believed him. She believed that they would find her, in one place or another. She was less convinced of whether or not it would be better for her with him. But her mother had said it might be pleasant with the right person.

Lumen took the servants stairs up to the second story, listening at the false panel until the hall was quiet and the right number of doors had been snapped shut. She tiptoed to the bedroom that no longer belonged to her and then raised her fist to knock.

No, he hadn't said to ask. He'd said to come or not come.

She opened the door and Westbrook's head jerked up from where he'd been perched on the edge of the bed, yanking at his boots. He had an angry twist to his expression as he saw her but it fell apart quickly, brief and stark surprise on his face. She stepped inside and shut the door.

"What if I don't know how to please a man?" she asked, breaking the silence abruptly.

His jaw went slack and then snapped shut and he swallowed, eyes falling back to his hands wrapped around his boot. "We're not especially complicated. Undress. I'll... wash a bit."

"I can help—" she said, starting to cross over, kneel at his feet and he jerked away from her, his eyes narrowing on her face.

"Undress," he said, words harder. "Light a candle. Smelling the inside of my boots won't make this night any easier for you."

There was a candle flickering in the far corner of the room. Did she *want* him to see her? It'd been years since there was anyone else at the Manor with her and the last time she was naked in front of someone it was one of the nannies, readying her for a bath. And did she really want to see *him*? The men of her family had left the Manor one by one, all gone before she reached womanhood. She and Oliver Spragg worked together in the fields but they were never alone with walls surrounding them.

She glanced out of the corner of her eye, watched him tugging the shirt—once white, now stained brown and yellow with old blood and sweat—over his head. His back was marred with shiny slashes, puckering scars from blades and whips, but his shoulders were broad and knotted with muscle and his waist tapered in. He was a little slighter than Oliver but more like carved gold and… yes, she did want to look at him, the warmth below her belly said as much.

She lit the candle by her bed and then twisted her arms behind her back, pulling the knot of her laces and starting the frustrating process of freeing herself. She hadn't bothered properly taking this dress off since she went swimming the week before, it was too difficult to get in and out of the thing.

A shadow moved across the wall and Lumen's breath stilled in her chest as a hand wrapped around her side, another batting her hands out of the way. Quick fingers tugged laces free, yanking the fabric taut around her breasts with each pull.

"Not all the way out," she said—blurted—and winced as he stilled at her back. "I'll- I'll just have to put them through again."

He's going to toss me out, she thought in the following silence. And then, with a little more care, the dress began to sag around her chest. His breath stirred on the back of her neck, brushing against the curling hairs that'd escaped her braid. He didn't wait for her to be ready, hooking thumbs into the shoulders of the dress and yanking it down to her hips, hands sliding under the fabric against her hip bones, shimmying her free until she was standing in nothing but her shift, candlelight running through the thin material.

"You can leave that on if you want, but it's not going to stop me from touching you," he said.

He pressed his chest to her back as if to prove his point, hands stroking over her stomach, the shift rising with his touch until he was holding her breasts gently in his hands, weighing them. He squeezed and Lumen gasped, arching, her body landing against his, feeling his length softly nudging her back. She swallowed and craned her neck to look at him and then he was gone, sliding onto the bed.

She pulled the tie at her neck free and let the shift fall to the floor where her dress lay. Lunars weren't shy about their bodies, but she was. *He might just as easily have seen me bare if he passed the road near the lake where I swam,* she told herself as she turned to the bed, feeling his eyes traveling her skin. He didn't look pleased or angry or disappointed. He looked as if he was mapping her.

There was dark hair curling over his chest, a new terrain of scars on his skin, all the work of blades. The hair turned into a trail down between thick thighs, nestling his cock, which twitched at her attention.

"You have to be in the bed for this to work," he said without expression, just a deepening of his voice to prove his interest.

She took a deep breath, watching him stare at her breasts as they rose and fell, and followed him onto the mattress. It was barely wide enough for the pair of them but since he took her by the hips dragging her down to her back and then flicked her thighs apart with a soft touch, his knees landing between hers, the space didn't matter. When his skin hit hers, scorching and heavy, Lumen stiffened on the mattress, eyes staring wide up at the canopy of her bed. He was everywhere, chest pressing to hers and hip bones digging into her soft thighs.

Fingers tilted her face to the wall and Lumen froze as hot breath cascaded over her neck, sour like beer, salted from meat.

Like a dragon, she thought. And then his mouth was on her skin, just below her ear, a wet, fiery tongue flicking out, lips sucking. His thumb stroked up from her chin, pressing to her bottom lip until she opened to him. He scraped the pad over her teeth, a purr rumbling against her throat as he dressed her neck in licks and nibbles. His hips shifted against hers and Lumen felt his cock nudging against the delicate flesh between her thighs.

She knew a little about the matter from the words of her mother and in the five years since, occasionally, in curiosity, she tried to mimic the act of sex with herself, nudging her fingers around and inside herself. It had mostly been an odd feeling, sometimes stirring. She braced herself for his intrusion. He was much larger than the two fingers she'd tested herself with.

But he didn't push in. His thumb slid into her mouth, over her tongue, and then his index finger, as he continued the soft mouthing up and down her neck.

"Suck," he said in the hollow of her throat.

She sucked on his finger, surprised at the odd instruction, at the way it made her squirm softly beneath him as he pumped the digit against her tongue.

Westbrook was nibbling on her collarbone when his hand pulled free of her lips. His back arched and then that hand was between her legs, stroking lazily against her cunt.

"Ah!" She froze again, fingers digging into the sheets as he touched her. It was as if he didn't know where to find her opening. Were they not all in roughly the same place? He seemed to be searching and in the searching he was… Lumen shook on the mattress, voice choking in her throat as he fumbled his thumb too high, sparking fire under her skin.

"Touch me, Lady Fenn," he ordered, and her fists flew off the bed and against his neck and back, holding him to her. He huffed a laugh and she realized he'd meant his cock, but then his thumb swirled over that same spot and Lumen dug her nails into his skin. He groaned, mouth open wide over her skin, like he was nursing on her flavor, and she knew more by instinct that she'd done the first thing right.

Please him, she remembered. So she raked her nails over his back, feeling the ridges of scars, marveling at the way he stiffened and shook on top of her. She was so distracted by the needy clasp of his lips, by the pattern his thumb made on the height of her sex, that it caught her by surprise when the first finger slid inside.

She stiffened again and he growled, head ducking down between her breasts. Coarse stubble scraped over delicate skin and then his tongue traced the outline of her nipple, drawing it between his teeth, toying with the tip.

Her lips were open on a silent, terrified, awed scream. His free hand worked its way beneath her waist, tipping her hips up to the mercy of his hand between her thighs, one finger pumping softly inside of her, thumb making her sizzle on the sheets. She forgot her orders to touch, that she ought to attend to his cock so that he could start the matter, and instead slid one hand up into the dark tangle of curls on his head. It was as if he'd hooked a line between his teeth around her breast and his finger inside of her. She started to move in time with his mouth and finger, feeling him slide easily inside her, feeling that promise of pleasure her mother had mentioned.

He fit another finger inside of her and the pleasure skirted out of reach at the onslaught of strange, shocking fullness. Westbrook's fingers were thicker and longer than hers and she wished she could push him out, let his thumb carry on its business without the trouble of having anything forced inside of her.

"No," she whimpered, as he lifted his head from her breast. She thought she caught a glimpse of a grin, dark eyes glancing against hers, and then she was arching, gasping out as he reached the neglected breast, biting against the flesh before delivering the same treatment to her nipple.

His fingers inside of her stretched and pumped, thumb petting at that same little nub of thrilling nerves. Her heels dug into the mattress as she started to ride his hand until there was a wet, slipping sound, his tongue lapping at her breasts, hot breath panting over the wet marks and drawing out gooseflesh.

The third finger was suddenly a welcome thing, filling a need she hadn't realized she was craving until it was being satisfied.

She sobbed softly as he pulled his fingers free of her, thumb retreating, and he hissed as she tugged hard on his hair.

"What a wanton little lady," he hummed, surging up over her.

Seeing his face above hers was a startling reminder of what was happening, skin and fevered need cooling as he braced himself with one corded arm above her. The scar on his cheek was stark in the candlelight, skin barely seamed together and he was staring down between them, lining himself up. Lumen's thighs shone white around his bronzed hips and she released a strangled squeak as he stroked his cock between her thighs and then pushed inside. Her hands grasped his shoulders, watching stunned as he thrust softly, inch at a time until he was filling places he hadn't prepared her for.

His chest sank onto hers, one arm cradling her shoulders beneath him, the other tilting her hips until she thought she might choke with the feel of him inside of her. He groaned as his hips nestled into hers, body grinding, brief sparks of early pleasure stirred. She covered his back with her arms again, studying his muscles with her fingertips, watching his eyes shut and a sigh escape thin lips.

Her legs were hanging open like a butterfly's wings and when she drew her knees up, wrapping herself around him, she was rewarded with a furrowed brow and the first thrust.

It ached, a hollow, stinging feeling, with a brief exclamation of that bright pleasure as he nuzzled his pelvic bone against her. He lifted her shoulders, teeth wrapping around the curve of her shoulder as his hips churned and fucked into her. When she tightened her thighs around him his weight landed heavily against her, burying her beneath him, skin slapping, his growl vibrating into her shoulder.

There it was again, that shimmery warmth in her stomach. Lumen shut her eyes, lips parting, breath catching in tight sighs and gasps as the thunder of him inside her began to echo in her blood, turning sweeter. He was sucking on her skin like he might drink her and when she clutched her hands against his shoulders, trying to twist herself to take more, his rutting turned frenzied, riding her up the bed.

"Oh gods," she whispered, feeling a sudden cliff's edge arriving. "Oh Mother!"

Westbrook barked a laugh against her at her praise of the Lunar goddess and the vibration of him rang deep inside of her. She felt herself start to flutter around his length and his head arched back, a loud groan of pleasure singing in her ear, as he dug himself deeper inside of her, faster, harder, faster!

"Fuck," he snarled out, turning the word into a chant.

She was tight as a bowstring around him when there was a sudden gush of heat inside of her and Westbrook shook and shuddered and collapsed, hips kicking in softer, briefer thrusts. She was catching her breath beneath him as he grew heavy and still, her eyes wide and mouth open and nails digging into his back. And that steep, startling, brilliant edge began to back slowly away, her nerves crawling under her skin. His arms circled her back, holding her so tight she thought she might lose her breath, face buried into her neck.

She wanted to weep and she didn't understand why.

It hadn't hurt, not really, not for long. Moments had been... near perfect.

She... she hadn't wanted it to *end*.

He was breathing deeply on top of her and she wondered if he would sleep like this, crushing her beneath him. Then his thumb stroked the skin of her back and Lumen had to resist the urge to scream, to roll them on the bed and ride him as he had ridden her. But his cock was softening, slowly loosening from inside her, a wet dribbling following.

He turned them suddenly, rolling to his side and taking her with him and the jostling was- was almost enough to—

Lumen gasped, clutching tight, and he pulled away, arms retreating, dropping her to the mattress. He stared straight up at the canopy, a light glitter of sweat against his temples, and then his eyes shut, sighing heavily through his nose. He rolled, his back facing her, and his leg hooked a sheet, kicking it up to cover them to their hips.

She couldn't breathe, couldn't move. She ached, felt hollow, as if he'd carved away a piece of her and left nothing to replace the space. Her fingers slid over her belly, down to the sticky fluid leaking out of her.

"Go to Healer Brink in the morning," Westbrook said to the wall. "He'll have a tea you can drink to keep your courses steady. Avoid pregnancy."

She bit her lips between her teeth because any answer would be a scream or a sob. It hadn't hurt. It had been awkward and then thrilling, aching and then desperate. *She hadn't wanted it to end.*

Westbrook ended up on his stomach, snoring faintly into her pillow, before she remembered to blow out the candle. The world was a deep blue outside, the moon hanging somewhere above the eye of her window. She shifted on the bed, watching his back in its steady breathing rhythm, and then slid off the mattress, picking the shift up off the floor and dragging it over her head. He stayed sleeping and she watched him for a long time, anger growing warm in her blood.

She surrendered. Was it worth it to give up her home, her land, her food and all her family's valuables just to survive? Was it worth giving up her flesh, her own understanding of herself?

She would not be his last conquest. The armies would turn her fields into barren worthless land, they would strip her home of worth until it was a shell. And if he could do this to her, make her crave, with just one night's touch… what would she be before he left?

Lumen tiptoed to her dresser, watched him sleep as she opened the drawer, found the silver knife her brother Andrew left her with, the one she'd tucked away, knowing she could never use it. She took it back to the bed with her, waited for Westbrook to turn, to stare up at her with a mean, black gaze. But he slept, soft snuffling breaths, fingers clutched into her sheets, face slack with sleep.

She poised the tip of her knife by his throat. A few quick slashes and pricks of his pulse would do the work. She would be dead by morning if she did it, but so would he.

And the army would break down the doors of the chapel,

steal the Mother's idols and all the holy silver, sell it off like coin to buy themselves a new General.

She could not protect the Manor or the land or even herself. She'd already failed at those duties, but her mother had always told her her highest duty was her devotion to Mother Lune. So Westbrook may have conquered her body but Lumen would protect the Lunar chapel with her life. No, not her life. She would give her skin and her sight and her mouth and her soul to these men if she could protect Lune's shrine.

Westbrook slept like the dead as she returned the knife to its drawer, pulled her dress back over her head, leaving the laces loose, and snuck out of the room and down to the kitchen to retrieve her keys. She would go pray to the Mother.

Tall and lean, Healer Brink had to duck his head as he took the steps down into her kitchen, Lumen watching him from the table where she was counting eggs, trying to guess how many more the chickens were good for before the frosts hit and they stopped laying as quickly. He studied the room as he walked, eyes never landing on her even as he stood in front of her. He dropped a wad of herbs onto the table.

"These are the last of what I have. Eight leaves in boiling water every morning as long as the General keeps you. He won't be kind just because you bear his child," Brink ground out.

His eyes were pale, a washed out blue, dark brown hair frosted with silver. He looked around the same age as the General, older than Lumen but younger than most officials in an army. His cheeks and forehead were sunburnt rather than tanned like the others and there was a fine quality to his features that made Lumen wonder if he didn't have a bit of the northern blood in him.

"I've no interest in ending up pregnant," Lumen said, picking up the herbs from the table. She counted quickly. There was barely enough of the plant to last her the next few days.

"Then you better go looking for those in the woods. Dried works as well as fresh," he said. "I've enough to do without foraging for you."

"No one asked you to," Lumen muttered. She was tired. She'd dozed in the chapel, knees cold against the stone, and her body ached in unfamiliar ways now.

Thin fingers gripped her chin, dragging her up to her toes to stare into those ice blue eyes.

"You may be *fucked* by the General but if you think that means you can mouth off to the rest of us I think you'll be very surprised to see exactly how little he cares how we retaliate as long as he still gets his dick wet at night," the man snarled into her face.

"It's the full moon," she said, refusing to flinch even as his nails gouged her skin. "Lunars vow honesty on the day."

He blinked and drew his hand back as if she had scalded him, rather than the other way around. He stepped back.

"Then you'd better stay well away from the rest of us today," he said, but it sounded more like a warning now than a threat. He turned to the doorway and then paused. "Do you…need anything to numb pain?"

She needed something to numb the memory of Westbrook on top of her, inside of her. She could still feel his mouth on her breasts, red marks left from his stubble scratching at her. But it wasn't pain.

"No," she said. And then Healer Brink was storming out of the kitchen, back to his patients.

Lumen stood, staring down at the wad of leaves on the table, the basket of eggs, her cheeks hot with anger. She had given these men beds to sleep in, made them a broth and bread. They could manage their own damn breakfast, and if they ate all the eggs then they could all starve and her along with them. So be it.

She pocketed Brink's plant and walked out the back into the cold brisk morning, fall snapping in the air, and let the chill shock her skin into wakefulness. She recognized the leaves as something she used to pick in the woods across the lake with her mother in the fall. Her mother hadn't made the tea for herself, as far as Lumen knew, but she'd passed the herb out to the female tenants, stuffed in baskets with cured meat and eggs.

Lumen had assumed it was a seasoning, but she understood better now.

She thumped down the hill to the edge of the small lake, certain she felt eyes fixed to her back as she walked. There was a small row boat anchored at the edge of the little gazebo along the bank of the lake and she jumped into the belly. There were men watching her on the bank. Gideon, and two others, but they didn't shout for her or to Westbrook, just watched as she rowed herself away to the woods.

"LADY FENN."

Lumen had heard him coming, and she looked back from where she was gathering bundles of herbs—most for the tea she needed, others for her mother's office and the kitchen—to see Oliver Spragg crunching through the woods.

"You should have run," he said.

She paused in her collecting, words on the tip of her tongue. That she wouldn't have made it far. That last night could have gone much worse for her. But they weren't the truest words and she had to offer those.

"I would never have left my home," she said. "The chapel alone-"

"They'll ransack the chapel! They'll ransack you!" he shouted.

She startled, shuffling on her knees in the dirt to face him. His face was red, hair streaked with dirt, but he looked... safe. He hadn't run into Westbrook's army, or he hadn't interested them, but she wondered how long that would last.

"I'm the only Fenn left to care for the Manor," she said, neck craning back to stare up at Oliver's thunderous expression. "To care for its tenants."

"There's nothing you can do, Lady!" He lunged down, hand wrapped around her arm and dragged her up, her feet tangling in her skirt. "Don't you know what that man does to women?"

"Oi! Hands off the girl!"

Lumen bit down on her own tongue as Gideon Jones

stomped through the brush, making his way to where Oliver stood, fist around her arm.

"This is a private conversation," Oliver yelled back.

"Don't be an idiot," she whispered to him, trying to step away.

"That's my sweet lady host you've got your paws on," Gideon said, grinning as he neared them. "You hold on to her another second and you won't have an arm to block my fist as it lands on your face. You might be entirely out of hands once word gets back to the General."

Oliver looked between Lumen and the soldier and she ducked her head.

"Lady Fenn, have you lain with him?" Oliver asked.

Lumen ground her teeth together, blood hot and rushing at the whole lot of them. Gideon and the General and Healer Brink with his sharp fingers. Oliver too.

"Leave her be, you little pig swill garbage," Gideon said, words light as if he were joking amongst friends.

"Lady Fenn?" Oliver repeated.

Stupid full moon, Lumen thought. "Yes."

Oliver pulled his hand back like she'd bitten him, eyes fixed to her face. Over his shoulder Lumen could see Gideon's own eyes grow wide in surprise. When Oliver took a step closer to her—mouth parted, forehead tangling, dappled sunlight falling in his hair and *utter* betrayal on his face—Gideon's large, scraped and bruised hand held him back by the shoulder.

"There you go. She's the General's now. Piss off." Gideon said, spinning Oliver around and—Lumen nearly choked on her surprise—slapping him squarely on the ass to get him moving.

She watched Oliver's back as he crashed back through the woods.

"Is anyone going to harm him on his way back?" Lumen asked.

"Not on my command," Gideon said. "But that's the only pass he's getting from me, little spirit. If he's left bruises on that arm of yours he'll land himself in more trouble with Dom than anyone else."

"Dom?"

"Dominic," Gideon said, clicking on the last letter, and added in a laughing tone, "The lordly General himself."

Dominic. She filed that away and sank back into the patch of growth.

"Aren't you done?" Gideon asked.

"No. I can come back tomorrow if you want another chance to follow me. But I have more to collect."

She was counting the days in her head as she gathered. This bundle would get her through the month to the first frost. This would last her another. This much might take her to the solstice. How long would the men stay? Better to grab it all and save herself worry until spring.

"Don't mind following you, little spirit," he said, propping himself up against a tree, ankles crossed so the heels of his boots dug into the mud. "Sure as shit had worse jobs in my time."

He was watching her as she worked and Lumen shuffled around on her shins, careful not to throw her rump up in the air. He reminded her of the dogs that ran wild around the estate now. They'd belonged to families once but then the families had left in the wake of the war and now they were feral things, begging whines and biting teeth.

"He make you bleed last night, little spirit?" Gideon asked.

Lumen's breath shook in her chest, eyes on her hands, speckled with dirt. "No," she said.

He hummed in agreement. "He's got a way with virgins." Lumen glowered down at the ground as he added, "Better you went to him. I've never been so good with patience."

Lumen huffed and twisted, glaring up at the smiling man. "You are certainly trying mine," she said.

His laugh was a loud wild bark and it went on into little wheezes of humor. But he left her to her work as she moved to two more patches until she was finished collecting. She stood brushing mud and leaves off the knees of her skirt, bundling the plants up in linen and turning to find Gideon, popping rich purple berries into his mouth.

"You ready?" he asked. "I'll row us back. The others can walk."

Others? Of course. The woods seemed quiet but Gideon

hadn't come alone—she'd seen him on the bank with the other two men. She glanced at the berries in his hand and decided to keep her answer simple.

"I'm ready."

"Hungry?" he asked, holding out his handful. "They're everywhere."

She shook her head and passed him, tracking her footprints back through the woods until the sound of water was near enough to follow. Out of the corner of her eye she watched him, stopping and grabbing handfuls of the sweet wood berries at a time, munching steadily.

"You sure you aren't hungry?" he asked her, boots clomping as he jogged to catch up to her. He leaned in close enough that she could smell the tart juice on his lips as he purred, "I don't mind sharing."

Lumen chewed over the words in her head. How to follow Lunar law. There was true, saintly honesty. And then there was answering a question.

"I'll wait till we get back," she said. She would only answer these men's questions.

It was a few minutes later, near the break of the tree line, when Gideon's face took on a queer, puzzled expression. A few steps more and the remaining berries in his hand were tossed aside. His hand passed over his stomach, tunic rucking under the unlaced leather jacket. He came to a full stop as Lumen reached the boat and she met his eyes for a full second before he was bent in half, back heaving in dry gags.

She waited for him to recover, palms braced on dirty knees, face ashen as he looked up at her.

"Those berries poisonous?" he asked.

"Yes," Lumen said, a little flicker of a smile on her lips.

Gideon grinned and his skin turned grayer. "Am I dying, little spirit?"

"I don't know," Lumen admitted. "You ate an awful lot of them."

He stared at her a moment longer, grin stretching, and then he was laughing again, choking, and finally vomiting black poison out on the ground. She waited for the first bout to pass, wincing as he wiped his mouth with his sleeve.

"You leaving me here?" he asked.

"That depends on whether or not you get in the boat," she said, untying the rope from the log she'd anchored it to, and stepping into the belly.

He was sick again before he made it to her, back curved from the stomach cramps, a thin greenish-yellow fluid mixing with the black.

"Keep your head out of the boat," she said as he reached her.

GIDEON WAS DONE VOMITING by the time she rowed them back to the Manor but he still looked uncomfortable, arms wrapping his stomach, skin strangely pale beneath that Solar tan. The bruises around both his eyes were starkly purple, and he was leaning at an odd angle, but he followed her all the way back to the Manor and inside to the courtyard where she stopped still in an archway.

A wooden tub had been dragged into the courtyard, filled with steaming water, General Westbrook soaking inside, his legs and arms and head hanging over the edges. *Dominic.* The sun was anointing every droplet on wet skin, gleaming like fire in his black hair. Off to the side, the boy waited with a towel.

Gideon passed her, hunched over and crossing to a patch of grass working its way up between the stone tiles, puking again.

"What the hell is wrong with you?" Westbrook asked the man, sitting up in his bath.

"The little spirit poisoned me," Gideon moaned, winking at her.

Lumen said nothing until Westbrook turned to her, eyebrows raised. "He ate wood berries."

Westbrook sighed, sinking back into the water, scooping handfuls out and rinsing it over his head until it splashed down onto the stones behind him.

"Go see Finley," Westbrook said to Gideon.

"I'd rather have a turn in that bath," Gideon said, spitting on the ground and straightening with a wince.

"No one's fetching you fresh hot water," Westbrook said.

"You know I don't mind going after you," Gideon said and when Lumen glanced in his direction he winked at her.

"Leave me in peace, beast," Westbrook groaned.

Lumen ducked into the halls, finding the nearest stair and following it up. She could see over the hall windows, down into the courtyard, sunlight glaring off the reflection of water in the tub, obscuring the sight of the General. She rounded the Manor to the south western corner and shouldered open the door of her mother's office.

"Get out!"

Healer Brink had found the room. He was hunched over a man whose teeth gripped a leather strap to keep from shouting. The man, the soldier, was stretched across her mother's work table, upper half bare as Brink studied his back, sharp blade digging into swollen boils on the man's shoulder, an infection blooming in an old wound.

Lumen's fingers dug into the bundle of herbs cradled in her arms. She'd protected the chapel, but Brink using her mother's healing room in such a barbaric manner was another violation.

"I said, *get out!*" Brink roared without even looking at her.

She ignored him, crossing to the far table and putting down the bundle. She unlaced the cuffs of her sleeves and rolled them back above her elbows.

"Sit him up," she said, opening drawer after drawer until she found the collection of clean strips of cloth.

"I beg your pardon?" Brink said, in a manner that did not indicate any form of begging at all.

"Sit him up to drain the fluid," Lumen said. She found a jar of honey and another bottle filled with witch hazel and carried the lot to the table where Brink was standing, bloodied knife in one hand, the other bracing the man down to the table.

"How many times have you had to do this?" she asked looking at the litter of scars on the shoulder.

"Get up," Brink said, ignoring her question, releasing the man who scrambled up to sit on the table.

Lumen found a small dish and poured a little of the witch hazel into it, holding her hand out to Brink. "Give me that knife."

His jaw flexed and the soldier, an older man with gray and copper hair and a large belly that hung over the waist of his pants, stared at her with watery blue eyes. Brink passed her the knife and she swished the blade in the witch hazel.

"I boiled it before working," Brink said, just a little defensive.

Lumen hummed.

"What is that? Alcohol?"

"Clean water and witch hazel," she said, wiping the blade with one of the fresh cloths. To the soldier she said, "This will sting."

She did not wait for Brink to move out of her way, simply fitting herself between him and the soldier. "One, two," she warned the soldier and before he could brace himself at 'three', she stabbed the boil, pressing a wad of clean cloth over the wound as it leaked pus. The man howled as she pushed down and Brink grabbed his other shoulder to hold him still for her.

"Hold that there," Lumen said to the healer and then she returned to her station. "I'll prepare the rest of the swabs and a rinse of honey and witch hazel which will fight the infection." She looked at the man's skin and tilted her head, he looked to be a yellowy green around the edges. "There's a vinegar in the cellar he should drink a bit of too. He's the wrong color."

"This is your workroom?" Brink asked her as she tore the cloths in strips and rinsed the knife again.

"My mother's," Lumen said as she worked. "But I trained with her as a little girl. When she passed I read her journals so I could help with the tenants."

"I thought Lords and Ladies only worried about taking taxes from their tenants," Brink muttered, working on the next troubled spot on the soldier who growled at the abuse.

"Lunar faith requires generosity," Lumen recited. "A tenant does not serve without equal or greater care."

"I have met plenty of Lunars, Lady Fenn," Brink said. "They don't concern themselves with tending the sick."

She knew that was true. Her mother had always begged leniency from the Lunar priests and priestesses on behalf of the people who came to the chapel. She'd said it was a cold faith, generous but impersonal, and by being impersonal it made room for a loss of empathy. But she'd been raised and trained in the skills to apply that empathy where it was needed.

"I'll come back with clean water," she said instead. She stopped at the front of the table, chin tilted up at the wincing soldier. "Show me your gums."

The man twitched as if about to look back at his healer and Brink snapped, "Go on." He drew his lips back in a mockery of a smile. Lumen frowned at the pale gums, the way they drew back from his teeth.

She hummed in displeasure. "We'll have to make more vinegar. I'm going to need someone to bring cider."

"Colin brought some back with him for the troops, I think," Brink said. Colin must have been the boy. "I'll see what's left and have the boy bring it back here."

Lumen nodded and left the room, hurrying back to the kitchen for supplies. Down in the courtyard there was a splash and she stopped, watching as Westbrook rose up out of the bath water, slicking his hair back off his face, body dripping to the tiles. He didn't seem concerned by the brisk air, she supposed the armies were used to it, and the boy, Colin, didn't make any effort to rise and offer him his towel.

In another moment, Gideon Jones was there, naked, twice as scarred as the General with great chunks of flesh and muscle missing from an ancient wound in one thigh. Purple and blue bruises smeared color across his ribs and Lumen realized why he'd been tilted earlier. There must be a fracture or a break in the bone, now newly strained by his bouts of sickness.

A throat cleared and she realized she was being watched from the ground, Westbrook's eyes on her, rubbing the towel through his hair as he glared at her. She turned away, frowning at the sudden reminder of the weight of hips between her thighs and teeth dragging over flesh.

No one made another demand of her for the rest of the day. Brink seemed to ignore her wandering in and out of her mother's—his—workroom, but he followed her advice on cleaning wounds and let her administer cups of tart cider vinegar to the men who needed it. She baked loaves, left them cooling in an archway, and no one came to find her even through the smell of meat cooking on a fire again. She was free to be ignored and it suited her.

What she was less certain of was what do after the sounds of men bickering ceased, and the footsteps in the halls faded, and the doors shut. Westbrook hadn't said a single word to her all day. He hadn't hunted her down to stake a second claim, but no one else had touched her. Gideon said she belonged to the man now, and when she thought to rebuff the words she wasn't certain if it would be a lie or not. A person could not be owned, certainly, but if they could be possessed wasn't that what Westbrook had done to her the second he stepped onto her estate. Hadn't she let him in the bed the night before?

Lumen wished he'd been a little bit clearer about their terms. Had she pleased him? He hadn't said so and he hadn't tossed her out either.

There was a part of her that was absolutely certain of one thing. If she did not go to him tonight, Westbrook would not hunt her down. She wasn't sure what that meant for the next day or the day after, only that whatever Westbrook was, he wasn't a hunter. That was Gideon Jones' style, perhaps.

Still, she found herself at the bedroom door and this time she knocked.

"For fuck's sake, what?" he snarled.

Lumen was unable to answer that question. It would have been better if she let herself in. It would have been *best* if she'd locked herself in the chapel all night. She was about to turn away and do just that when the door swung open and Westbrook's usual growl died in his throat.

"Where have you been?" he asked.

"I wasn't sure if I was meant to come again," she said.

His eyebrows lifted on his face. "What made you wonder, Lady Fenn?"

Her breath caught in her throat, afraid of what she might say. It was still the full moon, after all. "You said I had to please you, and I wasn't certain I had."

His expression locked and Lumen thought it was distinctly unfair that she was bound to the truth when these men so clearly weren't. Whatever he thought of her claim, he kept it secret. But he stepped back and held the door open for her until she followed him inside.

FINLEY BRINK'S EYE CAUGHT ON A FLASH OF BRIGHT, PALE COLOR passing one of the open archways into the circuitous Manor. *The White Lady*, he thought, watching the young woman duck back out of sight. She was strange. He couldn't decide if she seemed frightened of them, or defiant. Some mix of the two and yet neither was quite right.

"How much longer til he tires of her, do you think?"

Finley turned back to his food. Salted meat. Stodgy bread. This time the broth was made from bones instead of onions.

"I listen to them at night," Gideon continued, keeping his voice quiet for once. Westbrook was more tolerant of him than most, but there was always a line with the General. "She barely makes a sound. I can hear him groaning and moaning and grunting, bed thumping. But she's as quiet as the grave."

Finley grimaced at the thought. Lady Fenn was outspoken enough when she bullied him and his patients into her gentle treatments. He wasn't sure how he felt about the idea of her being silenced alone with Westbrook at night.

"Bet I could make her scream," Gideon added.

"Would you shut your foul mouth while I'm eating?" Finley asked. "Westbrook won't let you within five feet of her." Not that it stopped the rabid man from orbiting around the woman every time he had a minute to spare.

"Course he will," Gideon said, shoveling a wet handful of bread into his mouth. "He always does near the end. And I bet it's me he calls on to entertain her this time."

"I find that unlikely, Jones," Finley said. Gideon scoffed and went back to his food and Finley sighed in silent relief. Better to let the subject drop.

It was true, Dominic tired of the women who tried to sway his decisions by warming his bed. And it was true too that when he grew bored he liked to prove exactly how much power he had by dragging in Gideon, or Finley, to join them in that bed. It was one thing for a woman to think she held a man's head by riding his cock. It was quite another when she was faced with two who took what they desired.

But Lady Fenn had yet to press her case with anyone as far as Finley could tell. She didn't appear to speak to Westbrook. She only spoke to Finley enough to tell him how to better care for the men in the house. Since the full moon she'd taken to ignoring whatever Gideon said to her.

If Dom *did* exhaust his interest in the strange woman, Finley wasn't certain whether he *wanted* to be the one invited to torment her, or if he feared the opportunity. She had a strange effect on him. Even now he could smell her, passing the halls behind him, filling the air with a pure, clean, stinging flavor, like ice and salt.

THIS WAS a strange kind of ritual, she thought, the sound of flesh slapping loud in her ears, Westbrook's hips driving into faint bruises he'd built on the backs of her thighs over the course of a week. There was heat in her skin, a desperate aching need between her legs, his voice groaning in her ear, their chests sticking together.

She knew what would come next. She would rake her nails down his back, wrap her legs behind him and dig her heels into his ass. She would feel ready to burst, her voice frozen in her chest, vision blind. And then he would fill her with his seed, collapsing on top of her, holding her like a vice and she would simmer beneath him, ready to scream.

Lumen was almost numb to it now. This dizzying sense of nearing an edge, these bright flashes under her skin, she both loved and hated them.

Better to have it done with. She reached her arms up to his back and suddenly the man was rearing back, catching her wrists in his hands.

"Not this time," he grunted, forehead furrowed, sweat on his brow. He fumbled her wrists together in one of his hands, his free arm sliding under her back, fastening himself deep inside of her as he shifted back onto his knees, her thighs draped over his lap.

"What-" she started but then he reared back, thrust in again, and some fiery brightness cascaded over her skin. She arched, voice crying out, and then Westbrook was touching her, that exact spot he always used to start their coupling until she was slippery on his fingers.

Lumen tried to twist away, all of the sizzling, ecstatic pressure she'd been savoring suddenly doubling. Westbrook released a sound, something like a laugh, and then his pace was set again, deep and steady and not the rough jerk before he finished. His fingers held her arms to her stomach so all Lumen could do was squirm and twist below him, breasts begging for his mouth, voice embarrassingly noisy and wordless.

"Finally," Westbrook growled above her. "Finally, you little witch."

His cock head struck inside her and Lumen gasped, eyes wide, body taut, toes scrambling in the sheets.

"Just promise me one thing, Lady Fenn," Westbrook said, panting with each thrust. In the back of Lumen's mind it struck her odd that he didn't know her first name, but it was something of her own to keep if he was going to drive her into madness now too. "That you won't call to the Mother."

"Oh gods!" Lumen cried, whimpering with every careening curl of pleasure that spurred her closer and closer.

He picked up his speed in answer and suddenly Lumen was

flying, shouting praises, his name somewhere in the mix. Something like lightning was rushing through her, except that it was velvety soft, and staggeringly hot, and swept dark and starlight across her eyes. Westbrook carried her through the feeling, hand extending the ride, cock nudging her gently until all the painful stark shock was fading and she was melting into the bed, whimpers trapped behind her lips.

He pulled free, and she could see how he shone with her wetness, heat rising in her cheeks at what he had witnessed, what he'd *done* to her. His breath was coming hard, eyes studying her, a hint of a smile on his lips.

"I've been remiss, Lady Fenn," he said, eyes fixed to her opening he'd just drawn free of.

She was still fluttering with the finish—the finish she'd been desperate for and not realized was *there* for the taking. He trapped her legs open, hands around her ankles, and crawled backwards on the bed, sinking down to his elbows and knees, face startlingly close to her core.

"And I don't like to carry debts," he added.

Lumen was still loose, dazed, baffled by the possibility of what she'd been missing, that she watched him lower his face between her legs and take the first soft lick of her skin. The touch, such a contrast from the hard grind of him fucking her, left her sighing, eyes widening.

"I don't understand," she said. She didn't understand why she hadn't fallen over that edge before. Why he was helping her there now. She didn't understand why a soft tongue might feel as nice as a determined cock and hand.

He was kissing every inch of skin he found there, sucking on her folds, tongue teasing at the little nub that she now knew was a key to ecstasy. He drew back, looking up the length of her to meet her gaze.

"I'm not finishing inside of you again until our score is even," he said. "Does that clarify the matter?"

It did not, but then his mouth wrapped around her, tongue probing inside of her, nose nudging and Lumen's head crashed back into the mattress, whining and panting at the new touch.

She couldn't possibly suffer that pleasure again, so soon, could she? He seemed determined to prove it so, and when she tried to scramble away, his hands clamped around the outside of her thighs, holding her to his face.

There was some kind of intolerable patience in the man now, content to lick and nibble and suck, seeking out whatever process left her writhing, made her moan. She was rolling her hips into him, eyes shut, lips parted and every thrust of his tongue inside her elicited a soft begging sound from her throat. When her own arousal had been kissed over every inch of her cunt and even the inside of her thighs, finally Westbrook focused his attack. His mouth surrounded her clit and sucked until she was shouting, cresting, hands fluttering. Two fingers slid inside her, thrusting her through the climax as he lapped and sipped at her sex until she was limp again.

Her arm was draped over her face, still rocking into the touch of his fingers, breath erratic. "I can't," she whispered.

"You just did, witch," he whispered. "Only six times more."

She snarled, pulling her arm away, and her voice stuttered at the sight of him, propped up, lips wet, a slight grin on his face as he watched his hand teasing her. His thumb stroked over its favorite spot and Lumen's eyes slammed shut, the feeling in her something between a stab and a craving.

This pleases him, she thought, her own brain grumbling at the realization. Another voice answered, *this pleases you too*.

"Relax, Lady Fenn," he murmured, eyes glancing at her face, body shifting slightly to press against hers, hand still patiently toying with her.

His cheek pressed to one breast and then nuzzled, and when he mouthed against her skin Lumen forced herself to relax, digging her fingers into his hair and making him hum.

SHE WAS RUINED NOW. She knew it must be so. Every inch of her had been touched, kissed, bitten. The bed was soaked with sweat and release. He'd rolled her onto her belly after the fourth finish, when she couldn't keep herself from weakly trying to push him away. Now she was sobbing into her pillow, body riding his fingers mindlessly, uncertain of where the waves crashing over her began and ended.

When he pulled his hand away she started to beg for their return.

"Please, please, I can't,"

"Hush," he said, turning her onto her back again.

Her skin was pink, roughened by the coarse hair on his cheeks, tender from attention. Lumen moaned, head rolling to the side, teeth in her pillow, as Westbrook finally slid his cock inside her again. He felt huge. She was still pulsing, but he pressed in without a single retreat. His chest pressed to hers and stole her breath and Lumen had to force herself to focus, to see his face hovering over hers.

"I owe you nothing," he said, eyes scanning her face. "Do you understand?"

Lumen frowned and his fingers wrapped around her jaw, tilted her chin back to force her stare to his.

"I want nothing from you," she said, voice hoarse with shouting.

His brow tangled and his fingers pressed to her skin harder as he leaned down, taking her mouth with his, tongue forcing its way in, stroking the taste of her against her own tongue.

It was her first kiss and it was a mean, punishing thing. Or something greedy and demanding. But it was a distraction from the sudden shift of him inside her as he finally began to work to his own end. She wrapped her arms around his neck, her weak and wobbling legs around his hips, and fought for her own brief moments of command in the kiss. She learned his patterns and used them against him until they were both scratching and groaning at one another, bodies churning and shifting in rhythm.

Lumen pulled his hair and he pressed a hand between their chests to pinch at one of her nipples until she sucked and nearly bit down on his tongue. His other hand curled over her neck, the softest squeeze, the gentlest threat. She used her last bit of strength for the night to squeeze her core around him, the pressure turning her wild again.

They came together in anger and argument until the fire burned away and the clutching was needy and the kiss was soft and hands were stroking to soothe instead of scratch. Dominic shuddered on top of her as Lumen trembled through a delicate, rushing release. When he turned heavy and still she held him there, the weight suddenly became a comfort instead of a burden, a promise that she wouldn't float away.

For the first time in over a week, Lumen woke in her bed instead of on the cold stone tile of the chapel. The sun was high, well past the windows, but she winced at the brightness all the same, rolling over into the pillow. Her body complained, skin irritated, limbs stiff and sore. The pillow smelled like him.

It had been an agonizing introduction to what sex was meant to feel like and Lumen wanted to shut her eyes, fall back into oblivious slumber and forget where the night had taken her. Where *he* had taken her. At least he wasn't still in the bed.

Outside the window, men's voices shouted in the yard.

Lumen hissed as she stretched, marveling at how *used* her body felt without anything really being in proper pain. She pushed herself up, squinting out the window, one hand reaching up to untangle a matted mess of hair. Too much tossing her head about, it was a rat's nest now.

Then she saw them, out on the lawn, troops in the squash patch, turning pumpkins. More out in the fields beyond, hoeing wheat and pulling in corn.

"Mother, what are they doing!"

Her legs were nearly numb and she tumbled out of the bed, yelping as she hit the floor and then dragging herself upright again. It was the first night that she'd slept in her room again, the first time she'd been in the room alone without Dominic. Watching the door, ready to duck behind something in case he—or worse, Gideon—came charging in, Lumen darted over to her armoire, searching for a fresh shift and dress. Her thighs were sticky.

She grimaced, tossing a shift on and then stopped in front of the small dresser. The water in the pitchers was faintly steaming, fresh. She poured it into a bowl and washed herself as thoroughly as she could with a cloth before dressing.

The Manor was silent, a few murmurs from the patients convalescing in the dining room. All the activity was outside the house in the fields. She ran out to meet them, Gideon Jones standing with Domin- *the General.*

"What are they doing?" she asked, staring out at rows of men working her land.

"Harvesting," Westbrook said.

His stare was heavy on her face and she felt the color rising up her neck, refusing to meet his gaze.

"Why?" she asked.

Gideon snorted. "Because we'll all starve if they don't."

In all the rumors that spread of General Westbrook's army, not one ever mentioned his troops helping during a harvest.

"My tenants-"

"Will get their share, Lady Fenn," Westbrook said.

This time when she turned to stare at him, his gaze twitched away from hers, watching his troops with a frown, arms crossed over his chest.

 Sarah Blythe said, gnarled fingers wrapped around Lumen's face.

The old woman was hunched at her side and Lumen was acutely aware of the watching eyes of Westbrook, Jones, and Brink, seated around her at the table and studying the interaction. Her chest was tight at the mention of her mother from the old nursemaid to the family. She didn't see her mother in those rare flashes of reflection she caught while dressing in the morning. She saw the bitten swell of her lips, the red scratch of an unshaven beard against her neck, the bruise of greedy kisses.

"Thank you, Sarah." Lumen kissed the woman's cheeks. "Do you need more of the Golden tea?"

Her mother had found a brew of spices and leaves that seemed to help those twisted joints from cramping and it had been awhile since she took a batch over to the Blythe cottage.

"I have a little saved yet," Sarah said.

Lumen pushed back from the table and the men shifted around. "I'll get some now," she said.

"Fetch me another ale while you're up, little spirit?" Gideon asked, grin bright and eyes laughing. Westbrook scoffed behind her back and Lumen snatched the mug from Gideon's hand, leaving the table, Sarah Blythe hobbling back to her table behind her.

For the first time in five years, the harvest gathering was taking place at Fenn Manor. It was planned before Lumen even realized, busy as she was sorting out her mother's workroom and helping Healer Brink with his patients. She was getting used to sleeping in late in the mornings—decadently occupied as she now was at night—and she barely noticed the soldiers filling her kitchen, the men hauling some thin hog in on a spike and starting its roasting over a fire.

And then Westbrook stopped her in the hall, frowning down at the bloodied basin of water she was taking to dump somewhere safe, and told her to dress and prepare to dine with her people.

Now she passed them, the few that were left on the estate, hunched together around a table, smiling, their hands reaching out to her as if she had gifted them this night of feasting. It hadn't been her. She could work fields and waive taxes but she hadn't hosted a harvest feast in years. Seeing fat shine on their lips she realized she didn't even mind that the hog had likely been paid for with more of what lingered in the house. Why hadn't she done the same before? Why save the belongings of family who would never return to retrieve them?

Oliver Spragg was sitting at the table, a dark bruise on his jaw, and she kept her eyes away from him. Maybe he saw her contribution to this dinner the way that she did. Earned on her back.

There were soldiers in the halls on the second floor, watching the festivities with mugs of ale in hand, and they gave Lumen a wide berth as she walked. She enjoyed the peace of her mother's workroom without Healer Brink looming over her shoulder, watching every move she made and refusing to ask the questions to satisfy his curiosity. She tied the herbs up in a little bit of scrap material and headed back down to the others.

Oliver was waiting for her on the stairs.

"Lady Fenn, I wanted to make amends for how I spoke to you

in the woods," he whispered, catching her on the landing and blocking her route to the courtyard.

"It isn't necessary," she said, stepping forward, hoping he would move out of her way. He didn't and she shrunk back to the wall.

"You don't deserve to be used up and treated like- like…" he sputtered, face turning red, refusing to put a name to what he thought of her.

Lumen thought of the way the General seemed to cradle her, cheek pressed to hers, hips driving her higher.

"Just because you learned a truth from me in the confidence of the full moon does not give you the right to speak to me in this manner," Lumen said, using the wall at her back to keep her spine straight.

"Just because a man puts food on your plate does not mean he has a right to your virtue!" Oliver answered, eyes wide and earnest. His hand reached up and yanked at his own hair in frustration.

"That food is on your plate too," Lumen said. "On the Blythe's. Feeding Widow Ramsey and those two little children."

"We should have scorched the fields at night and let the soldiers starve," Oliver answered.

And let her people starve with them? No, Westbrook would take care of his men but he'd give nothing to the estate if it weren't for those crops.

"Let me pass," she said, eyes trying to watch the stairs at either side before they were discovered.

"I can take you across the new border, you'll be safe," Oliver whispered.

She finally looked at him, body numb, head spinning.

His expression softened, brow wrinkling with worry. "You don't have to stay. Sooner or later Westbrook's generosity will dry up. You prolong the suffering by being here. Your own suffering, Lady Fenn. Let me take you away."

She knew in her heart the answer and even though it was not the full moon and she owed him no truth, she gave it to him. "I will not abandon my family's estate."

"You are damning yourself," he whispered.

"So be it," she said.

"Lady Fenn."

Her first thought was that she had been caught, but at what? Her second was that it was best for Oliver that this time it was Healer Brink finding them instead of Gideon.

"I was on my way down," she said, leaning to see him past Oliver's shoulder.

Brink was glowering at Oliver's back, eyes dagger sharp and just as silver in the darkness.

"I'll escort you," he said, and Oliver shifted just enough to let her skirt out from behind him.

Healer Brink's elbow was held out for her hand, a gesture she hadn't been the recipient of in so many years, but she curled her fingers around the crook of his sleeve and walked down with him, heart hammering in her ears.

"If he harms you, touches you..." Brink said, voice lowered for her ear only.

"He hasn't," she interrupted quickly. "Wouldn't."

"Westbrook would have him killed," he continued. He turned, his eyes cutting across her face. "Protection or possession or jealousy. He wouldn't hesitate."

Lumen turned her face away. Without a word between them Brink pulled his arm free just as she dropped her hand. He ushered her ahead of him, turning back up the stairs and she walked out to the courtyard on her own. She filled Gideon's mug at the table holding the ale cask, the crowd of soldiers parting for her to step ahead of them, and returned to Westbrook after dropping off the tea with Sarah Blythe.

"Did you see Finley while you were upstairs?" Westbrook asked her as she took her seat.

She thought of Brink's words. Protection or possession or jealousy. "He was talking to one of the tenants."

Westbrook grunted, and Lumen felt she'd chosen the right answer. Neither men were with her in her version of events.

"Your people seem to hold no ill will for sharing their feast with my soldiers," he said.

She picked at the meat on her plate, wondering why his eyes seemed to follow the path of her fingers up to her lips. "I'm sure my people are very grateful for this night," she said.

"They should be grateful you managed to keep the fields from turning fallow all this time."

Lumen paused in her eating, turning and resisting the urge to squirm beneath his gaze. Tonight she felt more vulnerable to his stare than in those naked candlelit hours upstairs.

"Eat," he said, glancing at her plate. "Winter will be thin."

LUMEN WAS COMING up from checking on the cider vinegar when she caught Colin in the kitchen, rustling in the bread bin for scraps.

He was a small boy, and very thin, and Lumen remembered as a very young girl hearing her mother speak of her brothers, that there wasn't enough food in the world to round a young boy's belly. Colin had gritty dark hair that Lumen suspected might lighten if it were ever washed, and enormous glass green eyes which were staring at her as if they were about to fall out.

"There are warm buns nearly out of the oven if you can sit still a minute," she said.

His eyes skidded around the room and out into the hall before dropping the lid of the bin and bouncing his way up onto her table. The cuff of his pants hiked up as he sat, revealing skin dusted with mud. She smiled and crossed to the oven, grabbing out the brownest bun she could find and cracking it with a knife to let the steam out. She found her wild berry preserves and spooned it into the hole.

"Count to one hundred before you take a bite," she said.

"Don't know that high," Colin answered, staring at the bun with greedy eyes.

Lumen hummed and rustled through the kitchen until she found a bit of dried deer meat she'd been saving.

"Chew through that before you take a bite, then," she said.

His eyes grew big again as he got the first bite of salt on his tongue. She found a clean rag, and wiped all the dirt from his hands as he ate.

"Watchu doing?" he asked her, staring down at his hands as if he didn't recognize them.

"I was checking to see if you were made of mud," she said. "But apparently there's a boy underneath."

Colin grinned at her. "Haven't had a bath in a whole year, I think. I bit the last man that tried to wash me."

"Then I am very grateful not to be sporting your teeth marks," Lumen said, smiling.

"Nah. Wouldn't bite a lady, don't think."

"And if I tossed you into a bath?"

His eyes narrowed and he took another bite of the jerky, teeth pulling hard at the meat in a way that made Lumen worry about them coming loose. "Would'nyone else be watchin'?" he asked her.

She hid her fisting hands behind her back. "No, just me to help if you needed me to."

"S'pose it'd be alright."

Lumen left the boy to his food and walked down into the cellar where a large basin sat with a water pump. She put the plug in and began to pump. It would be a nice quiet place for the boy and no one was likely to come in. She was fairly sure some of the men were still sleeping off a heavy hangover from the festivities the night before. She came back with a kettle of water to heat on the stove.

"Whas'sa Lunar?" Colin asked and she glanced over her shoulder, spying jam dribbling at the corner of his mouth, each hand now full with precious food.

"Someone who follows the Mother Lune's teachings as a guideline for good behavior and healthy living."

"But the moon don't talk," he said and Lumen laughed.

"Doesn't she?" Lumen asked, raising her eyebrows before pulling the rest of the buns from the oven. She'd give the boy another once they cooled.

Colin gave her a dubious look and Lumen grinned. "She shifts and changes, is full and open and then hides herself, over and over again. Change is good for people. Being honest is good. Being private is too. She's gentle enough to stare up to at night. She lights dark places."

"Healer Brink says the sun makes things grow," Colin said.

"He's right."

"So why don't you love the god that makes things grow?"

"I do love that god," Lumen said with a shrug. "But He also says that things must burn and bleed."

"Moon keeps secrets."

"It protects the things in the dark too," Lumen said. "And the sun gives joy, shows us horizons beyond our grasp. It's what makes armies move and push, the desire to claim the land out of reach. And the moon teaches that things will leave us, but also that things repeat."

Colin frowned down at the meat in his hand and then shoved the last bite roughly into his mouth, chewing as he spoke. "Why don't people just follow both?"

"I think they used to," Lumen said. "And then they chose the one they liked best."

"Who's the god for where we live?"

Lumen blinked at that. The god for this place? The god of the ground and the trees and the animals? She had never wondered that before.

"I suppose we are," she said. Colin grinned, a wicked little light in his eyes at the answer. The kettle whistled.

"I'll fill another roll with jam and butter after you've bathed," she said, watching as he stuffed the last of the bun in his mouth and jumped down from the table, a bit of dust left as a print behind him.

She pumped more water into the basin and then added heat from the kettle until the touch was warm but wouldn't scald the boy. He stood at the basin, chin just able to rest on the edge, nose wrinkled as he looked at the water.

"I think if I check the old laundry room I'll find some of my brother's clothes that might fit you," Lumen said.

"I'll wait here," he told her.

The laundry was just down the hall but by the time she

returned with a new set of clothes for the boy that didn't stand up on their own with the dirt in their seams, he had found his way into the basin, bare and huddled in the water. There was an overturned bucket he must have used to climb in.

"How's the temperature?" she asked.

"Could be warmer."

She saw the scars on his back as she added more hot water to the tub. She dipped a cloth into the water, staring down at her own reflection on the dark surface.

"Arm up," she said, and then began to scrub him clean. "Who took that belt to your back? General Westbrook?"

"No. He ain't seen 'em," Colin said, cheek on one dirty knee as he watched her work. "I stabbed the man."

Lumen wasn't certain if that was just a boy's bragging boast or the truth, but decided she didn't care.

"Scoot around, time for the other arm."

She flicked water at him and waited for him to grin before splashing more over the back of his hair. It rinsed out dark but he cackled with laughter. Bit by bit he let her wash him until the basin was murky and his hair rinsed clean and a light ash brown. She hauled him out by his armpits, dripping water all over her skirts, and handed him the nicest towel she'd found in the laundry.

"I can dress m'self," he said when she started to show him the pile of clothing.

"Course you can. Come out when you're ready."

She busied herself making him a new sweet bun until he reappeared, pink cheeked and dressed and bright hair dripping, just as Gideon Jones came stomping into the kitchen.

"Where you been? What the hell have you been up to?" he barked at the boy who froze in place, eyes shifting.

"I threw him in a bath," Lumen said, and then she passed between them, sliding the bun into Colin's hands. "Go on. I'm done with you now."

Colin went darting out the back door into the yard, flashing her a grin over his shoulder as he ran.

"If you're going to spoil someone, little spirit, I wish it'd be me," Gideon said at her back.

When she faced him she found him smiling out the door, like he was happy watching Colin run off clean and fed.

"Is your room not to your liking?" she asked, gathering up the rest of the buns and taking them over to the bin where the men who came and went in the house seemed happy enough to pilfer them.

"It's lonely and I like the view of you," Gideon said, words gritty in her ear, but he continued before she could blush. "Don't even mind watching you be sweet to another. Suppose he's due for a little soft touch. Helps a lad grow. Anymore of that jam left?"

She went ahead and made him a helping identical to Colin's and he beamed—a gruesome, crooked smile, but happy all the same—and left her to her kitchen in peace.

THE BEDROOM DOOR BANGED OPEN AND LUMEN WOKE, Westbrook twisting away from her bare back and turning on the intruder.

"Out!"

"Skirmishes at the border," Gideon said, loud in the sudden quiet of the morning and almost joyous.

She was shrinking on the bed and Westbrook flicked the sheet up over her shoulder.

"Fine. Out. I'll be down."

The door slammed shut and Westbrook collapsed at her side with a huff. Lumen wondered if she was meant to get up too, was about to move, when suddenly he was at her back again. His arms wrapped around her waist, one reaching up to clutch at a breast. She could feel him burying his face into her hair, breathing her in at her neck, legs curving up to tuck beneath hers, feet trapping hers. It only lasted a few beats and then he groaned and rolled away again, stepping out of the bed.

"You'll have the Manor to yourself today, I'm sure you'll enjoy that," he said.

Lumen rolled onto her back, sheet up to her chin, although she wasn't sure what the point was when he'd seen everything of her so often now.

"Are there many injuries in a skirmish?"

He smiled as he dressed. "Many injuries in war? Yes, Lady Fenn, there are."

"I'll prepare supplies in Healer Brink's makeshift hospital." Most of the patients convalescing in the dining room had since been moved back into their tents and the few who were left were still in too poor of shape to disturb her.

He was tugging a loose white shirt over his head as she spoke and he appeared from the collar, frowning at her. "I can't tell if you really disapprove of Finley's methods so much you must correct them, or if you've forgotten who your enemy is."

"I haven't forgotten that," she said.

His frown deepened. "Do as you please. If you're very lucky none of us may make it back this evening."

She had nothing to say to that. Except—

"I hope Colin comes out of it all right."

Westbrook laughed, head thrown back and shaking, turning and hiding his smile from her. Which was a shame, really, if she spent too much time thinking of it.

"Callous woman," he said, almost sweetly. Then he put on his overcoat and became the General again, leaving the room.

She rolled on the mattress as the door shut behind him, tugging the blankets back up over her head.

COLIN DID MAKE it back alright, dashing through the entry, his feet clapping against tile and echoing in the quiet Manor. She left the hospital, now full of clean bowls of water, rags boiled and rinsed and boiled again, all of her herbal tinctures and Healer Brink's torturous tools. Colin met her in the courtyard, face red with effort and breaths panting.

"He's coming," he managed and Lumen knew at once who he meant. "Think he's injured. Riding funny. Blood."

Lumen meant to run back to the hospital, to double check that she was ready. Healer Brink would be with the General and then work would begin. Instead she heard the horse hooves riding up the gravel and ran to the door. Westbrook was hunched low on his horse's back, blood dripping from his hair-line into his eye and over his cheek.

She ran, catching him as he slid sideways off his saddle, feet barely beneath him.

"M'fine, witch," he growled, but he leaned into her.

"Good," she said, the smell of blood and sweat heavy on him. "Let's wash your face."

"You're not taking me into that sickbed waiting room with the others," he growled, pulling himself up to standing, although Lumen could see in the twisted grimace that it cost him.

"Were you stabbed?" she asked.

He snorted. "Knocked on the head with a butt of sword... kicked by a horse."

He'd been on the ground? With the rest of his men, rather than the cavalry?

"Take me up to our room. Nurse me there, if you must," he said, and he seemed to steer them in that direction, pulling her across the courtyard and away from the dining room.

Our room. She shook the phrase out of her head. "Can you get yourself up there? Go on. I'll follow you then."

She raced in and out of the Manor, snatching up what the hospital could spare. What would she do if there was a broken bone, she wondered. Wrestle the man as she bound him? If she had to. When she made it back to the stairs leading in the direction of her own room he was only just pushing open the door to the room, hissing with effort. She followed him in, dropping her bundle on the bedside table and starting on the buckles of black and gold armor.

"Can't see for the damn blood in my eye," he muttered.

She handed him a rag and continued her work until she was lifting the plating off his shoulders, listening to him groan with relief. When his overcoat was off and he'd smeared the blood away, Lumen rose up on her toes, sweeping his hair back. The wound on his head was bloody but it wasn't too deep. She wadded up one of the bandages and soaked it with the witch hazel rinse, pressing it down on the gash.

"Argh!" Westbrook yowled, thrashing for a moment before grinding his teeth and glaring at her. "Merciless."

"Callous too," she reminded him. "How far can you lift your arms?"

He raised them slowly but they both made it up into the air. She took the right one and then pressed it down onto the cloth over the wound. "Press," she instructed.

She lifted his shirt and frowned at the reddened hoof print in the center of his chest. He held his breath as she pressed carefully, touching around and over the spot, but she watched his face and he didn't change colors. Stoic or not there was no hiding a reaction to someone poking at your broken rib.

"I was stepping out of the way," he said.

"Then you probably avoided the worst of it. I can make something for the bruise. In the meantime, chew this for the pain." She went back to the table retrieving a thin strip of willow bark and sliding it between his lips before he could object. He chewed, grimacing.

"I don't mind you as a nurse," he said after a moment.

She took a second look at his face and found his pupils too large and black. "A moment ago I was merciless."

"Brink's not any better and he's less pleasant to look at."

"A little over a week ago I was a fish."

He hummed and for some reason it was *her* that was blushing, wanting to shift away under the warmth of his stare. "Hmm, you're right. Not a fish. A doe perhaps? You certainly aren't cold blooded in bed, my Lady." His eyes narrowed and he stepped closer to her, lowering the hand with the bloodied bandage in it, and tossing it aside. She rose up to check the wound again, and his hand steadied her waist. "And what is the name of my gentle nurse?"

"Now I'm gentle, am I? How hard did that sword hit your head?"

He stepped into her space and it took every last bit of steel in her spine to keep from moving back, but it gave him room to wrap his left arm around her waist.

"What is your name, little witch?"

"Lady Fenn."

He crowded her and this time she *had* to stumble backwards to keep from hitting at the bruise on his chest. Her back knocked against the corner poster of the bed and Westbrook's hand settled on her hip, gathering her skirt up in his fist.

"That's a bit formal to be calling out as I bury my cock inside of you," he said, crowding her until her legs spread to make room for him, until his hand was sliding under the hem of her skirts and seeking her center. "Wouldn't you rather hear your name in your ear?"

"Why should my name matter?" Her breath hitched as his fingers slid around the lips of her sex, teasing briefly at her clit. "I've known it all my life."

Her head tilted back to meet his gaze, startled by the way he towered over her. Somehow in bed he seemed a better size for her than he did now, looming.

"I know I always enjoy it when you beg me by name while I'm fucking you," he said, dipping one digit inside of her, pumping softly, rubbing at her clit with another until she was squirming on his hand.

"What are you doing?" She wanted to ask herself the same question, hands lifting to clasp his arms so she could balance herself, already starting to rock into the touch.

"Interrogating," he said, grinning.

Why was she laughing? Why was she holding him just a bit closer, tilting her head as if to invite his mouth back to her neck for more abuse? He took the invitation, kisses featherlight, the hand under her skirt careful and cautious. When she thrust her hips to grind on his hand, he pulled away just enough to skim the pads of his fingers through the gathering wetness.

"Tell me your name and I will let you come," he said.

Lumen whimpered, frowning. Why wasn't she allowed to simply enjoy the pleasure? Why must she give something up in return?

"Tell me your name," he repeated.

"No," she moaned.

"Don't witches have names?" he asked, teeth scraping over her shoulder, touch gentling to an agonizing tease.

"M'not a witch," she mumbled.

"I beg to differ," he said, head lifting, and then two fingers were plunging inside her, rough and quick.

Lumen moaned, head thrown back, legs spreading father apart. She raised her hands behind her to grasp at the bed frame and Westbrook looked up and down the length of her.

"That's a pretty view."

Lumen's brow tangled as she realized he was careful not to touch her clit, to keep her suspended at a height without hope of completion.

"Please," she begged.

"Name," he said.

Just tell him, the back of her thoughts whined as she bounced on her toes. He was speeding up, her breath frantic in her chest. When his fingers crooked inside of her Lumen shouted, high on her tiptoes, certain she would cum or shatter.

He stopped abruptly and Lumen sobbed, falling forward, knees nearly buckling until he crowded her against the wooden bed frame.

"Tell me," he said. "I want to own that too. To have that lone claim of knowing."

Lumen shuddered, her mind as settled in refusal as her body was in accepting. And then there was a knock on the door.

"Not now!" Westbrook shouted, thumb brushing over her clit so that she was burying sighs and cries behind her lips.

"I need Lady Fenn." Healer Brink, on the other side of the door, *listening to them.*

"She's busy," Westbrook answered, nose nuzzling her cheek, torturing her back to the edge again as she tried to stay silent.

"I can't stitch Charlie up. She's going to have to do the sutures," Brink answered.

"You're not stepping outside this room until I have my answer," Dominic whispered in her ear.

She clawed at his shoulders, nearly ready to finish and his hand pulled free, stroking arousal over the insides of her thighs as her body wrestled its way down again. She moaned and from the other side of the door she heard Brink huff.

"Dom!"

"Not now, Finley!"

The door opened and Lumen was scrambling on her toes, eyes squeezed shut, as Westbrook began to fuck her onto his hand again.

"This is ridiculous. You're going to let Charlie bleed out while you frigg a maid?" Brink asked, but the door shut behind him.

Lumen's face was flaming hot, breasts aching, and when she opened her eyes she found Brink's eyes locked on her, something other than disgust in their pale depths. Westbrook was racing her to another brick wall and she didn't doubt he would pull her back before she had her satisfaction.

"Fuck off, Fin," Westbrook muttered, and he reached his free hand up, turning her face to focus on him. "Do you want to tell me or do you want the healer watching this?"

"We *don't* have time to waste," Brink barked.

Lumen's eyes slid back to the Healer and Dominic growled. "You *do* like him watching, don't you?" His thumb was rolling hard over her clit, her hips grinding against his hand, desperate for every last bit of contact.

"A man is going to die," Brink said, every word heavy, his eyes locked with Lumen's.

And gods, she was *so* close.

"Lumen! My name is Lumen," she shouted finally.

Westbrook snarled, teeth latching onto her throat, and then he was brutal in efficiency, Lumen shouting as he barreled her into oblivion, Finley watching her face as it went slack. She held his gaze, not understanding why but only knowing she wanted him to be a witness. And in her way she had thwarted Westbrook's wishes, sharing her name with the other man too.

Sunlight flooded through her, body undulating with every wave of release, skin of her throat sore with Westbrook's bite. Finley's eyes seemed to be changing color as he watched her, turning from glass to winter green, his lips white with pressing firm. When Lumen trembled down to the ground again he turned to the door.

"If you're done wasting time…"

"I'll send her along," Westbrook grumbled.

The door shut behind the healer and Westbrook pulled his touch away, slow and gentle as Lumen caught her breath.

"Lumen," he said, so quiet she almost didn't hear him under the racing beat of her heart in her ears. "You're bleeding."

She blinked and then his hand was raised between them, thin streaks of blood mixed with the fluid on his fingers.

"My courses are starting," she said. He frowned at the sight as if it offended him and she resisted the urge to snort, smoothing her skirts back down. Maybe he would banish her from his bed for *that* if nothing else.

She left him behind, rushing back down to the hospital, managing to catch Healer Brink before he entered.

"Dominic's priorities are warped," he said to Gideon who was waiting at the door and for once the other man wasn't grinning, only raised his eyebrows and let them in.

Lumen went to wash her hands at the small station she'd set up and then crossed to where the Stalor army was waiting for her. Charlie, as it turned out, was one of the two men she'd been doubly wary of since the army's arrival. Charlie seemed an oddly friendly name for a man who looked like he could crush her skull between his hands. Behind him, cradling the woozy, fading man was the other of the two strange and silent men, tears coursing down his cheeks.

Brink passed her a cloth bundle, needle and thread waiting inside, and moved to the man's side, slowly raising Charlie's bloodied right arm to reveal a gashing wound just below his armpit.

"You'll have to hold it together for me," Lumen said to Brink. "And it needs rinsed."

"There's no time," Brink said, eyebrow raised, as if *she* had been responsible for Westbrook's game.

"What's the point of stitching him shut if he's dead from infection a day later?" she asked, threading the needle.

"Gideon, go grab that bowl, yes, that one."

Brink poured some of the rinse over the wound and Charlie's eyes blinked, breath hitching at the sting, blood washing down to the table and dripping to the floor.

"Pinch the wound shut."

She bent, studying the torn flesh and then began her work, piercing through skin. Charlie made a garbled sound and the other man—

"What's your name?" Lumen asked, glancing at him as he watched her thread her needle like he thought he could do better.

"Danvers," he grunted.

"Someone will need to cut away the rest of your friend's clothes so we can bandage him," she said.

Danvers looked at Brink who nodded in confirmation.

"I'll manage it, little spirit," Gideon offered.

Westbrook had arrived in the hustle, joining his men at managing Charlie, keeping him still and steady as Lumen made quick, even stitches to seal the gash.

"It's not embroidery, Lady Fenn," Finley muttered, watching her fingers work.

"I can make a mess of him or I can leave a thin scar, which would you prefer Healer Brink?"

"She'd've made a tidier job of my face then you, eh Fin?" Westbrook asked.

"There was never any saving *your* face," Brink answered.

Lumen almost smiled. It was as if she hadn't just been undone by Westbrook's touch while Brink watched with a not quite clinical detachment. She followed the path of the wound until Brink was able to pull his hand away and she tied off her work.

"Rinse again," she said, walking away to wash her hands and put together the necessary bandages.

"Gideon, make a trip and find some women to keep the men company while we're here. They earned it and I suspect we'll be skirmishing through winter."

A skirmish didn't win a battle. It didn't move an army into

new territory. Lumen's fingers shook beneath the bandages. A winter of this, of these men, of guarding herself by piecemeal measures.

"Hold him still," she murmured to the men, before pressing the stinging bandage to the wound, Charlie yowling in their arms like an angry cat.

"WHAT'RE you doing down here at this hour?"

Lumen jerked her chin up off her hand, startling at her seat in the kitchen. It was dark and the ovens were cold and the shadow in the doorway was a too familiar shape. Westbrook had come to find her.

"Finishing up," she said. She'd been dozing after dinner, uncertain of where to take herself. To the chapel? To his bed?

"Come."

She opened her mouth to argue and then realized that her body was already starting to cramp, and she was cold. She followed him up to the bedroom, watching his back, his slow steps, and remembered he was still sore from being kicked by a horse.

"How's your head?" she asked.

"Hurts."

They undressed in the dark and Lumen pulled out her red petticoat to deal with her period, slipping it on under her shift. She shivered, some of the cold from the changing season was already starting to leak into the rooms of the Manor. When she finally slid under the covers, followed shortly by the General, she waited for him to touch her, tug her beneath him, as he usually did. Instead he pulled the stockpile of blankets up, spread the sheepskin over the top. His arm wrapped around her waist until they were curled on their sides.

He was warm, skin hot through the thin layer of her shift, and the heat spread into the aching muscles of her back, the arm over her belly dulling the cramps.

"You haven't even used my name yet," she said, eyes studying the shadows of the stone wall in front of her.

He was quiet, almost so much so she might have believed he were sleeping if she weren't so familiar with the sounds he made in slumber.

"Sleep, Lumen," he murmured. His free hand swept thin blonde hair off the back of her neck and he pressed a kiss over the spot.

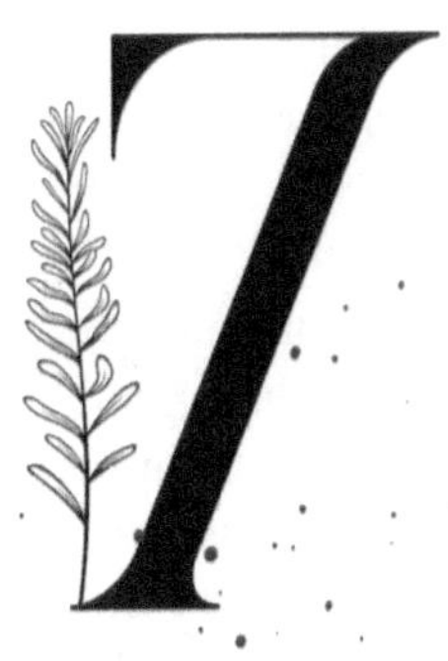

determined to hold the line when his orders were to *push*, conquer. But his men were weary and winter was coming. It wouldn't serve them to force their way north into worse weather when they were barely coping with the first frosts. He wondered what the south really wanted from this country. Certainly not its weather.

Dominic supposed there were worse places to be stuck for a winter than Fenn Manor. His eyes scanned the office he'd commandeered. The late Lord Fenn seemed to enjoy his books, the shelves lined from knee high, up to the rafters. But he wasn't in the mood for reading and he was sick to death of dealing with the correspondence of old men sitting by sun streaked windows trying to orchestrate a war they'd never seen a minute of.

A round white face appeared in his thoughts, silver eyes demurring. He knew what those white lashes hid, a gaze sharp as a dagger. He blinked and pushed himself out of the desk chair in pursuit of better entertainment. Finley likely had the girl locked away in an office, sniffing herbs and talking about... bones. He frowned at the thought of them together and went on the hunt. She'd been missing from the bed before he woke and he hadn't caught so much as a glimpse of her since.

He wanted a bit of sport and Lady Lumen Fenn—*Lumen*, like the moonlight she resembled—was his new favorite kind.

The way she tried to bury her reactions to his touch, the sounds she made when she couldn't hide them any longer. He hadn't felt her pulsing around his cock in three days now and he was finding his patience to be a thinner thread than he expected. He'd certainly gone longer without sex before but never with a craving to hold a woman close and still take nothing for his own pleasure.

He didn't remember how to make a woman laugh. He'd learned new ways to keep them warm.

Now he was craving the sight of one glaring at him from beneath ghostly lashes as he made her cheeks flush with that heat.

He stopped in an arch of the open courtyard, frowning at the sight of an old woman toddling her way across the tiles, Colin close on her heels.

"What's she doing here?" he barked at the boy.

"It's the new moon, sir," Colin said, skidding to a stop.

"And?"

"The Lunars come and pray in the chapel with Lady Lumen."

Dominic nearly growled. Had he won her name simply to share it with the entire Stalor army?

"Do you know how to med- meditate, sir?" Colin asked him, frowning over the unfamiliar word.

"Do I *what?*"

"Lady Lumen says it's like sitting in quiet with yourself and your god. She don't eat all day, either," Colin said. "I don't think I could skip one meal let alone all three."

Dominic frowned until his face hurt. "Take me to the chapel."

It was in a far corner of the Manor, down a long hall that separated it from the main ring of the building. He'd never heard of a chapel in a home, not even as they travelled deeper north. In Stalor what temple remained sat at the heart of cities, not in private houses.

There was something heavier than silence in the air as they reached the room, and when he opened the door Dominic realized what that feeling was. The chapel felt like a tomb, bodies lined evenly along the floor, heads touching stone, backs bowed. The room was blue, walls washed and stained, trimmed in silver. There were glittering ornaments in every corner, stars and moons and delicate figurine women draped in veils and crowned with round mirrors.

Lumen was in the heart of the room, her arms stretched forward, fingertips almost touching the pooling stone skirt of the Mother Lune idol at the front of the room, back shifting faintly with every breath.

"How long do they do this?" Dominic asked the boy at his side. One of the devout on the floor twitched at the sound of his voice.

"Dunno. Lady says till the Mother shows herself again."

His teeth hurt for how hard he clenched his jaw. He hated religion.

THE SUNSET OUTSIDE was mixing with the blue stained glass of the chapel windows, a dappled bruised rainbow of light filling the room. The last of the tenants left the chapel for their dinner, leaving Lumen in a lovely quiet. She'd stretched out to her belly hours ago, after her legs had gone numb from too long on the floor, and the stone was finally warmed by her skin. Soon the chapel would chill and go dark with night and she could stumble her way back into bed.

The thought of bed brought the thought of Westbrook and Lumen inhaled slowly, measuring the breath to the beat of her heart, and then exhaled, releasing Westbrook from her mind.

Now was a time to connect with her Lady, not think of the man who'd taken up residence in her head for the better part of two weeks.

In the quiet, watched over by the Goddess, Lumen's skin was her own again, the memory of touches receding in her thoughts. She was not Lady Fenn who fought to keep her land and home her own, but simply a vessel waiting to be filled again by the Mother's grace and light.

All the worries of the past month, all the blood, the sweat, the invasion, the heartache and conflict, were gone. She was hollow. She would be clean again with the first sliver of reappearing moon.

Most Lunars spent the new moon in prayer, waiting for the light to return. Lumen had always loved the momentary darkness, the reprieve from the burden of life, forcing her head to quiet and body to still. Life would return again soon, louder than she liked, faster than she could keep up with, harsher and leaner than she could sometimes bear. For now she would embrace the brief interlude of emptiness.

But something was coming to interrupt that hollow pause of the day, footsteps in the stone hall, voices low as rockfall, a vibration under her fingertips.

The door swung open and a winter chill swept into the chapel from the courtyard, twining around Lumen's ankles. She tried to breathe through the sound of men, to wash them out of her head with every exhale but already Dominic Westbrook's presence was overwhelming the room. His boots were too loud on the floor, and he shed heat like the sun even from feet away.

"We'll start small, we don't want to waste the best haul before it's really needed."

Lumen's spine stiffened, the stone beneath her cheek, under her fingers, suddenly jagged and abrasive. They'd come for the silver. She'd forgotten what these men wanted from her, from the Manor, and left the chapel vulnerable on its weakest day. Now they were on their way to pillage her sanctuary.

"If the lads get wind there's a load—" Gideon's voice bounced down the hall to her.

"Then don't tell the damn lads, Jones," Westbrook rumbled. "It's food on their plates, they don't need to know where the coin came from."

They were inside and Lumen was still face down on the stone. Every puff of their breath and scuff of their shoe—the startled, abbreviated stutter as one of them spotted her—was loud in the silence of the temple.

Her mind was twirling fast as a top but her body was heavy with meditation. The men were already rifling through the little figurines on shelves and the candlesticks in windowsills when Lumen tried to move. Her limbs were stiff and cold, knees numb, and all her muscles twinged as she rolled onto her side. Danvers and Healer Brink were inside too, Danvers edging dangerously close to the delicate silver charms Lumen had strung together as a child to hang from a chapel window. Trinkets she'd saved up for for months, made from the holy silver the priestess mined from the mountains in the east.

She lurched to her feet, nearly falling again when her body rebelled at the sudden motion and then righting, determined to stop the man.

Her throat was silent, a scream stifled out of respect to the New Moon's frozen pact, and she struck the man's back and neck hard with her fists before he'd ever realized she was up from the floor. Danvers grunted, stumbling forward and knocking the little figurines on the window ledge into a pile, a few landing on the tile floor with bright *tinks!* of music. Westbrook shouted behind her and Lumen climbed onto the quiet man's back, yanking on his hair until he released the silver pieces to better scratch in retaliation at her hands.

"What in Sol's Fire is she doing?" Westbrook hollered.

Tight arms wrapped around Lumen's waist, pulling her off Danvers, loose strands of hair clutched in her fists like trophies. She thrashed in the arms that held, kicked out as she was turned to face Westbrook who tried to catch her. Her elbow thrust backwards and she felt the crunch of bone, heard Brink's injured yelp, and then she was dropped to the stone.

Gideon was across the room, bent over with raucous laughter that bounced off the walls and floors, like a percussive symphony of sound in what was meant to be still perfection. Lumen scrambled across the floor before any of the men could catch her, darting out of the way of Westbrook's arms and launching herself into Gideon's gut, slamming him against the wall, crushing her own arms against stone and hearing all the breath rush out of him in one collapsed 'Oof!'

"Enough!" Westbrook roared.

Lumen rounded, chest heaving, binding fury in her lungs to keep the sound contained. But the world rang around her, vision flashing lightning bright and she met Westbrook in the heart of the room. She wasn't afraid of the rage on his expression, she didn't care about the white knuckled fists clenched at his sides. Her own fist flew, knuckles screaming as the first hit landed against his chest. The force pushed him back a step.

She threw another, and another, until his hands were wrapped around her wrists. Her face was twisted up into something painful and there were hot tears dribbling down her cheeks, dripping salt into her slack mouth. She was struggling to stay silent, breaths catching and a squeaking whimper trying to strangle her throat shut.

"Out," Westbrook said as she continued to punch between them. He looked over his shoulder and bellowed at the other men, "Out!"

Brink's nose was bleeding, Danvers had his hand covering his head like she'd ripped his scalp straight off, and Gideon groaned as he straightened, staggering to the door.

Lumen saw the glimpse of silver out of the corner of her eye and she tore herself out Westbrook's grasp, wrists burning from his touch. She reached Gideon just before he got to the door, broken fingernails scratching at his hands until he dropped the candlesticks.

"Leave the silver! Get out!"

Brink knelt by the door where Lumen was hunched, gathering up Gideon's haul into her skirt. She was ready to scratch him too, to spit in his face, break his nose again, until his expression stopped her. There was no anger, only red blood smeared beneath his nose, and a furrowed worry around his eyes as he dropped two silver lady figurines into her hands. He stood, and pushed Danvers out the door, Westbrook just behind them. The heavy wood door slammed shut behind the other men, leaving her alone with the General.

She folded the silver into the fabric of her skirt, tucked it out of his sight, just as he bent, his hand clasping around her face, dragging her up from the floor and throwing her to the wall, stone hard against her back.

"What the *fuck* do you think you're doing?" he growled.

Lumen's lips pressed together, eyes lifting his, and no amount of fire in his gaze could burn through the hard ice in her chest.

"You are a *guest* in this house now, Lady Fenn. This silver you guard belongs to the Stalor Army." His thumb dug into her cheek, smearing the tears into her skin. "You attacked my men, attacked me. You better be coming up with a damn good apology in that head of yours."

Mother Lune forgive her, she would have to speak. Speak for the silver and the chapel and the Mother herself. Her tongue wet her lips and Westbrook's eyes fixed to the sight, fingers relenting a fraction against her skin.

"Not this room," she said, voice a hollow scratch. "Not here. Anything else in this house, but not here."

His eyes narrowed and he scoffed. "That's it? That's all you can say?"

Fresh tears spilled out of her eyes. "Not here, Dominic. Anywhere else."

His touch was a scorching brand but it loosened on her face, tears coating his fingers as he stared at her, watched them track over her skin. All the hot anger on his face cooled until his eyes were stony with suspicion, lips pressed to a white line.

"Not here," she whispered again.

He released her and escaped out the chapel door.

Lumen collapsed to the floor, silver clicking and clanking together in the lap of her skirt. She wrapped her teeth around her knee, biting the skin and tasting the salt of her skin and tears mingling, trying to breathe instead of scream. Deep sobs shook in her chest but she refused to give them notes. She had broken the silence enough.

She let her thoughts wash out with the crying and fell asleep against the wall, collar soaked.

"Well?" Danvers asked as Dominic met them in the courtyard.

He looked around but it was only them, just Gideon and Brink and he to hear.

"Leave it," he said, teeth grinding in his jaw.

"All that—"

"Forget you saw it," Dominic hissed at Danvers. The other man blinked, eyes narrowing. How could he justify this? Silver enough to keep the army warm, fed. Enough to move them into new territory even. And he was giving an order for it remain untouched. "We strip the rest of the rooms bare. Bring more men in for the winter. Just keep that area clear."

Brink had wiped the blood from under his nose and Gideon landed himself on an archway seat.

"How is she?" Jones asked.

"Why?" Dominic snapped, fingers of his fist still damp from her tears.

"Because she broke my damn nose and nearly made Danvers bald, that's why," Brink supplied, eyes wide. "What did you do to her?"

He'd made her cry, that's what he'd done. Made himself sick in the process.

She had done something to him. Plenty of women had asked favors, mercies of him. He'd taken special joy in not granting them. The only thing she'd ever begged him for until now was release. He'd disregarded that more than often with other women too, but he craved watching her, feeling her, undoing her completely until she was senseless. But not like this.

One thing. She could have one thing. It was not a mercy.

"I left her precious chapel untouched," Dominic said, biting around the words as he met Brink's gaze.

Religions were for fools. Wasting away on a stone floor. Telling humiliating truths. Starving yourself. Binding your tongue.

She deserves better than to bow to someone who does not exist, he thought. He didn't even want her to bow to him.

"Someone find me the boy," he said.

Gideon pushed up, grinning. "Shall I tell him you made his sweetheart weep?"

"Fuck off, Jones, just fetch him for me."

"Lady. Lady Lumen."

A soft hand shook against her shoulder.

"She's back, Lady Lumen. Your Lady Mother is back in the sky."

The delicate fingers brushed over her cheeks and eyelashes, around her lips, over her forehead, like some kitten touch, gentle and teasing. Lumen's eyes stung as they opened, finding Colin in front of her, small face watching hers.

"He says you have to drink this," Colin said, passing a warm mug into her frozen fingers.

It was broth, warm on her tongue, stinging her bitten lips, and she sipped it down, eyes tracing over Colin's face, around the chapel. The room was deep blue with night, glittering with new candles. Her skirt was empty of silver but her trinkets hung in the window again, the candlesticks on the ledge, the figurines in their places.

"I put it back to rights for her," Colin whispered. "He didn't tell me that part, but I did. Didn't speak while I was in here, neither, just like you said."

"Thank you," Lumen rasped.

"'Course."

He stayed crouched in front of her, thin arms wrapped around his knees, as he watched her drink the broth. Her eyes felt bruised from crying, body stiff with cold, with the pain of cramps, with fighting men nearly twice her size.

"Can anybody be a Lunar, Lady?"

She hummed and nodded, a shaking hand reaching out and brushing Colin's bright hair out of his eyes. He shook his head and the locks fell right back in place.

"He says you're to come up and sleep," Colin whispered, as if there were someone else listening in the room, and then he looked over his shoulder to glance at the statue of Mother Lune. Lumen's lips twitched. Colin looked back to her and added in a hush, "Told him to leave you 'lone and he nearly kicked me. But I'm fast."

Lumen's chest hurt and she blinked away new wetness. "I'll be alright, Colin."

"I know," he said, bright and quick.

He took the mug from her when she finished the broth, darting out of the chapel and down the hall into darkness before she managed to drag herself up onto aching feet.

The Manor was silent, the fire long since died out in the courtyard. The bedroom was dark when she reached it, the silhouette of Westbrook barely visible in the bed.

Lumen went to the dresser. She opened the drawer, fingers sliding through fabric, searching for the dagger. It was gone and her eyes slid shut, a shattered moan falling free from her lips. She checked another drawer but there was no sign of the cold silver blade. Westbrook had found the thing and sold it by now.

"The argument has passed, Lumen," he whispered from the bed. "Your chapel is safe. Now come to bed."

His arms were gentle as she slid beneath the covers, circling her back, and she found it too easy to lay her cheek against his warm chest. *He is a different man here, at night,* she told herself. *It's alright that I don't hate him here.* The longer this went on the less certain she was of when she was telling herself lies.

Lumen was hiding in the gazebo, by the water, face lifted to the sun to soak up the last rays before winter. In the north they called it Final Sun. There would be more days as bright as this, but only when it was bitter cold and the world was cloaked in white snow.

Finley Brink was bringing men in from the fields, all the spare rooms of the Manor filled with beds and sour-mouthed soldiers who eyed her home like they were being asked to sleep in a pigsty. Fenn Manor may have been more rustic than the Mallen estate but if her home lacked any glamour the army only had itself to blame. And when she'd gone down to the kitchen it'd been full of busy women washing their clothes and hair and bodies and working on food all at once. The women Gideon had hired to entertain the men.

"Don't worry milady, we'll handle this mess for you now. General said so," one of the women said. She was pretty with bright copper blonde hair and full hips, and looked to be older than Lumen. She stood at the sink down in the cellar, bare chested and washing the linens of the hospital beds while the others crowded the kitchen counter and bickered over what could be cooked without using more than could be spared.

Lumen didn't mind the women, she liked their chatter and

their laughter and their smiles, but they shooed her out of their way and she was left without anything to occupy herself.

There were bruises around her wrists from where Dominic had held her while she fought against him in the chapel, the color stark beneath her delicate skin. Her courses had ended and Westbrook had seemed to know without her saying a word, simply pulling her beneath him and swallowing any attempt to speak with a kiss. His attentions had shifted from desperate and hungry to delicate and tender until she felt she was relearning the act completely.

"Little spirit, by the lake," Gideon called.

Lumen rested her head against the post, listening as the man thumped across the wooden floorboards until his boots—leather that was barely holding together at the seams—were at her side. Then he crashed down, legs folded in front of him as he sat to face her.

"You know Dominic likes to pretend he doesn't notice you, but then you move five feet away from the Manor and he sends me out after you," Gideon said, grinning. "Never seen him smitten before."

Lumen thought of the slow cooling of Westbrook's expression in the chapel, the heat of rage bleeding out of his face and leaving confusion and exhaustion behind. Was that smitten?

"If he doesn't please you, little spirit, I can certainly do my best to see you satisfied."

His voice purred and his breath washed over her cheeks as he leaned across the space. Lumen flicked her gaze across his face. He was handsome in an odd sort of way, all his features broken and distorted. And what she had mistaken for menace in the first week she now recognized as playful joy in the package of a rabid creature who'd forgotten how to smile without baring fangs.

"I don't mind that he keeps you so long but I wish he'd let me join you," Gideon said, watching her eyes as they widened. "Would you like that, little spirit? I'd be patient, wait till he'd spent you both, and then I'd take my time with you until you thought you couldn't stand another second."

His hand ducked beneath the hem of her skirt and Lumen remained still, the pair of them watching each other, as heat travelled higher from his fingertips, skimming her legs without actually touching her skin.

"I like to make women beg," Gideon said, eyes fixed to hers. "I like them dripping before I haul them onto my cock, like those wet sounds they make as they scream for more."

There was an arrow of warmth pointing directly toward her center, her knees parted to accommodate the threat of his touch. Lumen stilled the breath in her chest rather than let him watch her pant with desire. She didn't mind that these men could undo her, she didn't even mind the way they tricked her body into raptures. She only wished it wasn't done in displays of power and control.

"Why don't you lay with the women you brought for the others?" she asked—almost whispered—to keep her catching breaths a secret from him.

His crooked eyebrows shot up.

"Your General told me," she said. "He said you wouldn't touch them and I wouldn't be able to hide from you."

His eyes narrowed slightly and his hand skidded away from her skin, a brief touch against her ankle. He braced his elbows on his knees and faced the water, jagged smile returning.

"My mother was a whore, and the whole house of women raised me with her," he said. His eyes brightened at the memory. "Nice ladies. But whores have enough work on their back and I don't have coin to waste. 'Sides, like I said, I like my women to beg."

Lumen joined him in watching the water. It was a still day and the reflection was almost glassy, a dark mirror of the sky. She imagined sliding beneath the surface into a world that was just a little dimmer than her own, and quieter too, filled with water to bar the echoes of noise in her head.

"Does he hurt you, little spirit?" Gideon asked.

Lumen's mind drew up the memory of the thousand kisses laid upon her skin the night before, wet and pressing patterns left until she was drowsy and desirous. She shook her head.

"What would you do if he did?" she asked, mostly out of curiosity. It seemed that Dominic owned his men as thoroughly as he now owned her. Even more so in the case of Gideon and Healer Brink, who she would have called his friends if she'd ever seen a sign of real affection between the three of them.

Gideon turned until his warm knees were against hers, leaned in so close his lips were hovering above the skin of her shoulder.

"What would you ask me to do?"

Lumen licked her lips, trying to ignore the tingling thrill of his mouth barely on her. "Take me away from here."

"And would I stay with you, little spirit?" he asked, voice thick with gravel, the sound vibrating between her legs. His hands rose, bracing heat over her belly and against her back. "Would I keep you warm at night once we escaped?"

"No."

The moment froze between them and then Gideon drew away, a cracking, rasping laugh bellowing out of him, on and on until bright tears were creasing out of the corners of his eyes. Lumen turned her head away before joining him with a smile.

IT HAD ONLY BEEN a day and already Finley missed the austere silence of the Manor. There was a headboard banging against the thin wall of the attic room he'd taken, a pair of whores riding Charlie and Danvers hard to their pleasures. He wasn't going to ask Lumen to repair those stitches if they tore.

Thinking of her, his White Lady, conjured the vision of her held at the edge of ecstasy on Dominic's fingers. The ringing of the women's cries in the room next door mingled with the memory of Lumen burying her own cries behind pressed lips.

His fingers dug into the straw mattress beneath him, wished for wrists to hold, a body beneath his, and then he rolled off the bed and paced out of the room and down the stairs.

"Charlie boy, oh! Oh, Charlie!"

There was laughter down in the courtyard, and Finley leaned

over the hall banister to look down at the revelers. A group of men sat around the fire, chugging from ales and watching one of the girls crouched between a prone man's thighs, head bobbing over his lap, as another knelt behind her. Her skirts were flipped up and Finley watched her rump bounce and ripple as the second man thrust inside of her.

She tore her lips away from the cock she'd been working to release a loud, praising moan and the men around the fire cheered as she bounced herself back in earnest pleasure.

Gideon had good taste in whores, even if he never sampled them for himself. The women he brought to the army enjoyed their work and in return Gideon made sure they were well treated.

The men all clapped as the woman came with whimpering shouts and then immediately set back to her greedy work of sucking at the cock waiting by her cheek while the fellow behind her continued to chase his release.

Finley wanted company. He paced the halls until he reached Dominic's door.

It'd been nearly three weeks in the Manor, three weeks of *her* in the General's bed, and Finley and Gideon had yet to receive their invitation to share the night with the woman. Finley had never enjoyed those nights for more than casual relief, and now he was *craving* the opportunity. Not to get his cock wet but to have Lumen beneath him, surrounding him, the bright cold clean scent of her filling his lungs.

Breaths hitched behind the door—sweet, melodic sighs and a low, masculine murmur. The girl had been claimed but Finley wasn't fooled. Dominic was caught, had built himself a trap out of pale skin and sharp eyes and a cheek that turned away.

"Dominic, please."

Finley shivered at the sound of her, a voice so different than the one he heard in the workroom. He dragged himself away from the door. Better to be locked back in his room listening to Charlie and Danvers grunt and groan, than to listen to another note of her.

He made it as far as Gideon's door, heard the laughing grunt, and shouldered his way inside.

Gideon was naked, all his muddled scars and bruises on display, carved into his skin with harsh lines of muscle. His throat was arched, flexing, as he fisted a hand around a hard, massive cock.

"Can you hear them?" Gideon rasped, fingers flexing around the full base, sac twitching as his fingers brushed the skin.

Lumen was crying out in the next room, a high, pretty sound mixed with pleas and Dominic's name, finally escalating into an exclaiming refrain of 'yes!'

Finley wrestled himself out of his shirt, untying the belt of his pants and stumbling out of them on the way to the bed. Gideon laughed as he tripped out of a pant leg, shin knocking against the bed-frame.

"They're finishing?" Finley asked.

Gideon shook his head, grunting as he squeezed the tip of his cock, smearing the little beads of sticky fluid already gathered there. "He's just getting started with her. Finishes her a handful of times these nights before fucking her. *Glory* I want in that bed," he hissed.

Finley braced his knees on either side of Gideon's hips and took his own cock in hand, blood rushing south with every squeaking sigh that floated overhead through a crack at the top of the ceiling.

"It's a nice sound," Gideon whispered.

"Tell me, little witch," Dominic demanded from the other side of the wall and then a small, answering murmur, just a delicate sound. Whatever Lumen said must have been rewarded because soon her voice was breaking again, quick high notes, and Finley's cock grew hard at every beat of her breath.

"Get down here," Gideon said, pushing up on an elbow. "What's the point of coming in here if we're not touching?"

"Better than finishing myself off in the hall," Finley answered.

Gideon snorted. "Why? Who would care but our Lady?"

Our Lady.

Finley rolled down to the mattress, a softer thing than the

one he'd picked out for himself and Gideon wrestled him flat until both their cocks were trapped between their bellies. Gideon was bigger, wider, and his skin was rough with old scars. Finley didn't like the feeling of being trapped beneath him but he would tolerate it for the moment. Gideon nuzzled their lengths together as Finley arched his head back, staring at the wall as if he could see into the next room.

"Do you know how he does it?" he asked. He had the vivid picture of Lumen against the bedpost, body hidden by the folds of her skirt, but all the agony of approaching release written in the bright flush of her cheeks.

"If he's quiet he's got his head between her thighs," Gideon answered, pausing his slow grind to listen.

Dominic's voice was hissing, too quiet to make out the words, and Lumen was sobbing brightly, begging for more. "He's fucking her with his fingers now," Finley said and Gideon huffed a shaky breath, face nuzzling against his neck.

Gideon was an odd mix, all the need and affection of a woman with the desire to be in control like a man. They didn't suit one another in bed, Finley required the same control, but they were so...*used* to one another. Until Lumen, Finley would have said he preferred the smell of Gideon or Dominic to most women. He'd rather be beneath Gideon than on top of one of the whores.

He stroked his hands over Gideon's back, listening to the faint whine from the other man's throat, the anxious thrust of hips crushing against his.

"Dominic! Yes! Yes, there!"

Their heads turned in unison, mouths locking together in a mess of tongue and teeth. Finley spread his legs wide apart until Gideon was stretched too far, and began to thrust his hips up, sensitive skin of his cock sticking against Gideon's sweaty stomach, scratching through coarse hair.

"I want her," Gideon growled. "Want to watch you drive her mad, wait for Dominic to soothe her until she's limp..."

"And then you want to slide around in both our messes as she clings to you, begging," Finley whispered in his ear and Gideon went briefly limp and heavy against him.

"Yesss."

Finley slid a hand between their chests, wrapping long fingers around them both, barely able to circle them completely with Gideon's girth. The man was a beast in every sense of the word. He'd watched as women begged to be filled by the heavy inches of that cock, felt it nearly split his own hole. It had rarely been more than an object to him but now, thinking of Gideon stretching Lumen after he'd had his own time with her…

Sharing women had been a perverse entertainment. Now it was a *longing*.

Lumen was falling apart, breathy and delighted, almost laughing, and there was something warm in Dominic's voice. Was the General *falling in love*? It seemed impossible.

He pumped them in his hands, sliding through sweat and thin drips of arousal, listened to Dominic release a long, relieved groan.

"He's in her now," Gideon murmured.

"When will he share? When can we have her?" Finley asked.

If the sounds Dominic was making were anything to judge by, being inside Lumen was a path to Sol's Light.

"Don't say anything to him," Gideon said. He pushed up onto his knees and Finley took a deep breath, that secret oppressive stress lifted off him. Their hands bumped together around their cocks and he bit his lip to bury his groan as Gideon fumbled around their sacs.

"You say a word and he'll hoard her to himself for another month," Gideon muttered, bouncing slightly over Finley's lap.

"You're too goddamn heavy to ride me, you beast," Finley muttered, but he was rocking back in answer, the crush a glorious kind of painful.

Gideon only laughed anyway, fingers teasing lower, sending Finley in a high arch off the bed, a loud yelp of surprise. Lumen answered it with an equally noisy moan.

"She likes being watched," Finley muttered, eyes blinking at the ceiling.

"Bet she likes being heard too," Gideon said, and then he grinned and aimed a hearty groan up to the crack of the ceiling.

His finger furrowed around Finley's hole again, drawing out another longer cry and Finley retaliated with a twist of fingers around their heads. Soon the sounds were a chorus. There was skin slapping in the next room, Dominic grunting as their Lady sang joyously for more, for relief, for whatever Dominic was doing to her to be done again and again.

Gideon rolled on the bed and Finley scrambled to follow, so close that bright sparks were shooting up his spine, balls tightening. He took Gideon's face in his free hand, holding him firm to take his kiss, tongue plunging in as he thrust fast and hard inside their twin holds.

"Come, come for me, little witch."

Gideon moaned, twisting hard beneath him, licking back, sloppy animal kisses.

"Come, Lumen,"

She shouted as she met Dominic's demand, and Finley felt her voice hook directly beneath his balls, hot lightning shooting through him, spurting out in waves, sticky fluid rinsing over his fingers. Gideon trembled as he came too, head hanging off the edge of the bed, hand rubbing almost painfully between them.

Finley tugged away his hand when he couldn't take any more, pinning Gideon's wrists to the mattress, relaxing the full weight of himself on top of the man. They kissed, the clumsy sounds layered with the light echo of their neighbors in the next room. Lumen's mild voice, Dominic's dry rumble.

Did the Stone General say sweet things to his White Lady? Had she tamed him somehow? Could she do the same for Finley? Could Gideon be calmed in his wildness, made restful and human again? They were costing her peace every minute they stayed in the Manor, he could see the wear of it in her shoulders, her eyes. But if Dominic told him tomorrow that they would leave, move forward in Oshain, Finley would hate the news. *Would I follow that order?*

"I want her," Gideon breathed, rubbing his stubble coarse cheek against Finley's.

"I know."

Heavy arms wrapped around his back and Finley turned them slightly, dragging Gideon fully onto the bed, letting the big man wrap himself around him, ignoring the mess they made between them.

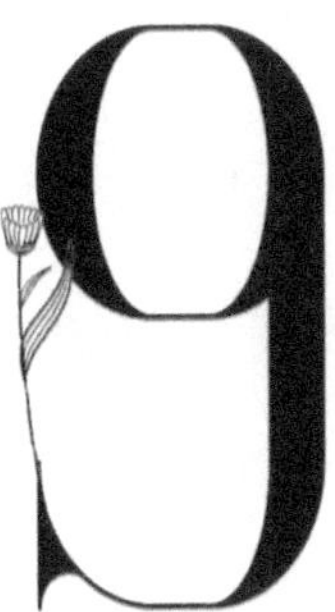

"IT'S TOO COLD FOR THERE TO BE ANYTHING OUT TO EAT," COLIN moaned, feet taking special joy in crunching through the brush of the woods.

"We're not looking for eating," Lumen said, and then thought of Gideon vomiting the berry poison—and thinking of Gideon conjured the sound of him from the night before and a flushing heat in her cheeks. She shook away the blushing memory and called back to Colin. "Don't eat anything you find unless you ask me first. These woods aren't kind to strangers."

"Serves Jones for stuffing his mouth with whatever fits," Colin muttered.

Lumen laughed under her breath. "The moon is growing fuller in the sky. It's a good time for gathering. I want to make sure the medic cupboards are full for the winter now that the house is—"

"Full of rank soldiers," Colin finished for her.

Lumen smiled at the boy over her shoulder and then spotted the little plant he was about to crunch beneath his boot. "Oh wait!"

He froze still for her, perfectly balanced as she rushed to pull the mint up from its roots. "Of all the men Westbrook sends to follow me about, you are certainly my favorite," Lumen said, glancing up in time to catch Colin's cheerful pink cheeks and sheepish smile.

"I'm the handsomest," he added, grinning.

When they started on their walk again Colin followed her footsteps with more care. He spotted another bundle of mint and went to gather it for her.

"What do Lunars do when the moon starts to get thinner?" Colin asked. "Eat less?"

Lumen smiled and stopped at a willow tree near the water's edge, gathering long strips of bark. "We only fast during the New Moon. We... release things while the moon wanes," she said. When he frowned at her she added, "While it shrinks."

"Whaddya mean by 'release'?" he asked. "Like birds?"

"Like anger. Or bad feelings. Or things we've kept that we don't need."

"How do you get rid of being angry?"

Lumen thought of how sometimes her jaw was clenched tight when she woke up in Westbrook's arms, about how out of seemingly nowhere she imagined clawing at his face as easily as she raked her nails down his back while she clung to him. How the violence of those moments contrasted with the way a nervous edge in her thoughts would soften when he caught her round her waist and tugged her against his chest at night. How tension passed out of her chest as her lungs filled with the raw smell of him and he peppered kisses over her skin as he laid her down in bed.

"You find a different way to think of the thing you're angry about," Lumen said.

"How?"

"I'm not sure how to explain it," she said.

"Are you angry at the army for taking your home?" Colin asked.

Lumen popped a thin sliver of willow bark to the back of her teeth and began to chew. She looked over her shoulder at Colin who was sniffing at a mint leaf while he watched her. "I am. But I... if I tend to the men who are ill or injured, then I see them as patients. If I cook food for you, then you are my guests." She stopped herself there. That was as much as the boy needed to know.

"Don't know if I could stop being angry," Colin said in a voice that was amusingly mild for the notion. "Don't know if I could skip three meals in one day either."

"Most Lunars don't really skip their meals. They just eat before the sun rises and after it sets so that it's a secret."

Colin kicked a fallen branch out of his way. "Sounds like cheatin.' If you're going to do a religion you should do it properly. Do you tell the honest truth on the Full Moon like Gideon was saying, Lady?"

"I do."

"What if someone asks you 'bout something that's supposed to be secret?"

"I could say that I didn't want to tell them, or I could try and change the subject," Lumen said with a shrug, starting to toe through the underbrush to look for medicines. "But it's better just to have out with the truth, I think. Full moon or not."

Colin mulled the words over as Lumen led them deeper into the woods.

"I'll show you how to find the good mushrooms," she said. "But you can't tell the other men."

The boy chased her heels, taking the basket off her arm and carrying their goods for the rest of the hunt.

DOMINIC WAS SKETCHING a pattern on her back with his fingernail and Lumen couldn't decide if she liked the drowsy hypnotic feeling or if she wished it would stop so she could fall properly asleep.

"How many brothers did you have?"

She blinked in the dark. His voice was so low it was nearly a whisper, fingertip still swirling over the planes of her back.

"Six," she said.

"Did they all go to war?"

"Brandon, the middle one, refused. And then he caught ill

and died in the next winter. Locals said it was some kind of divine punishment," Lumen said. She rolled, turning onto her back, Dominic's finger tracing around the curve of a breast as she moved, landing at the center of her chest. He was propped up on one side, the bed too thin for them to share it without piling close together.

"And are you sure the others are all dead?" he asked.

"Are you sure that your army takes no survivors?" Lumen asked, because that was what they said about General Westbrook and his troops.

He frowned at the question and stared back at her. All his heat and fire was washed into shadows at this time of night—after they had finished their attentions to one another and the candle was blown out. She thought she could see him better this way, less of the bright glare of the sun reflecting off of him, softened and blurred by darkness.

"I am," he said.

"Then they are lost," Lumen said. She reached up, studying the shape of his jaw with her touch and he leaned into her palm, stubble scrubbing over the skin there.

"I don't take prisoners," he said, and before Lumen could say that she'd heard as much, he ducked down, biting at her lips. "It's an ugly business and a mercy for them in the end to be killed."

"I believe you, Dom," she murmured, combing loose strands of hair back behind his ears.

He kissed her again, a slow easy lick and pull of tongue and lips, arms sliding beneath her back to hold her against his warmth. The kiss turned lazy and then wet lips dragged across her jaw and down to her neck where he nuzzled and rested. She scratched at the roots of his hair and felt the steady puff of his breath on her neck. He was restless, which meant there'd be no sleep for either of them yet.

"How did the war begin?"

Dominic stiffened against her and then his head popped up, brow furrowed. "What?"

Lumen blushed. "I wasn't even walking yet when it began

and I... by the time I was old enough to understand half my brothers were gone and my mother never spoke of it."

"And your brothers?"

"Held their breath until they were old enough to join." Lumen turned her cheek away from the stare burning over her face. "I listened to what I could from the locals after... after I was on my own but it wasn't a complete education and no one really had an answer."

"Wars aren't waged for villages more often than not," Dominic said and Lumen faced him again, frowning in confusion.

"Then who are they for?"

Dominic smiled but it wasn't happy. "The men who make money dressing an army for battle. Or the ones who want richer territory, better trading ports."

"And this war?"

"Both," he said, head tipping down to kiss one breast, and then the other. "Oshain kept raising the taxes on grain and Stalor decided it was time to take some of the farmland for themselves."

"Is that why you joined the army?" she asked.

He grunted, wedging himself on his back between her and the wall, his arm around her waist holding her tight to his chest. "No. I was given a choice, Army or Labor."

Lumen blinked. Either his family was very poor or—

A hand reached up to cup the back of her neck, the chest beneath her cheek rising and falling with a sigh. "I was an orphan, Lumen. I grew up on the streets. Begging until they caught me at it. Stealing until caught at it. I was lucky to even have a choice but the old knights liked having boys to lug things around for them back then. Plus it's easier to start young. Easier to fight later when you're used to seeing a battlefield at its worst."

If you weren't killed in battle before you were old enough to fight, from what Lumen heard.

"Jones joined up not long after me. We kept each other alive until we could age in."

"How old are you?"

"Thirty-six, snoop," he said, tugging on a strand of her hair. He froze next to her. "Why? How old are you?"

She kept her eyes pointing to his chest and rolled them. Spooked that she might be too young but not bothering to have thought about it before now.

"Twenty-three," she said, patting his chest as he relaxed.

"It's a wonder they didn't marry you off already," he muttered.

"To who? Everyone my mother might have considered went into the war a decade ago." And didn't come back out.

Dominic only grunted again, fingers softening and stroking up into her hair. She arched her head back into his touch, feeling a bit like a cat.

"What about Healer Brink? Was he a page boy with you and Gide-Jones?" she asked, tripping over the name as his touch stilled in her hair. When she found him staring at her she added, "The three of you seem like...friends."

It was the wrong word but it was as near as she could figure to their relationship.

"Fin is some rich lord's bastard as far as we can tell," Dominic grumbled. "He was thrown into all the finest schools until he was too old, given an allowance long enough to find an occupation. And instead he took it all and nearly poisoned himself. Whoever paid for the school arranged for him to be thrown in the army with the rest of us and he found his own way of being useful."

He tugged her closer, nose stroking against hers, teeth nipping at her lips. "I think he's rather sour at you knowing all your little hedge witch ways around his schooling."

Lumen hummed, her touch feathering over his cheekbones as she retaliated the kisses with her own. "He should be sour his schooling left so much untaught."

"I should've gone to school," Dominic said, hands grasping at her hips and turning them until she was straddled over his lap, blankets sliding off her back. "Maybe then I'd have been smart enough to lock you up in an attic from the beginning. I'm too selfish to be wise now."

"I'm glad to hear my opinion factors so little in this dilemma of yours," Lumen snapped, but the only real heat she felt was between her legs at the moment, his skin barely brushing her, cock stirring against the cleft of her ass.

"Hmph," he said in answer and she narrowed her eyes at him. "Speaking of schooling, how are you at riding?"

His hips jerked beneath hers, body nudging clumsily around her entrance.

"I've been told I have a very bad seat," Lumen said.

The white of his grin was bright even in the darkness. "I beg to differ," and then he squeezed at soft, twin rounds of flesh and lined himself up, drawing her down onto his length.

Lumen didn't know how he was so certain she would be ready for him, unless he had learned the somewhat embarrassing truth that was lately she was *always* ready for him. At least, if he was near enough to be touched, for the smell of him to be filling up her lungs until she breathed it out again, the shape of him tugging her eyes in his direction.

She sighed as he filled her and his hands stroked down to her knees, pushing them farther apart, her lips forming an 'o' at the angle. She shifted and moaned, head falling back, clit scraping against his skin, body hiccuping on top of his lap.

"Go on, little witch," he said, rocking himself up into her.

Lumen whimpered, every move of her thighs shifting him inside of her and distracting her from her rhythm. His hands wrapped around her hips, helping, and she braced her palms onto his knees using the leverage to rise and fall over his length.

"There you are," he grunted as she began a canting motion, steady and breathtaking. "Natural."

This is not really like riding, she thought. "You're much more comfortable than a horse," she said instead, biting at her smile.

He laughed and Lumen felt his heels brace behind her, crying out as he started to buck as if he meant to throw her off. The force of his thrusts, the weight of her fall, brought them together with the sudden crash of a drumbeat and Lumen felt she continued more by momentum and a need to see the crescendo than by an intentional effort on her part.

"Oh gods, Dom, Dominic, please!"

"Take it from me, little witch," he hissed beneath her. "Take your pleasure. Fuck!"

She groaned, brow furrowing and discovered that she could mimic the same dip and grind he always used to leave her whimpering. It did the same now, made her thighs tremble, and she whined, body burning, wishing he would turn them over and rut her into her pleasure.

"Help, please, Dominic," she begged.

His right hand abandoned her hip, fingers pressing quick and hard and rapid against her clit, swirling. The effect was immediate, her motions stuttering into a shallow nudging grind as she jerked and shimmied against his touch. Her knees tried to close around the onslaught of ecstasy, back bowing and nearly tipping her over if not for the grip on her side.

"Yes, yes, yes," she chanted, nails scratching at his skin, eyes falling shut and body trembling through the soft flutters of release that came first. She shook, Dominic carrying her through the next wave with his touch, her body doing little more than rocking against his, as she fell apart with high cries of joy.

He pulled her down to his chest, face cradled against his neck, hands stroking her back as she came down in soft, weak aftershocks.

"Little moon," he whispered into her hair.

She blinked, eyelashes tickling at his skin, and he thrust slow and soft inside of her, still hard. She started to lift up off his chest but he held her fast.

"Stay. I want you close," he said, the words almost bitter as if it cost him to speak them.

Lumen nuzzled against his neck, sucking at the skin there and humming as he began to plunge, arms wrapped tight around her, clasping her to him, skin sticking. His breath was heavy in her ear, fingers studying her greedily, teasing down her spine, between the flesh of her ass, hinting farther and then skidding back up again.

"Want you everywhere." One hand gripped at her hair, drawing a handful up to his nose and taking a long breath. The other splayed over the base of her spine holding her in place to take his thrusts.

"You have me," she said into his skin and listened to his answering groan, felt it from head to toe, vibrating against her sensitive skin as he pounded inside of her. *You own me*, she thought but every inch of her skin proved that he already knew as much.

But he moaned beneath her as if she had said the words out loud, crushing her in his hold, tight enough that every snap of him inside her was joined by a drag of skin over her clit until she was clutching him in return, panting and sobbing into his neck.

"Lumen," he growled, fucking her fast and hard and with every determination to take her over the edge with him. "Say it."

"You have me," she whimpered.

"Say it."

"Dominic, please!"

She didn't know what it was he wanted to hear but he didn't seem to be able to wait, body frantic beneath hers, the first hot burst of him inside of her, tipping her over the edge with a bright cry. His lips fumbled for hers, groaning into the kiss as she sucked at his tongue, mimicking the way her body milked his cock.

He held her tight until his breath steadied, arms loosening enough for her to lean back, see his eyelids drooping.

"Pull the blankets up and stay as you are," he mumbled, a hint of the General in his tone. "I like your touching."

Lumen smiled, catching the blankets with her toes and kicking them up. She shifted in spite of his order. It was alright for him, but she'd be walking bowlegged tomorrow if she slept like that. Never mind the mess he always ignored after the act was done. She wiped them up as best she could and snuggled against his side, one leg thrown over his.

"If you'd been smart, you'd've run," he murmured, falling into sleep.

Lumen wasn't sure if he was speaking to himself or to her and she preferred not to think on it. Things were as they were and for the night at least it was better than she had feared while listening to the thunder of the army's approach those weeks ago. Dominic's lips brushed over her forehead once more and then they were both asleep.

"He's getting too attached to her," Dom growled, eyes fixed to where Colin was chasing the skirts of Gideon's favorite view of Oshain.

The little spirit, white braid patting her spine as she marched back from the lake to the Manor, basket full of the fall's last harvest. Her eyes flicked up to their window in her father's old office—silver gaze cutting through glass to knick at Gideon's skin—and then fell back to the ground again. He wanted to take a bite out of her.

"Are you jealous?" Gideon asked, laughing. He knew the answer. Dominic was jealous of the grass under the young woman's feet, and the sun that pinked her cheeks. Of course he was jealous of the boy she spoiled with jams and gentle touches.

Dom's frown deepened. "War is only going to be harder on him if he gets used to her sweetness."

"I wonder how you will manage then," Finley muttered from the other end of the room, his back turned to them, nose in a book.

Gideon waited for the snarl, for Dominic to snap back at Finley, their natures too suited to clashing. But Dominic's eyes were fixed on the last glimpse of Lumen Fenn as she ducked out of sight, back into the Manor. He was good and lost to her then. Gideon wondered what that meant for him and Fin. His cock ached to fill the woman, hands itched to touch her. If she had turned Dominic into a new kind of creature then he might be out of luck.

"Go get the boy," Dominic said. "We'll need information for tomorrow's strike. And those women you found are drinking us out again."

"It's the men as much as the ladies," Gideon said. "It's cold up here. They need something to warm them."

"I thought that was what the whores were for," Finley snipped from behind his pages.

"You feeling tense again, Fin?" Gideon asked on his way to the door, grinning. "You can always come by."

Finley sniffed, a little color rising to his cheeks. The pair of them fucking to the sounds of his little spirit was better than nothing, at least.

Lumen was crossing the courtyard below and Gideon called down as Colin's bright hair appeared in her wake.

"Oi! She can manage from there. General needs you."

Colin grumbled and Gideon brushed some of the loose dust and dirt collecting on the ledge down onto his head.

"Oh cut it out, you surly old bastard," Colin snarled.

Across the courtyard Lumen made a bright, surprised sound, almost like a giggle, and then ducked out of sight. Gideon's fingers clenched around the stone, body tense with want. Colin came skidding up the stairs and Gideon decided he wasn't needed back in Dominic's court. If he was they could send someone to find him. He started down the open hall towards the lady's workshop.

"Where you going?" Colin called, feet slapping on stone.

"Never you mind," Gideon answered.

The boy ran up to his back and Gideon turned to glare down at him. "She don't need you panting on her too," Colin said, teeth clenched, and then his foot lashed out, kicking at Gideon's shin before he spun and took off in the other direction like there was Sol's fire at his back.

Gideon nearly fell over laughing, his voice echoing all around the Manor. The little shit was probably right. And Dominic was too. The boy was getting too attached to Lumen.

Not that he could blame him. He certainly wasn't going to take the warning seriously, and he continued on his path.

The office was on the opposite side of the Manor, room fragrant with the must of drying herbs, Lumen moving as quietly as a ghost through the space as she strung up her gatherings.

"More poisons, little spirit?"

She didn't jump or squeak at the sound of him, although he supposed he didn't move near as quiet as she did.

"It depends on if you're foolish enough to eat them," she answered, her back to him.

He stepped loud on the floor, letting her hear his steady approach, waiting for her to skid out of reach. But she hadn't pulled away when he'd reached beneath her skirt by the water, and the heat of her against his fingertips was a haunting memory. She remained working until he was close enough to stir the fine hairs at the back of her neck. When he braced his hands on the shelf in front of her she stilled.

"Did you like our little performance?" he asked. "Listening to Finley and I. Us listening to *you*."

Her breath hitched and her head cocked, neck bared and nearly close enough to kiss, to bite, to suck.

"That was Healer Brink?" she asked.

Gideon blinked. He could see the pink on her cheeks, the flush spreading down her neck beneath the collar of her dress. But that wasn't the mewling, bashful answer he expected. Words were stolen straight from his lips when she spoke again.

"Yes. I liked it. Did you?"

One of Dominic's growls escaped his throat. He'd forgotten it was the full moon. And instead of drawing secrets from her lips, she was using them against him, cutting through his teasing to torture him with desire.

"Not as much as I might have if I'd been in the bed with you."

The flush turned darker on her skin and Gideon lifted one hand away from the shelf, skimming it above her skin, watching goosebumps appear in the path.

"Is that something you do?" she asked, voice wavering.

He hummed. "Usually. Would you like that?"

She blinked and he watched the flutter of ghost pale eyelashes brushing over her cheeks. "It seems like an awful lot of work."

Gideon bellowed out a laugh, breath fluttering her hair, and rolled away, cock half hard and back landing against the shelf, jars rattling. Her lips were pursed tight as if she were trying to keep from smiling.

"You have him all tangled up in you," Gideon said, glancing at her from the corner of his eyes. "I don't blame him."

This at least made her demure, turning her cheek away, looking down at her hands and finding them empty of herbs to work with.

"I'd tell you to suggest inviting me into your bed but I think he might break my neck for it," he added.

She frowned at that. "I suppose I'm meant to feel grateful for not already being passed around."

Gideon didn't like the queasy turn of his stomach that followed. Usually women *were* grateful for that...until Dominic grew tired of them. Not that Gideon let the women be treated poorly. Perhaps by their standards but...

He'd seen a lot worse growing up.

Is that enough? a voice asked in his head, sounding like the woman in front of him. And a bit like his mother too, or what he could remember of her.

Lumen was continuing in her work, tying branches to the rafters in long, spindling streamers, and Gideon was trying to brush a feeling away that was too much like guilt. A cold pit in his stomach and the hot flick of shame on the back of his neck.

What if Dominic *did* tire of his little spirit?

She'd be mine, he thought, with a certainty that felt hard as stone.

"If anything happens, you come to me," Gideon said. The hem of her skirt whispered against the stone and then stilled. She turned, those sharp silver eyes wide. "You come to me, you'll be safe. No one will touch you without your permission. Right?"

When she looked at him with that stunned, frozen expression, he could almost imagine her vanishing with a little flicker of light.

"Alright?" he asked, lowering his chin and staring back at her.

"Yes," she said, nodding.

"Jones."

Shit. Of course Dominic would come looking for him. The little lad probably made a point of mentioning that Gideon went dancing after Lumen. Spies didn't learn to keep information like that secret until they were older.

"Sir," Gideon said, pushing away from the shelf.

Dominic stood in the doorway, studying Lumen who seemed to have lost sense of where she was or what she was meaning to do. Gideon didn't blame her for her surprise. He'd never offered as much to anyone else. He didn't even know rightly how he would *keep* his promise. But he'd figure it out if he had to, if Dominic lost his brains and tossed the girl out to her ruin.

"Do you mind doing your fucking job and joining this meeting?" Dominic asked, eyes narrowing at him.

For nearly twenty years Gideon had taken orders from the younger man, and never minded that he could be a demanding, prickly little shit when he was in the mood. Those moods had come more and more frequently the longer the war lasted. And up until this moment Gideon had never really felt like decking the man.

Lumen was a lovely kind of poison on her own, berries or not, he realized. He didn't even mind. He would take her by the handfuls too if he could.

"Only a bit," Gideon answered, rolling his shoulders and crossing the room.

Dominic huffed, some of the tension puffing out of him with Gideon's humor. They entered the hall together.

"If I want you tracking her, I'll tell you," Dominic said, words so low Gideon almost couldn't hear them. But he was nearly deaf in one ear, anyway.

"Yes, sir," Gideon said and Dominic's eyes narrowed at the obedience. So Gideon grinned and added, "Can't help looking for a nice view on a gray day."

Dominic grunted, head nearly turning back as if he wanted another view himself.

Lumen was returning to the Manor after sitting out by the water, when Dominic appeared at the kitchen door, mug of ale held loose in his fingers. He was glaring at her. No, only staring. She was learning the hard shapes of his face and the occasional softer meanings behind them.

"Why don't I find you fluttering around my side at all hours?" he asked. "Or at least during meals, taking bites from my fingers."

Lumen's nose wrinkled at the suggestion. "Is that something that would please you?"

Dominic's face relaxed, all the usual firm furrow of his brow and downturn of his lips easing into something strangely bright. "Not usually," he said, smiling. "Have you eaten?"

"Yes."

"Then come to bed with me," he said.

Lumen glanced over her shoulder. There was still a fiery red edge of sunset bleeding through the tree line. Normally Dominic didn't make it up to the bedroom before the sun was down for the night and the men had settled around the fire or into the cots.

"I go to war tomorrow, little witch," he murmured, snagging his fingers around her wrist and tugging her to his chest.

There was that bonfire smell on his skin, the salt of sweat, and tart cider on his breath. It made her dizzy, fingers catching on the coarse wool of his coat, burrowing into his warmth as if she'd suddenly realized how chilly the night was. And then she remembered.

"Is Colin back yet?" she asked.

"Your little lover will be home soon, Lumen," he said, nuzzling into her hair, the hand at her wrist pulling her arm around his shoulder until she was arched against him. He pecked at her lips until she was gripping at his shirt, rising to her toes for more. "Come inside," he whispered in her ear, nipping at the lobe. "I want to enjoy my witch before tomorrow."

Was he worried about the outcome of a skirmish? Or simply excited by the thought of it?

She blinked and drew back, briefly dazed by the calm warmth on the face above hers. "What supplies did Colin need to fetch before a skirmish? And where could he go? The nearest city on this side of the battle line is more than a day's ride away."

Dominic groaned, head falling back and throat flexing before her eyes. "You are extremely difficult, do you know that?"

"Dominic…" Lumen thought of the other times the boy had run off on errands and come back by nightfall. "Dominic, you're not sending him across the line are you?"

"He's a *spy*, Lumen. He knows his business," Dominic said, brow arching.

Lumen reared back, his warm arm scrambling for her but not catching before she was out of reach. "Spy? He's a *child*. That's dangerous! What if the Oshain army catches him!"

He stared back at her, the easy, happy man being replaced again by the General. "Lady Fenn, I am sure you should know your people better than I do," he said.

Lumen's heart twisted painfully. She might know her people, but she did not know their army. What would they do if they caught Colin? She didn't trust one army more than another no matter what country they were from.

Dominic sighed, hands spread in front of him and taking slow steps in her direction. "He's a smart boy, Lumen. He knows what he's about and he's been doing it for months. It's safer for him to go on his own than to send someone like Danvers with him, believe me."

Lumen's shoulders relaxed as his hands skimmed down her arms. She told herself it was because she *did* believe he knew enough not to send Colin into a truly dangerous situation. It had nothing to do with the way she was always ready to be touched by him.

"Now will my lady lay me down in bed or am I to see to myself tonight?" he purred in her ear.

Lumen snorted. "Sir, I had assumed you did not know how and this was why you needed me."

Dominic's laugh was choked as he hauled her back to his side, all but lifting her from the ground with his arm around her waist. "And what did you do before me, then?"

Lumen tilted her head, cheeks flushing, tongue numb until he turned his head to look at her, carrying them both inside with a long stride.

"I had not learned how to… to do whatever it is you do," she said, when it was dark enough to hide her face.

His feet stumbled and then they were turning, and he was crowding her against the doorway leading from the kitchen to the hall. "Witch," he hissed, fitting his hips between her thighs until she was pinned in place. His fingers tipped her chin up to take his kiss, tongue flicking across the seam of her lips. She parted them with a hungry whimper and moaned as he filled her mouth with the taste of him, them together.

"We're going upstairs and I am going to teach you to take your pleasure for yourself as I watch you do it. And then teach you how I take mine. And then I'm going to have you every way I can think of before we are both too tired to move. What do you think of that, my lady?"

"I think we are wasting time in the kitchen," she said, pleased as he smiled for her again. Pleased as he dragged her down the hall, men laughing in the courtyard as they watched them flicker past the archways on their rush to the stairs.

LUMEN CAUGHT A BRIEF GLIMPSE OF COLIN THE NEXT MORNING, the pair of them equally bleary-eyed. But he was dashing through the courtyard below, head ducked low, carrying supplies from one man to the next. She waved at him from the archway above, body wrapped in a blanket pulled straight from the bed, until Dominic walked out of the room, dressed in his uniform, armor plating halfway strapped on.

His mouth was in a grim line, all the laughter from the night before buried away, but there was fire in his eyes as they flicked over her and then down to the ground where his troops waited.

"Get back into bed," he said, and Lumen arched a brow at the order. "We're making a risky move today. Brink will need your help later, no doubt."

She swallowed. Was that worry fluttering in her chest or expectation?

"I'll have the infirmary ready," she said.

Dominic took a step toward her and Lumen's spine straightened, almost a flinch. He was the General now, and not her lover, and instinct knew the difference even if logic told her they were the same man. She forced herself to wait for his approach.

"I will have need of you later too, Lady Fenn," he said, head leaning down to tap against hers.

She would have to do better this time to let the injured men receive her help before Westbrook had her cornered in a stair-well again.

"I thought you might have had enough of me by now, sir," she said lightly.

"No, my lady," he whispered. "Not yet."

She lifted her lips to his, expecting the kiss, but not for it to be so soft, so long. A perfect press to her mouth, breath exhaling out over her cheeks before he pulled away.

"Rest," he said again, turning away.

She took a last glimpse down into the courtyard, caught Brink and Jones' eyes as they stared up at her with a study she didn't entirely understand, and watched Colin ducking out of a doorway and through the house to the front yard. She pulled the blanket tighter around her shoulders, breath puffing clouds in the morning air, and went back to bed.

THERE WERE no soldiers left behind to rest during this skirmish. The Manor was empty but for Lumen and the other women. They seemed to keep mostly out of her way until they noticed her lugging hot water from the kitchen over to the dining room turned infirmary. Then they lended her their help, boiling every scrap of fabric till it was clean, keeping the fire lit, tidying up after Lumen everywhere she went.

But the skirmish didn't end. For the first time in a month, night fell and there were no men in the Manor. Lumen paced the infirmary until there was nothing unchecked, nothing left to be done to prepare for their return. The other women were sleeping in a pile in the sitting room, snoozing on men's cots, a shared cask of ale leaking gently on the floorboards.

Lumen wandered the halls, finding her route taking her back to the front door, eyes on the road. It was dark and silent, the moon was heavy and bone white in the sky, and there was no sign of torches, no sound of hooves.

She was worried. That was the crawling, churning, queasy turn in her stomach. Westbrook had turned her home into his fortress, her body into his conquest, and now he had done this to her too. Made her worry. For *him*.

"This is for Colin," she muttered up to her Mother Lune. It was not the full moon tonight and she could not be cursed for the lie. It was bad enough to know that she ached to see Dominic again, to know that he was safe. And not just him but Gideon, for all his strange and hungry brand of teasing. Even for Healer Brink.

She took herself back inside to where the women slept and drank two mugs of ale to put herself to sleep. When she could not sleep with the smell of Dominic so heavy in the bed, she took one blanket down with her to the infirmary to wait and drowse on a hospital cot.

SOUND CRACKED before dawn and Lumen sat up, gasping, blanket clutched to her throat and toes numb with cold. Horses neighed outside the window and another loud crack sounded. The doors of the Manor being slammed open.

She wadded the blanket up in her arms, tossing it onto a spare chair and barely jumping out of the way as the dining room doors burst open, bloodied men carrying in friends worse off than they were. All the worry of the night before, the exhaustion of two days with little sleep, was shocked away by the bodies coated in dark scarlet and drying brown. It didn't matter who these men were—not that she could tell through all the blood—they needed her more than she needed to find Dominic.

The first two men to make it to the table were already dead, her fingers slipping in the blood on their neck as she searched for their heartbeat, eyes watching her like empty windows.

"Too late. Move them," she said, barely loud enough to be heard over the storm of the army returning.

The next man was frozen, pulse weak, stiff and unmovable as she searched for the injury. There was a swelling at the back of his neck, but no other sign of pain and she stripped him out of his jacket and passed him to one of the women who'd come in with the hustle.

"Clean him up, put him by the fire. Get him to drink something warm if you can."

The man was walking at least. She busied herself with the next, no sign of Healer Brink in the first wave of soldiers. But Gideon's ladies were quick hands and remembered the names of tools and herbs she'd explained the day before. They kept their hands clean and bandaged men with tight and tidy care. When the clean water ran out, muddled and dark with blood and dirt, they were already carrying more in for her.

"Jones!"

Lumen's hand dropped the rag she'd been using to wipe the blood off the table at the sound of Westbrook's bellow.

"Bring the boy!"

Her breath hitched in her chest, unable to keep herself from turning to the door. Colin? Was he—

"Let me, lady," one of the women said, one about her age with southern tanned skin and dark eyes. Rosie was her name, taken after the bright red bloom of a birthmark on her shoulder.

"Clean them, bandage," Lumen said, and she nodded. "If you can see bone, or the blood still runs fast, call for me."

If the blood still ran quick, the man was more than likely near to dead, but if she could try something to help them, she would.

"Yes, lady."

Lumen ran to the hall, squirming past the men until she was jumping through an archway to the courtyard. Westbrook was there, skin painted red, and her heart froze in her chest until his head turned in her direction, eyes bright with life, face hard as stone. He was tearing his jacket off his shoulders in such a fervor she was sure he must not be injured.

Next came Gideon, equally bloodied, equally ferocious and alive, one huge hand cuffed around little Colin's neck, dragging the boy with every kicking squirming step.

"What is it? What's happened?"

She ran to the boy, stumbling down to her knees, skirts wet with blood, and tore the boy from Gideon's grasp, patting him over to check for harm.

"I didn't mean to, lady, I swear it," Colin said, and Lumen's breath was short in her chest, finding his face clean but for mud and tears. "Only it was the full moon and you's said t'was better to be out with the truth."

Westbrook's shadow layered over hers, looming over her back and Lumen bundled the boy to her chest, arms around his shoulders.

"He sold us out to the Oshain army, gave them our plans for the morning," Dominic thundered at her back.

"It was the full moon, lady," Colin whispered into her throat, voice hiccuping on the tears. "I didn't want to fail you."

Dread was an icy coat of frost through her veins, up into her throat. She lifted her eyes to Gideon's face, and found him unreadable, too thick with war, no smile to be found. Over his shoulder Brink appeared.

"How many dead?" he asked.

"Three," she said, swallowing through fear. "Two more soon."

"And will they be better served with you out here?" he snapped. He looked to be in similar shape to Colin, muddied, and she felt more certain that whatever blood he wore was someone else's.

"The women are taking care of them for the moment."

"The whores?" Dominic barked.

"The women who are just as neat with bandages as I," Lumen answered, sharp and sudden, Colin tight in her arms. "There's not much they can do for your army on their backs at the moment, Sir."

Fingers snagged at her back and Lumen released the boy as Dominic twisted her to face him.

"Do you know what your preaching and saintly care has cost my soldiers?" he asked, voice deadly, words slithering into her ears with a viper's grace.

"He's just a boy," Lumen said, straightening her spine as stiff as steel to withstand his rage.

"And now he has killed men," Dominic answered.

"You made him into a spy at ten years old!"

"And you made him *worthless* to me!" Blood creased in the

lines of his face, stubble thick and a gash cracking open on his jaw.

She wanted to slam his head against the stone and then wash the whole mess tenderly away, as if that might take his anger and violence with it.

"Enough!"

Neither Lumen nor Westbrook backed down despite Brink's order. She felt as if she had caught some of the man's fire and she was determined to turn it back on him.

"Lady Fenn, I need you in the infirmary."

"Come, Colin," Lumen said, turning way.

"If you think—" Dominic started on a snarl, fingers still tight in the fabric of her waist.

"Leave it for the hour, Dom," Gideon said, taking hold of Colin's arm. "I'll keep the lad under my eye."

"He's going to be punished and hiding in your skirts won't change that," Dominic said to her, and then pushed her away from him.

Lumen opened her mouth to tell the man off—she'd have his head if he hurt the boy—but Colin spoke first.

"I understand, sir."

"Hush," Lumen said, combing her fingers through the boy's hair and following Brink back to the infirmary.

"I shouldn'a gone, Lady," he said, but his hand reached up for hers, holding on tight. "I knew it'd come to no good."

Lumen wanted to weep. She looked to Gideon who was frowning, staring straight ahead, but his eyes flicked to hers after a moment.

"He'll be punished and things will be set to rights again," Gideon said softly. "Better that than the men carry anger. This'll put all that aside."

"If it's my fault—" Lumen started.

"It's not, Lady," Colin said quick. "I shoulda said somethin' before we rode out."

"Come on, lad," Gideon said, pulling the boy away. "Let the lady be useful to the men."

Brink was striding into the infirmary, jacket shrugged off

and shirtsleeves rolling up. There was a red stain on his shoulder but he was moving well enough that Lumen figured he could decide if it was worth worrying or not. Beds were already filling up around the room, the other ladies bustling in and out as they organized the men by need.

"It won't be easy on the boy, but Westbrook will be fair," Brink said to her under his breath as they paused for a moment, in the middle of all the wreckage.

Lumen looked around and found a man hissing, hand hovering over his shoulder that hung too low.

"He needs his arm reset," she said, ignoring Brink's words. "I'll deal with the stitches."

They parted at the center of the room and went to their work.

SIX MEN DEAD. Four more near to it but Healer Brink said they looked better than he'd expected. Lumen was numb to hope, to worry, to the pain that ran up from her feet to her hips, straight through her spine and into her shoulders. To the pounding in her head. To the way her eyelids stuck and scraped over her eyes every time she blinked. To the thick lines of dark stain that turned her fingernails brown no matter how long she scrubbed and washed until her knuckles were nearly raw.

The last thing they needed was someone else bleeding.

She couldn't stop herself, skin stinging, still scratching under water tinted murky pink.

"That's enough, little spirit," Gideon said, at her side, hands wrapping around her wrists and pulling them from the water. He dried them with a clean cloth, gentle on the fragile skin.

"Where's Colin?" Her throat was dry and the room was dark except for candlelight. The boy had kept faithfully to the soldier's side every moment Lumen could spare to check on him.

"It's time, and—hold, lady," Gideon said, catching her around the shoulders, "it may be better for you not to see."

"I'll cut his cock clean off if he hurts that boy," Lumen growled, struggling in Gideon's hold.

The man choked at her answer, eyes wide and Lumen noticed for the first time that he was still grimy from the battle. She took the cloth from his hands and raised it between them wiping roughly at his cheeks to take the worst away.

"I don't doubt you mean what you say but trust me, little spirit, it would be better for Colin to take the lashes dealt. He was right. He should've told me if he didn't think he could keep his trap shut. Or he should have told the General what was said as soon as he got back that night," Gideon reasoned.

"Lashes," Lumen repeated dumbly.

"One for each of the men dead," Gideon said. There was a deep line between his eyebrows and a sorrow in his eyes that she didn't expect to see, could barely read in all her exhaustion.

"He's a boy," she said.

"He agreed to the punishment, didn't even flinch," Gideon said. "Let me walk you upstairs, little spirit."

"Where's Brink?" she asked. The infirmary had cleared out but for the patients and she hadn't even noticed.

"Ready to care for the lad."

Lumen blinked. That little white back, already pocked with scars. And now more and these were *her* fault.

"If he can take the punishment, I can watch," Lumen whispered. "I want to see him through."

Gideon hesitated and Lumen pushed herself out of his hands. He raced her to the door.

"Let him do this for the men's respect," Gideon said.

Lumen stalked through the corridor, out to the courtyard, pushing aside the men she had nursed just an hour ago. The fire was high, and with the space surrounded by a watchful crowd it was almost warm. Brink stood at the edge of the ring not far away, face haggard with exhaustion, arms folded over his chest. There was a wooden post not far from the fire, upright and waiting, with Colin standing near, head hanging low.

Westbrook stood with his back to the boy, hands gripped tight around a cat o'nine tails. Lumen wanted to rush between them. Wanted to run at Westbrook and take the flogger from his hand, stripe his back with it and rub salt into the wound.

The faces of the crowd were grim, even flickers of sympathy, but Lumen understood. The boy had cost them the lives of friends, brothers. He was a child, yes, but he was living under men's laws. Maybe Gideon had been right and she shouldn't watch but she couldn't bear not to.

The moon was high above, her face turned to the scene, and Lumen thought the Mother must have understood the boy's sacrifice best of all. He had told the truth when even Lumen would have found a way to lie, obeyed the goddess' law and would pay man's price.

"Shirt off," Westbrook said, turning to the boy.

"I'd rather keep it on, sir," Colin said, chin lifting, lips wobbling.

Westbrook, who was nearly as filthy as Gideon still, frowned but Lumen knew the expression. He would waver.

"It'll be better for you if it's bare," Brink said, tone soft but carrying in the muffled quiet of the scene.

Colin's eyes skittered around and Lumen's heart panged, eyes already filling with tears. She blinked them away. It wouldn't help him to see her cry for him until later. The boy undid the buttons of his shirt with trembling fingers.

Six lashes. Six lashes. It would be done soon. She would slit Westbrook from neck to belly, perhaps, and that would be done soon too. She and Colin would sleep in the chapel together from now on. And when the army finally moved on she would lock him up and let Westbrook leave without his little spy.

Six lashes.

Colin folded the clothes she had given him into a tidy pile, setting them out of the way and turned his back to Westbrook. She watched the man flinch at the sight of Colin's scars, broad shoulders sinking and eyes falling to the ground. His chest heaved with a breath and Colin stepped up to the post, thin arms hugging the wood.

Westbrook's eyes found hers, searching her face. She didn't know what he wanted to see and she was too tired to show him anything but the truth, too heartbroken to care. He would never touch her again. Not after this. He closed his eyes briefly, and then squared his shoulders stepping up to the boy.

"I will count," he said, tone as gentle as it had been during their last night in bed together. His arm rose with the flogger in hand, the thin leather tails dangling, and then cut through the air.

Colin's breath caught and the leather hissed against his skin, scratching. The boy's eyes were wide and Lumen's chest was frozen but she could see the relief on his face, narrow shoulders softening. It hadn't been what he expected. She could see little marks of pink blooming in the wake but it hadn't hurt the way he'd expected.

"One," Westbrook said, word flat. He repeated the action and Colin flinched and whimpered behind closed lips but relaxed again.

Gideon's palm landed on Lumen's rigid back briefly, a soft brush. She understood what he said.

See? Not so bad. As if she were supposed to think of West-brook as merciful. She stepped out of reach and Gideon's hand fell away.

A third strike landed and Colin's feet skittered, as if he were ready to run, and then steadied. His face was white, breaths panting. The pain may have been light but it cost the boy to stand still for the act, not to run, too close to what he had already suffered.

Around the fire, soldiers began to shift, faces hardening, arms crossing. Unsatisfied. Westbrook's eyes skimmed his troops, and Lumen watched the transformation. The man who had been watching the boy for signs of terror was now watching his men to judge their satisfaction. The light strikes were not enough.

"No," Lumen mouthed but she could raise no sound to her lips.

The next strike cracked and Colin went taut, screaming bright in shock, and small voice cracking out. His arms held tight to the post as tears spilled onto his cheeks again. Westbrook eyes were fixed to his own fingers around the handle of the flogger, chest heaving with breath.

Lumen understood him. He would satisfy his men's anger for the boy's sake. And Colin had only done what he thought was required of him. What she herself had suggested.

When the flogger rose again, she was ready, running between the man and boy, a scream in her throat but no further.

"Lady, no!" Gideon barked from behind her.

But it was too late, Westbrook's eyes were wide as the delicate braids of leather and their cruel knots landed across her face and neck and chest, the pain as bright as starlight. The scream burst free, sudden and startling, and the fiery sting turned the world white. Her worn body toppled under the wave that followed, the sight of Westbrook's boots staggering back all she saw as she fell.

Overhead the sleeping roosts of birds in the Manor rafters cried out and took flight, cluttering the sky with black silhouettes until the moon was tucked behind wings.

⸙

"Leave him, Dom, he'll be more devoted to her than ever now."

Lumen flinched, head pounding, and then froze. The scent of herbs was strong in her nose, right side of her body aching and left side of her face burning and swollen. The strike on her skin. The little pinching tugs in her flesh now. Finley had made delicate stitches for her.

"You say that like that's a good thing," Westbrook hissed. Lumen kept her eyes shut, head spinning as she listened. "His devotion to her cost us lives."

"His not telling us straight the next morning cost us lives," Gideon said. "We could've stayed in bed and left those Oshits sitting out in the cold, freezing their bits off."

"What are you saying?"

"I'm saying we let him keep doing his job. They'll trust him now. They nearly had us."

"What should it matter if he is devoted to her?" Brink, near to her. Her hair stirred under a soft touch and then it vanished again.

"What?"

"Why do you care if the boy is devoted to her?" Brink asked again.

Lumen thought it must be obvious by now that she was listening. She couldn't stand to take a breath through the tense quiet.

"Oh, I'm sorry, Brink," Dominic snarled. "Did you miss the part where we were ambushed because the boy gave our plans for the day away?"

"No. I obviously didn't. He learned his lesson."

"Did he?"

"Six lashes, Dominic? On that back?" Brink snapped.

"Of which he only received four!" Dominic answered, adding with a mutter, "Three were barely swats, I swear."

Brink moved behind her, and a shadow dimmed the glow sinking through her closed eyelids. "His love for her only gives you pain if you plan on hurting her again."

Lumen's ears rang. Westbrook's breath sucked in with a noisy hiss and then was silent. She should open her eyes, sit up. Tell them all to get out of her home and leave her in peace.

"I don't plan on touching her again," Dominic said, low and hard.

There was a brief stabbing between her lungs but it dulled quickly. It was done. She was done with him.

"Let her be your problem now, Brink, if you're so concerned," he said. The words were light and felt like razors in her chest. Brief, skimming, tearing pain that left licks of pain behind.

"Dom, what the hell do you think you're doing?" Gideon sounded feral, words rumbling like a warning growl.

"You heard me, Jones," Westbrook answered, voice flattening. "She's the good doctor's now. You'll have to keep your hands to yourself at night."

A door shut and Lumen's eyes opened, skin complaining the faint movement just below on her cheekbone.

"Finley," Gideon said, name heavy in the air.

"Oh forget it, Gideon. You're an idiot if you don't think he'll be back for her in a matter of days."

"I told her I'd keep her safe. That she could come to me."

Finley laughed above her and then paused. "You're serious."

"I promised her."

"I won't touch her," Finley whispered. "Not just because I think Dom'll come to his senses and kill me for it."

"But the other men—"

"I'll keep her safe, Gid."

"See that you do."

The door opened and shut again. Finley sighed, long and weary and his footsteps shuffled away from her, until wood creaked as he sank into a chair.

"You can quit pretending to sleep now," he muttered.

Lumen gasped and shifted, head spinning. Overhead the shadows of hanging herbs loomed. Her mother's workroom. She was stretched out on the table. Brink had given her something for the pain that made her woozy as she tried to move.

"Where's Colin?" she asked.

"Asleep on the bench," Finley said, nodding in the direction. The bench was piled with blankets, the boy nested inside, his back striped with bandages and only little flecks of blood staining the cloth. "Dom didn't break the skin until... until the last lash. He'll be back to rights in a day or two. Can you see alright?"

She blinked. "I think so. Dizzy."

"Sorry. Laudanum for the..." And then he seemed to run out of things to say as she pushed herself slowly up into sitting. "He'll be back."

Dominic. Westbrook. That was who he meant. Not Gideon.

"I'd rather he wasn't," Lumen said, staring at Colin's back.

Finley huffed, leaning forward, hands scrubbing at his face. "That complicates things. Can you walk?"

The room was spinning. She couldn't even shake her head to say no.

"I can't carry you *and* the boy. We'll have to sleep here for the night."

Lumen's head jerked to him and she nearly tipped back down to the table at the wave of nausea that came after.

"I meant what I said to Gideon," Finley said, glancing at her out of the corner of his eye. "I won't touch you. You'll stay with me to keep the others from circling. But if Dom comes I'll... you'll have to go to Gideon. I can't disobey him."

"What does it have to do with you? What does it have to do with Jones?" she asked, voice rising. "Why can't I take a space for myself and keep it without one of you demanding it belongs to you too?"

Finley blinked at her, fingers draped across his jaw, eyes bruise purple with exhaustion. "Are you going to find that space tonight? Get up and walk out of here?"

She opened her mouth. Tried to move, to let herself spill off the table, but with the slightest movement everything seemed to slip away beneath her and she wrapped her fingers around the ledge to hold herself up. When a dizzy turn took her forward, nearly face down to the floor, Finley jerked in his seat as if he meant to catch her. She fell back again, collapsing, eyes shut, brain and stomach twirling in opposite directions.

"I'm too tired to leave," Finley said. "So tonight at least, you'll have to share."

She thought of answering, using one of the rude phrases she'd heard volleyed between the men. Her mother's voice hushed the thought and her stomach warned that any attempt to speak might end in being sick. Her heart beat in her chest and the rhythm echoed in her head.

Finley rose up from the chair, shifting behind her and she tried to ignore the sound of him. A moment later her head was lifted gingerly. She flinched, more for being touched than any twinging pain of her injury. That was dulled beneath the laudanum. He tucked a blanket beneath her head and then spread another over her.

"Sleep, Lady Fenn."

She wanted to say that she had ceased to be the lady of the house the day that they arrived. Maybe even sooner, when the last of her brothers died in the war and she was alone. She wanted to curse him, curse Gideon. Curse Westbrook. Already her skin betrayed her, recalling the touch of Dominic surrounding her, as if she needed the memory to help her sleep.

"Your trials aren't ended yet," Finley said, soft as breath, retreating back to his chair.

Spiky hot tears slipped free, trickling over one of the flogger's sharp little wounds, stinging with salt before rinsing down into her hair.

II
THE HEALER'S PLEASURE

FINLEY STORMED INTO THE WORKSHOP WITHOUT A WORD, rattling the jars on shelves before digging through drawers. Lumen pressed her lips together and waited. She'd asked once what he needed and he nearly snapped her head off assuring her he'd find it himself.

"Where's that damned flower of yours?" he asked, slamming a drawer shut.

Lumen blinked and shook her head at the bottles of solutions in front of her. 'Damned flowers' made up the majority of the ingredients in the workshop.

"What's the ailment?"

"Fever, it's spreading downstairs. Too fast for coincidence. Nausea, aches."

"Did you quarter off the sick?"

"Of course I did! Do you have the flower or not?"

"Gensen," she said, hopping down from her stool. "The flower is poisonous—"

"Well then it's not the one I want, is it?" Finley asked with a parsing tone.

"—but the root will burn through their fever. Sedate them. Use it sparingly." She crossed to him and stood on her toes to reach the top shelf where the more risky herbs were kept, fingers fumbling till she found the narrow little bottle.

Finley was at her side as her heels landed back on the floor, studying the brown grit in the bottle. "How do I administer it?" he asked.

She was learning this way of him too. Brittle and sharp one moment, calm and demure the next. She didn't mind his temper now. He had touched her once in anger, in the very beginning, but in the week since Dominic had washed his hands of her, Finley had become a kind of… protective shadow. The fury of a storm followed by quiet, fresh stillness was his nature and Lumen decided she could weather that and more.

She stirred her fingers over the countertop until she found a small spoon. "This much into broth for twenty men. No more than a sprinkle per man really. And don't give it to anyone who isn't sick."

He nodded, taking the spoon and the bottle from her and turning to the door before pausing again. "You should come with me."

"I'd rather just meet you in the room," she said.

"I know, Lady Fenn, believe me," he said, frowning. "But for appearance's sake…"

"I hate to parade for him," she whispered, frowning back at her work on the counter. She was trying to find a tincture to help the men who were weak with blood loss from the failed skirmish. Surely that was more important than giving the rest of the company a glimpse of her at Finley's side.

"You're right," Finley said. "I'll see you upstairs."

Lumen sighed, rubbing at her forehead with the heel of her hand. "No, wait. I'll come. I should give the dosage. Then if I poison the men it's not your fault." She managed a weak smile to let him know she was joking and went to her workspace, bottling everything away and leaving it for the night.

Those who were well enough were rowdy down in the court-yard, Gideon's hired ladies' voices bright with laughter and something sharper. She glanced through the arches down below and saw Gideon watching in the corner, ankles crossed, lifting ale to his lips. He was keeping an eye on things. The army was restless. Losing a battle had soured their mood and having downtime left them bored.

She didn't glance at the crowd again as they made their way downstairs and toward the infirmary. Dominic might be somewhere in the mix. He might even be one of the men making a woman squeal with anxious humor. She didn't want to watch.

There was a jug of broth waiting in the infirmary, almost cold and forgotten by now, and Lumen used the Gensen sparingly. They could administer another round tomorrow evening if it didn't have enough effect.

"Wait here for me. You don't need to risk catching this," Finley said, leaving her at the table and carrying the jug over to the men.

She wasn't sure what good it would do her to avoid the sick men and then share a room with Finley, but she waited, eyes turned to the floor, until he was finished. They left together, his fingers wrapping around her wrist as they reached the corridor.

"Let's go around," she whispered.

"Walk through with me. Tomorrow you can hide away, I promise," he said, tugging gently on her arm. When she stared out at the crowd he added, "The night after too. Come."

They pushed into the heart of the crowd, past the men, past one of the women clinging around a neck, head thrown back on a moan as another man pressed to her back, her skirts rising by the handfuls. Gideon appeared near the fire, eyes watching her, face strangely grim for a night of revelry.

"Aye, now there's the little lady herself!" one man cried, and heads turned to stare, tracking her around the fire.

Finley's fingers slid down, tangling with hers and squeezing gently, tugging her closer to his back.

"Come now, good doctor, you've had her for a week. Surely she could use a softer touch by now," another man shouted.

"She's better off with us than you!"

It brought a roar of laughter with it, Lumen's eyes fixed to the back of Finley's neck as he hunched and pushed through. She skirted out of reach of pinching fingers, and he wrapped his arm over her shoulder, drawing her closer.

What did this serve, she wondered? Was the idea to be laughed at? It didn't seem to keep those hands from trying to touch. Maybe during the day, but she kept to herself as much as she could—tucked away in the workshop or the attic room she shared with Finley or down at the gazebo when she couldn't stand the constant noise inside the Manor.

She looked up when they were nearly through and found Dominic watching from above, alone and surrounded by the shadow of the hall. Their stares grazed one another and then she was out of his sight, her lungs burning in her chest as if she'd run instead of walked and the small wounds along her face and neck stinging as if struck anew.

Finley was silent as they wound up the stairs and through the Manor. Lumen had asked once, days ago, what the snide jokes meant but all he had said was, 'Nothing you need worry about.' Had he hurt women? Not the ones staying here, she was certain of that. Not her.

When they hit the landing of the hall above, the space was empty, a door snapping shut. Dominic's retreat. Every time she thought of the man she was equal parts rage for all the pain he'd caused, and regret for all she'd shared with him, and a faint sliver of longing she hated more than him and more than herself.

The door to the attic bedroom creaked open, and a bright head popped up from the blankets of the bed, Colin's eyes heavy with sleep.

"Just us," Lumen whispered to the boy as Finley shut the door behind him.

"Did anyone see you come up here?" he asked.

"No one ever does," Colin said.

"The General was out—"

"The General don't look at me if he can help it," Colin huffed, sinking back into the thin mattress. "I started a fire."

Finley's feet paused then continued to the other end of the room where the little stove in the corner had wood burning for the night. The man stretched, long arms reaching high, fingers grazing against the beams of the roof above. He shrugged his coat off, hanging it over a beam, and landed heavily on the narrow camp cot he'd set up on the opposite side of the room.

One week. One week of this strange balancing act. Finley sleeping on a cot, Lumen in his old bed, Colin sneaking in to curl up with her when no one could catch him at it.

"Show me your back," she said, going to the boy.

"'M alright," he grumbled, but he rolled onto his stomach, face stuffed into a pillow and let her flick his shirt up over his back.

The scabs were little dark spots on his skin but they were nicely healed. Better than her own, which were too often stretched and abused to heal quickly. She had received the worst blow from Westbrook's flogger and she was grateful for it. Her fingers stroked over Colin's back—the old scars puckered under her touch—and she pulled the shirt down again. The blankets were warm as she slid beneath them and the boy curled into her side, her arms wrapping around him, cheek pressed to his soft head.

The men in the infirmary ran through her thoughts, eyes glassy, skin flushed. "If the Gensen doesn't work we could try—"

"Sleep, Lumen," Finley snapped from the other end of the room.

"Rest, Lady," Colin mumbled, nudging the blankets up over his nose.

It was easier said than done.

LUMEN WAS LOADING the last of the medicines she needed into her basket when Finley entered the workroom looking for supplies.

"Where are you going?"

"To see to the tenants," she said. "It's been too long since I checked on them."

"It's freezing out."

"I have a shawl."

She ignored the huff of irritation, the clack of glass against wood counters, but when fabric began to rustle she looked over her shoulder. He was shrugging his sweater up over his head, a thick knitted thing with twisting cables over every inch.

"Take this, I'll find my coat if I need it," he said, holding the sweater out to her.

The workroom was large and spacious and it meant that Lumen and Finley could exist while they worked without crowding each other. She crossed the gap and caught the sweater as he released it. It was heavy and the wool was a little coarse but when she drew it over her head she could feel the warmth from his skin wrapping around her. He'd made the sweater smell like dark tea, earthy and bitter, and a sharp smoke scent that wasn't from campfires. She had to resist a strange child-like urge to remain inside the body of the sweater, light bleeding through the stitches, breathing him in. When she emerged, she took a longer look at the man.

He was tall enough that she had to crane her head back to look at him. She'd always thought of him as slender, but his shoulders were as broad as Dominic's. There were lines across his forehead and his nose was long and just a little wider from where she'd broken it with her elbow, fighting him off her silver in the chapel. Glass green eyes skirted away as she stared—thin, chapped, and torn lips pressing tight.

"Take Colin with you," he said. "He's better than nothing."

The boy was out in the front yard, turning a hoop over the gravel path with a stick, looking young and careless and not the part of a spy at all. He danced to a stop as he spotted her, slinging the hoop around his shoulders and hooking his wrists through. Up ahead on the road, horses approached, bright red coats blinking through glittering black armor. Westbrook and Jones by the look of them, returning from an errand.

"Come with me to see my people?" Lumen asked, holding out her hand.

Colin glanced over his shoulder at the road and then abandoned his hoop and stick in haste, taking her hand and running through the yard with her, to the side road that would take them to her tenants.

"Will you get into trouble?" She asked him, breath thin in her chest, the frozen air making her head bright and awake.

"No more'n you, Lady," Colin answered, which might have been a reassurance or a warning. Lumen chose not to think on it.

"AND YOU'RE sure it's just croup, Lady Fenn?" Widow Ramsey asked, bouncing the toddler in her arms.

The woman wasn't much older than Lumen herself but she was a widow now with both children under five. One hugged her skirts while the other buried a cough into his mother's shoulder, her fingers rising up to stroke through russet locks and soothe down his back.

"There's talk something's going round the army," she whispered, dark eyes wide.

"It's only croup. Better to get him inside. Warm everything you can before he eats. Plenty of clean water. Do you have someone to bring you wood?"

"I manage some," Widow Ramsey said and then pink rose to her cheeks as she added. "Oliver Spragg helps too."

Ah, that would make a kind of sense, the two of them together. They were neighbors and Wid- *Gretchen* Ramsey was young. Oliver was handsome and he worked hard and tended land even after the loss of his arm in the war. Lumen had once thought of him in her moments alone, but she didn't feel an ache of jealousy now at the idea of him pursuing the other woman. Maybe a little one, a kind of wistfulness for something that seemed more peaceful than argument and struggle.

"Good. I'll check on you again next week," Lumen said.

Colin followed her away from the cottage. "Some of the soldiers talk about her," he said.

"Have any harassed her?" Lumen asked, fingers clenching around her basket.

"Don't think so. Gideon would have words. And I think that bloke Spragg kicked one round, one arm and all."

Spragg's cottage was up ahead. It had been his parents' and they'd passed while he was at war, leaving the house and land attached only in time for him to return home injured. It was small, barely three rooms, but kept well. Smoke piped out of a thin chimney at the peak of the roof.

"We stopping there too?" Colin asked. The sun was high in the sky and even Lumen's stomach was starting to rumble with hunger. She pulled a small hand pie she'd made with scraps out of her basket and handed it to Colin, stopping at an apple tree.

"Do you climb well?" she asked.

"And fast!" he said, already eyeing the branches.

"Eat and then run up and see if you can find any late apples for my cider," she said. "I'll meet you back here."

"If you're going to see a man, I ought to come with you," Colin said, back straightening, chin lifted. "I don't trust none of them."

Lumen beamed at him, wrapping her arm around his shoulders and pressing a firm kiss to the top of his head. "Neither do I," she said. "You'll be able to see me from the tree. It's just a quick check and I'll be right back."

Colin stuffed the pie into his mouth and jumped up to catch the lowest branch. Lumen left him to it, walking up the path to Spragg's cottage. She heard him shuffling inside as she knocked.

"Comin'!"

"It's just me," Lumen called back and heard the footsteps rush to the door.

It swung open and she held her breath. The full lips and broad nose and blue eyes. She'd forgotten his face somehow in the weeks that had passed.

"Lady Fenn." His lips were parted in surprise, collar of his shirt untied and revealing tanned skin even after weeks of winter creeping in.

Lumen took a step back from the doorway. "I've been neglecting the tenants," she said catching her breath and forcing a smile. Oliver only frowned and looked more confused so she added, "There's a fever running around. I came to see if anyone needed anything."

He looked over her shoulder down to the Ramsey cottage and she said, "You're my last stop."

"I am well enough, Lady Fenn," Oliver said, eyes studying her, sliding down her front and up again.

"Good." She closed her lips, parted them again to speak and realized there was nothing to say. "I'll leave you to your day," she said, half-laughing and starting to skirt away.

"Lady Fenn, wait," Oliver called, hand reaching out and dropping before any touch. "What happened?"

His fingers hovered over her scars and she forced a smile. "Icy patch in the woods. I fell into some brambles." It was a lie she'd perfected over the course of the day and thankfully the wounds were well enough healed now not to giveaway her secret.

Oliver only frowned, stare fixed to the spots. "Have you... have you given any thought to my offer?"

Lumen's eyes widened. She could only think of one offer and it was hardly the kind of thing Oliver would suggest to her.

"You do not have to stay simply for your people's sake, my Lady," Oliver said, frowning. "They can manage for themselves or they can leave too. The cost is not so high for them."

"How can you say such a thing?" Lumen asked, awkwardness washed away under indignant shock. "The cost may be the food on their tables or their homes or their well being, Oli- Mister Spragg. I will not abandon them. I will not abandon the chapel."

"The chapel?" Oliver asked, jerking back. "They haven't- I thought by now- Westbrook's men aren't known for sparing anyone their silver."

Lumen's face flushed hot. She had begged for that mercy. She had given Westbrook pieces of herself she'd never shared with anyone else. It hadn't occurred to her since the night Westbrook tossed her aside, but she wondered now how long that mercy would last.

"My lady, the things that man has put you through. Not one of us would ask it of you," Oliver said, hand reaching to her elbow and stopping just shy of touching her. "Please. Let me take you to safety."

Lumen sighed and looked down the path to the tree. She couldn't spot Colin in the branches but she didn't doubt the boy had his eye on her.

"I am safe," she said, thinking of him and smiling for it. "I will do as much as I can for the Manor and its people. And I will do it as long as I am able. Let that be an end to it."

"Perhaps I am wrong about your treatment," Oliver bit out, and his hand retreated to clutch at his doorframe. "Perhaps you are satisfied with the arrangement."

The anger in her heart cooled her blush. Not just anger at Oliver but at Dominic too. She had been satisfied for a time, fooled, and it had cost her.

"Remember who it is you speak to," she said, holding Oliver's gaze until he turned away, red spots of color at the top of his cheeks. "Good day, Mister Spragg."

The door shut behind him with a heavy slam and Lumen turned away quickly, feeling the flush of shame spreading around her collar. She was just edging past the cottage when Colin appeared with a basket full of apples. She glanced at the corner he'd ducked around and her eyes widened.

"Where did you come from?"

"I was only waitin' for you," Colin said, as innocent as a babe and twice as suspicious for it.

Lumen stared down her nose at him and narrowed her eyes. "You may spy for Westbrook but not on my tenants, good sir."

Colin snorted at the name, nearly tripping over the basket as they walked together, taking turns carrying all the way back to the Manor.

Finley regretted forcing Lumen through the hoards the night before. They were docile tonight, the slight bounce in decent weather ridding them of some of the urge to burn and drink and fuck. He supposed she didn't care what their temperament was as long as she was left in peace. He didn't blame her.

"Where is she?" Gideon asked, appearing at his side, shoving a plate of squash and thin scraps of chicken into Finley's empty hands.

"Upstairs," Finley said, keeping his voice low.

Gideon had been unbearable all week, quizzing after the woman. But he was the only one aside from the boy who knew the arrangement between Lumen and Finley. Sometimes he wondered if Dominic could tell that Finley hadn't touched her, much as he might want, much as he *thought* about it. What was the point of the facade on the General's part? And when would it end?

It won't, he reminded himself. Because Lumen wanted nothing to do with Dom and Finley had promised her safety.

He was going to get himself killed. Or at least punched.

"The boy with her?" Gideon asked.

Finley huffed and nodded to where the boy was hanging in an archway, jabbering at a pair of soldiers. "No, he's there trying to get Bevins and Unsell to fight one another."

"You left her unprotected?" Gideon hissed.

"All she wants is to be alone," Finley spat back.

"And where is Dom?"

Finley startled at that, nearly choking on a bite of food. His eyes scanned the crowd around them and came up empty, equally so in the archways up above. His heart pounded in his chest as he searched again. No sign of the man.

It didn't have to be sinister, did it? How far would Dominic really push a woman? None had ever taken much effort before. They saw the General as an advantage to make use of and were always surprised when he made use of them.

"Let's go," Gideon said, tugging on Finley's arm.

Before they could move Colin skidded in front of them, cheeks bright and rosy. "Need to talk to you two."

"Not now, boy," Finley said, trying to pass.

But Colin was quick on his feet, blocking the way. "Yes now. It's important. 'Bout my Lady."

Finley opened his mouth to argue that he had enough worries when it came to the lady in question but Gideon beat him to speaking.

"Where's the General?"

"Out riding," Colin said, answer at the ready. "Follow me."

The boy went dashing through the crowd and Finley jerked to follow him, Gideon holding him back by the waist of his coat.

"Easy. Men don't need to wonder what's so important."

Colin was waiting for them in the hall before vanishing into the kitchen. When they reached the doorway they found the boy jumping up onto the counter and rifling through the breadbox, pulling out small hand-pies from the bottom.

"Did you drag us in here to watch you stuff your face?" Finley asked.

"Was gonna offer you one, but not no more," Colin said, blinking at him. When Finley growled in answer Colin rushed to add, "Whatchu know about a man named Spragg? One of Lady's tenants."

Finley's brow furrowed in confusion and Gideon answered. "Oshain army man. One arm. He give her trouble again?"

"Again?" Colin cried as Finley hissed, "I thought I chased him off once already."

"I warned him as well," Gideon said, expression turning dark.

"She went to see him herself but I can tell she don't like him none," Colin said and Finley froze, watching the boy.

He wasn't certain the boy was a true judge of whether or not a woman was interested in a man. He may only have one arm but Finley wasn't an idiot. Spragg's face was certainly pleasing to a woman's eye.

"He offered her a trip across the border."

Silence rang in Finley's ears. "What border?" he asked.

"He fucking *what?*" Gideon growled, low and feral, shoulders rising up.

"Said he could take her to safety, Oshain territory," Colin said through munching bites of pie.

"When are they planning on leaving?" Finley asked. He could keep Dominic occupied for her at least, give her time to get away.

"I'll kill him," Gideon said.

Finley's head whipped to stare at the soldier. "What? Why? She *should* get away."

Gideon turned his thunderous glare on him. "What are you talking about? Our lady? Leave?"

Finley swallowed. Gideon's attachment had been clear from the beginning but he hadn't realized that it was blocking all reason. *How much reason was left in the man before now?* Somewhere in a decade of fighting, serving Dominic and becoming his berserker, Gideon was losing the happy gentleness that Finley remembered from the early days.

"We promised to protect her," Finley said slowly, voice soft and coaxing. "She will be safest away from here."

"She would be safest with me," Gideon said, eyes narrowed.

"She told him no," Colin chirped and they both spun to stare at him. "Said she's got a duty to the Manor and she won't leave. But you lot better keep her chapel safe cause I don't think she'd stay if not for her Mother Lune."

Gideon's shoulders relaxed, expression easing as a lopsided grin spread. "Course she wouldn't go."

Finley's teeth ground. It would be better for her to leave. It might even be better for them if she was gone. Dominic could get his head on straight again. Gideon would put himself into the fight. And maybe he too could clear his own mind of the woman's strange influence.

"Do you really think now that Dominic's lost interest he'll keep his word to her about the chapel?" Finley asked.

Gideon's eyes narrowed. "I'll think of the right thing to say. She's not leaving, Fin."

It sounded like a warning more than a reassurance. Finley sighed as Gideon ducked out of the kitchen, hunching to avoid crashing his head on the doorway. Colin's legs kicked as he sat on the counter, licking his fingers of crust.

"Find me another one of those," Finley said, trying to sound as ferocious as Gideon.

The boy snorted but rummaged into the bin, pulling out one for each of them. "There's a hidden bottom Lady told me 'bout. But if you tell the others I'll cut your bollocks off," the boy said lightly.

Finley blinked and took a bite of the pie. It was dry but a great deal better than what they were eating out by the bonfire. "Consider me warned," he said and followed the boy out.

It was early enough still, and he wasn't really tired. If he took himself up to the room it would be that much more time spent laying awake, thinking of how close Lumen was, breathing her in, trying not to fixate on her. He turned to the stairs and cursed himself. Torture or not, silence with her was preferable.

LUMEN SPENT the earliest part of the mornings—before the sun was properly up and the Mother had hidden herself away—in the chapel praying, cleaning, and paying her respects. The men slept in late when it wasn't a day for fighting and she could be in and out before the rest of the house woke. Usually.

This morning she was locking the door behind her when she heard a scuff of sound in the hall at her back. She turned to find the hulking presence of Gideon Jones.

None of the soldiers had come down this hall since the day of the New Moon. She wondered if her concerns from the day before were coming to pass. Had Dominic's unspoken promise to leave the chapel untouched expired already? What would she offer to win it back?

"Little spirit," Gideon greeted, a low rattle in his voice that made her spine stiffen and her belly warm.

Lumen's eyes searched for a route of escape but Gideon took up the width of the narrow hall but for a handful of inches and she found it unlikely that he would let her pass. She tucked the chapel key deep into the folds of her skirt and lifted her chin, pressing forward to meet him.

"Mister Jones."

"A little bird told me you had an offer to fly the coop," Gideon said. Step after step, closer and closer until she had no choice but to retreat or let him press against her. His hands were folded behind his back but with a gentle nudge of his boot against her shoe she was turning, back to the wall and fingers scratching into the stone as he crowded her.

"I'm not quitting the Manor," she said quickly, her breaths weak as she forced herself to look up into the haggard shadows of his face.

His feet braced hers, just close enough for her to feel the trap of them. She looked down the hall to where the courtyard waited, gray and dim before dawn. She could escape, squeeze past Gideon and return to her bed or up to the workshop. But Gideon's warmth was radiating against the front of her and she found the feeling a comfort. He was a puzzle of kindness and unpredictable will and it drew a guilty thrill out of her blood to be near him.

She relaxed against the wall and turned back to find him studying her throat. "You once offered to escort me away."

Gideon grinned, smile white in the dark. "Only in my company, little spirit."

"Then I have not broken our pact," she said.

Gideon's chuckle was something like an earthquake, echoing through her. Lumen found the tension in her shoulders easing the longer they stayed together in the hall, all but pressed together.

"I would hunt you through the woods, my lady, before I let you escape from me," Gideon said.

A strange impulse ran through her at the threat, a determination to prove her own power. She lifted her hand between them and stroked a finger down the wide, sharp angle of his jaw. His eyes widened and she could have sworn the large man shivered in front of her.

"I believe you," she said, watching him relax, feeling the belt on his trousers tap against her stomach, his chest brushing hers with every breath they took together. "But I don't wish to give up my home. And I would rather not be hunted."

His eyes blinked, a drowsy peace settling over the broad face. "When you're sweet, it makes me feel like a shit for being a beast."

Lumen's laugh was bright and surprised and a shadow passed right across his cheeks and over his nose. He started to pull away from her. "I'll escort you to your next destination," he said.

She caught him at his sides, marveling at the way he went as still as a statue beneath her faintest touch. "I think I would rather stay a moment like this."

Her eyes fell shut as his widened and she hummed as his warmth returned, covering her head to toe like a blanket.

"Does Fin touch you?" he asked.

"Not more than he has to," she murmured.

"Less than he'd like, I promise you that, little spirit." She ignored his words and tugged at the front of his shirt until he was against her. His voice vibrated against her breasts as he spoke again. "Would you like him to?"

What Lumen wanted was to rise to her toes and rub herself against the man. She hadn't realized until this moment how much physical touch she'd learned to appreciate while Dominic had... made use of her. Not only that. She craved sex. The act itself. She'd gone twenty two years without. Now after one week of abstinence it was as if she was missing meals and left constantly hungry.

"I don't know," she said. Finley's presence was certainly as strongly felt as Dominic's had been, and sometimes it was more... companionable. But she hadn't given much thought to him as a bed partner until Gideon suggested the idea.

"Do you want the General's touch?"

"No," she said. The touch, yes. The man? No.

"Mine?"

Her throat was tight. He was touching her now, in a way, even with his hands behind his back. They were upright but his proximity was a weight on her skin. His head dropped, stirring her hair, the breath of his words kissing her ear.

"I crave yours, my lady," he said.

"Don't move," she said, *whispered*, and the man froze.

Lumen pushed herself against him as if she were trying to soak his heat up like a sponge. His cock was nudging at the front of his pants and she rose up on her toes, notching him against herself through the gathers of her skirt. He made one sound, an abbreviated moan, and then swallowed it down as her hands stroked across his shoulders, face pressed to his neck.

Gideon was rigid against her, almost shaking with the effort of holding still, and she wasn't entirely certain what to do with herself. A part of her wanted to command him to move, to crush her to the wall and play the part of the beast against her. Another part of her wanted to be the beast herself, rut herself against him as he imitated stone, if only to see how long his self-control lasted.

Even his scent was animal, leather and smoke and hay, his shoulders flexing under her fingers, chest heaving with breaths against hers. She rolled her hips against his once, lips parted as her body sang with the memory of this breed of friction, and then again, a soft moan into his pulse. There was a taste of him on her tongue, bitter and tangy and just a shade sweeter than Dominic, and Gideon rattled in her arms.

Enough. She released him, sliding out from beneath his chest as he sagged against the wall, fists pounding to stone to brace himself. She could see the outline of arousal, startlingly thick against his trousers, and a stray thought whipped through her mind. *I couldn't really feel that properly through the clothes.* Lumen blushed and turned away.

"You are cruel," Gideon rasped, and then laughed.

Fingertips skimmed down her spine and Lumen looked over her shoulder to find him leaning against the wall, a giddy little smile stretched across his face.

"I'm sorry," she said, voice small.

He snorted. "Don't be. Sweetest touch that ever killed a man." He winked at her, hand reaching down to adjust himself. Lumen tried not to stare. "Who are you off to curse with those deadly eyes of yours next?"

I like him, she thought, and it hurt her heart to know it.

"My patients," she said.

"Then let me join you," he said pushing off the wall.

Her eyes skimmed down to his cock again and he cleared his throat before she forced her stare away. "Can you walk like that?" she teased.

"Oh I can do a lot like this," he said, grinning.

⸙

"Sweet Lady Moon!"

"Come and sit upon my lap a little while, my lady! I'll kiss those bruises Healer Brink does leave!"

"Nay, he'll leave more, lady!"

The soldiers sang with laughter as Finley appeared from the dark cover of an arch. She shook her head once at him and he waited for her to meet him there. Westbrook was not far, sitting with his men, his eyes tracing her and then dragging away only to return again.

"I'll go up with you," Finley murmured.

"It won't stop their jokes," she said, sitting down in the arch and waiting for him to follow. She picked a potato wedge off his plate, pleased to find it still warm and ignored the way he watched her bite.

"You are in better spirits tonight," he said, passing her the entire plate.

Which was good. She was hungry and had worked straight through the day without remembering to eat before now.

"The men are improving," she said.

Finley turned, bracing his back against the column to face her. He was half fire orange and half deep night blue by the light, almost mythic in appearance, and Lumen found it easier to focus on her food than look at him and think of Gideon's questions from the morning.

"You put a great deal of effort into keeping the Stalor army in decent health, Lady Fenn," he said.

"They are only men." There was sausage on the plate tonight, and she wondered which of her family belongings had purchased the extravagance.

"I'd love to see Dom's face as you said that," Finley said, sounding dry and tired.

Lumen's eyes skidded over to where Dominic was sitting, watching them. She turned her back to the fire and the courtyard, lifting her legs to hang over the other side, her thigh pressed to Finley's. He looked down at where they were touching as if the nearness startled him.

"I can't say it wouldn't be..." she sighed, not knowing the right word, "...easier for me if you..."

"Had never come here," he said, barely audible above the festivities around the fire.

She looked up from the plate and lost the track of her speech as she met his gaze. He was handsome but in a stranger way than Dominic—more elegant, almost fae. And when he stared at her she felt pinned by his eyes, as if she were offering him more of her thoughts than those she spoke aloud.

"I don't believe my conscience would be easy if I ignored my knowledge of healing in favor of letting another human suffer. Enemy or not."

His lips quirked, the slightest curl and he leaned forward, elbows balanced on his knees. "I know you are a Lunar, Lady Fenn, but I believe Sol smiled on us when we reached your land."

His smile dropped as quickly as hers, as if they were sharing the same thought. *Then what had Sol done to her?* Spat sparks and fire and blood down on her peaceful world?

"You have done enough for us," he whispered, leaning closer and when his shoulder was against hers she answered the touch until they were balanced together, facing in opposite directions but sharing the moment.

"I would rather be busy tending the men than idle and hiding from them," she said.

He sighed, head tipping against hers. It gave Lumen a view of Dominic, jaw ticking, eyes fixed on the fire, hands clenched around the sheath of his sword like he was ready to draw it out. Finley shifted, just a fraction, breath stirring on her neck and she reached up, sliding her fingers into the hair at the back of his neck. It was softer than she expected, slipping like water through her touch. He stiffened and then sagged into her side as she stroked his hair.

"If you want to stop..." Finley started but never finished.

She didn't want to stop. Like earlier in the morning, she missed having the permission to touch, to be touched, and as long as Finley didn't mind...

"Let it be part of the lie," she whispered and he nodded slightly.

Dominic's head twitched in their direction and Lumen's gaze dropped before she could be caught staring.

LUMEN WOKE TO THE RUSTLING OF FINLEY, DRESSING ON THE other side of the room. Colin was gone from the bed and through the window the thinnest sliver of moon was left in the sky. It would be the New Moon soon and she was afraid to return to the chapel, to leave it unlocked and at risk of another pillage.

She rolled on the mattress, startled to find herself faced with the pale, smooth back of a man still in the midst of dressing. Finley's knuckles knocked against a beam overhead as he pulled a shirt down over his shoulders, hiding away knots of muscle and a tapered waist. He bent, rifling beneath the bed and Lumen found herself appreciating a new view of the man before he reappeared, red coat in hand.

"Is there a battle?"

Finley spun to face her, eyes wide and staring, collar of his shirt untied, planes of his chest peeking out with winking dark freckles.

"You usually wear the black coat," she said, nodding at the wool coat hanging over the beam.

His throat cleared and he finished pulling on his uniform. "Skirmish. Colin's down rousing the others. You'll manage the men who stay alright?"

"Rosie and the others will help," she said.

Finley paused, hands at his throat as he readied himself. "You've taken whores and turned them into nurses."

"Do they mind being called that?"

He shook his head. "I haven't bothered to wonder. Next you'll have me bowing to them."

"It's never wrong to be polite."

He stopped in front of the bed, drinking her in, and she checked herself to be certain she was decent. His hands twitched at his side.

"Right. I- I'll see you in the infirmary later."

She nearly found herself saying "good luck" and then remembered he was going to fight her countrymen and she'd rather there were no skirmishes and battles at all. Stalor had taken enough of Oshain in the last two decades. So instead she watched him stumble his way to the door and out of the room.

THE WOMEN HUSHED as Lumen entered the laundry room, bundles of sheets in her arms, a few hurrying to stand, their own arms full.

"We'll be out of your hair here in a moment, milady," Rosie said with an abbreviated curtsey, reaching to scoop her sodding clothing out of the water.

"Nonsense," Lumen said. "You've as much right to be here as I do. I'm in no rush."

One of the younger women snorted but dropped back down into her crouch against the wall as she waited for a turn at the washing. The others relaxed after a few glances between each other.

Rosie propped herself against the wash tub, churning the handle herself and watching suds bloom on the surface of the water.

"How are the men in the infirmary?" one woman asked. She was pale and pretty with dark hair and a gap in her smile.

"They are no worse at least, which is a good sign," Lumen said. "It would be better if it were a good season for getting fresh fruit."

The woman bit her lip and frowned down at the bundle in

her arms. A tall friend at her side with close cropped honey blonde hair and heavy breasts nudged at her, smiling and saying, "Inda only worries because her sweetheart Philip is lying in one of those beds."

"Mia," Inda hissed.

"He is just a bit of work, Inda," another woman muttered.

"Pfft," Rosie said to the soap bubbles. "Is that what you call your 'Charlie-boy', Jennie?"

Jennie, an older redhead, short and stout and sweetly faced if not for her sour look, frowned and tossed her hair. And then, for no particular reason that Lumen could tell, all the women turned to stare at her.

"And how is *your* new gentleman, milady?" Jennie asked.

"Jennie Greer, if you don't watch your mouth," Mia snapped, swatting the woman on the arm hard enough to make a cracking sound.

"He is quite different," Lumen said and as one they hushed.

In truth, Lumen didn't mind being asked. She would have to watch what she said, because it did seem important that no one know Finley hadn't taken the liberties the General had awarded him. But she didn't see herself so differently from these women. There had been a kind of repayment for those nights in Dominic's arms, even if it wasn't coin in her hand. And what was so really wrong about their profession anyway?

"Are all men so unique from one another?" she asked. Finley and Dominic were equal parts heat and cold, but in entirely different directions.

"From what I hear, your healer is a little more unique than most," said the girl on the floor and the other women giggled and then rushed to quiet themselves.

Lumen smiled and looked down at the sheets in her arm, feigning embarrassment. "Maybe. Less than you might have heard."

"I watched him bathe once," Inda whispered, locking wide eyes with Lumen. "He's...you know. Quite long, isn't he?"

Lumen swallowed. Here information failed her, but luckily Jennie was not satisfied.

"Who cares about the healer. I want to know about the General. Tell me, is it terrible? Is he huge?" And then she stuffed a bundle of clothing beneath one arm and held her hands out so wide apart from each other that the other women squealed and Lumen wasn't sure what she even meant. Until suddenly she did.

"Sol, no!" She laughed and the women laughed with her. "No. More like…" She frowned and then estimated in the air.

"No!" Jennie said, stomping her foot. "Average, damn him. Never would've guessed it."

The women tittered and Lumen felt a strange tightness in her chest. They had not seen for themselves then. She'd thought maybe… but what did it matter?

"Does he at least know what he's doing with it?" Mia asked her.

Lumen blinked, a little thrill running through her at memories she did her best to suppress. "When he cares to," she said, thinking of that first week where he'd taken care not to hurt her, but hadn't been interested enough to see her to her own pleasure.

The ladies hummed with understanding, Rosie rolling her eyes. "Good riddance to him then," she said.

Lumen smiled weakly.

"'S'it true you were a virgin a'fore the men came?" the girl on the floor asked.

Lumen nodded and the room seemed to hold its breath for a moment.

"Well if you gets any questions you just come'n ask me. I'll see you rights," she said with a lofty nod.

Jennie bellowed out a laugh from the other side of the room. "Bea Smith you only know how to be loud and eat cock."

"Aye, and it sees me alright, doesn't it?" Bea lobbed back, wadding up a sock and throwing it across the room. It didn't make it nearly far enough to hit anyone but all the occupants laughed. "Let's just wait till the men get back and then we'll just have ourselves a little contest. Let the men be the judge!"

"Listen to the pair of you," Rosie said, an attempt to sound firm that failed under the grin on her face. "Talkin' this way in front of a well bred lady."

"I'm not sure any of the usual methods would suit my new gentleman," Lumen said with a shrug, lashes lowered and smile faint.

Inda gasped and Mia screamed with laughter.

"Oh, lady, now you've gone and got them going again," Rosie groaned, flapping a weak hand in Lumen's direction.

"Ohhh but he *is* delicious," Bea said, scooting forward on the floor, tossing her washing in the belly of her skirt and staring eagerly up at Lumen. "Does he make you scream proper?"

"Not everyone thinks volume is a measure of pleasure, Bea," Rosie said, nudging the girl with her foot.

"I never hear a peep," Jennie said, eyes keen on Lumen's face.

"You're not meant to," Lumen said, lifting a brow. She released a slow, silent sigh as the words sent the room into another fit of thrilled giggles.

AFTER THE LAST round of fighting had brought more men wounded than safe, Lumen thought she was prepared for any outcome.

Watching Dominic and Gideon burst through the doors, Finley sagged limp on a stretcher carried in their bloodied hands, she realized that was not true. She had not considered this.

"Tell me you know what to do," Dominic said, voice ragged in his chest, skin white beneath the red sunburn of his skin, heels slipping on the stone beneath him as he marched backwards to the infirmary.

She didn't have the faintest idea and the thought of Finley—who often made the diagnosis and then compromised with her on treatment—being the injured one himself... how was she to proceed? Her jaw was hanging loose as she ran in after them, watching blood drip from his side as he lay on his stomach.

"Where- where is the injury?" she asked.

"His back. An arrow wound," Gideon said.

She could see it now. They had stripped him of his armor but a small wedge of the arrow shaft was still protruding from the back of his coat, below his shoulder blade and to the right of his spine.

"I need to get to the wound. Can the coat be removed?" she asked. Her hands were shaking and she hid them in a bowl of water, rinsing and scrubbing herself clean. The men lowered the stretcher onto the dining table, soldiers walking calmly in after them.

"How many others?"

"Just Fin. Got him while his back was turned tending another man's shoulder," Dominic said. "Do you know what to do? His only assistant was killed weeks ago."

She blinked at him and then shook the surprise away. No one had ever said anything. Why should they tell her at all?

"I need a clean knife. And the strongest alcohol your men have hiding. And send one of the girls to get me the stitching supplies."

There was a rush of activity around her and she returned to Finley's side. His eyes were barely open, lips parted with the shallowest breaths. The coat was peeled off his back, and she held him down, elbows on his shoulders, as he moaned and stiffened. The shirt beneath was soaked in blood, and she nodded for them to lift that out of her way too, biting her own lip as Finley hissed when the fabric snagged on the shaft of the arrow. She mopped the blood pooled on his back away with a cloth and touched softly around the wound, feeling the shape of the arrow below.

Finley whimpered and Dominic stared at her. "Don't torture the man."

"It would be better if I knew what the arrow looked like, I think," she murmured, ignoring his fretting.

Gideon barked to the men behind her and then Dominic set a bright, shining dagger, still in its ornate star stamped sheath, by her hand. It was *her* dagger. The one from her brother Alan, given before he vanished into the red folds of war. It looked untouched. Where had he even produced it from?

Gideon brought back a flask of alcohol and Lumen frowned as she listened to the thin swish of liquid inside. Barely enough. She soaked a new cloth and wiped the knife down before poising it at the ragged edge of the entrance wound.

"Wait, lady," Gideon said.

A moment later a soldier reached the table, breaths panting, clean arrow in hand. "It landed near me in the fight. Saved it for use later."

She studied the shaft and head. It looked right. Looked like it could have come from a military stock rather than handmade.

"Alright." She met Dominic's eyes once, saw the worry there for his friend, and nodded. "Alright. Hold him for me."

She splashed a few quick drops of alcohol down and as Finley went rigid she cut careful, quick marks into his skin. The shaft fell away and Gideon growled.

"Damnit, he won't heal without—"

Lumen already knew and Gideon's words died off with a gasp as she spread the wound open, trying not to grimace, to admit that she felt queasy, as she pinched a slippery, bloodied arrowhead with her free fingers, pulling it slowly free, careful not to cause more damage than was already done. Finley moaned and then roared behind gritted teeth as she retrieved the black metal.

"Sol," Dominic muttered.

"Pour the rest in the wound and keep him still," Lumen ordered, breathing through her teeth and wiping her hands clean. They were shaking and she didn't have the faintest idea how she would manage to stitch him neatly like this.

"Ghosts sure can't do that," Gideon murmured in an affectionate kind of awe.

Lumen laughed, a little hysterical and fumbled her way to the stitching kit, dragging it back to Finley's back and opening it over his squirming spine.

"Settle yourself," she snapped at him and the men all froze.

Just as well. She tried to thread the needle but with every tremble of her fingers she missed the eye.

"Drink a little, Lady."

Colin pushed past the men at her back, a new flask in his hands and his bright gaze undaunted by the sight of the wound and the blood leaking down the table.

"Thank you," she said, the liquor hot and tearing its way down her throat. But she held her cough and blinked the tears that gathered in her eyes and took a long, slow breath, wondering if she had the power like Dominic to command the room cleared out so she might think without dozens of eyes on her.

But this is their Healer, she reminded herself. And they had put him in her care. *Finley* was putting himself in her care, whether he'd agreed to or not.

The needle was ready and the task was waiting. She nodded to Gideon and Dominic and then poured more alcohol onto the wound, wincing as Finley struggled on the table.

"I'm sorry," she whispered, without meaning to, and began to set to the work. She could hear his teeth grinding. "Laudanum?" she asked.

Finley had mentioned the drug when she had woken up after being struck in the face by the flogger. He'd only given it to her the once and she didn't know how to administer it, but maybe Dominic would have seen him—

"He won't take it," Dominic said, adding as she glanced at him, "he *can't.*"

"Fine." She didn't blame him. The laudanum had made her woozy and there was a strange sort of dimming effect to the drug, like blowing the candle out on the world around her. "Will he let me use something for that spot alone?"

"He'll want to decide, little spirit," Gideon said, ever so gentle even as he pinned his friend while she worked her stitches through skin.

Fine. If Finley could bear the pain then she would let him and she'd do what she could to speed the healing. In the corner of the room, one of the other patients began to cough.

"He can't stay in here with them," she murmured as she tugged the thread and Finley hissed. "He'll get infected for sure."

"My room," Gideon said. "You'll take my room while he heals."

The room next to Dominic's. But better than dragging him all the way up to the freezing attic. Gideon's bedroom had a proper fireplace at least.

"Very well. Colin, ask Rosie to clean the room."

"I can clean my own room," Gideon protested as the boy dashed away.

"You're a walking stain, Gid," Dominic said, and it was the first time in almost two weeks that she'd heard that bone dry humor, low and rumbling beneath her skin.

"I'd rather you stayed and waited for me to finish here. You'll have to help him up the stairs."

"How long till he heals?" Dominic asked.

"I... I don't know. It depends on how well the wound heals." If he healed, or if the wound grew infected. "Rest for a week," she said. She expected the General to argue with her and just in case he might she continued, "I'll handle the infirmary."

"You already handle the infirmary," Dominic said.

She didn't like this. This ease between them. She focused on her stitches, wondered if it wouldn't have been better to cauterize the wound. He'd been pale that morning but now he looked nearly sheet white, too much blood lost.

"There is... there is some jewelry in a compartment at the bottom of my wardrobe. It was my mother's. It should be used to buy good food, meat. Fruit if it can be found," she said, refusing to look up.

"Very well," Dominic said in an echo of her own words.

The stitches ended and Finley was bandaged, tight and secure, his eyes almost transparent as he blinked slowly at her. Lumen swore a year of her life drained out of her as she finished, some anxious energy that had driven her through the challenge now burnt out, leaving her limp and exhausted. Hands caught her round the waist, directing her over to a chair, and it wasn't until she was steadied and sitting that she realized the hands belonged to Dominic.

He strode back across the room to his men and together they carried Finley out of the room, abandoning her to her cluttered thoughts.

Finley stirred and then flinched and relaxed back into the bedding on his stomach. She'd already managed small cups of broth in bickering dosages three times. Now it was nearing midnight. Lumen had sent word to the tenants, by way of Colin, that the chapel would remain closed for the day. She would be busy and it was better not to tempt Dominic's hospitality now that he was finished with her.

"My New Moon observances must start," she whispered, reluctant to wake him.

He grunted into the mattress. "It's fine. Go. Wait, help me up first? Need to piss."

She slid her arm beneath his chest and helped him slide off the bed and upright, ignoring the warmth of his skin on hers. Trying to ignore it.

"I'm not leaving," she said as he turned away and walked slow and careful over to the small bathroom compartment at the opposite side of the room. "I'll just fast and abstain from speech."

She heard Finley's snort through the doorway. "I can help you with the men."

"You're not even going downstairs," Lumen said, tone firm. "I can manage fine. Gideon and Colin are under orders to keep you resting." She listened to his sigh and waited for him to reappear. "Do you want anything for the pain?"

He shook his head and then grimaced, body wobbling as he shuffled closer. "I won't take anything."

"Willow bark won't start cravings," Lumen said. Finley stilled, glaring at her by candlelight and she tilted her head. "How far is the pain spread?"

"Straight up into my skull," Finley muttered, continuing in his slow path to the bed.

She waited until he'd made his slow crawl back down onto the mattress, arms pressed to his side and face smushed down. Her hand shook a little as she reached out, and his eye peeked open as she rolled onto her side. He stiffened as she touched the back of his neck, his gaze watchful and narrowed, and then his lids fell shut and he sighed, her thumb stroking up the curve of his shoulder and neck.

"If you won't accept medicine you'll have to settle for this treatment," she said.

He snorted, soft and weak, shoulders easing as she stroked muscles loose in long sweeps until he was practically limp. She started up into the hair at the back of his neck, brushing flakes of blood away as she worked her touch up and down his neck, behind his ears, up to the top of his head, until she was certain he was asleep and she was the only one benefitting from the care. She dropped her head onto her pillow and carried on all the same.

"This is a kind of drug too, Lady Fenn," Finley whispered, words barely escaping his throat.

Lumen thought it must be the time of the New Moon by then, and refrained from answering.

FASTING WAS one thing when she was laying still for the day. Doing it when she was running through the halls of the Manor, up into the workshop, over to the kitchen... she realized why Lunars meditated on New Moon day. And she was beginning to question the entire structure of the Manor. Why this enormous, drafty, ring of halls and rooms?

Her cheeks burned with cold and her head floated, untethered from her body, as she hurried back to the infirmary from the kitchen, a large basin of warm water in her arms.

Idle men filled the arches, playing cards and checkers, each pair pausing as she passed.

"Think of it, a whole day without a woman speaking," one of them said as she passed.

"I can keep that mouth busy for you, milady!"

Laughter followed, rolling out around the ring. Lumen kept her eyes fixed to the floor and the basin in her hands. The last thing she needed was to trip, not in this weather. She'd leave an icy patch on the stones and land herself with another patient in the infirmary with a broken bone.

"Poor lady," another murmured, rising from his seat, his friend grinning with dark gaps in his smile. "Her healer is laid up and now there's no one to lay her. I could do the job, milady. Can't guarantee you'll keep quiet."

Lumen tried to hurry. There was no sign of the General, and Finley wasn't coming to her aid from where he was tucked away upstairs. But the sudden anxiety only made her vision swim, hallway wavering ahead of her feet.

"Nay, Devon, she'll be weeping you ain't big enough to please her!"

What good would it do her to get to the infirmary, anyway? The men could follow her there just as easily and she doubted any of the patients had the strength to intervene, if they even cared to.

"Let's just fucking see once I've got inside her, shall we —Argh!!"

Gideon appeared from a parlor, barreling behind her, fists clenching into Devon's coat collar, throwing him against a pillar and scattering a game of checkers onto the stone.

"You so much as lift your eyes to that woman and you won't be riding anything, woman, horse, or cart, for the rest of your life. What little of it I leave you with."

Devon bared yellow teeth, heels kicking in a futile effort, toes scraping on the stone as Gideon growled down at the soldier.

Eyes red with exhaustion and effort began to slide to Lumen and Gideon rattled the man, knocking his head against the pillar.

"What did I just say?"

"Yes, sir," Devon wheezed.

"Will you look at her?"

"No, sir."

Lumen was torn between trying to stop Gideon and leaving in the midst of the scene, but she couldn't speak and the dozens of prickling stares that had fixed themselves to her as she walked were now finding new directions to look to.

"Speak to her?"

"No, sir."

"Think of her?"

Devon's throat was white where he was held, face blushed red and turning purple. "No, sir," he mouthed.

He crumpled as Gideon released him, and Lumen turned her back to the scene, cheeks hot and heart pounding. She only made it a few steps before Gideon appeared at her side.

"I'll find the boy to run your errands for you," he said, glancing at the basin of water. "Or I'll do it myself. We'll put the men back in training tomorrow morning, burn the bastards back into... well, not gentlemen." He grinned at her and Lumen ducked her head as he opened the door into the infirmary for her.

"Try to stay out of their way until Fin is back on his feet, little spirit," Gideon whispered. "I'll keep my eye out for you."

There was no good answer to his reassurance and she was glad for the excuse to remain mute. She didn't want to feel like a coward in her own home. She didn't want to leave the doors open for men that made a game of terrorizing her or anyone else.

A dark part of her head had felt a spiteful pleasure at watching Gideon grind the man into the pillar. She was not grateful for the violence but she was a petty and ugly breed of flattered.

For once Gideon did not tease at her silence, only shadowed her around the room as she continued her work, arms folded over his chest and eyes glaring at men too unwell to defend themselves. Colin replaced him at Lumen's side just before sunset, infinitely more helpful and less distressing to the men whose beds she tended. They left together as the bonfire was being lit in the courtyard, Colin's fingers wrapped around hers and tugged, weaving them through the loitering men.

"Lady, come look," he whispered, so quiet Lumen suspected he was trying to keep his speech a secret from Mother Lune herself.

She smiled and let him drag her to the heart of the courtyard, just feet away from the fire. He stopped, nudging her into place and then pointing east through an arch and the entrance hall, straight out the front doors where the first sliver of moon was rising over the horizon. She smiled down at him and he shook his head, turning her in place to the west. Someone had left the door to an old staff quarter room open and through the window on the opposite wall, the sunset was red and swollen as it sank into the woods beyond. She turned her head back to the front entrance, Colin's eyes on her face, the moon curling like a tilted smile in the sky.

"Did you know?" he whispered. "That they face one another at the start and end of the day?"

She tried to remember if she'd ever stopped to watch, if the doors and windows had ever been opened together in the right places at the right time? In summer perhaps, but it'd been a long time since the house was full of enough people to warrant throwing all the doors wide.

"I never noticed," she whispered back. Lune was up again, and she'd made terrible observances that day anyway, head full of patients, of Gideon, of Finley upstairs. "But by the solstice they'll have shifted. We'll have to wait and see."

Colin nodded solemnly and then Lumen's stomach rumbled angrily and he snorted. "Go upstairs and check on Brink, Lady," Colin said. "He was being a prickly shit when I left. I'll bring you both somethin' to eat!"

Lumen kissed the boy on the top of the head and ran up to the room, feeling watched but never seeing the evidence of it as the soldiers gave her a wide berth. She heard the shouting coming from inside her borrowed bedroom and rushed in, Gideon and Finley's voices dying off as she appeared.

"Your turn," Gideon said, voice rough and shoulders hunched as he squeezed past her and into the hall.

Lumen raised her brows at Finley who was standing with his bare back to her, neck twisted around and arms contorted as he tried to fuss with his own bandage.

"Did I sew you shut after getting shot with an arrow just for you to rip through the stitches?"

Finley huffed and sagged, all but stomping over to the bed as Lumen followed him, finding where she'd hidden the ends of the bandage and unravelling the wrappings from around his chest.

"I can't stand being locked in here with nothing to do," Finley muttered, head hanging and nudging briefly against her arm. She huffed and sat down next to him since he didn't seem willing to move his arms out of her way.

"I'll bring you something to read," she said.

"How are the men?"

"Healing, growing stronger. Better patients than you."

"Have you checked for any swelling in the digits?"

"I remembered all your notes very well," she said.

She pulled the last of the wrap away and then held him still when he started to turn to her. She softened the bandage on his back with some honey water and then wiped away dried and crusted blood. The wound wasn't elegant, it would leave a jagged scar, and it was a little puffy. But there was no sign of fever or infection. She replaced the bandage with a fresh one and started to wrap him up again.

"You'll live."

Finley snorted and then rolled his neck, a sharp cracking sound released as he moved.

"How's your head?" she asked.

"If you're asking if I want your attentions again... my answer is yes." He shifted to face her, the snarl of the expression he'd been wearing when she first walked in now dissolved.

Lumen scooted back against the headboard and Finley

followed on his stomach, his head landing in her lap. He sighed as one hand sifted through soft strands, the other attending to the back of his neck where knots of tension had returned since the night before.

"Is this another skill your mother taught you?" he mumbled, cheek pressed to her thigh.

Lumen closed her eyes, head propped against the wooden bedframe. "No. I learned it on my own, I suppose. She would get headaches and I would tend her."

Finley sighed, one hand clasping around her thigh. "Always tending others."

LUMEN PAUSED OUTSIDE of her father's study, listening at the door, waiting for the rustle of a page or the huff of a breath, but all was quiet.

Westbrook was hard to track within the Manor lately, she felt his eyes on her even when he was out of sight and she wasn't sure if she was imagining his presence. But the room sounded empty and Finley was going through books like glasses of water, even now that he was up out of bed. She was keeping him strictly to the second story until the wound on his back was better healed.

She snuck in before anyone caught her loitering outside of Westbrook's claimed office. She knew the arrangement of the shelves as well as she knew the herbs in her mother's workroom. Finley's tastes were wide enough and he seemed to skip from one book to another at the whim of a moment so she grabbed something new for every book she replaced.

The door creaked as she finished with her selections and Lumen's stomach dropped to the floor.

"Stealing from me?"

The shock of surprise and being caught hardened in her veins. These were her father's books. *Her* books. But hadn't Westbrook already told her she was nothing but a guest now?

"Running an errand for your healer," she said, wrapping her

arms around the haul of books, as if she might use them as a shield. She kept her eyes on the rich pattern of carpet between their feet, the landscape shrinking as Westbrook stepped closer.

"My healer?" He hummed and the sound was a predator's warning. "He's yours now, isn't he?"

By your command, she thought. "I'm just leaving." She tried to make a quick step to the right, avoid his approach, but he was too fast.

His feet rushed and his arms reached out and then Lumen was pinned to a bookshelf, eyes wide and staring up at that dark face she'd been pushing out of her mind for weeks. There was a black and silver peppered beard properly growing over his face now and dark circles beneath his eyes. His lips were pressed into a white line as he stared down at her, his chest pinned to where she held the books between them. Shield, indeed.

"Stay a little while, witch," he said, head leaning down until she had to turn her cheeks to keep from finding herself nearly kissed.

The anger building in her chest wrapped itself around her tongue, sparking words behind her teeth. "What do you want, Dominic?"

He huffed a laugh. "What have I ever wanted from you, Lady Fenn?"

"You dismissed that duty of mine," she snapped, narrowed eyes flicking to his, watching him flinch.

"And if I were to change my mind and ask for your favors again?" He painted a smile on his lips but it read as a lie. She'd seen smiles on his face before, burst free so fast it surprised even him, and this moved her to nothing more than further fury.

"You would be denied," she said.

The smile vanished and his eyes darkened. "Do you really think that's wise?"

"I will fight you tooth and nail if you touch me."

His chest scraped against her knuckles as he bent his head, tip of his nose running around her ear and down to her jaw. "Oh but you forget, I like your teeth and nails. You were partial to mine too."

There was a tickle of desire curling around her neck but her belly was cold with rage. Perhaps he would always provide a kind of temptation, and there had certainly been pleasure once. She'd lived in fear for two weeks of this invitation, of what it might drive her to, and it was a relief to know the answer. She hated him. She wanted her knife driven into his flesh. Whatever stirrings his touch might have caused, they were nothing compared to the twisting, coiling thorns of loathing that now rooted themselves inside of her.

"Does he satisfy you?" Dominic whispered against her ear and she jerked away with the first flick of his tongue, using the books in her arms to push and shove him back.

His stumbled back on his heels, his eyes wide and brow furrowed in genuine shock. It drew more irritation out of her to know he was surprised to be rebuffed.

"I am satisfied, sir," Lumen said, louder and faster than she meant to speak but enjoying the way he winced as the words landed. "I would be more so if you left me in peace. You have passed me on and I wish you would keep it so. Is that enough?"

His jaw clenched as his shoulders straightened, chest puffing. "I could just as easily command you mine again."

"I could just as easily poison your ale," Lumen spat at him.

"Are you threatening me?" he asked, laughing.

"Yes." Her nails dug into the leather bindings of the books as she stared back at him until his laughter died. "If that is all, sir." She bent in a brief parody of a curtsey and turned her back on him, storming to the door.

"Lumen." Her feet didn't stop at the demand in his voice and he had to rush to speak. "All I have to do is say the word and he will drop you. I am still his General."

Lumen bit her tongue as she broke into the hall. She wouldn't dare him to follow through, she wasn't fool enough to think he wouldn't. He only misunderstood how little she cared what he demanded of her now.

Lumen gasped as hands wrapped around her hips, her nose bumping against a firm chest as she rushed up the stairs to check on Finley, only to find him in front of her.

"What are you doing here?" they asked in unison.

"You should be resting," she added, pressing her palms to his chest and trying to herd him back upstairs. "I'll bring you a meal."

"I've had enough of resting and Gideon says the men are well again," Finley said, dodging her grasp and then wrapping his arm around her waist. "Eat downstairs with me."

"It's cold, and you've only just healed."

"Lady Fenn, I'm near madness and I handle that very poorly." His hand urged at her side, long fingers cupping around her ribs and a shockingly stirring touch. "If you must escape, go up without me."

Lumen's breath rattled in her chest and she dug her heels into the stone, the pair of them coming to a stop halfway down the flight of stairs. "Westbrook is out with the others this evening."

Finley hummed and cocked his head at the news. "Then we better stick together. But he's kept his distance, hasn't he? Come down with me for a meal. Only long enough for me to remember how much I hate the company at least."

She snorted and let him nudge her along at his side, hiding the way he leaned into her for support.

Gideon was with Dominic when they reached the courtyard and he grinned at the pair of them, but that was as all she was willing to see. She hadn't told Finley or Gideon about the scene in her father's study and she had no intention of telling them. Westbrook hadn't tried to touch her again, hadn't spoken to her.

And clearly, despite his threat, he hadn't demanded Finley "drop her."

Which was good, because she wasn't convinced the healer wouldn't. He tolerated her. He didn't seem to mind her care while he was healing, but it wasn't like with Gideon. There was no clear display of desire or humor or anything else. At least not since the time he'd watched her fall apart under Dominic's ministrations, and she may have misunderstood his expression in her own pleasure.

"Don't worry," Finley said in her ear as her steps began to drag. "We won't test his tolerance tonight."

"I've an open spot just here lady," a man muttered, thrusting his hips in her direction until Finley stopped to glare him into a surly retreat.

They found a spot behind a group of younger soldiers and Finley jerked his head at the two who sat in an arch until they scampered out of the way.

"I'll get us food," Lumen said, starting to pull away but he wrapped his hands around her hips and pulled her down with him onto his lap, her legs hanging over his.

"Your favorite suitor will find us something," Finley said nodding to the fire where Colin was fixing up two bowls, a hunk of meat hanging from his own lips as he chewed. "Gideon said the soldiers have been at you. Better to make a show of it."

Lumen sat primly over his legs, bracing herself with a hand on his shoulder, her toes straining to balance against the stone tile. She hadn't sat on anyone's lap since she was a little girl, and it was strange to do it for the sake of an audience.

"But you're injured."

"Only on my back," Finley said, lips quirking at her. "Relax. Any harm you do me I'm sure your magic fingers will set to rights later."

Finley leaned his side into a pillar and Lumen settled her back there, softening in small increments. Colin brought them steaming bowls of stew and two cups of ale pinched between his fingers. She relaxed as the boy joined them, giving her somewhere for her eyes to land that wasn't a glaring General or an audience of soldiers waiting for she-didn't-know-what from her and Finley.

One of the other women, Inda, caught Lumen's eyes. She had her own lap for a seat and it was Philip, her sweetheart. She was curled in his embrace, his hand clamped tightly against her ass as his nose nuzzled against her neck, leaving her squirming and him panting. Inda winked at her and Lumen blushed and tore her eyes away, but the couple lingered in the corners, curling closer together.

"You're blushing," Finley said in her ear.

She flinched and his arm wrapped tighter around her waist, keeping her from skittering away.

"I didn't mean to stare," she said, looking back at him.

"Who am I to judge?" he asked, raising his eyebrows. He smirked as her cheeks heated further.

"Bet you're looking forward to being healed again, eh Healer Brink?" One of the young men asked, the others snickering around him, hands patting at his arm as if to reward his bravery in speaking.

"Nay lad, Our Lady Lune is a good little nurse," an older man called out. "She's seen him through on her knees no doubt."

Finley made to stand but Lumen planted herself firmly and he grimaced as the wound healing on his back pulled.

"Leave it," she whispered, her fingers digging into the wool of his coat, eyes fixing to his as the rumble of the crowd grew with every added laugh.

"Ladies ain't sucking cock, ya daft prick," Jennie barked at the men.

"Maybe not, but all the nurses I ever met sure did!"

The whole gathered army roared with laughter, the bonfire flaring and showering the sky with sparks.

"*Enough!*"

The single bellowed word shook through the humor, a familiar order demanding response, and the laughter settled, all the faces turning and then ducking shamefully under Westbrook's stare. The General settled back into the shadow of the courtyard but the effect remained, faces turned back to their small parties.

Finley's fingers dug into her side as Lumen looked to him. Colin slipped away, into the crowd in the rush of quiet, likely to look for more scraps to eat.

"A man like that doesn't even know what to do with a woman."

It was only a whisper from one of the young men nearby but a breeze carried it further than it was meant to travel and Lumen was watching Finley as the words landed. His jaw ticked and his eyes dragged away from hers briefly.

"You were right," he said, one corner of his mouth turning up in a bitter smile. "We should have stayed upstairs. Are you ready?"

"Not quite," Lumen said.

She had to hunch, because for all her time with Dominic she hadn't really learned how to *take* from a man, only to be prepared for when she was needed. Her forehead bumped against his, breath stuttering over his nose and lips and he leaned back, face lifted and eyes wide. She pressed their noses together, felt his body stiffen against hers, and then tilted her face, lips landing. It wasn't a kiss. Not at first. He was too surprised and she wasn't practiced.

Then she pressed in, and he breathed out, and she fit her mouth to his. A caress. Awkward and hesitant. If anyone was watching they would know this had never been attempted before. It had been a poorly considered plan to start with.

She made to pull away and Finley caught her by the chin, a familiar mirror of that one angry touch from so many weeks ago. But this wasn't anger, it was instruction to stay. His lips surrounded hers, dragged on them, tongue flicking out to taste her. She was being sipped at, a kiss so gentle it made her tremble. Such brief, teasing caresses as if at any second she could pull away—except he held her to receive, not to allow escape.

A deeper hush was rolling out over the crowd. Or was it only in Lumen's ears as Finley pecked and pressed and sucked at her lips? She hummed and clutched his coat in her fist and his arm around her waist squeezed until her chest was pressed to his, hand trapped between them. The kiss deepened and the quiet at her back gave way to huffing laughter and new conversation, the interest drifting away from them.

She didn't stop, only opened her mouth to Finley's searching kiss, shifting on his lap as her body remembered its interest in friction, in wrapping itself around another person. His fingers stroked up her jaw, into the tangles of hair at the back of her neck, tongue sliding against hers, a soft hum of approval vibrating between them.

All at once she felt the stare, hot on the back of her neck, twin pokers of anger digging against where Finley touched her. Dominic watched them. Then Finley nipped at her lip, as if in penalty for letting her thoughts stray, and she was consumed again, one long, decadent kiss at a time.

FINLEY SHUT the bedroom door behind them and she was there, rising up to her tiptoes, those gentle fingers of hers sliding into his hair to pull him down to meet her lips. He followed like it was a reflex, hands grasping at her hips to brace them against his, bowing over her until she was arched in his arms. She made sweet, brief, pleading sounds at the back of her throat and they drugged his dizzy head like opium.

"I may have underestimated my madness," he breathed into the soft flesh of her throat as she panted, breaths stirring his hair.

"Perhaps it's contagious," she said, sighing. Her hands burrowed beneath the shoulders of his coat, lifting it away from his back before sliding it down his arms, ever careful not to harm him.

And what are you doing? He asked himself as the coat landed on the floor in a quiet rush. Was taking what she suddenly offered any breed of kindness or just greed?

Lumen's arms twined over his shoulders, drawing him back to her lips, tilting her chin to offer her throat again, hips nudging in a teasing rhythm. Needy and sweet. Begging. Finley licked over her pulse, hands swarming and surrounding her back as she moaned, sliding down over the swell of her ass to pin her against him, let her feel the length of him waking and rising to meet her.

"Is this for his benefit or mine?" Finley asked, fingers digging through Lumen's skirt to grasp the soft swell of flesh.

Lumen stilled in his arms and he scraped his teeth over her pulse. If she would only admit that this was about Dominic, he could call the farce to an end. Although laying next to her in the bed after tasting her would be a new kind of torture. It was bad enough to feel her warmth, to flood his senses with that snow bright smell of her. Every brush of their skin left him startling to wakefulness at night and now it would likely leave him hard and aching.

She pulled herself out of his arms and the loss was a sharp pang running from his chest down to his cock. But it was better this way. Until she spoke.

"I suppose I meant it for my benefit," she said. His eyes darted up to stare at her, found her lips soft and curling, cheeks blushing with the shining white flecks of her scars littering her skin like stars in the dim room. "But I imagine it would be to yours too."

There was a crunching, cracking feeling in his chest, pounded beneath a wave of possessive desire. He prowled after her, but she was a strange and fearless creature and instead of backing away to the bed she waited for him, fingertips scratching through his shirt over his stomach as she stared up at him.

"Would you do it because he commanded you to take me on?" she asked.

Finley frowned. "I don't think that was really his intention.

But no. If I have you, Lumen, it will be for entirely selfish reasons."

She sighed and rose up, lips lifted for the taking and he tried to steel his nerves, setting a palm on her shoulder.

"You've heard rumors," he said, hand sliding up her neck, thumb stroking her jaw, covering one scar with the pad of his finger.

Lumen blinked, a slow, lazy skim of pale lashes over her cheeks and then her eyes grew wide, breath catching. She'd heard the rumors and forgot them in the daze of the kiss.

"I don't want to hurt you," he reassured her. "Do you trust me?"

Her eyes dropped, tongue wetting her lips as her brow tangled and Finley realized. Of course she didn't trust him. Why should she? Why would she trust any of them after Dominic had twisted her thoughts in every direction for his own satisfaction.

He frowned and nudged her to the bed, sitting down on the mattress first and watching with an overwhelming relief as she followed him.

"I played games in bed with women before, at Dominic's bidding," he said, trying to read her expression and finding only her usual stillness, secrets held behind pale eyes. "Some of them were cruel. That's not what I'm asking for. But I prefer control."

Lumen's head tilted and she glanced up again. "Don't most men?"

He huffed and found himself smiling. "Does Gideon seem in control to you?" He wanted to feel the blush that followed against his lips, the rush of blood warming her skin. "I only take the control you offer me. Say the word and it's yours again."

Her shoulders eased and he wondered if it was right to feel the victory burning through him. He was accepting a hand in her ruin.

"Such complicated terms for such a simple act," Lumen mused. Then she leaned in until her arm brushed against him. "What are my instructions?"

His head spun. She was agreeing. She was *his* if only for the night, or until his tastes sent her running. Or until Dominic called her back.

"Stand in front of me here," he said, spreading his knees and taking her hand in his to guide her between his legs, turning until her back was to him.

Her head turned, listening as he reached up to the laces of her dress, sliding them loose. She was small and the bed was high enough that with a slight tug at her waist he could reach the nape of her neck with his mouth, pressing kisses and sucking at the spot until she was shivering, a little giggle rising from her throat. She lifted her hands to tug her dress down and he caught them by her fingers, locking them with his and holding her still, a soft nip of teeth against her shoulder.

"Don't lift a hand unless I tell you," he said, squeezing lightly.

Her breath shuddered and she nodded and he released her, his own hands returning to her waist. He kissed every inch of skin between her neck and shoulder, tongue flicking out to find each flavor of her, sweeter and sharper than he'd expected. He kissed the pattern of healing marks left with the flogger, his nose nudging the fabric of her dress out of the way until it sagged over her arm. Her shoulder shone damp as he drew away, moving to the other side to repeat the process.

She was perfect—still but pliant, her only sound the rapid and soft pant of her breath. His hands stroked over her stomach, up to her breasts, scratching his nails over the fabric covering her nipples, and she made her first whimpering cry. He found the collar of the dress at the front, his cheek pressed to her warm back, and tugged it down to her waist, arms trapped to her sides in her sleeves. His tongue lapped up her spine and Lumen's body swayed as he toyed with her breasts, tweaked at her nipples.

"You're being very patient," he said. He was stiff as stone, tempted to toss her to the bed, tangled as she was in her own skirt, and show her the rougher edge of his pleasures.

"Acting patient is not the same as being patient," she said, voice thin, and Finley hid his grin against her back.

"Pull your arms free."

She did and he pushed the dress down of her hips, watching with interest as it pinched around her soft hips and ass before giving way. She shivered again and he stood, arms surrounding her, one hand tucking between her legs to cup at her sex. She moaned, thighs parting in invitation and squirmed as his touch didn't advance.

"Undress me," he said, pulling her earlobe with his lips, worrying at it with his teeth.

She was wet against his fingertips and he was tempted to hold her there and drive her straight to orgasm. But he wanted to show her what there was to appreciate in restraint. And, more secretly and in a darker place in his mind, he wanted to savor an experience that didn't feel rightfully his.

She turned in his arms, silver eyes glassy, and lips pink from being bitten between her teeth. He had to duck for her to lift his shirt over his shoulders but she was careful not to scrape against the bandage still covering his wound. She frowned at the sight of his wrappings and he lifted her chin for another kiss to distract her. Sex would take some thinking but he was well enough healed to manage the act and desperate enough to ignore any pain as a result.

Her hands found his belt while he busied her mouth and he grunted as her fingers dipped inside, stroking around the base of his cock, her belly rubbing against the aching length. She pushed the trousers down his hips and reached to pull herself up against him.

Finley caught her wrists and pulled away from the kiss, heart hammering at the sound of Lumen's whine. "Hold your elbows behind your back."

This was a step further, an instruction she wasn't familiar with, but she only smiled at him and did as told. He swallowed and sat on the bed, gut and cock heavy with wanting. He pulled her closer, her knees on either side of his, pussy glistening with desire. A feast for the taking right before his eyes. He leaned in, lifted one breast to kiss the crease beneath it, found her scented more strongly of salt and something sugary sweet, and then drew away again, Lumen's body following his mouth for more.

"Lay down. I'll help you," he said, bracing his palms around her belly and back.

Her cheeks were stained with pink and he locked his ankle around hers when she made to step over. "No, like this, over my lap and stretched back across the mattress."

He ushered her down, steadying her as her chest hit the coverlet, her breath hissing as her breasts scraped against fabric. Finley grinned at the sight of her, ass high, her delicate hands knotting her arms at her back, toes balanced precariously on the floor. He ran fingertips down her back and she shuddered.

"Relax, I'm not about to let you fall off," he teased, stroking over the soft rounds of her ass as her legs relaxed, feet dangling. "If your arms get tired you can let go, but you have to leave them at your sides and not move them."

Her head turned in the blankets. "Why?" she whispered.

Finley slid his hand between her spread legs, thrilled with how slippery wet she was, marveling at the way her breath broke in a cry at the first touch. Her legs kicked at air as he skimmed the soaked flesh, teasing at her entrance, gentle exploring pets of touch until she squeaked as he found her clit.

"Because this is about what I want you to feel, not you demanding what you want," he said.

She hummed and softened further over his lap. Her chin tucked to her shoulder and she waited for him to look at her again before she asked, "But it won't just be touching, will it?"

Finley's hand cupped at the back of her thigh and squeezed, his cock twitching. "Depends on how well you do," he said. A complete lie. The only way this wouldn't end with him burying himself inside of her sweet cunt was if she called it to an end before he reached his limit of patience.

Lumen's back melted, her hands loosening their grip around her elbows, as if to prove how good she could be for him. Finley turned his face away, that tender crushing sensation returning to his chest. But he rewarded her, one fingertip swirling over her entrance before pressing inside. His breath was hard to catch as her cunt gripped him, slick and giving and clutching as he pumped and plunged. Lumen held still, remained relaxed, but all the torment of his treatment came out in muffled cries against the bedding. Finley glanced up at the crack in the wall and remembered.

Shit. If he was lucky Dominic would remain down in the courtyard for hours still. If he was unlucky...

He gave her up. She's mine now. If only the thought felt true.

"Oh gods, yes," Lumen gasped as he pulled free and teased down to her clit.

Her thighs and sex were coated in glossy arousal and it had just started to drip down to his lap. He wanted to coat his cock with her wetness and fit himself inside her tight heat and never draw free again.

I am damned, he thought. And rather than dwell on the fact, he focused on the woman draped over his legs.

He played a delicate rhythm around her clit, until the sound of her ragged moans drove his fingers up inside her, fucking her roughly enough she rattled on his lap. Sweat dewed on her back but her arms remained resting, toes never touching the floor and trying to take control of the pace.

"You're too good at this," Finley said, watching her gasp for breath as he slowed his touch and continued back to her clit for another round of driving her up to the edge.

"Isn't that what you want?" she asked, a little pout of lips appearing, her face red with frustration.

Did he know what he wanted? He wanted *her*. Exactly like this. Surrounding him. Pressed to the bed beneath him. A hundred ways. His head in her lap as she soothed him to sleep. Curled against his chest and kissing him in front of Westbrook's army.

He pressed hard on her clit and her head arched back, cry brittle. Her hips kicked once against his hand and then she trembled and forced herself still again, releasing a long breath as she relaxed. It was all the submission he had ever craved from a partner during sex and instead of triumph he felt... captured.

"I think I want to watch you come for me," he said, very soft.

He spread his knees wider apart, and Lumen grunted at the stretch in her own thighs. His right hand covered her clit, grinding fully and she made a sweet, high sound of relief which shattered as he filled her up with the fingers of his left, pumping and twisting. All the control of a moment ago vanished and Finley watched as her fingertips left white prints on her elbows and her back shifted and twisted, head tossing in the blankets.

The orgasm ran through her, rippling muscle all the way down to her toes and up to her shoulders and he watched the path of pleasure as she coated his fingers in release.

"Finley! Finley, yes!"

His cock pulsed at the sound of his name on her lips and he pushed her through orgasm until she was wiggling away from his touch. She giggled into the bedsheets as he drew free, lifting her leg over his to let it drop next to the other.

He opened his mouth to order her to turn over and then swallowed the demand, reaching out to untangle her fingers from around her elbows. "Are your shoulders sore?"

Lumen hummed and stretched her arms and then pushed herself up on them. "Maybe a little."

She crawled up the mattress to the headboard and he caught himself staring at the swollen red lips of her sex, glistening. He turned and followed her on his knees.

"Let me take care of you," he said. It was the only order that felt right on his tongue the entire night.

Lumen twisted and fell onto her back against the pillows, trying to force the giddy smile off her face and finding herself completely unable. She had missed this. Sex. Pleasure. And Finley was different. More discussion and less demand. A new kind of seduction and a refreshing one.

Or maybe she was just a little dizzy with her finish.

"You just took care of me," she said, raising her eyebrows.

He knelt in front of her, cock jutting out, bobbing with its own weight. Inda was right. Finley *was* long. In body as well as manhood. His muscles were lean, but dense with strength, corded and carved down long limbs. His hand reached down and she thought he meant to cover himself until his fingers were wrapping around his cock and pumping the flesh, a bead of fluid leaking at the tip. She looked up to find him smirking.

"And I intend to do so again," he said, words purring in her ears. She parted her legs to welcome him between them and smiled as his chest shook at the sight of her, eyes fixing to her core. "Are you teasing me?"

"I only meant to do as I was asked," Lumen said, lips shaking with the effort not to smile.

Finley huffed and shook his head, a lock of hair falling forward into his eyes. "Stretch your arms up above to the headboard."

Lumen pursed her lips and obeyed, wincing as her muscles stretched to the new arrangement, stiff after being locked behind her back for so long. Finley's knees burrowed beneath her thighs and then he was reaching out, hands working over her shoulders and upper arms, body leaning in to kiss her. The tip of his cock nudged between her legs and Lumen hummed and bumped her hips closer.

"So eager?"

"A little," she admitted, tilting her head back.

She couldn't see him clearly from here, with the fire beyond the bed putting him in a golden outline. But she could feel his eyes on her face, the warmth of him softening the air. He smelled like that bitter smoke of his, and the honey ointment she'd been spreading into his skin each day.

"Better?" he asked, pulling her arms down, running his hands over the length until he reached hers, linking their fingers together.

The twinging stiffness was gone and Lumen squeezed at his hands and nodded. "Am I meant to behave again?"

Finley nipped at her nose, body sinking over hers. "Only as much as you want to."

She wanted one thing, very badly. Her heels dug into the bed and she rocked herself against his length, feeling him slide against her damp skin, watching as his eyes fell shut and a breath panted out.

"I take that back," he said, glaring down at her as she landed into the mattress again. "You are too eager to undo me."

"To be undone," she said, smiling, watching his cheeks twitch. So much control to stay stern, calm, when all he really seemed to want to do was laugh.

He released one of her hands and she slipped it into his hair, drawing him down by the back of his neck for a deep kiss, tongue stroking against his. His own went to his cock, knuckles brushing briefly against her center before lining himself up and pushing in. Lumen's lips parted on a moan and Finley drew back, rising above her, watching himself sink in, watching her face as he started to pump and shift inside.

"Oh gods," she breathed. It was deep, the fullness rolling like a wave up to her throat as he continued to delve. Her knees rose to cradle his hips and her breath froze in her lungs.

"Can you take more?"

She nodded, although with the next soft roll of his hips she thought she might be mad for doing so. She groaned and his head ducked, breath rushing over her breasts as his thrusts shortened and grew quicker.

"Finley!" Her body rose up to meet his and his hand squeezed around hers as he lifted his head and pressed his mouth over hers, tongue pressing inside to mimic the act between her thighs.

He pulled away and groaned her name into her cheek as her legs wrapped around his hips. "Hands back," he rasped into her ear.

She didn't hesitate, grasping onto the cut out in the headboard. Spread out over his lap and onto the mattress, unable to really move for her own pleasure, had been a new brand of intoxication. She would accept any more he had to offer.

He drew back and already she felt the loss of him, back arching to try and drive him in again. But his hands went to her hips and his lips peppered kisses over her breasts, the tip of him just barely nudging in and out at her opening.

"I think you *are* the madness," Finley murmured against her skin. "And you've taken us all under."

She opened her mouth to object but then he was biting around her nipple and she was shouting, dazed by the way the pain followed with a rich pang of pleasure in her cunt.

"You handed me control and yet the sound of your voice is a command of its own," he said.

He treated the other breast the same and Lumen whined, the sound breaking off suddenly as he surged up again, filling her in one stroke. One hand reached up to cup beneath her neck, the other digging his fingers into her ass as he rocked inside of her in long, full strokes ending with a percussive pressure that ran down to her toes at every strike.

Her fingers itched to touch him, heels digging into his ass as she churned up to grind herself against him with every deep thrust. His eyes were fixed to her face, watching her, and she couldn't decide between shutting her own to let the pounding sensation drown her, or fixing her stare to his. She clenched around him and his chest dropped to hers, pressing her to the bed, anchoring her beneath hot skin and hard muscle. His lips latched to the pulse on her throat and then he whispered.

"Touch me."

It wasn't an order but a plea and Lumen met it just as easily as any command, crossing her arms over his shoulders. She tugged him up, a clumsy request, and he followed, nose bumping against hers just like it had an hour or more ago down in the courtyard. They shared quick, wet kisses between gasps and moans as Finley drove them forward. He was everywhere inside of her, up in her chest, voice in her ear begging her name, echoing in her head, down to her toes curling like the tongue against her jaw.

His hips ground against hers, working her clit over his pelvic bone as he thrust deep and high. Lumen shattered with a brief scream, arms strangling around his neck, legs around his waist pinning him against her. He moaned into her skin, rutting anxiously against her, their bodies thumping into the mattress. The heat of his seed splashed inside of her and Finley shuddered, gathering her up tight in his arms, so tight she couldn't move. His teeth bit at her throat with the last moan and then they collapsed together, bodies knotted by clinging limbs.

"Don't stir," he said into her cheek.

Her hand on his back smoothed over skin and she nodded. "Don't pull away," she answered.

"CRATE THEM UP," DOMINIC SAID, POINTING TO THE ROWS AND rows of bookshelves. "Don't just try and sell them all off to the same buyer. Get every penny you can for them."

Charlie and Danvers stood in front of the desk, arms folded, foreheads creased with deep lines as they looked around the office room.

"Silver would make a fair hand more for the army than paper, sir," Danvers said, his voice a natural whisper.

Dominic glared at his scout. "I daresay it would, if there were any available for sale."

Charlie's eyes slid to Danvers and then back to the General. Dominic wasn't a fool, he was sure Danvers had told his partner about the night in the chapel, about the horde of good silver left untouched. As long as it had gone in Charlie's ear and no further, he had no issue. Danvers and Charlie were good soldiers. They took his word as law, just as they should.

Before Fenn Manor he'd never given them reason to doubt that law.

This is her fault.

"The books first," Dominic said. "Sell them off piece by piece if it makes you more change but that is my command."

Charlie nodded but Danvers locked eyes with Dominic. "We should push North. To another estate. Or better yet a town."

"Towns resist harder," Dominic said on reflex.

It was one thing to suppress a handful of elderly and *one* injured man from the war who hadn't wanted to abandon their lady. But a village of local folk who had business of their own, ones who hadn't wanted to fight for their cottage but would feel stronger amongst a pack of neighbors? The Stalor Army would win, of course, but it would be costly for both sides and while Dominic understood the price of a soldier's life on a battlefield, the thought of destroying a village who were seeking lives outside of the war left him uneasy.

"The men are growing restless," Danvers pushed. "There's not enough food. There's not enough fighting."

"Not near enough fucking," Charlie added with a brief grin.

"You both seem to be doing fine from what I've heard," Dominic muttered.

Better than him of late, that was for certain. He forced his stare to his hands as the back of his thoughts began to conjure that same nagging image. Chaste and agonizing, Lumen circled in Finley's arms, her face lifted to his, body swooning as one kiss after another was laid against her lips. Dominic's eyes traced the lines of his knuckles, the scar that ran down the side of his thumb, trying to fill his head with the mundane to chase out the taunting vision.

"There are attachments growing," Danvers said. "One way or another fights will break out amongst the men."

Dominic's nails dug into the surface of the desk for a moment. "I understand. Sell the books, buy what we must have, save the rest. We'll march to the field when you're back."

He met Danvers' stare and waited for the other man to flinch away, nod and turn his back. Charlie gave him that brief, mild grin and followed his partner out of the office. Dominic clenched his hands around the edge of the desk, gripping until his knuckles hurt, until he could almost feel the wood give beneath his fingers, and then let go. He needed to find somewhere else to be when they came back. Let them pack up the books and bitch his name under their breath, relieve a little of their frustration and then follow his orders, like them or not.

He found Gideon out at the stables, brushing down horses like they used to do as boys for the knights. The huge man made the horses nervous, shifting and huffing in their stalls, but they soothed him, tension falling off his shoulders and some of the wild energy dimming in his eyes. Dominic leaned against the open doorway, watched massive gnarled hands coaxing flanks to relax.

"Bored?" Gideon asked.

Dominic didn't know what he was. Bored, antsy, a constant tangle of anger and frustration and resentment.

At her. At *himself*. He should have dragged her to a chapel and bound her to him the moment he realized the sway she had on his mind. He should have left her to the wolves of men in the company. No, even thinking that made him see red.

"I want you to keep an eye on Danvers and Charlie," Dominic said.

Gideon paused and the horse beneath his hands knickered and tried to dance away at the first sign of life stirring back into the man.

"They just asked for their horses to be ready. Colin went to get their things."

"Not while they're away," Dominic said. "While they're here. Danvers won't let the chapel go."

Gideon turned and left the stall, propping himself against a post, arms folded over his chest. "We could use the money."

Dominic's eyebrows raised. "You think we should clean it out?"

Gideon grinned and rolled his eyes to the roof. "It would break my little spirit right in two. And that I'd hate to see."

Anger burned hot in Dominic's chest. "Why should it matter how she hurts?"

"I didn't say it should," Gideon said with a shrug. "Only that it would."

Dominic huffed and covered his mouth with his hand to try and contain the growl of frustration. She had bled into his thoughts at every hour. She was shifting his mind, affecting his decisions. He felt as if he was losing his senses, not just when it came to the army, but as if every day that she was away from him he lost the ability to taste because she was not on his tongue. The world was dimmer, or was it just winter? The bed he slept in was colder, rougher, and despite no longer having to share it, the space grew small without her.

And now the farce of her time with Finley had become reality. He'd turned her away to punish her and put her in the arms of a man who made punishment pleasure in more ways than one. And she looked happy.

He hated her for existing without him. He hated himself for pushing her into Finley's arms. Hated the healer for resisting her for weeks—because there was no confusion for Dominic that Brink had left her to her own devices until recently— when he was never once able to ignore the temptation she presented.

"A good day or two of training would burn some of the fight out of the men," Gideon pointed out.

He'd ignored the suggestion days ago when Gideon had first brought it to him. "Or make them hungrier. We'll go out on the field when Danvers and Charlie get back."

For the first time since they had aged into service, Gideon Jones frowned at the news he would be fighting in battle soon. "You want to push north?"

Dominic's stomach weighed like a brick at the very words and he refused to consider why. Any reason to stay was worthless now. It had been worthless before and he'd been trying force a fantasy out of... a threat. He'd told her to please him or put her body and home at further risk.

"I want to fight the war we came here for," Dominic said, scuffing the stones beneath his boots. "You're right. Train today. Let them be hungry for new territory when we go to battle again."

THE WORLD STARTED to turn sideways and all Finley could see were the faces of soldiers watching their healer land on his ass. Again.

Gideon grabbed him by the elbow and hauled him up onto his feet again. "Don't want you ruining all of our lady's handiwork on that wound."

Finley resisted the urge to say it—*my lady's*—just barely. "Can't this wait?" he asked instead.

"We wait too long and you'll end up with another arrow in your back, or worse," Gideon said. He stepped back, shoulders rolling and his sword lifting into the air between them.

The field was busy with bodies grappling in the snow, and all Finley could think of was whether Lumen had risen from bed yet. They'd moved back up to the attic now that his back was healed and he had celebrated by paying Danvers and Charlie back for all the nights they'd kept him up with their choice of women. Not that he'd told Lumen that was his reason for ducking beneath her skirts and teasing her until she was begging.

"Besides," Gideon continued, interrupting Finley's reverie, "it wouldn't be bad for the men to see you fighting a bit. Roughing it up. You know, for her sake."

Because if they thought he could *fight* they might be less likely to harass his woman. The logic was flawed.

"Oh and watching you knock me to the ground a dozen times will make them respect me, is that it?" Finley snapped back, but he shuffled himself into position, raising his sword with a weary arm.

"If you took my advice and moved into your block instead of flinching, I wouldn't knock you down." Gideon grinned and Finley caught the twitch of his heel in the icy slush as a warning before the man leapt into action.

When the army enlisted him—a single note from that mysterious force who governed his path in life, bidding him to turn up at the barracks or lose access to any future funds—Finley assumed he would be kicked out as fast as he was accepted in. His body was broken down after too many months in the opium dens, and even at peak health he wasn't built to fight. The training had been light and the goal was clear. His medical education was paid for and it would see him into one of the army's companies. It wasn't until he was assigned to Dominic and Gideon got ahold of him that he really learned anything of sword fighting. He was alive thanks to the pair of them.

Finley's shoulder burned as he fought back against Gideon, trying to push with every blow, ignoring the vibrating ache that ran up his arm as they clashed. Gideon wasn't really putting full effort into the sparing but Gideon at half force was closer to an average, farm-plucked, soldier anyway.

"Dominic's thinking of pushing north," Gideon said, grunting as Finley managed to charge him back a step.

"Finally," Finley answered, jaw grinding.

"You're ready to leave?" Gideon asked. "Leave her behind?"

The mention of Lumen, the picture it conjured in his mind—pale hair spreading over the sheets, smile curling up her lips as she caught her breath—nearly gave Gideon room to knock him off his feet and Finley dodged the swing of the blade at the last minute.

"Isn't it time? This is the longest we've stayed yet."

Gideon frowned, shoulders relaxing, and it gave Finley time to dance around. He didn't land a blow, which was good because he never remembered to turn and smack with the flat edge, but if any of the soldier's were watching now he was putting on a good show, at least.

"S'pose that's true," Gideon mused.

"I thought you'd be pleased to be moving again."

"It's not the thought of a victory I mind," Gideon said. "But what will happen to her once we've moved on?"

Finley opened his mouth and shut it just as quickly. The reply he should have made was 'what did it matter to them what happened to her?' Except it *did* matter. Even Gideon could see that.

"She'll have peace," Finley said. "She'll... have her home back."

Gideon 'hmm'd and then his body tensed, refocusing into the the fight, and Finley caught his breath while he could. It was only a matter of minutes before he was sliding into the snow again. His body ached, his arms were tired, and he didn't really *care* about this fight. He was just waiting for Gideon to call it to an end so he could get back inside. If they were leaving soon, he wanted to enjoy every stolen minute left with the Lady of the Manor.

THE DOORKNOB OF THE WORKROOM RATTLED AND FINLEY STILLED inside of her, Lumen's fingernails digging into the wood grain of the table, swallowing her frustrated moan.

"Quiet," Finley hissed, nudging his cock against her front walls, hipbones digging into the soft flesh of her ass.

Her thighs trembled, his hands wrapped around her hips and holding her up to take his thrusts, braced away from the rough edge of the worktable. The doorknob rattled again as Finley began to draw out, a painful, slow pace that accentuated every place inside of her he touched. She wanted to cry as he pulled nearly all the way out, only the head of him still teasing at her entrance, and then gasped as he began to push in again.

"What is it?" he called to the door.

Lumen made to turn her head, eyes huge with shock, and Finley released one hip, the hand stroking up her covered spine to halt her, cheek pressed to wood grain.

"You're needed down in the yard," a man's voice said, blessedly unfamiliar.

"In a minute," Finley answered, taking his time with every gentle press and retreat, Lumen squirming needfully between him and the table.

"Please," she whispered.

Finley grunted, grinding deep and make her lips part on a stifled moan, her face rolling against the table, the scent of old herbal remedies worn into the grain. Feet shuffled away in the hall outside the door and with the first real withdrawal and slam back, skin slapping, Lumen cried out. Finley's brief patience from the moment before was gone again, his fervor doubled as he fucked her fast with vivid thrusts.

"Please," she repeated, as his hand gripped her hip tighter, the fingers of his right hand framing the back of her neck and pinning her in place.

"Do you want to come, dear lady?" Finley rasped, voice thin with effort and panting breaths, every strike inside of her more urgent.

"Yes. Yes, please Finley."

"Clasp me tight," he ordered.

Lumen's brow furrowed and she hiccuped on a groan, one deep buck of his hips taking her near her finish and still somehow far too distant away from the climax she craved. She squeezed herself around his cock, doing her best to press back into every rut, but there was no teasing touch on her clit to take her over the edge and she whimpered in frustration.

Finley, behind her, arched in pleasure, moaning loud and long up to the beamed ceiling, his rhythm breaking and his grip tightening until he was driving her against the table, jars at the far end rattling dangerously and the legs squeaking in warning. She felt his release burst inside of her, scratched her nails on the table with how close she was to her own end and then he pulled free, yanking her back to standing and spinning her on weak legs to face him. He crowded her into the table, mouth landing harsh against hers, tongue forcing his way in as she tried to grind herself against him, a hand, anything at all that might offer her the friction she needed. But nothing was enough.

Lumen wrapped her arms around his shoulders as Finley kissed her with all the hunger he'd shown when he'd bent her over the table and teased her to dripping with his bare cock before fucking her senseless. She was breathless as he pushed her away, dazed and weak and wanting.

"Please, please touch me," she begged, too desperate to mind the keen and triumphant turn of his expression.

"Do you crave me, my lady?" he asked.

"Yes," she whined, tipping toward him.

He met her halfway, pressing a sweet lingering kiss to her lips, his hand stroking down her stomach over her skirt as she leaned into the touch.

"Stay this way for me today," he said.

Lumen froze, drowsy eyes popping wide and the gray morning haze of desire sharpening the view of Finley's face above hers. His cheeks were bright with the flush of release, smirk curling on bitten pink lips.

"Wha-what do you mean?" she asked.

He pressed his forehead to hers and brushed his nose against hers. "You want to relieve that need don't you?" He cupped her through her skirt, the touch too soft to do more than remind her of her need. She nodded. He kissed her again and then pulled away smiling. "And I'm telling you not to. Don't touch yourself. You have to wait for me, for tonight."

"Please," Lumen whispered, lifting to her toes and pressing herself to his front.

He rained kisses down the line of her jaw. "No." Her breath hitched and then he raised her face to gaze back at him, a gentler look softening the wicked glare of his eyes. "I promise you won't regret the wait when I'm done with you, my lady."

His hands settled on her shoulders, smoothing down the outside of her arms. He pressed a last kiss to her jaw and then stepped away, leaving Lumen feverish and tender, staring back at him.

"Yes?" he asked, eyebrow raised.

She breathed out, slow and weak and then nodded. "I'll wait."

There was a brief, bright smile, crinkling lines at the corner of his eyes, a thin gap between two teeth revealed at the corner of his mouth. "Good. Good. I'll see you later. And don't forget to try the—"

"Milkweed with the mint, yes, I know," Lumen said, wiping loose hairs off her cheeks with dews of sweat. Her eyes landed on the herbs she'd been comparing with her mother's notes before Finley had decided to distract her from her own mind completely. "It was my idea," she reminded him.

"So it was," he said, bright and cheerful as he turned away to the door.

Nice for him to have a skip in his step. Her thoughts were edgy and sharp, like the sweet ache left in her empty core, as if at any moment Finley might return to fill and finish her. The door shut and she huffed, elbows landing on the table and her face in her hands, cheeks hot.

Finley Brink made her head spin. She'd learned his restraint just in time to watch that restraint crumble as he cornered her beneath him, pressing kisses to her lips like they gave life to the pair of them. He was as sudden to embrace her as he was to temper, and he could draw away from a passionate moment as fast as that same temper would gentle.

But every touch between them was her choice. Even the demands made were followed with his pause as he waited for her to agree to his terms. She may be left sore and hollow now but she believed his promise that any ache would be made sweeter by the relief to come.

The door of the workroom scratched against stone and Lumen pushed up, expecting Brink or one of the women or a soldier. Instead there was Gideon Jones, propped up against the doorframe, grinning crooked and razor sharp at her.

"Finley's gone down to the yard," she said, ignoring the blush that rose on her cheeks. "Was it serious? Should I follow?"

"Nay, lady," Gideon said with a wave of his hand. "I think it was a sprain or something trifling. I came to see you not Brink."

"Me?" she asked. Her breath in her chest was tight as Gideon stepped into the room, pulling the door shut again behind him, tugging the lock into place.

"I was walking through the halls not ten minutes ago when I thought I heard the sound of lovers coming from this room," Gideon said, that hungry toothy grin bright on his face as he made a slow approach.

Lumen held her breath in her chest, her feet twitching on the floor beneath her, debating whether to run or freeze like a rabbit caught in the predator's gaze.

"The sweetest sounds of skin slapping and your little voice crying out for more." He drew the last word out on a breath, one hand reaching out and resting on the table, his knuckles scraping over the outside of her arm and drawing a shiver. "Did you soak his cock, little spirit? Is he dripping out of you?"

His arm was warm against hers, body thick with the scent of the bonfire and the horses, as if it put an actual weight on her flesh. She remembered his teasing words, the hints, the open interest in sharing her with the others.

"Did you come find me in the hopes of taking your turn?" Lumen asked, trying to ignore the tight squeeze of her own throat, her thighs pressing together beneath her skirt and feeling the exact sticky evidence Gideon asked her about.

"Could you take another? Or has he worn you sore with all your begging?"

Lumen's cheeks went hot as fire and she dragged her eyes away from the rough scratch of beard growing on Gideon's jaw and turned to stare out the window. Gideon laughed at the sight of her blush and reached over, plucking at the front of her dress, rumpled and scratched from the wood of the table.

"Did he play his games with you, little spirit?"

"I've had enough of teasing," Lumen snapped, turning her bright cheeks around again and doing her best to glare. But her breaths were heavy in her chest, body squirming with the knowledge that Gideon was there, waiting to relieve her.

His eyebrows raised and he leaned in closer, shifting until his hip was barely against hers, just the subtlest hint of what the weight of him against her might feel like. "Didn't he see right by you?"

"It's one of his *games*, as you put it," Lumen whispered, ducking down her eyes. It was a mistake, the entire view was Gideon, the coarse weave of his brown shirt nearly thin to holes at his elbows, the broad width of him blocking out the rest of the world, softly rounded stomach pressing to her with every breath. "I have to wait," she whispered, certain that any minute her face might go up in actual flames.

"Poor little spirit," Gideon said, voice so low she thought she felt the vibration right down to her cunt. He was pressing closer but she wasn't certain which of them it was who started first. Probably her.

She looked up into the rough face, scars glinting white against his skin, carving through the frame of his beard, and her hands were fisting into his shirt. They were kissing before she knew what was what, and Gideon tasted bright and spiky—he'd found a mint patch somewhere and been chewing the leaves. His lips were full and strong, molding her mouth against his. She moaned with the first sweep of his tongue against hers and then she was wrapped in a tight, warm hold, pressed to his chest. Her hold on the floor was gone, on anything other than Gideon, and his arm was sliding down to press her hips hard against his, letting her feel the growing cock pressing at the place she wanted him most.

"I promised," she said, arching her neck to tear her lips away.

Gideon's mouth dragged, spiky prickles of stubble branding over her cheek and jaw and throat, until his tongue landed on her pulse, lapping at the spot. The slick wet press echoed between her legs and she squirmed in his hold, only making the friction of his cock against her crease more appealing.

"Tell me," Gideon rasped into her skin.

"I wouldn't- I wouldn't come until tonight. I wouldn't touch myself."

Gideon pressed wet open mouthed kisses up to her ear, nipping and tugging at the skin and drawing out brief little puffs and needy sounds from her lips. "Let me touch you, little spirit. Let me lick you clean. Our secret. I'll finish you sweet and fast and he'll never know." Gideon's free hand scooped into her hair, pulling her face back to his, thrusting his tongue between her lips and swallowing all her resistant sounds.

Her spine pressed to the edge of the table and then her thighs parted around his, the fat head of his cock dulled through layers of fabric but grinding against her. Arousal had skittered away after Finley left the room but it was rushing back with the promise of release approaching and an exchange of words seemed so much less powerful than the feel of Gideon between her legs.

The orgasm was soft and fast and Lumen sobbed in frustration, for having broken her vow to Finley, for a finish less than she wanted. Gideon purred into her mouth as she shook, her hands digging into his shoulders.

"There now, little spirit," he said against her bruised lips. "There, it's done. Let me taste you. I'll show you how gentle I can be."

Lumen growled and ground her answer out, "I don't *want* gentle."

Gideon grunted and then laughed, his grin scratching at her lips. "Let me worship you." He sank to his knees, his hands cupping her ass and squeezing once as she tracked his smile on its path down. "I'm a coarse man, little spirit. My worship won't be gentle."

Lumen wasn't sure what kind of idol she could be. *One for broken men*, she thought, and then Gideon was burrowing his face into her skirts, mouthing and growling like a beast. She laughed and her elbows fell back to the table as he nuzzled against her core. When he bit her sensitive skin, the scrape muffled by fabric, her breath caught in her chest. He did it again and all the quiet sparks of desire returned to her cunt.

She slid her fingers into his hair, held his face to her center and rolled her hips against him, sighing at the rattle of his groan. His hands squeezed the cheeks of her ass and then flashed down to her hem, scooping fabric up out of his way, scratching callouses against the bare skin of her legs. She scratched at his scalp and he lifted his face, eyes blacked out with hunger.

His fingers curled around the back of her legs, teasing in little tapping presses up her thighs and she lifted her skirt high for him. "You smell like sex."

He was going to taste Finley on her skin and the realization left her flushing with a new wave of shame and excitement, made stronger as his fingers dipped into the slick dripping out of her. She watched as he drew the fingers back to his mouth, sucking them clean with an obscene thoroughness.

"I know this flavor too," he said, grinning at her. "Let me find yours."

He nudged her legs to open, drawing the left one over his shoulder and steadying her with one hand wrapped tight around her hip. She braced herself against the table, their stares fixed together as he leaned in, running his nose against the soft seam of her sex. His tongue flicked out and he grinned as her chest heaved with the first gasp.

"Put your fist in my hair again, little spirit. I want to know when you've reached madness."

Lumen thought madness may have passed her weeks ago. She gripped the hair at the back of his head, staring down at him, felt his breath panting on her damp skin.

"Don't tease," she commanded.

Gideon answered with a growl that dived into her cunt, his tongue flat against her sex and scouring her skin clean of every drop of Finley's release. She knew the moment he found her own flavor. His eyelids fell closed and he groaned long and deep, his tongue dipping into her entrance and making her whine. His teasing fingers pushed deep and drew free again and she could hear him lapping the wetness away before returning for more, pumping her roughly with one thick finger, and then two until she was bouncing on her toes, head hanging back and hair brushing the table.

"Harder," she whispered and then cried out as his lips scratched over her clit and began to suck while his fingers fucked her fast and deep, thick knuckles dragging against her opening.

She writhed on his face as he burrowed closer, stubble scratching at tender skin, finger curling in her cunt. She tugged hard on his hair for that, thrusting her hips into the touch so he knew she wanted more. He gasped against her skin, laughed against her sex, and twisted his fingers inside of her, staying deep and drilling against her with his knuckles.

Loud, sharp cries curled around the beams of the ceiling,

feathered into the hanging herbs over head, and Lumen had a brief horror, thinking of what her mother would say if she could see the scene. The entire morning. Taken by one man from behind. Served by another on his knees.

And then she was tense as a bowstring as she came with a shocking rush, heat skimming under her skin, the room noisy with her own gasps, bright with light behind her eyes.

Gideon was sucking at her skin, kissing at her wet lips, making her clit burn with the scrape of his stubble. His touch tapped inside of her and she made a crude and guttural sound. He was slurping against her and Lumen wanted to laugh or wince or shove him away. She pulled at the strands of his hair but he only growled against her and the vibration made her toes curl until it was painful.

"Enough, enough," she said.

Except that Gideon was her wild man and she had invited him between her thighs. He hummed at the hard tug of his hair and lapped at her opening, every slow plunge of his fingers bringing more release for him to taste. Lumen whined as he cleaned her, she tried to squirm away, and he held her fast with his grip around her hip.

He was so rough and she was so sensitive already that every lick of his tongue against her, every scratch of his beard on her skin, was a kind of fire. But it was one she recognized, the longer he pushed her, kissed her, the tighter the tension turned in her veins, the more she fought to escape, to reach a new height. Soon she was working herself onto his hand again, holding him to her, begging.

How many times could he do this to her, torture her back to need? Her knees were useless, feet holding to nothing, only skidding against the floor as she transformed into an answering creature to Gideon's hunger.

"Your cock," she gasped. "I need- Oh gods, Gideon, please!"

She thought he would be on her the second she begged. Instead he only laughed against her cunt and then wrapped his pouting lips around her clit and suckled hard, a third finger joining the others to fill and stretch her. Lumen came with a collapsing sigh, her body bowing backwards, legs kicking and elbows barely catching her before she melted to the floor. She shook, trying to escape the assault of Gideon's mouth against her.

"Ah! Stop! Stop, please!"

His fingers pulled free and she trembled, listening to the wet sounds of him sucking her flavor away. He lapped one long stripe against her and she hissed. Her leg over his shoulder trembled as he shrugged it off, kissing her mound and then rising, dragging her away from the table and against his chest. She leaned with limp effort, allowing him to turn her face to his, taking his deep kiss and tasting the tart and too rich flavor of herself on his tongue. She struggled briefly and he softened until she relaxed, kissing patterns across one cheek and then the other.

"I thought you would want to—"

"I'll get to," Gideon said in her ear, and then nipped the lobe. "I can be patient." He rubbed her against his hips, rutting his hardness against her soft form as he buried his face against her neck.

If he had lifted her into his arms and taken her to a bed in that moment, Lumen would have let him take whatever he liked of her. The fight was all washed out of her now, drank down by his lips and tongue.

"Will you tell him?" he asked.

Finley. Lumen's fever cooled at the thought of the man. Of what she had agreed to and then promptly broken. "What will he do?"

Gideon hummed with thought. "The others think he likes to hurt women, but that isn't true. He likes for them to surrender. He'll punish you, but no more than you ask him to."

She'd thought the surrender began and ended when she opened the Manor doors to the army, but these men constantly required more. Worse, they made her desire each act.

Lumen pressed her lips to Gideon's again, and he purred into the kiss. Could she ask Gideon to intervene on her behalf? Ask

Finley for mercy? Did she even want mercy when Finley could make torment pleasurable?

"The taste of you on my tongue's going to keep me hard all day, little spirit," Gideon murmured, kissing her again.

She thought the burn of his beard might leave her cunt tender and sensitive all day too, so that was fair.

LUMEN MADE HERSELF SCARCE FOR THE REST OF THE DAY, AFRAID if she saw Finley he would read her broken promise on her face. Or if she saw Gideon she might beg him to throw her into a bed and fuck her into further oblivion. She thought even Westbrook might be able to see her shame and thrill from the morning if they were to meet in a hall.

She busied herself in the workroom and then with laundry, the staccato sounds of men training floating in from the yard. Colin found her with her elbows deep in scalding water, scrubbing at sheets with a concentration that could only belong to a guilty mind.

"Lady, how much do you like that Spragg fellow?"

Lumen blinked at the murky water in front of her nose. "Who? Oh! Oliver Spragg?"

Colin shrugged and scrambled up onto the counter at Lumen's left. "The one who offered to help you escape over the border."

"You heard that?" Lumen asked, straightening and letting the sheets sink to the bottom of the basin as she stared at the boy.

"Why didn't you say yes?" Colin asked.

"This is my home," Lumen said and even to her own ears it was becoming a tired refrain.

"Westbrook don't think so."

She swallowed and blinked at the boy who relaxed against the wall behind him and stared back at her with wide eyes. He'd healed nicely from all his wounds and seemed to have returned to himself. He hadn't tried to sneak back into bed with her since the night she and Finley kissed in the courtyard. Even after she and Finley returned to the attic room, Colin never appeared. Lumen was relieved she hadn't needed to say anything on the topic. Maybe Gideon had warned him off.

Lumen pulled her hands from the water and looked down, wiping them dry on her skirt and letting her thoughts turn away from the relentless distraction of the men and back to Colin.

"The army will move on eventually," Lumen said. "I would like to be here when that happens. When my home is my home again."

Colin frowned at that, chewing at his lip and studying the room.

"Would you like to be here too, with me?" Lumen asked. The young boy froze in his seat, eyes going wide before turning to her. "It will only be farm work and dull days here. You may miss the excitement. The other men."

Colin snorted at that, thin legs kicking and drumming against the wooden post of the counter. "Not gonna miss those bastards. I'd gladly stay and work in the stables—"

"No, no!" Lumen crossed the space to the boy. "Not to stay to work. Just to stay, to be safe here. Well, there will be work, but no more than I do myself. Stay as my friend, Colin." She reached out and took his hand. He glanced at the hold and Lumen thought for a moment he would pull away, but then he squeezed back.

"I would stay, Lady," Colin whispered, but he looked sad as he said the words. "But the General won't let me go. Truth, Lady, I don't think he'll let you go either."

Lumen frowned. "He has to move on. The army can't just *stay* here."

"I know, I know," Colin said, nodding, but his lips curved down and his brow had a little furrow in it that shouldn't have existed in a child so young. "I would stay."

Lumen's chest hurt at the doubt in his tone, like the offer was a daydream and he was too wise to believe the words. "Help me squeeze these sheets out and get them drying by the stove. I may have an idea for something sweet to make for you."

Colin jumped down and together they wrestled the linens out of the water and over to the waiting poles by the burning stoves of the kitchen. Lumen found a secret stash of sugar, mostly remnants now, and made a syrup with wild ginger. They threw together a small batch of soft biscuits and drowned them in the syrup and the last of the cream, eating it out of the pan with wooden spoons, huddled over the table to keep their treat a secret.

Out the back door in the yard it began to snow fat, white flakes.

THE ENTIRE DAY had been a distraction from Finley's singular goal. Return to her, satisfy her, feel her fluttering around him, hear her calling his name in his ear, legs and arms wrapping him up in her hold. She was vanished from the workroom by the time he made it back and the space smelled of her in a way that stirred the interest of his cock all over again.

He was turning into an animal like Gideon. Every sight of Lumen Fenn at the corner of his eye made him a feral creature who only thought of flesh and fucking. And then when he couldn't find her nearby, he was barely capable of thinking at all.

He didn't catch sight of her again until there was food cooking over the fire and he barely kept himself from leaping over the flames to reach her. When she was within grasp he pressed her backwards until she was pinned to a pillar, her breath puffing out of her in surprise, cascading over his throat.

"Have you eaten?" he asked and he cleared his throat when he found the words too low and hungry.

"Earlier, with Colin," she said, and her eyes brushed over his shoulder widening and darting back to his chin.

He craned his neck to look behind him and found West-brook, watching them again, eyes narrowed, hands clenched. There was a thrill in his gut. Westbrook had given her up and now she was well and truly *his*. There was also the churning knowledge that a display like this might just as easily tempt the General to make a new demand of her, to rip her out of Finley's arms.

And? What would you do? Would you fight for her?

Her hands slid inside his coat, fingers dancing up his chest and she sighed again as he pressed closer, her expression softening, eyelids growing heavy. She was perfect for him, far beyond any expectation. She was designed to please him, to be pleased by him.

"Have you been thinking of me?" he asked, unable to resist his own smile stretching.

Her hips circled against his and she wet her lips with her red tongue. "Yes."

"Wanting?"

She blushed and her eyes darted away.

Interesting. He wouldn't have guessed she'd break the vow, but it suited him just as well to take retribution as it did to reward.

"Come upstairs," he whispered in her ear, and she wiggled against him again, her hands circling to his back and sliding down, tugging him against her as if she wanted him to mount her right there for anyone to see.

Or just for Westbrook to see? some wicked part of his mind wondered.

"You've waited all day. Time for me to keep my word," he said, watching with amusement as her lips pursed.

"There's something I have to tell you," she said, voice small and tucked beneath his chin.

"Tell me in bed," he answered, taking one of her hands out and tugging her into the hall, over to the stairs.

On the way up to the attic a cold pit formed in his stomach. What if it hadn't been an innocent lack of patience on her part. What if it had been Westbrook himself? The way she'd squirmed at the sight of him shifted in his memory, was it discomfort or arousal? Had the General already called her back to his bed and if so where did that leave Finley?

"Have you been aching for your release all morning?" he asked as they climbed the stairs together, his voice turning dark.

"Finley, it... I... Gideon came into the workroom after you left."

His feet stopped dead on the stairs with surprise. "Gideon. Jones?"

She was picking at a scar on her jaw when he turned to face her. He pulled her fingers away from the spot and up to his lips. "I didn't mean to," she whispered, lower lip wobbling. "The first time I wasn't even—"

"The *first* time?" Oh Sol's Light he wanted to laugh, but she looked so worried.

"It really *was* an accident," she said, bright pale eyes shining up at him. "But I broke the promise."

He hadn't even needed to coax it out of her. Finley bent until his forehead was against hers, lips brushing her mouth as he spoke. "Up the stairs and then out with the truth, my lady."

They rushed up the stairs together, her fingers linked with his, alternately clinging and releasing. He opened the door on the cold, dark room, their breaths puffing pale blue and Finley left Lumen fidgeting by the bed as he went to the small stove and built a fire.

"You said first time. How many was it?" he asked, pausing in his work to wait for her answer.

It came after a long stretch of quiet. "Three."

Finley's lips fought with a smile. "How are three orgasms an accident, my lady?"

"It was only the first one," Lumen breathed. "He wasn't even trying."

He snorted. "I suspect Jones knew exactly what he was doing."

"I'm sorry. Are you angry?" He opened his mouth to tell her 'no' as he lit the fire but she rushed on. "I know I- I know I'm meant to be yours—"

Finley turned on his knees, eyes wide. "I'm not angry. Come here, please."

She looked exhausted as she stumbled over to the stove and

down to her knees at his side. Perhaps tonight *wasn't* the night to tease her with discipline, to play at punishment. Not seriously at least. He took her chin between his fingers, lifting her face to his.

"Whatever claim I have on your person is given by you and only you," he said. Her eyes widened and he tilted his head. "And I have no complaint with you enjoying yourself with Jones. I've done that myself."

She blushed by firelight and some of the weary droop in her shoulders relaxed away. "I remember. So I'm not in trouble then?"

Don't be a brute, he thought to himself, but his eyes traced the lines of her face, the sprinkle of scars down one side that burned like stars in the firelight. "Well. There is the matter of a broken promise."

She tensed but he could have sworn that there was expectancy in the gesture. And was that excitement shining in her stare as she met his gaze? When her lips quirked he was decided.

"Three times?" She nodded and he continued, "Tell me how."

Her breath hitched and she shifted on her knees. He knew that little motion, the twist of thighs touching to relieve a growing pressure. He reached out, barely setting his fingertips on her knees and watched as she followed the soft guide, parting her legs under the tangle of her skirts. Behind her shoulder, snow piled in the window sill and an idea began to brew in Finley's head.

"Once just by...by being close," she said and he raised his eyebrows, watching her blush. "You left me so... so close and he came in and—" She turned her cheek away, skin brightening even in the cool dark around the room. "The others with his fingers and mouth."

"You wouldn't let him fuck you?"

"I asked. He said- said it could wait."

Finley blinked at that. Gideon Jones had an opportunity to get his dick wet and turned it down for...for what? Patience? Self-torture? That was more Finley's speed and when it came to

Lumen Fenn he hadn't managed it for longer than it took her to flick her skirts. Maybe she wasn't the only one in need of learning patience.

He tugged at the fabric of her dress. "Will you pull that loose for me, my lady?"

She hesitated, watching him and then rolled back on her heels and released the fabric out from under her knees. He stopped her as she started to pull it up to her waist, pulling it free from her fingers, one of his hands hidden beneath as it fell to the floor.

"What will you do?" she asked, voice shaking.

A thrill ran down his spine and into his gut at the tremor in her words, a sick kind of response to her nerves, he thought. He leaned in, the hand under her skirt hunting in the warmth until he skimmed against the soft inside of a thigh. Lumen panted and jerked, leaning into him as if he were the sun to her bloom. He brushed the spot again, watching her breaths catch and heave in her chest.

"I haven't decided if you need to learn patience, or to be careful what you wish for," Finley admitted. "Possibly both."

"You're going to leave me wanting again?" Lumen asked, frowning, knees scooting forward as if he wouldn't notice her trying to find his touch beneath her skirt.

"Not for long," he said, and then he found her, already damp and hot to the touch. Her thighs stretched apart and she whimpered, face stretching up to his and small hands reaching for his shoulders. He caught them in his and held them captive as he swirled the pads of his fingers over her clit, faster and faster until her eyes were wide, hips churning against the touch.

"No touching," he said and she frowned. "Hold still."

She froze, barely perched up on her knees, his fingers working fast and her chest rising and falling at the same pace. "Please," she whispered, hips twitching and a whine rising up after the words.

"Please what?" he asked.

"Let me- let me come for you," she said.

He smiled. "For me? My lady, I think this time it would be for you. If you want to please me you will *hold still.*"

She swallowed, eyes falling shut, little squeaks and sighs as he worked her relentlessly to the edge. He had never found it especially complicated to take a woman through her orgasm—unlike some men. It was simply a pattern of observations. But Lumen seemed more than usually aroused, and pleasingly simple to drive over the edge. He needed to remember to take his time or he'd ruin the game for himself. As a moan rose in her throat, flush high in her cheeks, head nodding backwards with the rushing pleasure, Finley drew his fingers away.

She sobbed, all but throwing herself against him. He put his free hand to her stomach, his damp fingers under her skirt pinning one knee open so she couldn't find her own relief. Her face was close to his, a little furrow of frustration tangled between her brows and he found her mouth with his, sucking long kisses as she whimpered against him.

"Breathe, my lady," he whispered against her. She sucked a breath and he kissed her through it, her body sagging against him. "Twice more. One denial for each orgasm you took."

Lumen shuddered in his arms, sighing and nodding, biting at her lips. *It's not a punishment if she agrees so readily.*

"Go lay on the bed," he said. She looked up, staring in confusion and he pushed gently on her stomach until she sat up again. "You can stay dressed, but lift your skirts for me."

She staggered back to the bed and he stared at the laced front of her dress as she laid down. "Undo those ties, too," he added after another glance at the window.

Her eyes tracked him as he stood, skirts bundled around her waist to reveal her sex, swollen clit exposed to the cold air, skin goosebumping. She gasped as he opened the window, a handful of snow falling into his palm. It burned his hand with the cold contrast and Lumen was squirming backwards on the bed at his approach, eyes huge with shock.

"What are you—?"

"It won't hurt you," Finley said, grinning and laughing as the bed creaked as he jumped onto it, taking a bite out of the snow and letting it freeze the roof of his mouth.

"Finley. Finley! Ah!" She squealed and writhed as he pinned her beneath him, streaking rivulets of icy water up her thighs and the pressing the last, melting, handful against the skin of her sex. She arched and screamed. Finley tore the open laces of the front of her dress, fabric fraying and burning triumph in his chest. One breast lay exposed and Finley bent, wrapping frozen lips around her nipple. "Oh gods! Oh, Finley, you- you beast! Ahhh!"

But her fingers were digging into his hair, holding him to her breast, body writhing *into* the touch the longer it lasted, her heat melting the chill and turning the touch fiery for them both.

"Oh gods," she whimpered, hips thrusting against his hand.

He gave in, dipping two fingers inside her, letting her fuck herself, feel that control in her hands again. He would take it away from her, of course, but he loved the way she claimed it. He could almost imagine himself handing it over to her if she asked at another time.

He suckled at the breast in his mouth, feeling the nipple turn tight and puckered against his tongue, flicking it and savoring every grunt it drew from her lips. She hissed as he pressed his thumb to her clit, let her rut herself against the touch, as if she could race herself to an end without him noticing.

"Please," she whispered. "Please. Please, please, Finley, please."

He lifted his mouth from her breast, her fingers pulling hard enough on his hair to make him wince. "Are you close, my lady?"

She groaned, face scrunched and turned away from his gaze, hips rocking, his fingers soaked with cool water and warm, slippery arousal.

"Please," she repeated.

"Tell me. Are you close?"

Her voice was hiccuping, brief bright sounds, mouth parting on an 'o', brow relaxing, and he felt her flutter around his fingers.

He tore his hand away, body drawing back, and Lumen twisted on the mattress, crying out, "No!"

"You tried to fool me," he laughed. "What part of punishment don't you understand?"

"I don't *want* to be punished," Lumen growled, twisting and rolling onto her stomach.

Finley caught her hips just as she started to press them to the mattress. "Ah, ah! Careful now. You have a tendency to *accidentally* find yourself in the midst of orgasm." Lumen huffed and muttered, glaring at him over her shoulder. "I could think of games you'd like less, my lady. Believe me."

"Oh, I do," she said, shaking her head and then pressing her face to a pillow and groaning.

Finley pushed her skirt aside. Her cunt was glossy and red with desire. Her hips wiggled with every rustle of air against the skin. *Patience*, he reminded himself. He needed to give her more time to come down.

"Up on your knees," he said.

She obeyed, despite her complaints, and when he tugged on the back laces of her dress she fell into his arms, sighing.

"Will you be too cold if I undress you?"

"Are you planning on pressing snow to places it doesn't belong again?"

"Yes," he said, and kissed behind her ear. "I'll let it melt longer, if you like."

She huffed, head shaking, and relaxed. "Oh, alright."

He liked the act of undressing her, that she let him set his own pace of revealing her. *That she lets you touch her at all.* He lifted her breasts in his hands after pushing the bodice of the dress down and Lumen moaned. He twisted her nipples gently in his fingers and she arched backwards, gasping, hips nudging uselessly at the air. With every pluck and pinch and pull she got louder until he was gripping her flesh tight in his hands before he might discover that he could finish her from that treatment alone. Maybe she really did have accidental orgasms. What a beautiful thought.

"Does that count as my third?" Lumen asked after catching her breath.

He folded his arms around her ribs and buried his face against her neck. "No," he mumbled against her skin, listening to her irritable growl with a smile.

He'd been close to half hard since he slid his hand beneath her skirt, but holding her close like this made the need more difficult to ignore. He pushed her dress down over her hips and she shivered. He cupped his hand over her cunt, stroked his fingers over the wet lips and she bit off a moan as if to keep it a secret. Still too close.

"Hands and knees," he whispered in her ear and then sucked a fast line of kisses down her throat before releasing her. "No touching."

Lumen obeyed, a beautiful feast of flesh on display for him as she arranged herself on the bed. He dragged himself away, fetching a cup from beside his old cot. He'd be glad not to see that again tonight, even if their current bed wasn't as nice as the one in Jones' room. He opened the window again to fill the cup with snow, and then fastened it shut, ignoring his own shiver at the mean bite of winter.

He set the cup on the floor to melt and stared at Lumen, held perfectly still, breasts hanging heavy from her chest, and sex shining, waiting for him. He shrugged himself out of one layer after another. If she could bear the cold of the room, he ought to as well. Plus he wasn't sure how much longer he would be able to wait to be inside of her.

There was ice water in the cup when he picked it up off the floor again. "Part your legs for me," he said, waiting until she shifted to make room for him. He spilled droplets down onto her spine and she shouted, brief and bright, the water trembling on her back and spilling over her sides as she shook. He took a sip and then pressed the mouthful to her lower spine, letting it leak out from between his lips slowly, down between the cheeks of her ass.

"Damnit," she hissed, her thighs quaking.

"Down to your elbows," he said, eyeing the picture of her ass in front of him, and then—as she did as he asked—the open lips of her pussy. He took another sip of the water and lowered himself onto his belly, adjusting his cock, and then lapping at her cunt with his chilled tongue.

Lumen buried her face against her arm and groaned, body

tense as she struggled not to pull away from the bright contrast of temperatures. She burned on his tongue, tart and heady, and Finley understood now why Gideon had turned down fucking her for this. She was so soft here, her most vulnerable place, pushing back against his mouth and then trying to wiggle away.

He traded sips of water for every taste of her, the icy slush contrasting with the hot syrup of her in his mouth. He coated his lips with her, filled his lungs, and then craved more, licking up her thighs, over her ass, and then spreading her open there too. She stiffened and held her breath as he stared at this new hole he hadn't learned yet. Not hers, at least. He spilled a little water over the spot and Lumen shouted and jerked. He soothed the bite of ice with the heat of his tongue and her breath stopped, body stilling. He stared down her spine, watching as her back slowly, so carefully, relaxed. The moan from her lips as he pressed against her hole surprised them both.

Oh he would have this spot too, there was no arguing that.

He dipped his fingers into the last of the cold water and then slid them up inside of her, lapping at her ass as she threw her head back and cried out at the wall, hips sinking onto his fingers.

Finish her, he thought.

"Oh gods, Finley please. No more. Please, fuck me. Please."

He refused to be undone by her. He wanted her surrender, not to offer up his. The reminder was enough and he drew back, pinning her between his two hands, one finger teasing at her asshole, the other hand fucking her steadily with two fingers. She was gasping, fingers tearing into the thin flesh of the pillows in front of her, body trapped between the touches.

It was hypnotic, feeling her, watching her and he nearly lost the the sense to stop himself as she started to clutch. He pulled out and one small white fist pounded at the mattress.

He flipped her onto her back, spilling the water over her chest, just to shock her out of the haze for a moment. Then he lined himself up at her entrance before he lost his will and buried himself in the taste of her again. He pushed in, feeling her squeeze at him.

"Don't come," he said.

Lumen's face was torn, teeth biting hard into her lower lip, scars sparkling bright against the red flush of her skin. For every inch he pushed she discovered another layer of control over her body, keeping the orgasm at bay. He stopped just before bottoming out, bending over and dragging her face up to his for kissing. She pleaded wordlessly against his mouth but kept herself still beneath him, resisting the urge to grind their bodies together.

"I will let you come this time," he murmured and she nodded. "But that isn't the end. You had *three* orgasms after promising me you'd wait. So you're going to have three orgasms tonight. Just like this. For being greedy."

"Finley," she whispered, but instead of horror in those wide eyes he found laughter and... he didn't know the word. Something soft and horribly heavy, weaving its way into his chest, tearing him down and building him up all at once. His fingers clutched at the roots of her hair and she arched beneath him as he notched himself completely against her.

He wrapped his lips around her pulse and began to move, trying not to let her voice drive him into madness again.

"Yes. Yes, I'll do anything," she said. He bucked against her and her legs wrapped around his hips. "Anything. Please, just don't stop. Don't stop, Finley. Oh gods, yes!"

Sol's Fire. She had his head muddled completely. Every thrust inside of her, every deep clasp of her around his cock, the kiss pressed to his ear, the fingers digging into his shoulder, *every touch* felt like his reward. And he knew, without a doubt, he'd done nothing in life to earn this woman. The opposite. Life would ask for payment for this night, for every moment he stole with her. Stole from her.

Lumen turned his face back to hers, drank him up with kisses until even the sneaking fears began to wane and there was no concept of punishment or reward, only the perfect drowning heaven of being inside of her.

LUMEN WOKE, NECK SORE AND ONE ARM NUMB AFTER FALLING asleep tangled up in Finley's embrace. The rest of her body was magnificently tender and stretched and used. One of his arms was twined around her back, fingers tangled in strands of her pale hair, the other grasped possessively over her hip, just where it was when she sank into sleep.

He huffed and pressed his lips against her hairline and her eyelashes brushed against his jaw.

"I feel too lazy for the army today," he said, voice as soft as the moment she found herself in.

This was... peaceful. Not just a tentative ease framed by awkwardness and anger as it had been with Dominic. The contrasts in her relationship with the General had muddled the shape of any happiness there had been, but this—this exact morning with Finley—was simple. Easy.

"Can it be ignored?" she asked.

Finley hummed and kissed her hair again. "I think so."

"For how long?"

He stilled against her and then rolled them on the bed, the pair of them both grimacing at the dead weight of their sleeping arms. He glanced briefly down the length of her before covering her bare body with his, doing a better job of blocking out the biting chill of the room than the thin blankets they'd been under.

"How long will you want me, my lady?" His voice was light

but there was serious study in his gaze and Lumen busied herself with tracing the soft lines of muscle against his chest.

There was a weight in his question and the answers that came to Lumen's mind left her edgy and nervous. It was better to tease. To stay *simple*.

"The morning, at least," she said, smiling and glancing up into glass green eyes. His sleep-soft expression sharpened but he was ducking down before she could assure him she was only teasing, taking a heady, deep kiss from her lips until she was clinging to him, making room for him between her thighs. All the ache of the night turned into a hollow craving and he released her, his body tense and hers limp.

"And who will you be in need of once you are finished with me, hmm?" he purred against her lips.

Lumen stiffened and pulled away from the feel of his mouth on her neck. Their eyes met, both wary, and simplicity evaporated. She scrambled back on the bed, pulling herself out from under his body. Finley huffed, breath stroking over her breasts as he pushed himself up, wincing with eyes slammed shut.

"I didn't mean- Lumen, that's not what I..."

She found a blanket pushed aside, near to sliding to the floor and dragged it around her, her back pressed to a cold and rough headboard. Finley sighed and sat up on his heels, cock hanging half hard between his thighs, and a pale, scarred hand reaching up to scrub at his face.

"That came out wrong," he said, shoulders slumping. "I know none of this has been your choice."

Lumen bristled and snapped, "This *was*. You were my choice, Finley. Are you telling me you took me to bed because *he* told you to?"

"No! No." Finley's eyes widened and Lumen wished he would search for pants. Or a sheet at least. Instead he looked bright and warm and defenseless by the morning light. "If anything I've- I've let this happen *in spite* of him."

Lumen's eyes narrowed and Finley flinched, brow creasing in confusion. "Why won't you believe me when I say that Westbrook doesn't have any say in my body now?"

"I believe *you*. I just don't trust him not to change his mind."

"He changed his mind," Lumen said, words sharp and abrupt in the quiet. Finley's eyes widened and she resisted the urge to growl. "He changed his mind and I told him I'd poison him if he tried to touch me again."

Finley made a choked sound, something between shock and laughter and Lumen lost the battle with her frustration, snarling and climbing out of the bed, the blanket tangling around her legs.

"I haven't asked you to protect me from him," she said. "I can manage that myself. If he ordered you to 'drop me', would you?"

There was silence and Lumen risked a glance, finding Finley stunned where she left him, staring at the dent she'd left in the pillows. Peaceful. That had been barely more than a minute ago and now her thoughts were clashing in her head and anger was running through her veins. Her breath sucked disappointment into her chest.

Finley jerked at the sound, jumping out of the bed. "Lumen, wait!"

"No, this is ridiculous," Lumen said on a heavy sigh, hunting the floor for her clothes.

Finley caught her on her way around the bed, dashing in front of her, arms outstretched but not grabbing. "I don't know. Lumen, I don't know and I'm *sorry*."

She stopped, staring up at him. His fingertips skimmed her elbow and then pulled away as she flinched.

He was frowning back at her but it wasn't anger. Not at her at least. "I know the answer you deserve," he said. "I would give you that answer if I was absolutely positive it would be the choice I'd make. I take orders from him. He is my *General*."

"Yes," Lumen said head nodding and teeth grinding. "That's what he said too."

Finley swallowed, head drooping as she dodged out of his reach, finding her dress and shift on the floor at the corner of the bed.

I keep surrendering myself, Lumen thought, dressing with her back to the man, waiting for him to speak and a little relieved when he didn't. She offered what was asked of her, realizing too late she never asked for anything in return. Finley had asked her days ago if she had trusted him and the night before she'd let herself. He wanted her trust in sex, that was all, but she didn't know how to separate one feeling from another.

"Lumen," he whispered.

"Not now," she answered, not certain when later would be. He didn't stop her from leaving him there, naked and guilty at the center of the room and even her gratitude for *that* was weak.

The Manor was already awake as she made her way downstairs and realized too late that Finley had left a rip in the front of her dress. She laced it up as much as she was able, ignoring the stares of the few soldiers she passed in the hall, and then gathered up a shawl from the workroom. Now that snow had fallen there was no excuse to go foraging, nevermind the store of herbs was full after all her new spare time since the army had taken over the farming.

She grabbed a few treatments for colds and sore throats and filled her basket. Freezing weather or not she wanted to be away from the Manor today. Away from Finley shuffling around the workroom and Dominic storming around the halls. She considered hunting down Colin or Gideon and then decided her mood was too dark for any kind of company, especially the complicated variety Gideon presented.

She would go see the Blythe couple, their sweet old temperaments would soothe her and remind her of home, as it had been before the Stalor army arrived.

HER STOMACH WAS A THORNY, curdling thing by the time she was done with her visits and she tried to muffle the sound of her hunger beneath folded arms and the layer of her shawl. Winter was as thin in her tenants homes as it was in the Manor and she didn't want someone like Widow Ramsey trying to feed her when she had children to worry about.

"Are you going to see Oliver Spragg next mi'lady?" The woman asked.

Lumen swallowed and remembered her throat was dry as she stared back at Gretchen, children bundled close. She glanced out the window. The sun should have been high in the sky by now but it was hidden behind dense clouds.

"I should get back before it snows or worse," Lumen said.

Gretchen went on as if she hadn't even asked Lumen the question, "He talks of leaving for the north."

Lumen took in a slow, cold breath and nodded. "Yes. Would you go with him?"

The baby babbled and Gretchen smiled at Lumen, brittle and half-hearted, shaking her head. "The children couldn't make the trip in winter. You should go."

Lumen blinked. Oliver had said something to her. But there was kinship in the other woman's eyes as Lumen shook her head. "It wouldn't feel right."

"We'd manage, milady," she said but she only smiled and bounced the children on her knees.

Lumen left with a parting touch to each member of the family, happy to see the babes looking well after the rough turn in the weather. Snow crunched beneath her boots on the path back and even with the cold sinking through to her toes and making her feet stiff, she picked the long route home. Growling hunger in her stomach, toes turning to little knobs of ice, dark clouds overhead threatening snow—none of it outweighed the irritating thought of seeing Finley or Dominic at that moment.

She took a smaller path off the road and through the old orchards where the last foragers of winter, squirrels and fat black ravens, perched in bare branches and chittered at her from overhead. She was halfway through the brush when she heard the hum of low conversation ahead, the deep char of tobacco in the air.

Three soldiers huddled together at the edge of the orchard, passing a pipe between them, warming their hands against their trousers. Lumen paused on her way—they weren't familiar faces, but they wore the Stalor uniforms. No one had bothered her since Gideon warned the one man who'd dared in the courtyard and she was sure there was no doubt now about what she was doing in Healer Brink's bed.

The men on the path had hollow cheeks and their uniforms were threadbare and instinct told her to turn back. It was too late, one looked up and spotted her, his dark eyes narrowing, thin cheeks twitching with a smile. He nodded his head at her, or in her direction, some signal for the others, but that was all. She could turn now and offer them a chase or trust the word had gone through the ranks that she wasn't to be touched or tormented. Mutters passed between the men as she started forward again and Lumen couldn't make up her mind between keeping her eye on them or watching her feet as she walked, choosing some frantic combination of the two.

Maybe it was hunger, or stress from the morning, or maybe she'd spent weeks feeling the slow boiling anger rising in the ranks of the army as food grew thinner and days got colder and their swords sat idle. She hadn't felt this warning ringing in her ears since the first night. It wasn't about which officer laid claim to her company, it was about how little these soldiers cared what happened after they'd entertained themselves with her fear.

"G'day milady," one grunted as she began to pass them.

Lumen meant to speak but her voice was frozen in her throat and she only managed a jerky nod.

"Let us walk you back, Lady Fenn," the one who'd spotted her said. He had dull dark hair and three scratches over his chin.

"I know my own way home," she answered, swallowing down the tremble in the words and raising her face. She forced a hard smile at the men and nodded once more. *Walk steady,* she told herself. *Don't amuse them.*

But keeping her pace even only meant they caught up to her easier, one at either side and the third hovering at her back, staying out of sight as she walked.

"Curious, restless fellows out today," the first said. His face sagged, dark circles under his eyes, and she remembered treating him weeks ago, when she was still sleeping next to Dominic. He had watched her with a fixed stare as she cleaned a wound on his chest, leaning in closer than necessary and breathing against her neck. "Too cold to fight and too dull to think."

Lumen bit down on the inside of her mouth, resisting the urge to suggest they find a new occupation. There were parts of the Manor that could use cleaning, trails in the woods that wouldn't mind clearing. There was always more need now for wood for the fire.

"Nothing to do but feel hungry and want fucking," the man at her back muttered.

Lumen glared at the road ahead of her, fisting her hands against her sides as the men jostled her between them as they laughed.

"Poor Lady, you must be bitter after being handed over to that sick bastard," the dark-eyed one said, breathing smoke against her neck. "Sol's fire, he calls himself a healer? I've heard rumors of what he likes to do to women."

She ground her jaw, trying to brush the memory away of the softest mouth against her cunt. She doubted the men had heard rumors that included a feeling like what she'd suffered the night before. Worship was a dangerous game and it left her weaker for being the subject of the care.

"Must wonder what proper love-making feels like between him and that beast General of ours," said the one on her other side.

She wanted to snap back that she had very few questions left when it came to the act, but there was nothing in her head that didn't sound like an invitation for more trouble.

"I only wonder when I will have my home to myself again," she said quietly, trying to speed up. Her traitor boot, foot frozen inside by now, slipped on a patch of ice on the path in front of her. Hot hands grabbed at her waist, drawing her back against a bulky body that squeezed her close. "Let me go," she breathed.

"Steady now, Lady," the man behind her growled in her ear. "No one here wants you hurting yerself."

"Get her off the road where anyone can see us," the dark-eyed one said. "Last thing we want is more cocks to share her with."

Lumen snarled and thrashed in the big man's hold but his hands were clamped around her wrists, trapping her arms across her chest. A rigid bulge dug into her lower back as he hauled her against him and staggered off the path and behind a large oak. When her foot kicked backwards, colliding with his knee, he grunted and tossed her forward, her feet slipping and arms flailing.

The leader, scarred jaw and dark eyes, caught her by the ribs, twisting her on one ankle and slamming her back against the oak, knocking her head against the bark and slamming the breath out of her. Her vision swam but nothing disguised the grip of a greedy palm against one breast squeezing too hard. Knees knocked and crowded against hers, hard hips nailing her to the tree. Lumen shook off her dizziness, pushing at the body in front of her, screeching and twisting as a face nuzzled against her jaw, teeth biting the skin of her neck.

The biggest man took one of her hands in a firm grip, framing her on her side and grinding his clothed length against her palm, but the third grasped her wrist in a half-hearted grip, his eyes fixed to her breasts. She took the opportunity, tearing her hand away from him and pressing it between her and the leader, digging her nails hard into his chest where she remembered the wound she tended.

It worked. The man howled in pain, throwing her bodily away from him in reflex. Her other arm yanked and nearly popped but she was released in surprise, knocking against the third—a younger, weaker man.

"Bitch!" the leader snarled, one palm covering his chest. "Hold her down."

Lumen locked her wrists in her hands and then threw her elbow into the younger man's nose, dashing away as he yelped and reared back.

On the path an unmistakable rider was charging toward them, and for the first time in weeks, Lumen felt relief at the sight of Dominic Westbrook. The horse reared as Lumen staggered towards him, her ankle screaming with every step. Westbrook was jumping down from the saddle before the horse had come to a stop and the men were already stiff, studying the thin cover around them as if they were deciding between escape and facing their General.

"What do you think you're doing out here?" Dominic growled, pacing past Lumen, covering her view of them.

"We was only walking the lady home, sir," the leader said.

"Oh and I'm to believe you walk with your cock stiff as stone, do you?"

Lumen limped to the horse, trying to drown out the sound of the men with the quiet huffs of breath from the animal, replacing the heavy cloud of smoke in her nose with the thick, natural smell, her cheek pressed to warm flesh.

"You know my position on this. There are whores in the house."

"She's no better now."

A loud grunt cracked in the air, the sound of a body collapsing against snow. "Get back to the Manor," Dominic snarled. "If I don't see you there, I'll make sure you're tracked down and dragged back by the ankles. Either way you'll see the punishment."

Boots trudged away with grumbles and Lumen pressed her face to the chest of Westbrook's horse, feeling it snuffle at her shoulder. Even the rough heartbeat buried beneath coarse hair and strong flesh couldn't stifle the sounds of boots approaching behind her.

"What in Sol's Light were you doing out here alone?"

"Visiting my tenants," Lumen whispered.

"Look at me." He waited in the silence and then sighed when she refused to turn, breath heavy and uneven. "I don't know what left you oblivious but you're meant to take someone with you when you leave the Manor."

"It's my land," Lumen said.

"And it's my army! I know their appetites, Lumen. I know what this war has turned them into!"

Lumen nuzzled against the warm skin and then turned to look at Dominic out of the corner of her eye. His cheeks were red with anger and she could see the whites all around his own dark eyes. He looked… panicked.

"What has it turned you into?" she asked.

His expression hardened, jaw flexing as he turned his own face in the opposite direction, studying the backs of the men who trod back to the Manor. "Which of them tore your dress?"

"How many lashes for that punishment?"

Dominic cursed under his breath, head ducking and black curls covering his expression.

"It wasn't them," she said, softer, the anxious fight that stirred in her blood ever since spotting the men in the orchard finally starting to wane and leaving her weak and sore. "It was just an… accident from the night before."

Dominic scoffed, head shaking. "Are you alright?"

"My ankle is twisted," she said.

He turned and stepped toward her, freezing as she jumped and skittered in reflex. "I only want to put you on the horse," he said, palms outstretched. "So you don't have to walk back."

Lumen took a deep breath and nodded, bracing herself against the urge to run as Dominic marched forward, his shadow crossing her. The horse followed an unspoken order, scooting forward so all his master had to do was take her waist in a firm grip and lift her up in the saddle. Lumen grabbed the reins and horn as Dominic steadied her.

"How did you know to come find me?" Lumen asked, combing her fingers through the black hair of the horse's mane, eyes determined to avoid the upturned face staring at her.

"I *didn't*," Dominic bit out. "I was riding out to meet Danvers and Charlie. Can you ride like that?"

I've been told I have a very bad seat.

I beg to differ.

Lumen nodded, batting away the fond memory and nudging the horse forward into a turn back to the Manor.

"Find Brink or Jones," he said. "Stay out of the men's way until I make an example of that group."

"What good will it do?" Lumen asked, frowning and facing him.

Dominic's expression darkened and she realized she had forgotten the dichotomy of the man, the one she'd slept with and the one who'd prowled the halls of her home and turned it into a fortress for his war.

"Let me manage my army, Lady Fenn. I've better things to do with my time than chase you through snow."

Lumen bit off her response before she said something foolish, like she could have dealt with the men herself. She'd bought herself enough time to run but she had no doubt they would have caught her again and she doubted causing injury was likely to buy her any mercy from them. Instead she nudged Westbrook's horse down the road. She would tuck herself away in the kitchen where she could soak her ankle and eat scraps until she quit shaking like a leaf. She didn't think she'd make it up the stairs to her room in this state. She ignored the sound of boots stomping away behind her.

THE KNOCKING ON THE DOOR INCREASED TO A CRESCENDO BEFORE rousing Finley from his thoughts. Even then he considered ignoring the summons. His mood was sour, guts churning and head heavy with the weight of his own recriminating chorus. Why had he said those words to Lumen? Why had he bothered waking up at all? Why hadn't he chased her to the door, wrapped her up in his arms again and dragged her back to the bed?

He should have made vows, promises, choices. He should have kept his idiot mouth shut.

The door to the workroom creaked open behind Finley's back and Gideon grunted. "What the hell are you doing in here?"

"Working," Finley said, eyes squeezed shut.

If he'd gotten anything done today it was probably muddled into something toxic. His head was everywhere but on his shoulders.

"Did you hear about Lumen?"

Finley's eyes popped open, back stiffening fast enough to send a twinge up his neck. "What about her?"

"She went out to the tenants on her own. Wallin and his crony shits had her up against a tree."

He spun fast, knocking a jar of dried dandelion greens over to spill its contents across the wooden counter. Gideon was in the doorway, arms folded over his chest, eyes narrowed and all the crooked lines of his face pointing to warning.

"Where- how is she?"

"Kitchens with Colin. One of the lot has a broken nose and Wallin is bleeding. Dominic caught them..."

Before. There was a stone lodged in Finley's throat as he stared back at Jones. The word was unspoken but it wasn't a relief. He wasn't an idiot. She'd left the Manor in the temper he put her in and it'd been weeks since she tried to venture out without at least Colin with her.

"Is she alright?"

"I haven't seen her," Gideon said, voice grinding low. "I've been dealing with them."

Finley glanced down to Gideon's fists, his knuckles swollen, split, and bleeding.

"Westbrook will finish with them later, for now he needs you."

"What? Why?"

Gideon shrugged. "Something to do with Danvers and Charlie just getting back from their errand. I think they brought news."

Finley suddenly remembered to breathe, glancing around the workroom. He'd accomplished *nothing* for the day and Lumen had... his vision turned red at the thought. "I need to go see her." Or to see Wallin and break a few well-chosen bones.

"Leave her for now. Colin's a better guard dog for her and if you put Westbrook off he'll only go hunting for you."

Leading him straight to Lumen. Finley swallowed down the lump in his throat with a brief bout of bile and nodded in a jerky rhythm. "Alright. Alright."

He followed Gideon around the Manor loop, eyes flicking through the archways searching for... for some glimpse of her. Passing the stairs it took every muscle in his body to keep himself from running down the flight and over to the kitchen. If there had been any injury Gideon would have told him, wouldn't he? Or would Lumen simply take care of herself?

I want to care for her, Finley thought. Which was not quite the only thought in his head. He had to prove to her that he *did* care for her. It was the same and somehow not.

Finley followed Gideon into the office and stopped still as Danvers and Charlie crossed his path, leaving out the doorway he'd just entered. The shelves were stripped down to next to nothing, like sets of dark wood ribs showing against the walls. They'd sold the books. Her father's collection.

But he hasn't touched the silver yet.

He wondered if Lumen knew that was the compromise when she'd made it.

"There you are," Dominic muttered, papers in one hand as he tucked away money with another. How much time and food could the books have really bought the army compared to the collection of silver they were keeping secret? Dominic looked up from his seat at the bare desk and glared at Finley and Gideon. "I'll talk to him alone. Wait, how far did you get with Wallin and the others?"

"Popped a shoulder, maybe broke a rib," Gideon said with a shrug. "I could break their hands but I wasn't sure if you wanted to discharge them."

Dominic frowned, looking down in thought. "Let me decide. Wait outside."

Gideon nodded once, strangely solemn for himself. But Finley understood. Gideon had a kind of bond with Lumen, something deeper than his usual interest in bedding women.

And what is it you have? he asked himself. Something like a spike running through his chest, sharper than the arrow that had struck him in the back. More permanent. More welcome too.

Gideon left the room and Finley squared his shoulders. He knew what was coming.

"General Meades needs a new medic."

Finley stared back at Dominic, expression blank. The statement was so far from what he'd expected to hear it took him what felt like several minutes to puzzle the words out.

"It'd be easier work and no one would ask you to stand on the field," Dominic continued, the letter in his right hand tapping on the knuckles of his left. Then he held it out and Finley realized he was clear on the other side of the room. He crossed the space with unsteady steps but when the letter was in his grasp he found himself barely able to read it.

"Meades is finally catching up to our line, a bit more activity in his company than you're finding here at the moment, although we made his way easier for him," Dominic said with a shrug.

"You're telling me to leave our company?" Finley asked.

Dominic's eyes narrowed up at his face. "No. I'm not an idiot, Fin. I'd expect you back. But you're closer to Meades than the Stalor capitol where the next medic would be coming from. It's an opportunity for you if you want it."

Finley opened his mouth to ask if this was about Lumen. Did Dominic want him out of the way? Or was he angry that Lumen had been hurt while she was meant to be under Finley's care?

"It's an offer, not an assignment," Dominic said, watching him, tone so flat Finley was more certain than ever the man was hiding something beneath the words. Finally it came. "Have you seen her?"

Finley shook his head, looking down at the letter again."I'll go down to her next." Meades didn't sound hopeful in the note and Finley couldn't blame him. Armies weren't known for passing over their medics.

"Her dress was torn," Dominic said and Finley's head jerked up. "At the collar."

It was shame and not embarrassment that burned up from his neck to his cheeks. "Is this any of your business?"

"None of the men take you seriously, do they?" Dominic asked, head cocking. "They don't understand your work, and anyway Lady Fenn's remedies are easier to swallow than yours. All they remember about you is what the women you sleep with say."

The words layered over Finley like stones filling his pockets, ready to weigh him down as he sank into Dominic's game.

"I knew this wasn't about Meades," he said, fisting his hands behind his back. "This is about her."

"I thought you could keep her safe."

"You thought you could make her beg for you," Finley spat

back, brief triumph burning in his chest as shock spread over Dominic's face. "You thought if you tossed her aside she would crawl back tamer and weaker and apologizing for defying your orders. She's not your soldier, Dom."

"She's not your whore," Dominic hissed, hands slapping down on the wood of the desk. "Which is all the men see her as with you."

"Is that *my* fault? You traded her over like she was cattle!"

"You weren't meant to *take* her!" he answered back in a roar, pushing up from the desk and leaning forward. "You were meant to keep her out of *their* hands. She'd have been better off with Jones."

Finley tried to scoff but the sound choked in his throat.

"I'm serious. At least with him the men would have been too terrified to so much as look at her. You're weak and they've smelled it on you and it left her vulnerable."

"You want me to leave. Go to Meades. You really believe she'll just turn back up in your bed if I'm gone?"

Dominic sighed, shoulders sagging and head drooping to face the top of the desk. "No. I think she'll take Gideon up on his protection. I think within two days there won't be a soldier in this company who is confused as to how off limits she is no matter how bored and restless they are. I think Gideon's likely to cut off my hand before he lets me touch her without her permission. And that's fine. But this is out of hand today, do you understand?" He looked up again and Finley didn't recognize the look on his face, skin pale and eyes wide. "If I hadn't ridden out to meet Danvers and Charlie they would have raped her, Finley. It might have happened anyway, the timing was... it was *too* close."

Finley's blood ran cold and a shadow passed over Dominic's face.

"I know it wouldn't be the first time it happened but I—"

Dominic had always been swift and hard on any assault. He and Gideon had done their best to prevent them although Finley had his doubts about some of their methods. Taking high-born ladies into their beds to better keep them out of the soldiers reach seemed a weak kind of logic. One Finley himself had taken advantage of because he… because some days a battle seemed to numb any humanity he might have had left in his head.

Lumen deserved more than this, more than being the soft place for men like him and Dominic and Gideon to land. More than trading the threat of rape at the hands of someone like Wallin for the acceptance of sharing his bed. His *tastes*. He was a drug addict who demanded she *submit* to him. How was that better than Dominic's need for her to obey?

"You'd let the men go without a medic?" Finley asked and to his own ears his voice sounded lifeless.

His head felt like a boulder. He wanted to rewind to the morning when Lumen had been soft and warm and limp against him, a smile teasing her lips. Or to the night before when his senses had been drowned with her and he'd barely been able to think clearly enough to follow his own rules for their game. *A game where you demanded she beg and whine and still offered no mercy.*

"We have her now," Dominic said, low and quiet.

It was true. She'd manage everything and with fewer infections too, no doubt.

Dominic sank back into the chair at the desk, slow and weary and wincing. "If you decide to go I'll write."

"Don't bother," Finley muttered, and even his eyelids felt too heavy as he blinked. "I'll ride to them tonight."

Dominic froze in his chair. "You're certain?"

"It says the medics' old tools are all still there," Finley said. "I won't have much to pack and this trip won't take me more than the night to ride."

"Finley, I—"

Finley turned and walked to the office door. Whatever came next, he didn't want to hear. This was why he hadn't made that promise to Lumen this morning. It wasn't about Dominic's orders and his obeying. It was about what she deserved in a man who would be loyal to her. And she deserved more than *him*. She healed men. He barely ensured their survival. He was barely interested in his own survival most days.

Gideon perked up from where he waited against the wall, his eyes scanning Finley head to toe. "Well. You're not bleeding."

"I'm leaving," Finley said and when Gideon startled he added. "You need to keep her safe, Gid. Better than I did."

"You're *what*?" Gideon hissed, eyes narrowing and glancing over Finley's shoulder as the door to the office swung shut.

"Meades needs a medic. You have Lumen here until I get back and she'll see you all through."

"You're leaving." Gideon's head shook as he raced to catch up to Finley's thought. "This is Dominic's doing? You're coming back."

"It was my decision," Finley said, starting to walk. He'd pack his things from his room first and then what little he'd left in the workroom that he couldn't spare. Would he come back? Yes, Dominic had said so. *I do follow his orders.* "I'm going to pack. I want you to wait until I've left to tell her."

"Wait! Wait." Gideon rushed to follow him, feet slapping on the floor as he chased him to the attic stairs. "Tell her? Finley, Sol's Fire, what are you thinking? You can't leave without explaining to Lumen."

"She'll understand," Finley said.

Gideon's fist caught the back of Finley's coat, pulling hard and nearly dragging Finley down two stairs. He was shoved against a wall, Gideon's face close and thunderous.

"What are you doing?" Gideon growled. "Think of her. Why are you leaving?"

"Let me go, Jones."

Gideon crowded him to the wall and Finley's breath was thick in his chest. "No. Now maybe I'm too stupid to follow your educated logic but I want you to try to explain it to me all the same so I can at least say I tried."

"She'll be safe with you, won't she?" Finley asked, staring back at Gideon's thin black gaze.

"Safest," Gideon said with a shrug.

It pinched at every sore spot in Finley's head and he hid his flinch with a nod. "That's all that matters."

"You have to talk to her, Fin," Gideon said, face twisting in confusion.

"No, she'll understand," Finley said. He reached up and patted his… his friend's hand on his coat lapel until Gideon's fingers loosened. "Let me pack. Take a horse. Speak to her after I've left."

Gideon's forehead knotted. "You're running away and I can't understand why you'd be so stupid."

Is he right? No, that was the weak, hopeful part of his head. The one that craved more borrowed time with a woman who would have been better off never having met him.

"I'll be back when Meades' new medic arrives," Finley said, and then he wormed his way out from between the wall and Gideon, ignoring the heat of the other man's stare on his back.

⁎

"Here you are, Lady," Colin murmured and Lumen hummed and blinked her tired eyes open as he poured fresh hot water into the tub where she soaked her ankle. The other foot was in there too, just for symmetry… and warmth.

"Thank you," she said, smiling at the boy and tugging the blanket he'd brought her a little tighter around her shoulders. "You don't have to stay."

"You said that already, Lady. But here's nicer than anywhere else I can think of," Colin said answering her smile.

It'd taken her a good half hour when she first arrived back at the Manor to convince Colin to stay at her side rather than go 'saw Wallin's bollocks off with a dull spoon.' It did him as much good to curl up with her in front of the fire as it did her to have his little head rest in her lap while she waited for her tremors to subside.

But rest didn't stop her from jumping when footsteps shuffled in the doorway and a shadow loomed, huge and dark. And then Gideon stepped down into the kitchen and everything was right again.

"How are you, little spirit?" he asked, words gentle enough she imagined wrapping them around her with the blanket.

"Better."

"I hope you left 'em in their own shit," Colin said firmly.

Lumen tried to catch his eye but the boy only shrugged and kept his nose high in the air.

"Go and see for yourself," Gideon said, nodding his head out to the hall. Colin moved to run and then stopped and glanced at Lumen. "Go on," Gideon added. "I'll be with her the whole time."

Lumen nodded at Colin and he ran out of the kitchen with a cheerful 'whoop!' She raised her eyebrows at Gideon. "You didn't really, did you?"

He grinned and came to crouch in front of her, warm hands lowering slowly to her knees, slowly enough that she didn't flinch or squirm. "I didn't but I don't know what Dominic has planned for them."

Lumen sighed and looked down at her lap frowning, not sure if she felt relief or disappointment or shame at the thought of any violence on her behalf. It wasn't the Lunar way, but a dark, wounded part of her wanted the justice of the trade.

"It's not the first time we've punished for the like," Gideon murmured waiting for her gaze to lift before continuing. "I hate to think it, but it won't be the last. Dominic may decide to send them home and that won't be a surprise to any other soldier here, either."

It isn't about you, it's about disobeying a rule of the company. And strangely that was a kind of comfort to her. She didn't want Dominic taking personal revenge. Not on her behalf. There was a fantasy of her taking it for herself but it wasn't an idea that sat well in her stomach.

"How's the ankle?" Gideon asked.

"Needs wrapped up is all," she said. "And maybe a bed in here so I don't have to take the stairs."

"Do you have the wrappings?"

She nodded and pointed to the strips of cloth she'd torn and left in a pile at her side. "I suppose Finley can do it."

Gideon was quiet for a moment, thumbs brushing over her knees. "Better let me try, little spirit."

She stared at him. Was Finley angry with her for the morning? Or was he hiding because she was angry with him? Gideon lifted her leg from the water, taking a towel from the floor and patting her dry with a little furrow of concentration between his brows and a gentler touch than anyone would imagine him possessing. She relaxed under his care and waited to see if he needed her instructions on how to wrap the cloth. He must have had the practice because he pulled just tight enough to keep her secure but not enough to damage circulation.

"You have a secret skill," she said, smiling.

"Practiced enough on myself," Gideon said, one cheek full with a half-smile. "Brink straightened me out on the details later."

"Where is he? With Dominic?"

Gideon finished the last wrap around her ankle and up her leg, tucking the fabric into place as she waited in silence and a growing dread building between her heart and her stomach. When he finally looked up to her, bruised and crooked face open, she held her breath.

"He's left, little spirit."

Lumen's brow twitched. "Left?"

"Another company of the army farther west needed a medic until Stalor sends them a new one." Gideon lifted her other foot out of the water and dried it off with an equally soft touch as she stared at him, a crushing pressure growing in her chest.

"When did he leave?" While she was out? Before she'd made it back to the Manor, surely.

"He rode out..." Gideon released a heavy breath and tried again, "He rode out a few minutes ago. Just before I came in."

Lumen reared back. At the back of her thoughts words from the day spun themselves into circles, words from days ago. From her mouth and Finley's and Dominic's.

"Where is he?" she whispered, trying to push herself up.

"Lumen, you can't catch him," Gideon soothed, hands wrapping around her waist and lifting her to balance on her good foot. The floor was icy beneath her and he carried her to the table where she'd cried and torn her boots off hours ago.

"Not Finley. Westbrook. Where is he?" She tried to fit her

boot over her wrapped foot and nearly screamed, dropping it back to the floor.

Gideon boxed her in, cautious and crouched and careful. "He's got Wallin and Fisk and Judd in the infirmary. You don't want to see that."

"I don't care what he's doing. I want to speak to Westbrook." Wanted to scream at him.

She hopped down to one foot and then gasped as Gideon caught her up in his arms, as if it cost him nothing to lift her. "You'll freeze those toes. I'll take you."

It was not the storming approach her pounding pulse craved and truth be told, as Gideon shouldered the door open to the infirmary, she felt a little silly being carried in. Especially when she saw the scene before her.

The young man of the trio was braced to the floor by Danvers and Charlie, stronger than they looked. Westbrook stood with a boot on one of the man's hands, crushed and broken and bloodied. The man, Fisk or Judd, she didn't know, screamed into his own chest and Westbrook ground the boot and whipped his head around to stare at her. Behind them, chained to bracing posts like the one Colin had held while whipped, their hands already ruined and faces seeping with ugly wounds, sat her other two tormentors.

"What in Sol's fire are you doing bringing her in here?" Dominic barked.

"That's enough for him," Lumen said, nodding to the younger man. "He was barely interested."

It wasn't pity. His hand was already ruined and if Gideon was telling the truth the only person who had the skill to possibly save it was riding away for who knew how long.

Westbrook's boot shifted away and the screams turned to gasping sobs.

"Put me down," Lumen said, trying to throw herself out of Gideon's grasp. He put her down with careful balance and she steeled herself for the cold and any pain as she forced herself to step toward Westbrook. "You did it."

"They are my men to punish," Dominic bit out.

"Not them," she said, waving her hand to dismiss the men. "You told him to leave and off he ran. Just like you promised."

She watched him, anger wild in her chest, dragging up stinging tears to her eyes that she wished would burn away before he saw them.

"I did not."

"You did! And you were right! He jumped to your orders. But I *won't*, Dominic. I don't *want* you!"

The shout echoed off the stone floor and up to the high ceilings. She remembered faintly a time when this room had been filled with the sound of solstice revelry, before the war had consumed every family's men, had sent their women into hiding. Steps clapped against that stone, Westbrook's boots leaving bloody prints behind him as he answered her, face firm and even and eyes sparking anger.

"I am aware, Lady Fenn. And you are under no obligation. As Finley was under no obligation when I gave him the letter from General Meades. You have made your choice. So has he." If he had dismissed her in that moment he might not have seen, but he waited, eyes fixed to her face and the burning truth building up as her eyesight wavered with tears.

Finley had left, without a word. And she believed Dominic. Something deeper than weariness sank over her and those tears she'd fought a moment ago fell with the weight. She didn't care. She didn't care that Wallin and Danvers and Charlie were a witness. Dominic nodded, assured she understood, and turned his back on her.

"Come with me, little spirit," Gideon whispered, a hand on her side preparing her for when he lifted her up into his arms again, a little pang running up from her injured ankle.

She'd let a festering anger boil over, hoping for relief or change, and instead she only felt like some kind of tension that'd been holding her together was no longer there to support her. She sagged into Gideon's hold and he squeezed her close.

"Do you know why?" she whispered, closing her eyes as faces peered at their progress from the courtyard.

"Hm? Why he left?"

"Without speaking to me."

Gideon grunted and the sound echoed under her ear on his chest. "'M assuming it's 'cause he's an idiot. That's what I told him."

Lumen clutched at Gideon's shirt as the sobs crawled up from her throat, soundless and straining and shaking her body in his arms.

"Oh, little spirit," he whispered, tilting his head to press his cheek to her hair. But he didn't offer any comforting lies. Only carried her up the stairs to the second story and down the hall to his room. The one she'd shared with Finley briefly. The one next to her old room, now Dominic's.

She understood. "I'm yours now, aren't I?" she asked through cracking breaths.

"Yes," he said, and he pushed the door open as she nodded. "Sleep. I'll bring you up something warm to eat."

He carried her to the bed and set her down as if she were fragile. Oh Lune, she thought she might be, every inch of her was too raw, all bruised. He slipped the one boot she managed down to thunk against the floor and Lumen caught his hands in hers. The vision of him was wavy in front of her soaked eyes, he might have been grinning or frowning, she didn't know.

"Just lay down with me for now," she said. She didn't have the stomach for eating.

Gideon's boots landed heavier against the floor and then he scooted in next to her, drawing her down against his side and wrapping himself almost completely around her, hot and heavy and humming in her ear with every easy breath as she wept.

III
THE SOLDIER'S DESIRE

HOT BREATH TICKLED DOWN THE LENGTH OF LUMEN'S NECK, warm weight pinning her to the mattress, and rough fingers cupping a breast through the fabric of her dress. Her eyelids were swollen and scraped her eyes as she opened them to a dim room. Gideon Jones kept his curtains shut, faint light bleeding through dense brown fabric. The morning was cold against her nose but the rest of her was surrounded by the heat of the body at her side.

She squirmed, turning under the blanket of Gideon to face him and then drawing an actual blanket up over her nose as he sighed out. The mint leaves he chewed had worn off during his sleep and his breath was sour and too strong for her pounding head. His face was slack, all the muscles relaxed into a softness she'd never seen him wear before, eyebrows twitching with dreaming. Her lips curled beneath the blanket and one hand slid up between their chests to brush across a scar running down his jaw.

Gideon's lips smacked together, a little shine of drool at the corner of his mouth by his pillow, his forehead twitching. She continued her study, learning all the old breaks over the bridge of his nose, the cut healed just over his eye, the chip carved into his lower lip.

All at once, Gideon's teeth snapped, his eyes flashing open as he nipped the tip of her finger. Lumen screeched and jumped in the air only to be caught around the waist by banding arms. His laughter cracked through the morning silence, splintering the brief terror of surprise that froze the blood in her veins. Lumen sagged with a noisy sigh and Gideon rumbled as she collapsed atop his chest.

"Mmm, morning, little spirit," he said, voice thick and gravelly.

The picture of him beneath her—teeth bared in a grin and eyes narrow with sleep, hair ruffled at odd angles and his beard cut through with scars and flecks of gray—left Lumen warm and relaxed in his hold.

"Good morning," she answered, finding her smile returning at the sight of his.

Finley is gone. It was a snap inside of her, chest panging in response and eyes wincing. Gideon didn't miss the twist in her smile. Turning them onto her side, he hugged her against his body. His stomach pressed soft against hers and below that his length prodded, warm and stiff and heavy along her thigh.

She didn't want to think of Finley, his sudden vanishing act or their argument from only... only the morning before. She wrapped a hand around Gideon's shoulder and tugged, rolling onto her back and trying to take him with her. He followed, face thoughtful and Lumen moaned at the full weight of him on top of her, her thighs spreading to accommodate his width.

"You're bruised," Gideon murmured, hands reaching up to frame her face, a thumb scratching over her cheekbone as he stared down at her, dark eyes smiling.

Lumen frowned, head thick with sleep, thoughts full of Finley and trying to suppress them under Gideon's heat. "Where?"

He shifted, hands holding her head, fingernails scratching at her scalp as he nuzzled against her throat, drawing out a gasp and then lowered his head to the collar of her dress, lips pressing to the skin at the top of her left breast, just over her heart.

"Here," he said, kissing again.

Lumen's eyes stung and she squeezed them shut. Her feelings for Finley had developed without her realizing the full extent of them. She'd let herself become attached, to trust him, even when she *knew* better. He'd made her no vows but temporary pleasure. It was insanity to lose him one day and turn to Gideon the next, but if it would distract her, or apply a balm to the wound, she would take the comfort.

"Are you going to leave?" she asked, forcing the words out of her thick throat.

"No, little spirit," he growled against her breast, and he sank against her a little more.

"If Westbrook tells you to—"

"I'll feed him my sword," Gideon said. The words did more work to satisfy her than she was willing to admit.

"Are you going to force me?"

He stilled and started to lift off but all she had to do was press her hands to the hard shoulder blades on his back and he relaxed again, the weight a blissful kind of crush against her. Gideon kissed her skin again and then turned his head up, chin propped between her breasts and eyes wide.

"Never."

She reached up and ruffled his uneven mess of hair and his cheeks filled with a smile before he buried his face against a breast, mouthing over fabric until she was gasping.

"Come up and kiss me," she said.

He surged up, fingers tight in her hair, tilting her head just so and still landing crookedly over her mouth, tongue pressing in before she could catch her breath. It was a messy, lazy kiss, deep one moment and a brief nip to her lip the next, making her grin. He paused, lifted his head above hers and stared at her so long and so thoroughly that Lumen grew used to the gaze, wanted to arch and preen for him.

"More," she said.

Gideon purred, hips nudging between hers, swallowing her little moan and answering it with another, rougher thrust to make her gasp. She returned his kiss, tried to make it her own but she couldn't match him for hunger and was soon left clinging and panting, wanting to beg for exactly what he was already offering. He was rocking over her, fast and hard and steady as if he were already inside her, and the feeling of him nudging at her through layers of fabric was sweet and soft and somehow still filthy. The kiss was wet, driven by eager affection and Lumen found herself smiling through every nibble and suck. His hips ground harder, fighting against their clothing and she moaned as bubbling heat built in her cunt.

Quick, hard knocks came from the door and Lumen tore herself away from the kiss, ready to scramble out from beneath Gideon but he only continued to buck and rut against her, groaning and wrapping his mouth around her throat, teeth scraping as he tasted her sigh.

"General says we're to ride out!" a voice shouted through the wood door.

Gideon sucked at her pulse and Lumen bit a moan behind her lips, eyes falling shut and her own hips answering his with a frantic pace. If they only had minutes, would he let her finish or roll away now and leave her wanting?

"Fine," Gideon ground out and then he kissed his way down to her shoulder. "What do you need?"

"This," Lumen gasped, fingers clutching into his shirt, head turning back to soak up the smell of him, all salt and hay and bonfire. "Just this, don't stop."

He licked stripes up her throat, growling against her skin and riding her up the mattress until the bed began to thump and creak, covering her squeaks of surprise. Lumen laughed, breathless and dizzy and Gideon hummed, peppering kisses over her cheeks and then sucking at her lips in brief presses.

She wrapped her arms and legs around him tight and he pinned her with his full weight, less friction and more pure pressure and motion. The heady, curling pleasure came on slow, a moan rising up and out of her throat as she scratched at Gideon's back and whimpered while heavenly heat coiled up her spine and down to her toes. He groaned in her ear as if he felt the pleasure with her and continued his rolling thrusts until she was crying out in flashing gasps, body losing strength and falling limp beneath him. He was tense on top of her as he slowed to a stop, panting in her ear.

"Sweet," he whispered into her skin. "You're so sweet." And then he licked her for good measure.

Lumen only felt heavy, the giddy need of the moment now sinking beneath the painful reality. Finley was gone and she had been passed on, more complicit in the transaction this time. Gideon's vows or not, he would leave with the army one day.

And what of it? she wondered. Wouldn't she be relieved to see the backs of these men?

"Did you finish?" She asked, her own voice hollow as Gideon nuzzled and kissed along her jaw.

"No, little spirit," he said. Another kiss, a long pause of his lips by her ear. "I'm in no rush."

He turned them to their sides and Lumen burrowed down against his chest before he could see her face, see the wetness gathering in her eyes. This was shame and she wasn't certain the source. Moving on too quickly, or developing feelings for Finley at all, or smothering them beneath the distraction of sex. All of it.

Gideon kissed the top of her head, his hands soothing down her back and then tucking the blankets up over her shoulder as he slid away.

"If I come back with bruises, will you kiss them away?" he asked.

Like he'd kissed hers? By that pattern they'd be back again and just as sore. She nodded, glancing at him out of the corner of her eye and conjuring a smile on her lips as he rose from the bed, watching her.

"But try not to need stitches," she added, smiling in earnest as he barked a laugh.

She watched as he shrugged out of his shirt, barrel chest carved with scars that must have needed stitches or worse, and wondered if she should have demanded a promise rather than only teased.

"I'll do what I can, little spirit," he said with a wink and then he rummaged through a pile of clothes she would have guessed were dirty and dressed himself for war.

INDA FOUND her bathing in the kitchen hours later, swollen ankle still wrapped and hanging out over the edge of the basin. She leaned against the doorframe as Lumen stiffened, momentarily shy at being caught, but then Inda smiled, the gap in her teeth showing and Lumen answered in kind.

"Heard about Healer Brink," Inda murmured. Lumen's eyes fell to the murky water. She grabbed the floating washcloth up and began to scrub at her legs. "I'm sorry. I hope Jones is keeping his hands to himself."

Lumen blushed and flicked her fingers over the top of the water. "He might have done but... I didn't."

There was silence and then the other woman snorted and rushed over to the tub, falling to her knees in a heap, smile brighter.

"You didn't?" Inda hissed, a giggle at back of her throat.

Lumen shook her head, shaggy braid shaking against her back. Inda crawled around behind her, and before Lumen knew what was what soft fingers began to comb through the tangles.

"Finley left without saying a word to me," Lumen said to the water and the touch in her hair stilled for a breath and then landed softly against her shoulder before setting to its work again.

"Men are idiots. He probably had some burr up his ass about being noble. Woulda cried like a babe if he'd had to tell you straight."

And who will you be in need of once you are finished with me, hmm?

"Maybe," Lumen said, shrugging.

"Lean forward, milady, and I'll wash your hair," Inda said, brushing through the thin pale strands.

Lumen almost said no, it was cold and no time for wet hair. But there were no soldiers in the infirmary now but Wallins, Fisk, and Judd, and Gideon said Dominic's orders were to ignore them. It was cruel, but she would do it anyway and spend the day in the kitchen, letting her hair dry by the heat of the stove and scrounging the stock for ingredients to bake with.

Inda took cupfuls of water from the tub, pouring them over Lumen's head, cool air layering over the water to draw out goosebumps. She lathered a small pinch of soap between her hands and Lumen squeezed her eyes shut, sighing as gentle fingers dug into her hair, working against her scalp. It'd been years since anyone washed her hair for her and it left her chest tight with fond memories of when the Manor had been filled with family, and servants who were as good as family. Of the last time another woman touched her bare skin with care and affection. She missed her mother, and her nanny Grete, and Sarah Blythe who would come to work in the Manor for extra pay when her husband was laid up.

Inda rinsed the soap away and Lumen almost mourned the finish. Her eyes stung and she let tears run free, disguising melancholy for the bite of soap.

"Do you want the vinegar too, milady?"

"Call me Lumen, please," she whispered and then nodded.

The apple vinegar washed through her wet hair, bright and tart and bitter, but it would leave her strands softer than the soap. Lumen hummed as Inda continued to work magic, sorting out tangles with a touch softer than feathers.

"What's Jones like?" Inda asked.

"Warm," Lumen said without thinking and they both laughed. "Um, he's... sweet, really. A little..."

"Mad," Inda finished and Lumen nodded. "Is he good in bed?"

Lumen bit her lip and shifted to face the woman. "I don't know yet. Well, yes, I think so. He's... used his hands. And his mouth." She blushed and Inda only waggled her eyebrows.

"If he'll do that mi- Lumen, he's good in bed." She grinned and Lumen laughed again, wrapping her arms around her knees and pressing her blush to her cool skin.

"I think he's big," Lumen said, eyes growing wide.

"Bigger than the healer?" Inda asked, perking up, hands clutching around the lip of the tub.

Lumen nodded. "But I haven't seen yet. Does it make a difference?"

Inda grinned. "It might. It may hurt a bit at first, or if he rushes."

Lumen mused on Gideon for a moment, eyes drifting around the room. "He did say..." she lowered her voice to a whisper, "that he likes for women to be soaked and begging first."

Inda choked, red flushing to her cheeks. "Lady, if that's true he's *certainly* good in bed."

Lumen snorted and then Inda did until they were both blushing and giggling and unable to meet each other's eyes. Lumen cleared her throat and lifted her face, one thought clearing through the amusement.

"How do we make men beg?"

Inda hummed and then glanced at the water, a flash of wistfulness on her face.

"Do you want a bath?" Lumen asked, making to rise. "I'll heat more water. I can wash your hair for you too."

"If you do, I'll tell you everything I know that makes a man weak," Inda offered, eyes brightening.

It wasn't only Gideon's face that crossed her thoughts at the offer. Finley was there too, and Dominic. She brushed them aside, wrapping herself in the robe waiting for her on a chair and sliding her feet into slippers on her way to start the kettle again.

H E ' D   B R O K E N   H I S   P R O M I S E   T O   H I S   L I T T L E   S P I R I T ,   G IDEON
realized, glaring down at the slice on his shoulder near his
collarbone, the reins of his horse laying limp in his numb hand.
He pressed an old scarf to the wound and hissed as it burned
with the pressure. His eyes rose to glare at Westbrook's back,
covered in wet stains from the snow smothering them from the
black sky overhead. Another skirmish and nothing achieved
other than new wounds for Lumen to tend. Would she be angry
with him or play his sweet nurse? He wouldn't mind a bit of
both.

He jogged his horse up to Dominic's side. "Are you satisfied?"

Dominic grunted, head twitching in his direction but
refusing to turn. "What are you talking about?"

"With the outcome of the skirmish? Did you find it useful?"

"You said the men needed activity," Dominic said. "We had
activity. No one's dead. I am satisfied."

"The men want a *victory*," Gideon hissed, nudging forward
more, trying to catch a glimpse of his General's face.

It was there, gray in the night's dark shadow, eyes blank,
muscles slack. He'd never seen Dominic look so *tired*, especially
not after a fight. Not in decades of knowing one another. Not
even when they were boys going days without sleep as they ran
for their knights.

They thought they'd be knights one day, and then Stalor
changed. No lords and ladies, like his Lumen. Just men and

women in houses, no matter how big or small or cheap. No knights, either, only soldiers for an army.

"Did you see an opportunity to break Oshain's line today?" Dominic's shoulders hunched against a blast of cold that marched toward them up the road. The Manor wasn't far now.

"Since when do we wait for opportunities?" Gideon asked.

"Last I checked I had my position because I was skilled at leading this army and deciding the best plan of action. And you had your position because I *gave* it to you."

Gideon snorted, falling back and leaving Dominic to charge forward into the cold alone. He was second in command because it wasn't a General's role to be liked by his men. Gideon could be their friend, jostle their bad moods away when a new order came down the ranks, bitch and moan with them until they were ready to fall in line. Dominic was right about one thing, he *was* given the position of General because of skill. Not because he was someone's son or had the money to buy himself the medals. Stalor wanted Dominic fighting in the lead because if he was, they would win. Which meant these months of idle cat and mouse with Oshain's army were either a well thought out tactic or...

Or Dominic was stalling.

One candle in a window winked through the snow, a brief orange eye in the blue dark. For the first time in years Gideon looked forward to the bed waiting for him after battle. She would be there, his little spirit, warm against him.

And hopefully not too angry that he was in need of stitches.

One of the whores was waiting on her toes as they arrived, bouncing and searching over heads for her lover.

"Philip!" she cried as the young man came trudging in with the company, and she ran through inches of snow to barrel into the lad's arms.

There were other women peeking out through the doorway but Gideon knew Lumen wouldn't be one of them. She'd be inside, ready to wrestle men into bandages. He caught Dominic scanning their faces all the same and his lips twitched. The man had made himself a sorry bed to lie in and Gideon couldn't find it in himself to feel bad for Dominic.

As much as Gideon enjoyed sharing a woman in bed with his General there was something delicate and precious about holding his lady alone in the bed through the night.

Lumen caught sight of his arm as soon as he entered the infirmary, ahead of the others, walking as fast as his legs could take him. One pale eyebrow raised and his stomach flipped.

"What did I tell you?" she asked. Gideon grinned and she shook her head, pointing to her work table. "Over here, now. You're bleeding on the floor."

HER HEADACHE from the morning had returned, splitting through her skull like branches of lightning. Her stomach was more than hollow, carving away at itself from the inside. She was certain the floor had been replaced with nails to walk upon and every minute or so it felt as if someone was jabbing a knife into her lower back as she paced.

The army returned to the Manor late into the night and if it weren't for the snowstorm she thought it must have been time by now for the sun to be shining. She finished with the last patient—not even bothering to wake him from where he'd fallen asleep on one of the infirmary cots—and washed her hands, wincing at the way the winter cold and repeated washing had left the skin chapped.

When she turned to the door she stopped still, staring at Gideon Jones sprawled out in a chair that had all but disappeared beneath his huge form, head tilted back and short, sharp snores popping into the air.

You could leave him here to sleep, too, she thought. Gideon's bed was calling to her and the idea of hoarding it to herself was tempting.

Instead her toes tapped against his boot and he snorted and startled awake, eyes swollen nearly shut.

"All done?" he asked, the question crackling with his grit.

Lumen nodded and smiled as Gideon grunted and groaned, bones cracking as he pushed himself up out of the tiny chair and leaned backwards, nearly toppling over with the stretch. She gasped as he straightened, uninjured arm swooping around her hips and heaving her up to his side. Her own back cracked and Gideon grinned as she stared at him, eyes wide and body stiff with surprise.

"You're injured," she said, but her feet screamed with relief for every second he held her up.

"That's this arm," Gideon said, flapping his left arm before squeezing her with his right and adding, "this one's fine."

She meant to protest but he was already walking them out into the cold hall and the sudden, startling chill left her curling into his chest, her arms wrapping around his neck. The bonfire was high in the heart of the courtyard, as if a blaze bright enough might have been able to fight the snow still falling from the sky. Only small handfuls of men were huddled around the flames. Colin appeared with bright cheeks, dressed in the extra layer of clothing she'd found for him and left in the little attic room while the army was in battle.

"Food is stingy round here today but I snuck some up to your room," Colin whispered.

"Good lad," Gideon answered and he dashed away as quick as he'd come.

Gideon carried her past the men and Lumen let her weary eyes fall shut, waiting for the chuckles and the lewd asides to reach her ears. There were none and when she risked a glance she only caught sight of one brief nod in their direction. Nothing like the stares and whispers of walking through with Finley. She curled back into the warm chest and Gideon hummed, his cheek against the top of her head as he walked up the stairs.

The fire she'd built the night before was burnt to coals in the grate but the room was warm and when Gideon set her down on the mattress she didn't have the will to jump back on her feet. And her bed partner was a source of heat in himself.

He sank to his knees in front of her, undoing the laces of her boots and pulling her feet free as she winced. When his thumb dug into her arch she caught her breath, the ache exquisite.

"Aren't I meant to be kissing your bruises?" she asked. Somehow the relief from the pain in her foot was traveling straight up to her back and shoulders and she thought she might not be able to stay upright for much longer.

Gideon smiled, one warm hand wrapping around her foot and squeezing before starting the same treatment to the other. "Broke my promise," he said. "And anyways, little spirit, you look weary enough to fade away in front of me. I want you lively when I have you beneath me again," he added with a wicked grin and a glance up at her from beneath surprisingly thick, dark lashes.

Lumen swallowed some knot of relief and anger down in her throat, tears springing up in her eyes again. The teasing smile washed away and then Gideon studied her from head to toe and back again. Not with heat or hunger but that same rare kind of focus. He scooped her legs up in his uninjured arm and turned her on the bed to lay down, following her onto the mattress.

"Roll over," he said.

She did, eyes shutting and salty tracks coursing over her cheeks and down to the pillow, his clumsy fingers loosening the laces of her dress. She didn't know if this meant Gideon *was* planning on taking liberties with her, or if he only wanted her undressed to hold a little closer, and she realized she was too tired to care. She shifted in whatever direction was needed to help him wrestle her out of the dress and didn't speak as he dropped the garment on the floor followed quickly by his trousers.

His hand caught hers as she reached back to stir him to interest. His fingers tangled with hers and squeezed softly as he pulled her against his side. If sex was his aim he was taking the work out of it for her.

"You'll hurt your arm," she said, careful not to jostle it as he wrapped the arm around her shoulders and tucked her head against his chest.

"It was only a small cut," he said.

Lumen snorted. A small cut that had needed ten stitches and would keep him from doing any real lifting with his left arm for a couple weeks at least.

"You were fond of him," Gideon said. She stiffened against him and he released her fingers only to stroke his through her hair. "It's alright, little spirit," he said, so quiet it was only a low rumble against the ear she pressed to his chest.

Lumen released a watery sigh. "I thought… I felt as if I had made a *choice* with him." Gideon hummed at her answer and her body went boneless in the following quiet. "Maybe we were only following Westbrook's orders."

"Don't think that," Gideon said, chest shaking with a laugh. "Dominic hardly knows his own mind lately. Don't imagine him in yours."

His fingers trailed out of her hair and down to her cheek where he found the wet remains of tears.

"I'm a poor bedmate tonight," she whispered.

"I'd be a worse one if I let you think so," Gideon said, pressing wet lips and rough stubble to her forehead. "I don't know what Finley was thinking when he agreed to leave for Meades' army, Lumen. He made a choice too but it was a fool one. I'm glad you're here with me now, but you don't owe me lips or hands or any of your sweetness. You make that choice too."

Lumen fingered the frayed edge of his collar as the words sank in. Their wrestling, teasing imitation of sex the morning before had been a relief and also left her feeling less at home in her own skin, as if she didn't recognize herself in the wake of the thing. But Gideon wasn't Dominic, threatening to toss her to the wolves or onto the next man. And if he wasn't Finley…

"You won't leave?" she asked.

"No, little spirit. I won't leave."

She sat up, ignoring his hand trying to nudge her back down to his side, and drew the blankets up over them both before the winter wind could sneak through old cracks in the Manor and chill the room around them. Gideon purred as she arranged herself against his side and she was asleep before he'd finished wiping her cheeks dry with his thumb.

SOMEONE PUSHED a cup of tea beneath Finley's nose as he wavered in place, eyes staring blindly around the medical tent. A cold snap of air rushed down a line of beds, washing away some of the smell of blood and bile and the stark, burning scent alcohol, but it brought with it the piss and shit of the latrines not far off. He took the cup with shaking fingers and set it down on the nearest flat surface.

When was the last time he slept? He knew and hated to think of it, to remind himself of what he'd left behind.

A little more than two days ago he'd been wrapped around his lady in the weakest hours of the night, body soaked with sweat and the most satisfying soreness running through every muscle. And now this. He made it to Meades' country battlefield after a rough and freezing night of riding only to put himself straight to work in the roughshod tent at the heart of the camp. Almost a day ago. He couldn't count the hours that had passed through exhaustion. Better to let the tea go cold and close his eyes until someone demanded something of him than to keep pushing.

The last medic kept a cot in a far drafty corner of the tent and it'd been offered up to Finley by Meades' second in command as if it were some kind of luxury. What would this company think if they could have seen Fenn Manor and its lady when they'd first arrived?

Soft and pale, like some distant memory of a woman, standing in the broad doorway of the Manor, her eyes cutting through them on their path to Dominic. Who looked as if he were ready to charge inside, horse and all.

No wonder the old medic was dead, a fever had run through the ranks weeks ago and he'd been left sleeping in the heart of the outbreak. At the back of Finley's thoughts Lumen's voice was running a tally of all that was missing from the medical supplies. When Finley had asked for the water to be refreshed regularly the boy assigned to help acted as if he were just demoted to latrine duty.

What if the water is coming *from the latrine?* Finley wondered with a horror muted beneath weariness.

He took the shabby cot, that smelled rancid, and collapsed down with a groan, pulling his sweater up over his nose and stiffening. There, deep in the weave of the knit... a little bright, clean whiff of her. He closed his eyes and her voice was in his ear.

You shouldn't have left.

"I know," he said, words cutting at his aching throat.

He pulled the sweater away and dug into his coat, hunting for his small bag of tobacco and papers. Better to burn away his sense of smell than allow it to leave him drowning in bits of his lady he couldn't really savor.

THE NEW MOON CAME AND WENT AND WHILE LUMEN SPENT THE day in silence she didn't risk opening the doors of the chapel with the Manor so full of people. Most mornings now she skipped sneaking down to pray in favor of remaining near Gideon's warmth. Gideon kept to his word—he didn't push for sex but he wasn't shy about finding alternative means of pleasing them both, and she'd used more than one of Inda's lessons to do the same for him.

There was friendship between them, if nothing else, and Lumen found that rarer and more precious recently than any passing flare of pleasure that left her colder afterwards.

"Making me something sweet?"

Lumen startled from where she was standing, staring at a cold stove, and shoved the note in her pocket before Gideon saw it. Colin had brought it from Oliver and she was still deciding if she was more concerned by the contents or by the fact that Oliver had Colin's ear in some way. If Westbrook learned of it there might be trouble for the boy... or for Spragg for that matter.

"There's nothing to work with," Lumen muttered. After months of scraping for ingredients her kitchen was well and truly scant. Now the only food came from what Westbrook provided, spread thin among the company.

Gideon's steps scuffed against the floor as he crept up behind her back. "I can think of something sweet you could offer."

His arms wrapped around her waist, hauling her back to his chest, one hand burrowing into the folds of her skirt while the other stroked its way up to a breast. Lumen stiffened in his hold, thinking of the letter in the pocket and the pit in her stomach at the news.

Spragg was taking one of the families over the border tonight while the army celebrated the discovery of a set of old instruments hidden in a cupboard. Tonight there would be music. Tomorrow Westbrook would have the pieces sold for another day's meat. And three of her tenants would have moved on.

If you can make it to my cabin before Mother Lune is a quarter high, I'll take you too, Lady Fenn.

Gideon's arms loosened but he dragged her back as he perched himself on the edge of the table, the legs beneath him threatening to break with his weight.

"What is it? Were the pieces precious to you?"

Lumen frowned, head scrambling around the conversation before she realized he meant the instruments. "No, it's not that. I don't know if I've ever heard them played before." She turned in his hold and let him arch her back, meeting his gaze. "I'm only tired. Hungry. Cold."

His eyes narrowed and she knew he wasn't convinced. But he nodded and squeezed her once in his arms. "Let me feed you, and take your share of the beer tonight, it will help fill you up. It might even make the company more tolerable."

The hard knot in her chest loosened with the tease and Lumen rose to her toes, pressing her lips to the corner of his jaw, grinning as his hands slid to her skirt again and he tried to nestle himself between her legs.

"You'd better feed me before you try any of your usual tricks or I may faint," she said into his skin.

Gideon grunted a soft laugh in answer. "I don't mind the thought of taking your breath away but I'd like it to take a little more effort on my part. Come along, little spirit. Let's see if I can't put some life in those pale cheeks of yours."

"Gideon Jones, consummate gentleman," she said, the rest of

her darkened mood chased away by the bright bark of his laughter.

Someone, probably poor Colin, had swept the snowfall away and the courtyard was packed with bodies as if to fight back the cold by passing heat to one another. Gideon shooed a pack of young soldiers from an archway near the fire, close enough that Lumen could feel the warmth thawing her bones but tucked away to leave them in shadow together.

"Stay," Gideon said, pressing a messy kiss to her mouth and then leaving her to hunt for food.

She earned no more than a few nods from the men around her. Wallins' punishment was ripe in their minds perhaps, or maybe Gideon was a threat enough on his own.

"Don't tell me you've come down from your high tower, milady."

Jennie Greer carried two mugs in one hand, her skirt high in the other, teasing glimpses of her legs to the men around her. As if she hadn't shown them as much and more dozens of times before. Perhaps the reminder was enough.

"My dragon demanded my company," Lumen said and smiled as Jennie snorted, taking the mug the woman offered her.

"We're no proper dinner party, that's for damned sure," Jennie muttered, squatting at Lumen's side in the archway.

"You say that as if you think I ever liked dinner parties."

Jennie gave her a sideways glance, lips twitching. "Better suited to the convents, you are. Shoulda left for one when you had the chance, milady."

Lumen wondered what the woman would think if she knew Lumen had that very same chance tonight. She watched Gideon weave his way back to her through the crowd, one heaping and steaming plate of food held above his head and out of reach of the men who made a joke of reaching. Behind him a brief flash of Westbrook appeared, face cast in orange firelight, eyes fixed to her as if he'd been watching the whole time.

"I don't think they have ale in the convent," Lumen mused and then took a quick gulp, grimacing at the sticky, tart flavor on her tongue.

Jennie choked on her own sip and then rose to answer a call for her to warm a soldier's thighs, just in time for Gideon to return. He held his arms out wide and Lumen huffed, climbing into his hold and perching on his lap.

"I said I'd feed you," he said, one eyebrow raised as she took the plate from him.

"I had a better idea," she said, mimicking his expression and tearing a piece of chicken free from the bone, raising it to his lips. "I'll keep my hands busy... and you keep yours occupied with their own pursuits."

Gideon grinned, teeth nipping at her fingers as he took the bite, tongue licking fat from her fingers. She shifted on his lap, curling one leg around his hip and the other over his legs, her skirt bunching over his lap. Their eyes locked, Gideon studying her, waiting for a flinch or a wince. She only smiled, eyes laughing as he ducked one hand beneath her hem, his eyes sliding down her face to watch her eat her own bite, sucking grease off her thumb.

"How much of that ale have you had, hmm?" he asked.

"Thank you for reminding me," Lumen said, reaching for the mug and taking a mouthful, nearly spitting it out as his hand beneath her skin pinched at the soft inside of her thigh.

"Wicked little ghost, give us a kiss," Gideon said, leaning in and breath licking against the skin of her throat.

She gifted him with one which quickly turned to two and then three, his fingertips only tracing lines up and down the insides of her legs until she was squirming closer in the hopes of forcing the touch. His mouth dragged over her jaw and down to her throat as laughter roared at the far side of the courtyard.

"We'll never get our fill at this rate," Lumen breathed, finding the plate again and nudging Gideon's head up, popping a slice of roasted potato between his lips.

He chewed it down and grinned at her, hand stroking up one thigh and then sliding against her sex, one fingertip poised at her entrance, another brushing against her clit.

"I certainly promise to see you have yours, Lady Fenn," he said with a sweet purr that roughened at the edges of the words.

Lumen circled her hips against his touch and took a bite of her own while she could, before Gideon became too determined to steal her breath from her chest.

THE ALE WAS as dry as ash on his tongue as Dominic watched Lumen drop the empty plate to stone, her arms circling Gideon Jones' neck. She tucked her face against her shoulder but Dominic could see the planes of her back shift with gasping breaths, could almost hear her in his own ear as if it was him she clung to now.

He had a running tally in his head, all the moments from the past few months he would erase if he were able. The moment they met, the night he first pressed her down to her bed beneath him, the night in the chapel, the boy's beating. How many did he have to erase before he could cross the stone tile of the courtyard and cover her back from prying eyes, kiss the throat she bared, take her up to his bed and refresh his memory of the scent of her skin flushed with arousal?

Gideon damned Jones could come too if he had to. He'd never hated the man until this moment and even now the anger was dimmed beneath a warped kind of gratitude for being able to witness her pleasure again.

He saw the exact second she came, wrapped in Gideon's embrace. The man lifted his head, smile triumphant, eyes fixed to her wilting frame as she shuddered and twisted on his lap and then softened. There was one brief glimpse of her face, tilted up to the moon above, eyes fluttering shut, and then she turned back to Gideon's chest.

Had she begged for more as she reached the end, or bit the words off behind full lips?

Gideon's mouth peppered kisses down the side of her pale throat and Dominic tasted her salt on his tongue. Sol had damned him.

Or was it the Mother Lune for defiling her sweetest devotee?

His eyes burned, dry with the blaze of the fire and refusing to break his stare. Lumen slipped from Gideon's lap, her cheek pressing to his, and reached for the mugs at their side. When Gideon moved to stand she stilled him with a touch on his shoulder. Dominic understood the power of that small hand, the weight of the faintest brush against his skin had reformed his will, his thoughts.

He tracked her to the casks of ale, men parting in her wake, their eyes averted. It was a lesson in learning how little his men had respected Finley, or how much they feared and loved Gideon.

He met her there, her back stiffening as he reached around her to turn the nozzle and fill her mugs. "You seem to be enjoying yourself this evening," he said and even to his own ear he could hear the bitter drop in the words.

"It is meant to be a celebration," she said, hunting for space to put between their bodies and finding herself pinned in place.

"Gideon has good in his intentions, but he's got no sense. Don't let him sweep you under."

Lumen turned, eyes as sharp and leaden as daggers and all Dominic could feel was relief he hadn't forgotten their color. "Since when do you play the voyeur, General?"

"Since you offer my eyes a feast," he said, adding with a frown, "This isn't you, Lumen."

Her lips pressed thin and her stare slid away, the wound those eyes left behind finally feeling its sting. "Who I am and what I do is none of your business."

"I know I gave you up—"

"No!" Lumen hissed, eyes wide and linked with his again. "Maybe. But that doesn't matter. I gave *you* up. And I don't intend to change my mind. Watch whatever you like but keep your opinions to yourself, Dominic."

His palms itched to catch her waist, to haul her back to his chest, carry her up to his room and remind her that in the Manor now, his desires were law.

She'd claw your eyes out. He smiled at the thought and found Gideon watching him from the other end of the courtyard. Yes. Lumen would do whatever damage she could on her own and

Gideon would finish him off for her when she'd had her fill. The boy, Colin, might lend a hand as well. And they would be right to.

One of the whores took the mugs from Lumen's hand and passed them to Gideon before dragging her to the fire. Music was coming from the old instruments in creaks and wavers but the women were already dancing, half performing and half relieving themselves from their physical duties. Lumen looked tired, circles beneath her eyes, her dress tied tight around her narrowing waist and still hanging loose. He wanted to take her up the stairs and tuck her into a bed for sleeping. He wanted to deliver decent meals to her table and all the stolen art back to the walls of her home.

I don't want her surrender, he realized. But he didn't know how to win anything else from a woman.

LUMEN ARCHED WITH A MOAN, and if she pointed the sound up at the crack in the wall that lead to Dominic's room, so be it. Gideon drew his fingers free of her still fluttering cunt, cleaning them with greedy sounds that left her blushing. She tugged at his locks and he huffed a laugh, mouth returning to her core until she pulled harder on his hair.

"Enough, enough, please Gid!"

"Tired already, little spirit?" He laughed and dropped kisses up her stomach with soft smacking sounds, on his way to her breasts, where he'd burned her skin earlier with scratches from his beard and nips of his teeth.

"Tired of waiting, Gideon," she said, waiting for his eyes to land on hers. "You said you like women to beg for you to fill them, yes? I am begging. Fuck me. Please, Gideon."

"Hush, hush," he murmured, but his body was frantic, hauling her up into his arms and moving her deeper onto the mattress from where she'd had her hips hanging over the edge against his waiting mouth.

He landed on top of her and Lumen wrapped her arms and

legs around him to keep him from lifting his weight away. The mattress was soft beneath her and she liked the dizzy, breathless feeling of being pinned.

"I worry I'll hurt you without... the others first," he said in her ear, low voice scratching.

Lumen rolled her hips beneath Gideon, the front of his trousers rough and warm against her pussy, his thick cock twitching at her teasing. She'd gestured his size to Jennie after she'd finally seen it and the woman, well versed in cocks by her own admission, had gasped and thrown a towel at Lumen's face, calling her a boastful liar. Gideon was huge and Lumen had appreciated his reluctance to push her limits. But she was out of patience.

"I know better than anyone how gentle you can be," Lumen assured him, kissing his chin and combing her finger through his mess of black hair. "Start slow."

Gideon shuddered and Lumen felt that same giddy power as when she'd taken him in hand and mouth until he made weak sounds and begged for release.

She let him pull away long enough to fumble at the waist of his pants, nearly tearing his feet through the knees in his eagerness to step out of them. At the sight of his fingers shaking she took his hand in hers, stretching her arms back behind her head to hang over the edge of the bed. Gideon's chest, dusted with dark curls and thick with muscle, swelled against hers, her breasts flattened between them.

His kisses were full of breath, his tongue licking against her lips, teeth pulling, mouth sucking. He was bare against her, stiff cock nudging and sliding against her slick lower lips. She shifted, trying to line him up, but he was too content to simply bump and grind them together until Lumen thought she'd have to beg again, or come again before he was inside of her. Her nails raked his back and her heels pressed against his ass, full and tight.

"Don't tease," she whimpered.

Gideon huffed and groaned. "Want to do right by you."

Lumen hadn't realized that there was a frantic, sharp-edged

urge digging in her until he spoke the words. She softened completely beneath him and took his face in her hands, taking soft pecking kisses.

"You do," she said.

Gideon shuddered and finally, finally, the head of his cock, seeping and sticky, was pressing inside of her. The stretch was a burn and she hadn't even taken him in yet. She thought for a moment she might not be able to and then he licked the roof of her mouth and took her tongue between his lips to suckle and she sighed, remembering to relax again. He popped inside, and Lumen moaned as he immediately began to buck, small little jerks and pushes forward.

One of his hands slid between them, thumb circling over her clit and they both hissed as she began to squeeze around his length.

"More," she whined in his ear and then her voice vanished as he thrust, filling her. Another thrust and his pelvis hit his thumb, bright pressure on her clit sending her over the edge. Gideon groaned in her ear as she came, body clutching all around him as she gasped and shook.

"Sweet lady," he said, fingers in her hand squeezing, face nuzzling to hers to leave wet kisses.

"Fuck me," she said on a sigh, still soaking up her aftershocks. But she rocked beneath him and Gideon grunted, answering the call and shaking the bed. "Yes, like that! Please, Gideon. I want you. Don't hold back."

The breath whooshed out of his chest and his lips smacked soft against her jaw, an answering roll of his hips for every kiss. He began to piston, body churning faster, mouth sucking on her pulse and a low roll of a growl vibrating against her chest. Lumen cried out and quickly begged for more. He felt like thunder in her veins, pounding inside of her, finally the animal again after weeks of playing the man.

"Yes! Yes! More, Gideon," she shouted, laughing without air in her chest as his sweet rumble grew louder and uneven, breaking with his pace.

This was what she wanted. To be taken by him, consumed, all

at her own demand. His arms circled her back, and then slid down to wrap his fingers like irons around her hips, holding her to take his thrusts. It went on and on, her praises and his rough needful noises in her ear as he gave up any pretense of control and only chased what felt good. When it was too much, too deep, too hard, and her body was made of white noise that was both ecstatic and painful, Lumen went limp, relaxing into the sensation.

Gideon arched above her, eyes wild and mouth slack, throat working. "Fuck! Lumen, lady, my little spirit." He babbled praises and the buzzing in Lumen's bones sharpened, cutting through the dull confusion and turning into a shocking relief, flourishing through her veins just as Gideon bellowed and filled her to bursting with hot rushes of release.

He carried on, riding her into the mattress, bed creaking, until he was nearly collapsed, only little reflexive nudges and jerks inside of her. Her legs were too weak to hold onto him and they slid to the sheets. She thought she might not be able to breathe if he remained there on top of her but her head was still spinning and bright little sparks were still chasing under her skin, curling her toes and spiraling up to her head.

He rolled, nearly pulling free of her, and dragged her to his chest with the motion. Lumen felt feverish, the fire high in the grate, her body warm from beer and dancing and sex. Gideon stroked fingertips down from her throat, between her breasts, to her stomach, making her twitch. He huffed a laugh.

"Can you forgive me for being a beast?" he asked, and she saw his grin from the corner of her eye.

"I think we are well-matched," she said, her cheek turned away as he snorted. Whatever she'd known of herself before the army arrived was gone now. She could match Gideon's hunger, and Dominic's rage. She had Finley's sickness too, not for opium but for these men.

"I think you are starshine itself," Gideon said, curling himself around her back and dressing her shoulders in kisses.

"Lady! Lady! Come look!"

Lumen rose to meet Colin at the back door, but he was already waddling inside, his shoulders laden with bags of goods. A cart waited outside the door and Lumen rushed to it, slippers soaking in the snow. There were sacks of grain waiting in the back and no driver in sight.

"Colin! Whose are these?"

"Ours! Better get it all inside 'fore it starts snowing again."

When she returned inside, her own arms aching with the weight of the goods, three golden jars with thick, crystalizing honey waited on the table. Her breath caught in her chest at the sight of them. Honey wasn't cheap and it was worse out of season.

"Colin, where did this all come from? The instruments can't have paid for this," she said. They'd made poor music when the soldiers played them, but no one minded when it was the first new entertainment they'd had for months.

"No, don't think so. General gave me the coin and the list," Colin said with a shrug.

Which ruled out her other thought, that the goods had been stolen from someone.

"Where did he get the coin?" she asked. Her chapel was safe when she checked it only hours ago.

"Dunno. Can you bake pies? There's meat in here and a good amount of fat too."

Lumen's mouth watered at the very words and she swallowed it down along with her questions. It was better not to know where the army's money came from. She would see the absences sooner or later. Maybe there had been a fine lamp in a corner somewhere, or an old collection of jewelry. So be it. She was starving and wearing thin. They all were.

Colin brought in the rest of the supplies, fresh cloth for bandages and the usual order of ale and cider, while Lumen organized the kitchen, her belly loud with the promise of food. When the meat hit the stove Lumen poured herself and Colin small cups of ale to distract them from trying to steal bites straight from the sizzling pan.

She was rolling dough out on the counter, listening to Colin's chatter and feeling warm and safe in her little corner of the Manor for once, when the back door creaked in, ice and snow falling around a dark shadow.

"Whatchu doing here?" Colin asked.

Oliver Spragg's head ducked inside, followed slowly by the rest of the man, his eyes skittering around the room as if he were waiting for the entire army to appear.

"Mr. Spragg?"

He stopped, brushing snow down to the floor from his knitted hat, staring at the warm oven with a frown on his face. Lumen's guilt followed quickly. She was celebrating her own good fortune with a full kitchen and allowed herself to entirely forget her tenants, suffering through the winter in their own homes.

"Supplies just came in," she said, the words weak on her tongue. She would bake loaves after the pies and sneak them to Oliver and Gretchen Ramsey and the Blythes.

"Ben Blythe is dead."

The announcement layered with her thoughts of the man and his wife, too close together to make sense. When confusion cleared, Lumen's jaw tipped slowly open as Oliver stared at her.

"Soldiers broke into the cottage last night," he added and there was something in his gaze, as if he were waiting for her confession. "Ben tried to fight them off and they roughed him a bit before his heart had enough."

She looked at Colin, eyes wide and vision blurring, and he only shook his head and shrugged. He may not even have known Ben Blythe if he passed him on the road.

"Sarah?" she croaked.

"With Gretchen Ramsey," Oliver said. "You didn't know?"

"Of course not!" Her head whipped in denial. "Of course not. Colin, go fetch Gideon."

The boy was out of the room in the stuttering beat of Lumen's heart and she stared after him, not hearing Oliver's steps approaching.

"What good will it do Sarah now?" Oliver asked, hovering close at her side.

"The men aren't allowed to run rampant," she whispered. "If Westbrook isn't aware, he should be. There will be... some kind of punishment for this. There has to be."

"Because you ask it of him?"

Lumen faced Spragg and stumbled back at the realization of how close he'd come, her head forced to tilt back to meet his gaze. "I don't buy favors."

Oliver looked at the meat burning on the stove and raised an eyebrow. "Don't you?"

"You should leave before Gideon gets here," Lumen said, teeth grinding together as she took another step away from the man.

"You should leave before you don't recognize yourself," Oliver answered, eyes narrowing.

She caught the sight of a fist clenched at his side and opened her mouth to remind him who she was, and who he was, and then let it fall shut again. She didn't know who she was anymore. Asking for her title after everything that had happened, everything she'd done, seemed more like a joke than any sincere deference.

Gideon's voice rumbled in the hall and for all of Oliver's daring when it came to speaking out of turn to her, he flinched at the sound of the man in the hall.

"I'll take you, Lady Fenn," he whispered, backing away to the door. "When you're ready to leave, you find me."

She pressed her lips together, her knuckles white around the handle of the rolling pin and watched him vanish out of the kitchen and into the swirling dark of evening and snowfall. Gideon appeared as the door clicked shut.

"You heard," he said, brows drawn together and hands shoved into the pockets of a coat she'd found for him—the sleeves were too short and the shoulders too snug and he looked near to bursting out of it but there were fewer holes than the last one.

"How long did you know?" she asked, taking the meat off the heat. She would make a shepherd's pie instead, maybe.

Ben Blythe is dead and I am still thinking about food.

She stumbled back, catching herself against a stool and sitting down as Gideon came closer, hands stretched out.

"Dom had already heard from some of the men. I caught Danvers and Charlie rounding up the ones responsible."

She sighed, resting her forehead against her flour crusted palms. So Oliver was wrong then, she hadn't needed to say a word.

"Dominic's got something in mind for them and then he'll send them to Meades. No local folk there for them to cause trouble with."

Her eyelashes brushed her skin as she blinked. Finley's new army. And they were without a Manor? A lady? She felt strangely jealous in a way that followed no logic. As if she could have had Meades' army instead of Westbrook's and none of the trouble. Except that wasn't how it worked.

"Where did the money come from, Gideon?" she said, not raising her eyes from her lap.

She heard his steps stutter as he came closer. "You don't think—"

"I don't know what else there's left in the Manor by now but it can't have paid for all of this!"

His steps creaked and his knees cracked as he knelt at her side. "Dom wrote back to the army, got the quarterly funds doubled." Gideon waited until she peeked at him around her fingers. "It takes a lot of ass kissing and a fair number of promises. He hates to do it."

Lumen didn't exactly care what Westbrook hated at that moment, she was only relieved to know the army wasn't stealing from her people to buy her honey. "I want something done for Sarah," she murmured.

"Who?"

She brushed his hands away from her face and sat up. "Ben Blythe's wife- his widow."

"Alright, little spirit. You tell me what and I'll take care of it."

"No. I will. She's my tenant." Gideon only murmured his agreement and anger rose high and hot in Lumen's face. She wanted to *fight*, not be placated. "Where's Dominic?"

At that at least Gideon had a reaction, his eyebrows raising as he swayed back on his heels. "Getting his hands dirty. Better if you leave him to it. This is the second step out of his law the company has taken and he won't go easy on the men."

Had crushing men's hands under his boot been considered a lax punishment? If he was sending these men on to Meades surely he'd leave them intact enough to carry a weapon.

Gideon raised a hand, holding it in the air between them when Lumen reared back, waiting for her to relax before stroking his thumb over her cheek. "I see that anger in you, my lady. I don't mind you letting it out on me but we're all better off if you keep it away from the General at the moment, hmm?"

She sighed and the tears she swallowed down, crawled back up into her eyes and fell free. Her arms looped around his neck and he drew her down into his lap.

"You take the sport out of fighting," she mumbled and Gideon huffed.

"Make some food for the woman and I'll take you on horse-back," he said.

Lumen pressed her lips to his cheek and he squeezed her briefly. "I'll hide some for us and Colin too."

THE WATER in the bowl was a familiar, vivid shade of red, Dominic's knuckles swollen and burning. Gideon had taken Lumen somewhere an hour or so ago, but even if she'd been in the Manor he couldn't imagine her tending to him. Not now.

He was beginning to understand what she hated so much about him. In the beginning he hadn't needed her to understand him as more than a rule to be followed. Somewhere in the mix he'd wanted her to see him as a man. But that wasn't who he was now. He was the General, the Stalor Army itself. She had every right to hate him.

Hadn't he been someone else once? Or was that so long ago, that person ceased to exist?

A door behind him creaked open and Dominic blinked at the bloodied water and turned to find her there, footsteps silent as she approached, her eyes on the tray in her hands. Remedy bottles and white bandages and that fearsome little needle kit she used to save his men's lives.

"I can manage," he said, wanting to throttle his head against the wall for the words.

But she and Finley had been right, she shouldn't have to put up with him if she didn't want to.

He tried again. "It... must be late by now. Take yourself to bed." No that was wrong too, still an order. "Gideon will be waiting for you."

The quick slash of her silver stare cut him off and he almost felt relieved that something had put a stop to his blathering.

"Sarah Blythe is staying with Widow Ramsey and her children. I want your men to stay well away from her cottage until she is ready to make a decision on what to do with it." Lumen set the tray down and pushed his foul basin of water away. She opened a bottle and the air was full of a sharp and minty scent as she doused cloth with clear liquid. She held one hand out and waited, her eyes fixed to her work until he laid his palm into hers.

"Fine," he said. It would be easier said than done to keep a group of soldiers from helping themselves to the cottage, that had always been a liberty he'd allowed them when they were stuck at length in an area. He'd see to it somehow.

"I want to know when you're going to take the army to the battlefield again," she continued and then pressed the soaked cloth to his bleeding knuckles, pressing hard when he nearly yanked his hand away at the violent burn. He growled and it died abruptly as he caught the twitch of her lips in a brief smile.

"Why?"

"I want to hold a funeral for Ben in the chapel. It'd be better if none of you were here."

He blinked. Right. The silver, lining the walls of the chapel, still a secret from his army.

"Very well. Tell me when it would suit you and your people to have the funeral and I'll take the men to the field." Have Gideon come up with a chore for his hired women too, send them to a village or out to cheer on the men.

Lumen looked up, and he wanted to raise his palm to her cheek, smooth away her frown and cover the dark circles under her eyes, but his left hand was bleeding too, oozing down to the table top.

"That can't be how war works," she said, lines creasing over her forehead.

He was an idiot but he couldn't help feeling happy to be standing here with her this way—speaking, touching—even if he was fairly certain she was being rougher on him than medicine strictly called for.

"It isn't," he said. "But I don't know if you can call these past ten years a war. I'll take the men out for a battle when you ask. It should give you plenty of time for whatever service you can manage." Without a priestess. Without much of a congregation. "What will you do with the body?"

"Take it to the woods," Lumen said, raising an eyebrow as he reared back. "The ground is frozen so there'll be no burial. Lunars don't mind leaving themselves to the earth and our Mother's creatures."

To the earth, to the buzzards, and the wolves. And here he'd thought Sol was bloodthirsty. The supposed Mother Lune was no less dark in her demands.

"Does this hurt?" she asked, and then if he hadn't watched her pinch his middle finger softly, he would've sworn she'd taken a hammer to it. He bellowed, body twisting in response to the pain, and Lumen hummed. "You fractured your finger. It'll have to be wrapped."

He breathed through his teeth as the pain subsided in slow throbs that echoed up to his skull. "Witch," he muttered, and wished he could take the word back as her face went pale and her lips pursed thin. She didn't answer the tease and he thought swallowing his tongue might be a mercy, or at least a distraction from her brutal care to his hand.

SARAH BLYTHE'S FINGERS WRAPPED AROUND HERS LIKE A VICE AND Lumen clung to the woman just as fiercely. There should have been music, a priest singing, dozens of voices carrying the prayer together as one. Instead it was only a handful of them left. Gretchen Ramsey and her children, Oliver Spragg, Sarah, Lumen, and two older widows who shared a cottage together. Their prayers were broken and stumbling, as if they were all too out of practice to do the words justice.

Dominic had kept his promise, taking the men out to the battlefield and the women along as nurses. Lumen had gathered every last candle and stick of incense to burn around Ben Blythe's body, and she handed the children the strings of bells that would usually be rung during the prayer. The sound was close enough and the bright babbling chatter of the younger child brought a smile to Sarah's lips again.

"Oh, little moon, I have missed the chapel," Sarah whispered, fingers clutching tighter.

Lumen swallowed hard around the lump in her throat. "I've been too afraid to open it," she whispered, careful to speak low enough that Oliver wouldn't hear the admission.

Sarah nodded slow and steady, a shadow passing over her eyes. "I understand. I wonder if those men wouldn't benefit from a little bit of our Mother's shadow. Something to cool those mean tempers."

The statue of Lune stood, watching over Ben in the quiet of their audience together.

"I never thought of Mother Lune and Sol as foes," Lumen mused. "I don't see why our armies seem to find them so."

Sarah scoffed, her small nose wrinkling, eyes narrowing so tight Lumen wondered how she could see at all. "They only put their symbols on their flags. They don't follow their laws, do they? Why, when I was a young girl, Sol and Lune were lovers."

Lumen startled and stared at the old woman who grinned. "I never heard that story."

"Mmm, lovers," Sarah repeated, head nodding and gaze wandering. She was quiet long enough that Lumen thought that might be the end and beginning of her tale, or maybe she was only starting to nod off. And then she brightened and spoke again. "They have their own kingdoms of course. Their own duties to perform. But they meet in the morning and in the evening, sit at their table together, or their wedding bed, depending on what kind of story you're listening to," the old woman said with a wink.

Someone, one of the widows, cleared their throat at the back of the room, and Sarah's voice hummed to quiet, her vision foggy again.

Sol and Lune together, as lovers or spouses. The idea spun in Lumen's head and she thought of the moment in the courtyard, where she and Colin had seen the sun and moon meeting through windows in the evening.

"I'm ready, I think," Sarah said, one tear rolling into the wrinkles over her cheek. "Let's take him now."

Lumen nodded, twisting in her seat to look back to Oliver Spragg and nod. The chapel filled with smoke as one by one the candles were blown out. She and Oliver carried Ben in his bedding out to the small boat on the pond, followed by the women and the faint sound of children's fingers twitching silver bells.

She rowed the boat over the pond, Oliver breaking ice and pushing it away with a shovel. She kept her eyes fixed on the setting sun bleeding through the trees.

"I'm sorry for the way I spoke, Lady Fenn," Oliver whispered over the water, ice groaning as it was shoved aside.

Ben's body stretched between them, shrouded in white cloth, reminding Lumen of her brother's winter burial, her mother's. Given back to Mother Lune and her hungry scavengers.

"I wouldn't want my poor words to prevent you from trusting me to see you safely back into Oshain," he added.

"I understand, Mr. Spragg," she said, preferring they didn't speak at all.

Either he understood or simply ran out of apology because he kept silent for the rest of the trip. They carried Ben deeper into the woods, well out of sight of the shore, far away from any ignorant soldier's steps, unwrapping his body until the shroud blended into the snow on the ground. Lumen frowned at the bruises still marring the old man's chest, her vision blurring, and she turned her back on the sight.

"Let's get back. The army could return soon and I need to lock the chapel."

Oliver followed her in silence and they made it back to the Manor before the sun died on the horizon. She took her tenants into the kitchen where she'd saved small bottles of cider to be shared, and enough hand pies for seconds. When the Ramsey children began to doze at the table Lumen saw her people back to the front doors, army torches high and distant down the road.

"Thank you, little moon," Sarah whispered, pressing a dry kiss to Lumen's cheek, and wrapping her in a brittle hug.

Lumen locked the chapel and made it to the infirmary before the army reached the doors, supplies laid out and waiting for her since the morning.

"Don't see the damn point in going out at all if the General won't give us orders to break lines and push the damn border."

Lumen finished tying off a bandage, trimming the ends neatly and sharing a brief smile with the soldier.

"Don't see the damn point in having a General who ain't

interested in winning a battle," another soldier answered.

She busied herself with tidying her things on the table, listening to the hushed conversation of the soldiers recovering in beds behind her.

"He used to be," the first voice said, quiet following before he added, "You think he's waiting for Brink to get back?"

"If this were about Brink, we'd have moved on weeks ago before the healer left," his friend answered.

"You're right."

"It's her," someone hissed, and Lumen stood bolt upright, the voices dying off.

"There you are, little spirit."

She whirled, watching Gideon limp his way across the floor, the eyes of other men shifting away from her with every step he took.

"This sorry bunch looks as well as can be expected," Gideon said, smile warm on his face. "Better'n they deserve."

The injuries had been minor, it was true. She wondered what the Oshain army looked like after a day like this, imagined if she were across the border with Oliver. Would she be a nurse? It would be a good use of her skills and give her a position other than Lady of a Manor on the wrong side of the border. She doubted her title would buy her more than basic courtesy this long into a war, and she didn't have any possessions left to bargain with. But if she left her Manor she wouldn't want a new home, only something to keep her busy and her mind off the one she'd left behind.

It was the furthest she'd thought yet on the idea of leaving.

"Look at you, falling asleep where you stand," Gideon said.

"What happened to your leg?" Lumen said, shaking off her distraction and eyeing Gideon for any bloodstains she might have missed in the first wave of the army's return.

"Pulled muscle, that's all. Promise," he said, wiggling his brows. "You eaten?"

She nodded. It'd been hours since the little hand pies in the kitchen, surrounded by her tenants, but there was never enough food to spare so it would have to do.

"Up to bed with us, then," Gideon whispered, his hands wrapping around her shoulders and tugging her to his chest.

Lumen caught sight of a pair of soldiers, like the ones who'd been speaking earlier, ducking their gazes to a set of cards on a low table between their beds. She followed Gideon up to their room, her fingers linked with his.

"How was the wake?" Gideon whispered in her ear as they neared their door.

She hummed and shrugged. "Peaceful. How was battle?"

Gideon huffed, head rolling on his shoulders and neck cracking. "Peaceful isn't the word. But I've seen worse, I suppose."

She opened the door and stepped inside, watching Gideon cross in front of her, his shoulders shrugging out of his coat and letting it hit the floor in a heap, arms already pulling his shirt off over his head. There were fresh bruises, nasty webs of purple spreading out over his right rib, and little sharp fingerprints along another shoulder. She locked the door behind her and ducked out of the way of his reaching arms to go to the cupboard where she'd stashed some of the stronger salves.

Gideon grinned at her and she raised an eyebrow, waiting for him to strip down his pants too, revealing a whole rainbow running down the calf of the leg he'd been avoiding using.

"Pulled muscle, hmm?"

"Strained," he said. "Horse, I think."

"On the bed."

He huffed, arms stretching over head and body twisting, drawing a startled grunt of pain from his lips, as if he hadn't realized his ribs were bruised before now.

Lumen laughed as he hunched, one hand cupped over the spot. "Quit showing off and stretch out on the bed, Gid."

"I'd rather stretch out on you, little spirit," he said with a wink, but he went to the bed and followed her orders, and she smirked at the sight of him. A bear in the clothes of a man, some moments more well-disguised than others.

Her own dress hit the floor not long after and Gideon gave it a hopeful glance as she climbed on after him, starting at his legs. The salve smeared into his skin, oily and thick, making the dark hairs stand on end, and she worked in tender circles around the spot, watching his back to see if he flinched when she pressed too hard.

"You should stay off this for awhile," she said and he only grunted. 'Should' was barely a suggestion to Gideon, more like a passing thought. "And watch your ribs. They might be fractured and that's the fourth time the same spot has been badly hit."

"It is?" He stretched his neck enough to glance to her. "Must be missing something in my fighting."

"If you aren't careful you'll be missing a lung. Rest a few days."

"I get bored. Can't help it."

Mother Lune, he sounded like Colin. Just a little boy in a giant's body, mad with impatience and energy.

Lumen sighed as if very weary—it didn't take *much* pretending, she was weary. "I'll have to think of ways to keep you occupied then."

Gideon rumbled, back twitching, and then hissed as she dug her thumb into a tangled knot of muscle on the back of his thigh. She scooted up the bed to his side and started on the next bruise. "Is it normal to fight so much and... make so little progress?"

She studied the twitch of the muscles in his back, the pause of his breath, and then the way he relaxed as she soothed her palm down his spine.

"Everytime we move the line, it goes a little different. Oshain's digging their heels in to keep what they have left, that's for sure."

Can you blame them? she thought but didn't say aloud.

"Suppose this is a long wait," he mumbled, and she could see his cheek, soft on his folded hands, eyelids limp and drowsy. "Less fighting than usual too. But it's cold up here. Don't know how you stand this place in the winter."

Did he mean the Manor or the north? It didn't matter.

"How long do you think it will be before you leave?"

He stiffened again, eyes popping open, flicking to her. She focused on her work on his back, smoothing through muscles that'd gone too long without care, bruises so layered upon one another she wondered if they'd ever finish healing.

"You sick of me, already?" he asked, and for the first time she thought he had to force his grin.

"That's not what I'm asking," she said, reaching up into his hair, scratching at his head and waiting for his smile to soften. "But that's the army's goal, isn't it? To push North and take the rest of Oshain."

"I s'pose," Gideon said, stare going distant, brow furrowing. He pushed up onto his elbows and then rolled to his side and Lumen took a moment to appreciate the full sight of him in front of her, ugly and beautiful all at once, brutal and darling in his way. "Lumen. You'd come with me, wouldn't you?"

She blinked, vision clearing of affection and replaced with confusion. "With you?"

"When we win this land and march north, you'll be with me," he said.

Lumen swallowed the urge to repeat herself. "Leave the Manor and come to... to war?"

The puzzle of the idea was there on his face too, as if he understood that it made no sense but couldn't imagine it any other way. She couldn't imagine it at all. Wasn't it bad enough that the war had come to her door? Did that bind her to it, forced to follow even after it was done with her home?

Gideon reached a finger up, grin growing as he tapped at her cheek. "I won't take you onto the field with me."

"Gideon... I—"

She didn't have the faintest idea of how to explain all the thoughts racing through her head, hanging on the tip of her tongue. It was sinking in slow and heavy that Gideon had no notion that she was only... surviving the army's residence in the Manor. She didn't want to leave with them, she just wanted to make it to the day they *did* leave and watch their backs as they went.

"Not sure how it would work yet, either, tell the truth," he said, but he looked as if he were enjoying the thought as a daydream.

She lifted her hand to his and threaded her fingers through. "I'm not sure I would know how to... to travel the way you do, Gideon. To live in a tent or—"

He laughed, bright and cheerful. "No, I suppose you don't, lady."

But she had made him promise, hadn't she? She'd made him swear he wouldn't leave. She'd meant it... well, not like this.

"I should stay here, at the Manor," Lumen said slowly, watching as his smile fell and his laughter died. She licked at her lips, an offer in her throat that she wasn't sure if she meant sincerely. But it came out. "You'll come back, Gideon. When the war is done."

Twin creases appeared between his eyebrows and they sat together in silence and she knew in his own way he was finding all the ways those words didn't fit together.

"When the war is done..." he echoed.

The war that had been crawling its way north for nearly two decades. Would Gideon even survive to see the end of that? She hadn't seen him fight, but she'd seen the state he came back from battle in. He wasn't trained to live to an old age, he was trained to burn through an army. Sooner or later that fire would run out.

"This is why we haven't pushed north," he whispered, taking her in with a long, thorough stare. His knuckles brushed over her cheekbone, down to her jaw, carrying her hand with his. "Can't take our lady to the battlefield, can't bear to leave without her."

Lumen's heart burned in her chest, skin flushing at his words, and anger rising up her throat until she thought Gideon must be able to see it catching fire in her eyes.

"Back onto your stomach," she said, voice bound in her chest so only a whisper released. "Let me finish your bruises."

He was subdued by his own discovery, rolling onto his stomach without a word of teasing or seduction. Lumen returned to her work, head full of his words, fingers tight and wishing for a different neck to wrap around and *strangle*.

THERE WAS A LIST GROWING AT THE BACK OF HER MIND-- candlesticks, tea sets, furniture, jewelry, on and on it went. And now this, her father's collection of books. She wondered, with a detached numbness, how many meals those books had bought her. As many as she spent summer days in the gazebo reading their pages? No, not that many, maybe if she counted the entire army's stomachs.

"Lu- Lady Fenn."

She waited for the creak of the floorboards beneath his feet, for the scuff of his boots against the carpets.

"If this is about the books—" he said when she remained quiet.

"If I asked you to take the army out to the battlefield again, would you?"

There it was, a little whisper of movement at her back. She kept her eyes on the bare shelves in front of her.

"For the new moon? I don't see why not."

Her jaw hurt and her eyes stung and her nails bit into the flesh of her palms where she crossed her arms in front of her.

"And if I asked you to go and fight tomorrow?"

"I don't—"

"And the day after that? And all the days between now and the new moon and all the days after?"

His steps stopped, near enough for that familiar shedding heat to kiss the skin at the back of her neck.

"I'm afraid I miss your meaning, Lady Fenn."

She turned, forced herself to look at him even as her heart rioted in her chest. The sun was sharp through the window, sparkling over the dust still floating in the room, as if it had yet to recover from the loss of the books.

"Why hasn't your company moved on?" she asked, watching those coal eyes narrow, noting the hollows of his cheeks were deeper too now. He was as hungry as his men, at least. As hungry as her.

"I imagine you can thank the Oshain army for our progress or lack thereof," he said, jaw ticking, his tongue dealing the words in razor-edged doses.

"Hasn't this house paid for enough by now?" Lumen breathed the words, body shaking. "Haven't I?"

"Finer homes than yours have been scorched to the ground in this war," Dominic ground out. "If you think what follows after my army will be any easier for you to bear, you are mistaken. If you think Stalor will leave you with your title—"

"I want my life, Dominic! I want what little of my home and my people you've left me. Why won't you go?"

He rushed at her and she didn't care that her courage failed her in the face of his fury. She stumbled back, body bowing away from him as he caught her on the edge of the desk.

"Because you won't be there," he said, his face torn with tangles of anger but the words so quiet it was as if he were trying to trap them in silence. Once they were out, all the tension in him leaked away, shoulders sagging and the red flush of anger fading, revealing skin gray with exhaustion and a flat expression. "You can bid me to the battlefield every morning, if you wish, Lady Fenn, but until I land on someone's sword I think my feet will only carry me in one direction at the end of the day."

She was mute, trapped to the desk, skin scorched with his nearness, her fingernails digging into wood grain as he traced her face with his stare, her throat and shoulders, on and on past the collar of her dress.

"I know this is only a burden on you," he said, and she heard the apology in his tone although it was made useless by his words. "I was comfortable in the knowledge of how my life would end until I met you and now I... I can't stop myself from taking the smallest piece of relief I've found. Even if it is only a glimpse of you." He was inches away and she held herself as still as stone as he closed the distance, rough cheek sliding against hers. "The hints of your smell in the halls. The sound of you at night as I try to claw myself closer to that damned crack in the wall."

She shut her eyes on the blurry picture of his black clad shoulder in front of her nose. "There is nothing kind in caging me in my own home for your weak comforts, sir."

"I'm not asking for forgiveness, Lumen. Or even understanding."

"Then what?"

The conversation was barely more than the impression of words for how soft they spoke. When iron brand fingertips settled around her ribs, Lumen both knew and refused what was coming next.

"A reprieve," Dominic breathed, his mouth against her jaw.

She resisted the first kiss, the faint nudge of his lips below her ear. By the second her lungs were flooded with his smell, salt and fire and blood, his tongue tasting at her pulse. The anger in her belly stirred with the warmth of his nearness and her head was heavy and clouded as he sighed against her throat, the both of them waiting for the other to break the moment. His hands slid against her sides, forming to her ribs and Lumen couldn't tell where her heart's hurt ended and her body's betraying joy at having him close once more began.

The tip of his nose stroked down the length of her neck, drawing an involuntary shiver up her spine and her eyes flicked open as he kissed the hollow of her throat, thumbs brushing over the bottom curve of her breasts.

There's no victory in this, she thought. And then Dominic sucked a trail over her collarbone, sparks dancing in her chest, racing down to her core, flooding her head. No victory, but there was pleasure. She wasn't foolish enough to think it would last, but every other moment now was a battle between sacrifice and the greedy hoarding of one good feeling.

Lumen would take what she could get.

He nearly jumped as her hands landed at the back of his neck, as if he expected the violence she'd been weighing in her mind. Taut muscles shuddered under her touch as she cupped her hands around the back of his head, spine curving backwards, body pressed to his in offering. His moan sank into her skin and his lips and teeth transformed from reverent to hungry, clutching and soothing and claiming the space from one shoulder to the next.

She rose to her toes, perching herself on the edge of the desk, and shifted against the wall of him until her knees framed his thighs, making room for him to press his cause against her.

"Lumen, I—"

Her hands turned to claws, tearing him away from her skin and biting his words off, her teeth against his lips, tongue turning him away from speech and into wordless cries, muffled in the hollow of her mouth. She grasped the collar of his coat, drawing him hard against her, thought of stripping him bare. His fingers clutched at her hips, fixing her like a vise around his waist.

A small, passive voice at the back of her mind wished he would push and push and push, so that later she could look at the event and think of it as his fault. But he only clung to her, followed the urge of her kiss, and she knew that whatever came next would be her fault.

She left his coat on, sliding her hands between them to undo the front of his pants. His lips tore from hers and she snapped at his jaw before he could speak.

"Don't say anything," she warned. "Not if you want this."

She drew back, met his gaze, saw the fold of worry on his forehead, the flash of irritation in the depth of his eyes as they flicked over her face. And then she reached inside his trousers and teased her fingers down to his base, wrapping him in her hold, seeing the surrender fall over his face as his lips parted and a sigh rushed out. She pumped his length in her hand and he groaned and then shook himself, hands scrambling to gather her dress up and out of the way.

"Wait, wait," he breathed, hands shaking on her thighs and she pushed his pants down far enough and drew the tip of him to her entrance.

She opened her mouth to warn him again, the wiser part of her mind screaming in the background of her thoughts and the warmth of him barely drowning good sense out, but he caught her lips before she finished the thought. His thumb hooked in the shoulder of the dress dragging it to the side and pushing it down, his lips following, sucking and licking and biting until her hands and head were distracted. She arched up into the caress as he built a bruise on her shoulder, his fingers working at the back of her dress until he shoved her bodice down, breasts falling free. He hooked her by the laces at her back pulling her body into a curve and trailing his lips down to her breasts, her arms trapped in her sleeves, shoulders falling into piles of notes and papers.

She lifted herself, offering her skin, and he growled against her breast, "You thought I forgot your tastes, witch?"

His cock nudged at her entrance and Lumen relaxed, stretching her thighs, begging him to fill her. This was what she wanted, this dulling consumption of Dominic above her, teaching and reminding her body that it was designed to take satisfaction from him. He slid his length over her slit, soaking himself with her arousal with every stroke until she was rocking and tilting herself, broken begging grunts cracking through her lips.

It was better if there were no words, she thought, no admission of the act. Except the more control she offered him, the more she craved he would claim, and the harder it was to set the terms.

"You thought I forgot the way your breath catches as I fill you?" he asked, and then he was pressing in and she was choking, eyes staring up at the beamed ceiling, cobwebs clinging and catching light in their strands.

Her eyes shut as he stretched above her, his fist at her back raising her up, forcing their bodies against one another. His lips pressed to her ear and her hands slid of their own accord up the length of his back beneath his coat.

"Did you think I forgot how to make you moan too?" He twisted his hips, cock pumping inside of her, his groin rubbing at her clit. She bit her lips and all he got was a whimper for his efforts and the retaliation of her clutching his length inside of her, making him gasp against her neck.

Dominic turned her face to his, all the argument melting in a kiss too tender. She wanted to fight, not blend together in this old memory of their nights together. She forced herself up, nails tearing into his shirt, teeth digging into his bottom lip, hips kicking and calling for a faster rhythm. His breath broke in the kiss, one arm wrapped around her shoulder and the other gripping at a thigh, digging his thumb into the crease between leg and cunt.

"Give me what I want," she whispered and it was his voice that moaned in response.

His thrusts turned quick and hard and she swallowed his groan with her tongue twisting around his, the slap of their skin pounding straight up into her head, drowning out the whispers of oncoming regret. His thumb burrowed over her mound, hunting for her clit, a grunt of victory as she hiccuped and whined in relief at the pressure. His touch was uneven, all their focus on the rutting pace of his cock inside her, lips parted and voices breaking against the kiss.

The desk creaked, feet scratching at the floor as Dominic raced her to a high, lunatic point of pleasure, equal parts demanding her surrender and declaring his devotion. Their breaths muddied together and Lumen squeezed her eyes shut as the fire in her core blazed brighter, arms and legs clasped around her- her enemy... He found his pace, found the pattern of touch which turned her helpless, found the press and push that dragged her over the edge, and she came with a shivering cry, tears slipping out of the corners of her eyes. He licked them away as she clenched around him, trying to bury her face into his neck, to disappear into his skin while he drove himself faster and deeper as if he were trying to do the same.

She kissed his pulse and Dominic came with a groan, pushing her down against the desk as he bucked and shuddered to his finish, heat flaring in her still fluttering core.

His fingers were in her hair, lips against her temple kissing and kissing, over and over again, body still rocking even as he hissed, oversensitive and sore. She buried her nose against his skin as they went still but for heaving breaths brushing their chests together.

I wish he were someone else, she thought. Or that I was only one of Gideon's hired women.

"Come back to me," he whispered.

Her hands slid away from his back, legs falling down till her toes brushed the floor, and she turned her face away from the rich scent of him.

"No," she said.

He huffed, a thick, wet sound like a sob trapped in his chest. His palms braced the desk and he pulled out of her, Lumen wincing at the stark, empty feeling and the sting of use. Black curls of hair rested on her chest, his lips grazing at her breast.

"Then what was this for?" he asked.

Me, she thought. *I wanted this and I hated it.*

"Your reprieve," she said.

He growled, one fist thumping at the desk near her head, but there wasn't any energy left in her to flinch, not until he tore himself away from her, storming to a window and leaving her cold and exposed in the center of the room.

She let herself remain bared for a minute, waiting for the cold air to chase away the last flavor of him, and then flicked her skirt down over her knees, shrugging the shoulders of her dress back up, loose and stretched.

"You were right," she said, sitting up. "But it isn't Gideon I'm losing myself to."

"If it's him you want, or Finley—"

"I want my home, Dominic," she said, sudden and cracking

through the room. "I want you to leave. Take them with you. Before there's nothing left. Please. Please."

She rose up from the desk, felt his release slipping out of her, sticky and hot on her skin. The doorway was too far away, offering him time to volley back at her.

"You let Gideon poison himself on those wood berries and you let me poison myself on tastes of you, parceled out in kisses and touches," he said to the window.

Her lips gaped, fists straining at her side. It was like carving herself open to show her veins and organs and bones to an audience of the blind. She moved to the door, legs shaking beneath her with every step, her hand grasping around the doorframe to steady herself.

The world wasn't fitting together. She was somewhere outside of herself, still spread over the desk trying to sacrifice her skin for mercy or claim one mouthful of relief to bide her through the next hour. Or was she still facing Dominic's back, wondering how she could speak a truth and the words never be heard?

Men were down in the courtyard, filling the world with the sounds of arguing, covering the softer murmurs from the women. Lumen slid along the cold wall of the Manor hall, fingernails scratching over stone. She wished it were summer so she could go and throw herself into the lake, wash away the mistake she'd just made. And she thought of the ice on the water, what it might be like to fall beneath it and let it seal over her head, finally finding peace.

She made it as far as her mother's workroom before sobs tore at her lungs, silent and screaming. The room spun and her vision was black, breathing too much at once or not at all. She hit the floor on her palms and knees, back bowing as she gasped and retched dry heaves.

I think my feet will only carry me in one direction at the end of the day.

The sound in her mouth was all wrong, too long and low and circling around and around in her ears as she shook her head and tried to refuse the understanding building in her head.

He would not leave. Not until he was dead. And he had some kind of sun curse hanging around him. She could smell it in the air that trembled over his skin, some promise of Sol's to keep the man alive as long as he continued to fight and bleed and burn for Stalor. Or not for Stalor. Just the sake of it.

Stone scratched into Lumen's skin as she shattered one little piece at a time onto the floor, sobs bursting from her lips too fast to be controlled, no breath in her lungs. Her hands scrabbled, hunting for something to hold onto as her body quaked and twisted. And then there was too much at once, and nothing left inside of her, and she thought her spasming heart might give away and let her finally rest.

"Oh, Lady! Hush, hush."

Small hands skimmed her heaving back and tears slid into her open mouth, eyes swollen and sealed shut. Colin.

"It's alright, Lady. It's alright."

Lumen tried to speak and all that came was a cross between a shriek and a moan.

"I'll go get Jones," the boy said. Her hand flailed and he caught it in his as she shook her head, strain burning in her neck. "Alright. Okay. I'm here, Lady. I'll stay with you."

It was harder to stop crying once you'd let yourself start and Lumen thought her chest might open into some gory chasm, relieve the pressure buried there. Colin's fingers ran through her hair, down her back. He tidied the laces of her dress and Lumen wept fiercer for his gentleness until she couldn't breathe and was forced into gasping and choking.

Slowly the choking turned to breathing, broken up by more bouts of sobbing, until Lumen's stomach was sore and her face was wet with tears and snot. Colin wiped it all away with the sleeves of his coat as she curled around him like a cat that'd been too foolish to keep itself from getting kicked by the horse.

"It's alright, Lady," Colin murmured again when her face was cleaned and her dress was put to rights and her body was too weak to carry on in the same painful upheaval. "You just tell me who it was and I'll have them cut in slivers 'fore you can say 'piss.'"

She hiccuped, head shaking and cheek scraping against the floor.

"They don't deserve you, Lady," he said, and he bent and kissed her hair, smoothing strands away from her face.

"I'm- Don't call me that," she rasped, her fingers curling around the hem of his pants. "I'm not a Lady, Colin. I'm not a good person. Don't admire me—I don't deserve it."

Colin hummed, a small sound, and Lumen closed her eyes as he petted down her shoulder again, the touch too sweet, snagging at her heart. "You are. You do. It's alright. You're *my* Lady."

She whined and curled closer and he carried on, soft touch and words, until she fell asleep there on the floor.

LUMEN WOKE IN THE AIR. NO, IN A PAIR OF FAMILIAR ARMS, THE scent of the stables in her nose, Gideon's chest against her cheek. Clouds painted red streaked across the sky above the courtyard and she closed her eyes again at the first sound of voices below. Her body was sore and her head was thick and she was so... so *tired*. The bedroom door creaked open and the room was warm, a fire spitting behind the grate.

Gideon spread her over the bed, pausing as she brushed her fingers over the back of his hand in a silent greeting. He managed undressing her with hardly any effort on her part, handling her as if she were the most fragile doll. She shivered as he peeled her shift away, rough fingers touching briefly against the mess on the inside of her thighs. When he brought over a bowl of clean water and a soft cloth Lumen wondered what he had heard and from whom.

"Will you let me clean you up a bit?" he asked, voice heavy and quiet.

She nodded and pulled herself up on wobbling legs, standing in front of him as he sat on the bed and washed her in gentle sweeps until she was damp and cool and her head was clearer. It wasn't the deep scrubbing and scratching of her skin she wanted but Gideon's care was more soothing than any bath she could remember.

"Found this for you," he said, and he pulled a clean shift off the edge of the bed.

She stared at it and it took too long to remember her other clothes that remained tucked away in the room Dominic used. Gideon pulled the linen over her head and she held his hands as her arms slid through the sleeves. He squeezed her fingers and Lumen barely recognized the man in front of her, so solemn and still.

"Did he hurt you?" he asked.

She shook her head and tried to swallow down the fresh spring of tears that threatened to break. Her eyes already hurt from crying.

"Did he force you?"

"No. I made it happen," she said, and then she climbed onto Gideon's broad lap and let his arms block the rest of the room out.

He sighed, chest shifting against her. "I didn't relish the thought of killing him, but I wouldn't break my promise to you, little spirit."

Lumen shut her eyes and wondered if she could ask Gideon to kill Dominic for the sole cause of wanting the army out of her house. If she did, and Gideon agreed, it would likely only end with the pair of them dead as well.

"Whatever you want, I'll make it yours. You know that, don't you?" Gideon's hands passed up and down her back. "I'll ride out to Meades and drag Finley back here by his boot laces, if you like. I'll keep Dom on his knees for you too if that's what you want, though I don't think it'd take much from me."

"I don't want that. Either of those," Lumen said, shaking her head.

He hummed and tilted them slowly down onto the bed. "I only want to give you a reason to smile again."

She traced a pattern against the fabric on his chest, fingertip spiraling over his heart and smearing rays out from the center. "I wish the war would end," she whispered.

Gideon stilled beneath her. "End?" As if the thought had never occurred to him. "We've got a long road into Oshain before the war ends," he said.

Lumen wondered what words it would take to make Gideon

understand.

I would hunt you through the woods, my lady, before I let you escape from me, he'd said it to her and then gentled when she didn't let his rough edges intimidate her. But was it still true? What if Dominic wasn't the only one who'd drag battles into years just to trap her life against his?

"I'll fight harder if that's what you want, little spirit."

Her fingers dug into his shoulders and her eyes slammed shut, the picture of Gideon sprawled over a stretcher, bleeding and broken, scorched inside her mind.

"No. No stitches, remember? How about a little supper up here though?"

He kissed the top of her head and ruffled her hair in thick fingers. "That I can manage. Get yourself under those covers before you freeze and I'll be back with an army's fortune of hot food in a minute."

He leapt up from the bed, dumping her into the sheets and surprising the softest laugh up out of her chest. She brushed her hand over his grin and then bundled herself beneath the blankets to wait.

GIDEON WAS out of the bed so early the next morning Lumen barely remembered his goodbye, although she woke up with the bruise of a suckled kiss on her wrist that must have been from him. Colin was in Gideon's place on the bed, snoring louder than any of her other bed partners, legs and arms collecting every inch of available space. She watched him until the picture of his little body at peace led her back into her own sleep.

The next time she woke up she found Colin watching her and the smile she shared wasn't forced or half-hearted.

"I thought they always took you with them," she said.

Colin nodded and then shrugged and stretched as far as he could in the bed. "They do, but your man said I was to stay here with you." Colin looked at her and blinked. "I'm not stupid so I said 'yes, sir.'"

Lumen wondered vaguely which one was 'her man' and hoped he meant Gideon.

"It's the solstice today," he said.

Lumen pushed herself up on the mattress and squinted at the shaded window. She'd missed dawn by now.

"What do Lunars do for winter solstice?"

"When I was little there was a feast and the Manor was full and I was allowed to stay up as late as I could keep my eyes open," she said watching Colin's expression brighten. She flicked honey blond strands of hair out of his eyes and then smiled as he shook his head on the pillow and they fell right back.

Yes, it was Gideon who'd told the boy to stay at the Manor today. Something to make her smile. And she would be sure to share it with him later.

"Oliver can catch birds in the woods," Colin said. "He could bring us some and we could have a feast too, Lady."

Lumen swallowed the first words that came to mind, that it was illegal for Oliver to poach birds from her land. It was her brother's voice in her head instead of her own. She didn't care if Oliver was catching birds to eat, it was better than she could do for her people at the moment and she certainly wasn't hunting them herself.

Instead she cocked her head and narrowed her eyes at the boy. "How do you spend so much time with Oliver Spragg?"

"He goes out to the west woods," Colin said, shrugging and waving his arms in the sheets as if he were swimming in the bedding. "Soldiers don't go out that way but the trees are better for climbing. He catches rabbits too. I can run and tell him to bring some and we can have ourselves a proper feast."

Lumen didn't think Oliver could catch so much at such short notice to really make a feast, but Colin's excitement rubbed off on her all the same. "Will you go to the other tenants and invite them too?"

The boy pursed his lips in thought and stared up at the ceiling. "The eating won't be as good," he said. "But I suppose it's neighborly and more like a feast if we've got company."

"Spoken like a true Lord of Fenn Manor," Lumen said and

grinned as he gave her a sideways look that implied he thought she might still be suffering stress from the day before.

Her chest was tight and her stomach ached and if she thought for more than a second about—

"I s'pose we can't eat properly in the dining hall if the army gets back," Colin said.

Lumen thought of the chapel and decided that was too risky, especially since she wanted to invite Inda, Rosie, and the others to dine with them. "I'll clean out one of the larger rooms of cots," she said. "If the men get back before we're done they'll… just have to sleep a little closer together for a night. It's cold after all."

"Not sleeping with me. I *like* having a bed to myself for once."

"I can see why," she said, nudging at the leg that was sprawled out nearly to her lap.

One minute Colin was stretched over the mattress looking as if he had no intention of ever getting up, and in the next he was out of the bed and dressed, running down to the courtyard and out to find Oliver. Lumen gave herself a little more time to finish waking up before dressing and searching for the other women.

She found them scattered through rooms downstairs, mending trousers and dozing under sunny windows like cats. Inda was curled up on a cot, sniffling into a pillow, and Jennie grabbed Lumen by the elbow and dragged her out of the room before she could go to the girl.

"Don't bother. She's weeping over her Philip," Jennie said, eyes rolling to the sky.

"Why? What's happened." Lumen looked back into the office room and saw Mia perched at the edge of the cot, one hand stroking down Inda's back while her eyes drifted around the room and she yawned.

"The men have gone out to the field," Jennie said with a shrug and when Lumen raised her eyebrows the older woman huffed. "Every time they go she gets a little more hysterical. Like she don't know he'll leave one day for good."

"She won't go with them when they move on?"

Jennie sucked her teeth and studied Lumen's face with a quizzing expression, brow furrowed. "Would you, milady?"

Gideon thought so. Lumen knew she couldn't. "No. But then... where will you go?"

"Back to the taverns where Jones found us," Jennie said, lips quirking. "Where should you think?"

Lumen swallowed as she searched for the words and then found them, unexpected as they were. "You would be welcome to stay here as long as you like," she said.

Jennie stared at her for a long time. "No offense, milady, but I think we'd have better livings and heavier meals in the taverns."

The laugh was bright and noisy, and Lumen's stomach ached with the force of it, still sore from tears the day before. Jennie's shoulders softened at the sight of her laughter and she grinned and huffed.

"I suppose if I ever get sick of the work and long for...hay," Jennie said.

Lumen snorted and shook her head until she could think clearly again, telling Jennie of Colin's plan for the day.

"Aye, sure, I know a room that can be cleared up quick enough."

It was the brightest day Lumen could think of in many years, planning a celebration in the company of the women whom she liked and Colin whom she loved like a brother who hadn't been stolen away by the war. Not yet, she thought.

The food was thin between the whole crowd of them but the room was just the right size to make a small and strange collection of people feel like a real party, warm and noisy with elbows bumping and clumsy laughter. And then, at the end of evening and just before dark, they padded out to the back yard by the pond with a faint memory of what being full bellied felt like, and stood wrapped in scarves and shawls as they watched the sun touch down.

Colin tugged her hand, pulling her back from the small crowd lined up near the water as vivid gold turned to brilliant orange and burning red, sliced with the black of trees.

"Look, Lady," he whispered in her ear, turning her back to the

Manor where he'd left the kitchen door open. "There she is."

Lumen had to duck, kneeling in snow and squinting in the dark to stare through the kitchen and across the courtyard, and out all the way through front entry hall to see where the moon hung like a silver smile just above the horizon. She squeezed his hand and settled on freezing toes, looking one way to her Mother Lune, and through the legs of her company at the dying blaze of Sol and his fire.

❋

"DANVERS AND CHARLIE JUST GOT BACK," Gideon said. His stare was focused somewhere past Dominic's shoulder, and Dominic knew well enough by now not to look. Gideon wasn't distracted. He just rarely made eye contact now.

He wanted to say that it wasn't his fault. What happened in his office had been her. She'd used him, gouging truths out and then refusing... Except that he understood something a little better since she'd left the room and it was twisting his thoughts in new and uncomfortable directions.

"They say Oshain's waiting for us on the line with a fresh cavalry."

"We won't stand up to that," Dominic muttered.

And isn't that what she wants?

"Yesterday was rough enough on the men. Better to let them rest before marching out again," Gideon nodded and moved to turn away.

"How is she?" Dominic asked.

Gideon's eyes narrowed, stare pinning Dominic and he regretted speaking or even thinking the question. And then Gideon sighed, body slumping down into a chair that complained as he sat.

"I don't like it, Dom," he said, continuing before Dominic could ask what he meant. "Don't feel good about it, about how she looks when she gets in her head."

"Would you leave her?" Dominic asked and raised his hands in peace as Gideon tensed. "If *she* asked you to."

297

Gideon shook his head, slow and steady, not in refusal but in thought. "Don't know. You mean... really leave, don't you?"

"With a promise to not return," Dominic said with a nod.

"The thought leaves something hurting in here," and then he rubbed at his chest over his heart. "Would you?"

"I'm still deciding," Dominic whispered and he pushed out of his chair and paced to the end of the room when the sight of the desk was too large in his vision.

It wasn't that he thought he was winning a battle against Lumen. Those had been *her* orders he'd followed as he'd rushed to sate himself on her skin, filling her up with his cock as if it might leave him less hollow. He hadn't been in control. If he was, he would have resisted, but the lure of her was something that offered no room for a refusal. No, that was a lie too. He hadn't had the least interest in refusing her. He'd wanted to consume her and forget all the lapse of time between that ugly moment and the last previous, blissful occasion he'd been inside her.

He'd made his life about the army when it was the only thing that offered him any satisfaction, and now...

"We'll go out again in two days time on the new moon," he said to Gideon. "Cavalry or not. Tell the men to get rest now while they're able."

There was a brief grunt of acknowledgement but Dominic was already out into the hall. He passed her bedroom door—her new bedroom she shared with Gideon—and nearly stopped and made his way inside, as if fighting with her again might lead to fucking her again. As if that might lead to anything other than fracturing the mess between them even worse than the thin little shards that were left now.

He moved on, taking the first stairs down. Someone was having sex in the kitchen, bawdy and rough, with a table creaking and whichever of the women it was making a generous amount of noises.

And all he could think of was the funny little 'shoo shoo' Lumen made as she began to fall asleep.

He got to the long, cold hall that led to her chapel and all the sounds of the Manor died away against the dark stone. Lumen had the key still, he'd promised her that much and he had no intention of going back on that one single thing she'd asked of him. But it wasn't hard to work his way through a lock. Especially not an old one, just like the ones he'd turned as a boy, sneaking his way into the backs of bakeries in the dead of night.

The room smelled of incense and snow and wet stone, like the few dresses still hanging in the cupboard of his room. Silver glittered over every surface, white candles waiting dormant around the feet of the Mother Lune statue. He shut the door behind him and took silent steps up to her platform, as if to let her continue sleeping, or to sneak up without her knowledge.

Mother Lune didn't look old and grandmotherly as he'd always considered her. She wore a perfect, smooth face carved into gray marble, veins of the rock glittering eerily in the dim light. She wasn't round and craggy like the face of the moon in the sky, but tall and slender with a long nose and soft lips and—

And she reminded him too much of Lumen, as if one was descended from the other. Or as if Lumen had shaped herself in the goddesses image by devotion alone.

Voices passed too close to the hall and Dominic stiffened, the noise interrupting the lull of peace in the room.

This room was too vulnerable. Every day the soldiers found another trinket in a forgotten cupboard, another room to clear of its history and anything worth their portion of a meal. He'd given them that, claimed it for their taking, and he'd promised Lumen this one room in exchange. One room worth all the others combined.

If he was going to keep that promise something would need to be done.

Speak to her.

But the thought of seeking her out, finding Gideon glaring at her side and what that conversation might turn into, chilled him as thoroughly as the northern winter. If she crooked her finger, would he bend knee? If she didn't, would he beg?

He sneered up at the goddess's stone face and eyed the silver that surrounded her.

LUMEN'S THIGHS BURNED WITH EXERTION AS SHE CHASED HER finish on Gideon's lap, their bodies dewed with sweat even in the cool shiver of the morning. Gideon snarled and bucked beneath her, one hand bracing her hip while the other worked her clit until she was taut and shouting, bouncing in uneven jerks as he flashed hot inside of her. She kept moving, riding and rutting even as the wave turned to trembles, until his arms circled her waist, pulling her down to his warm chest and holding her steady as he kissed her hair.

She wasn't supposed to be speaking, it was the new moon. She certainly wasn't meant to be begging and shouting, but she'd woken in the night, Gideon puffing warm breath over her neck as he slept, his cock fitted between her thighs as he thrusted in his dreams. And even though she was already a little sore from the night's exertions, she'd rolled him onto his back and fitted him inside of her before he'd finished waking up. He was going back onto the battlefield and she was starting to understand Inda's anxious heart while Philip was away.

Months of waiting for the Stalor army to leave and now Lumen had a reason to want them to stay. Well, not the army, but Gideon and Colin.

"Time for me to dress," Gideon said in her hair. "Don't think I'm meant to feel *quite* this relaxed on my way to battle."

She snorted, nuzzling against his throat and tried to push herself up on weak arms. Gideon caught her before she could roll away, fingers tangling in her hair as he rolled them onto her back, his lips feasting on hers in a kiss that went on so long Lumen thought she would surrender her last breath before it ended. He pulled away, leaving a scorching path down her throat and between her breasts. She squirmed as he licked at her belly-button and then sucked her breath as he began to kiss at her cunt, cleaning and fondling every inch of skin.

Lumen groaned and pulled a pillow over her face. Gideon made a habit of taking the moment she was certain she was too exhausted to feel and proving her wrong. She shook her head beneath the pillow, toes curling into the mattress, and sighed when he finally drew away. There was a simmer of heat left on her skin but she was too satisfied to mind the tease.

Fingers tugged at the corner of the pillow and she let him toss it aside, finding his grin in the shadows and running her hand across the smile.

"Wish me luck," he said.

She nodded. "I do," she whispered.

They stared at one another and Lumen blamed lack of sleep or her recently departed cycle for why her throat felt tight.

"One more kiss, little spirit."

She sat up and wrapped her arms around his shoulders, trying to beat him at the game, pulling at his lips while he scooped her up, shifting her on the bed. Gideon grunted as she sucked his tongue and growled when she bit his lips, laughing at her attempts to be ferocious in her hunger. He released her again, pulled the blankets back up to her shoulders before finally drawing away from her demanding kiss.

"I'll bring you new bruises," he said, brushing her hair across the pillow. When she opened her mouth to speak he added, "And no stitches. Promise this time."

Lumen burrowed deeper into the bed, right into the spot he'd warmed with his own skin, eyes drooping shut as she watched him leave the room.

LUMEN FOUND Colin waiting for her in the hall when she finally rose from bed. He bounced on his toes and handed her a warm roll as she linked her fingers in his and nodded in the direction of the chapel.

"I was thinking it might be better if I keep the ladies from looking for you," Colin said, wincing and whispering. "Found Jennie snooping down the hall couple days ago and she had questions about the lock. I told her the General locked it himself but… well everyone's bored and hungry so…"

Lumen frowned. She wondered recently if it was necessary to keep the secret, not liking the thought of lying to women who felt like friends. But silver was only sacred to Lunars, to everyone else it was coin in the pocket and she had given everything else up. Maybe it would be better if she didn't go at all.

"It's alright, Lady," he said, tugging at her fingers. "You can have the day."

She'd missed two new moons of prayer already, and the army wouldn't be back until after dark which gave her plenty of time to break her fast and ready the infirmary. Which meant…

Lumen pressed the roll back into Colin's hand even though the smell left her mouth watering. If she was going to meditate again, she wanted to do it properly. She bent and kissed his cheek in thanks and smiled as he blushed and took off to the stairs ahead of her.

Something fragile inside of her had shattered that day in Dominic's office and she did her best to keep her mind off of him and the consequences, but something good had come in the wake of it even if she preferred not to study her part too closely. The Stalor army had been out to battle three times in one week and it was just enough added calm around the Manor to keep her head together.

She made it downstairs and whatever Colin had done had cleared the courtyard and surrounding hall, leaving her unobserved on her way to the chapel. Her key was heavy in her pocket, patting against her thigh and Lumen smiled at the thought of a day spent completely alone. There was no way of inviting the tenants and keeping the chapel a secret from the women which meant she would have the space entirely to herself.

The key turned and Lumen took a deep breath as she cracked it open, stone and incense and candlewax leaking out. She slipped inside, glancing behind her to make sure no one was watching and then snapped the door shut and turned.

All at once, there was no air in the room, no light to see by even as she stared at what...

It couldn't be true.

The windows were dull and empty, surrounding ledge stripped, and even Mother Lune's feet were bare and bereft of all her gifts. Someone had taken the silver. Stone cracked against her knees as she landed on the floor, a last breath collapsing out of her chest. The candles remained but the snuffer and the silver box of incense were gone. Her bells. All the figurines. Only Mother Lune in gray stone with her eyes on the empty floor.

"He did this," Lumen whispered, tongue dry and sticky in her mouth. Her heart was racing, or it had stopped altogether, or was being crushed from the inside out.

The space was the last piece of herself left untouched and now it too was ransacked. Lumen sat with her back pressed to the door, waiting and waiting for something to change, for this to have been a mistake.

This is for refusing him, she thought. *This is for taking what you wanted from him and then walking away.*

For asking him to leave.

Would he leave now? Was Gideon saying goodbye that morning, now that the army had silver to last them another month or more?

Her stomach turned as her eyes swept over the scene for the hundredth time. Not a candle knocked over, no dust to be seen. As if Dominic had meticulously removed piece by piece as if they'd never existed.

This was heartbreak.

She remained there at the door gazing up at the statue, her ears blind to the sound of the Manor behind her back and her hunger building into a roar, until the sun began to shine through the far window. What if the army came back? Could she lay next to Gideon at night? Or go to Dominic and claw his eyes right out of their sockets?

She pulled herself from the floor and opened the door to the chapel, left it hanging wide on the hinges. Colin and the others were the in kitchen, something savory cooking and voices raised together in cheerful conversation. The sound was dull in her ears, echoing painfully into her skull, and she continued through the courtyard, sun glaring onto her back as she crossed to the front hall. There was a blanket dropped into a cot and she picked it up and wrapped it around herself as she walked out the front door and down to the road.

It was cold enough to make her eyes water and her lashes freeze together when she blinked, and she didn't really know where she was going until she was almost all the way there.

Yes, she thought, it was this or drown under the sheet of ice laying over the pond.

Oliver Spragg's cottage sat ahead of her, and there was no smoke rising from the chimney. Maybe he was gone. Maybe he was crossing the new border of Oshain. Except she saw him pass by the window as she grew close, blonde hair disappearing out of sight for a moment and then turning back, face filling the window and watching her. He opened the door as she reached his front step.

"I want to leave," she said, voice hoarse from the cold.

"Come in, Lady Fenn." He stepped aside and there were coals in his fireplace, wood drying in stacks just out of the way. There was food, half-eaten on the table and he flushed and 'hmm'd when she saw it, caught at skipping his fasting. She didn't care.

"Will you take me into Oshain?" she asked.

"Of course I will, milady, you know I will," he said. He stepped towards her and Lumen retreated without meaning to, both of them freezing. "Say the word. Bring your things and—"

"I don't have things," she said. "I have nothing, Oliver. I want to leave, please."

There were tears in her eyes, coursing over her cheeks but she didn't mind them until she caught Oliver staring at them, looking squeamish and queasy. She wiped them away with the blanket as he looked around the room. It was a small cottage but it was warm and there was a chair near the fire that Lumen eyed with a surprising depth of longing in her chest.

"Alright. I'll keep an eye on the road. As soon as the army is back we'll leave. Give ourselves a head start before they realize you've gone."

"They won't care," Lumen said, crossing to the chair.

"I hope you won't take offense, milady, if I say I hope you're right," Oliver muttered. He eyed her head to toe. "I'll find you a coat and a sweater. Help yourself to what's on the table."

Her mouth watered at the mention of food but her stomach was turned to stone so instead she curled herself into the armchair, stretching her toes to point toward the fire. Oliver shuffled up a set of narrow stairs to a room above and Lumen closed her eyes to wait for nightfall.

GIDEON BOUNCED into the infirmary ahead of the rest of Stalor's finest—ready to boast that he'd come through the day's battle with little more than a torn thumbnail, and after killing at least three men—when he stopped still in the heart of the room. His sweet little ghost was missing.

"Colin's went to fetch her," one of the whores, ladies, told him as she passed by with a bowl of steaming, clean water.

"From where?" he asked.

She shrugged, resting the bowl on Lumen's work table and spreading her hands over the waist of her skirt. "From wherever she's been all day. Haven't seen her."

"It's the new moon," Finley whispered, appearing at Gideon's back.

"Welcome back, Healer," said the woman, eyebrows raising. "Where'd you come from?"

"He met us on the battlefield," Gideon said, eyes searching the room again as if she might appear in the hunt. He glanced at

Finley and added, "You might be better hanging back a bit. I don't know that you'll be a welcome surprise."

Finley glared back at him, one cheek swollen and bleeding from where he'd received Gideon's fist in greeting. "I'll make myself useful."

Gideon frowned, not sure he liked the idea of Lumen walking in unprepared to see Finley back so suddenly and without warning. He'd wanted to make his little spirit stronger but no matter how he tried to please her and brighten her moods, there was always something else coming to bruise her, until she was all but withering in front of him.

Colin appeared, ducking around the legs of soldiers, and stopped in the doorway, his small face twisted with worry. He spotted Gideon, freezing like prey in the woods, and then jerked away. The chase was on, soldiers darting out of the way as Gideon chased the boy. He caught him in the courtyard, Colin's feet skidding against ice just before crashing into Dominic's legs.

Gideon grabbed him by the shoulder and spun him around and Colin winced at the sight of his face overhead. "Where is she?"

"I- I don't know," Colin said, eyes darting. He lowered his voice to a whisper. "I went to the chapel and the door was open and she wasn't there. And sir, all her lady's silver is gone."

Dominic twitched in the corner of Gideon's eye and Colin tore himself out of a tightening grasp. Gideon's stare turned up at his General, a growl simmering in his chest as his eyes narrowed and dread pitted in his guts.

"What did you do, Dominic?"

IV
THE PRISONER OF OSHAIN

"JUST A LITTLE FURTHER, LADY FENN."

Lumen's lungs burned in her chest and brambles clawed at her skirt, as if trying to hold her back in her marching and keep her from escaping.

I would hunt you through the woods, my lady, before I let you escape from me. Oh, but she missed Gideon already, wished it was him she'd asked to take her away. He'd have scooped her off the ground and carried her into Oshain himself, enemy soil or not.

And they would have cut him down the first chance they had, and her too.

"There, that shadow ahead," Oliver said, stopping in calf-deep snow and thorny undergrowth to point through the woods to a blurry dark form of an old hunting cabin.

Lumen leaned against a tree and Oliver stepped in her direction before stopping himself.

"It will be better if you push yourself, Lady Fenn."

She ducked her head and shoved herself back into motion, feet numb bricks in her shoes, legs somehow both frozen and burning, skin chafed everywhere her dress brushed. If a root reached up to catch her ankle Lumen thought she might land in the snow and stay there. The sprain, which seemed healed a week earlier, now panged through her leg, searching out warm muscle to torture since her foot was too cold to feel the ache.

Oliver gave up on her by the end, rushing ahead to the cabin, peering into windows and disappearing around the back of the building. Dawn was turning the woods pink and foggy, mist wrapping around dark tree trunks.

If I had picked the pond nothing would hurt by now, Lumen thought as she reached the narrow, crooked door of the cabin and stopped. It opened a moment later, pulling in to reveal Oliver, breaths puffing.

"Come in, Lady Fenn," he said when she didn't move. "A fire might be spotted but I think we better risk it. There are blankets in the trunk. You should... you should take your outer things off at least."

The cabin was only one small little room with the narrowest bed she'd ever seen sitting at the opposite wall as an equally narrow fireplace—which looked as if it were designed to put smoke back into the room rather than up through the chimney. A trunk sat at the foot of the bed and Lumen opened it to discover that everything inside smelled of mouse piss. She shook the bedding out and shed her coat and boots. The hem of her skirt was soaked, but at the sound of Oliver chipping kindling off a log she realized she didn't want to be undressed with him in the cabin. Maybe it hardly mattered—after everything she'd done what was being vulnerable around one more man?

She took Oliver's sweater off, picked the least fragrant of the blankets, and pulled a chair over to where he was building a fire.

"There's dried meat in my bag, and a loaf we can share. Just plan for the rest of the road too."

"I'm not hungry."

Oliver's back stiffened and then relaxed as he sighed. He turned to her, balancing himself by setting the small hatchet in his hand against the floor. She couldn't see the blue of his eyes in the dark but she knew the color well enough, just a shade grayer than a sunny day. "La- Lumen. If you're going to walk tonight, you'll have to eat now. We'll make it over the border before morning and then everything will be... you'll be with your people again."

Her people had once been her family, but they were all dead.

After that her people were her tenants, but there was barely a handful of them left on the estate, and the others... Her heart clenched in her chest, for Colin, and maybe Inda and the other women, and Gideon too. It was all just deep pricks of pain to think of and she brushed it away and looked down to her feet where the sack of supplies waited, bending and searching for something to chew on.

"You should rest once you've eaten," Oliver said as the match caught the kindling. His back was to her again, hand using a stick to coax the flames. "I'll join you once this is ready to be dampened."

Lumen stiffened in the chair, stare fixed to his back. Did he mean he would join her in sleeping or in the small bed?

"We'll stay warmer if we lay together," he said, voice lowering and words quavering slightly.

Her skin burnt from the cold and her jaw hurt from clenching and chewing the dried meat, but every sensation was buried beneath a mental fog, as if she were wrapped in a stifling cocoon of wool.

Oliver shifted at her silence, face tense but open, some attempt at being reassuring. "I don't mean any offense, Lady Fenn. But we--"

"I think I will sit here by the fire and dry off," Lumen said. "I'm sorry but I... there are plenty more blankets."

"My lady, if you think I would ever hurt your or- or-" Oliver sputtered, eyes wide.

"I have had enough of the nearness of men," she said, head and heart cold as she answered. "My skirt needs to dry off. I'll rest here. I can manage the fire."

He blinked and turned back, staring at the flames rising, twining around the logs he'd placed. "Yes. Yes, of course. Wake me if you decide to sleep. We can trade places."

He rose, taking his bag with him to the bed, a brief huff of breath released as he sat down. Lumen closed her eyes and waited for the fire to rise and thaw her. She wouldn't step within three feet of that bed.

DOMINIC'S HORSE kicked stone up as it reared to a stop in front of the open front doorway, Danvers waiting in the arch.

"Has she been found?"

"She's nowhere on the property and..."

"And?!"

"And the men are sick of searching, sir," Danvers said blinking, body stiff as if waiting for the blow to land.

Dominic leapt down from his horse, hands clenching, and turned back to the horizon, red sun rising and eyeing him with the same infuriation that was burning like kindling in his heart. Of course the men were sick of hunting for Lumen. Now that their Healer was back what use was she to them?

What use was she to you when she hated you? he thought and the ugliness of his own mind made him queasy. The answer, lingering in the corners and whispering the truth, terrified him.

"Where's Jones?" Dominic asked, seeing Danvers' shoulders relax when he realized he wasn't about to get cut down for his answer.

"I think that's him on the road, sir," Danvers said, nodding out ahead to the sun.

Not just Gideon but Finley too, both alone on their horses, their search as fruitless as Dominic's. Danvers ducked back inside before he could be caught in the coming conversation, as if he knew what was waiting on all three men's tongues.

"We don't even know what kind of head start they had," Finley said, gentling his horse into an easy stop.

Gideon was silent as his side but there was a storm brewing inside the large man, and the heart of it was focusing its stare on Dominic.

"Why'd you do it?"

Dominic swallowed but raised his jaw, prepared to take his friend's rage. "It was only a matter of time before one of the men broke in and—"

"You could have told her," Finley snapped, jumping down

from his saddle. "Or Gideon if you find it so abhorrent to speak to her."

Dominic's jaw ticked painfully and he tore his eyes away from them both and the burning sun rising behind them.

"He wanted her to come running to him," Gideon growled, dismounting from his horse. "Did you think she'd beg? Or did you just want to hear her voice again, shouting at you?"

Hiding the silver had been a mistake. Dominic shut his eyes. The answer was yes, he had wanted to draw her out. Yes he'd wanted her to fight with him. If she had begged he would have told her it was safe, shown it to her. But if she had come with color in her cheeks, and eyes flashing, hands ready to pound at his chest... at least there would have been life in her.

"Perhaps it's for the best," Finley said. His fingers were wrapped around the reins of his horse and he flinched as Gideon spun to face him, gravel spitting under black boots. Finley raised his eyebrows. "She may be safer there."

"*May* be?" Gideon snarled.

"What was going to happen to her after you'd moved on?" Finley asked looking at them and when Gideon opened his mouth he rushed to add, "When the army moved farther north? What would Stalor have done with her? That estate wouldn't remain in her hands. This Manor is a relic, but they wouldn't let her keep it."

"I was going to stay!" Gideon charged at Finley, grabbing up his coat collar and dragging him into the air to balance on his toes. "I swore it to her after you fucked off and broke her heart."

Finley's eyes grew wide and pale and Dominic knew it had nothing to do with any threat of violence. Gideon dropped Finley abruptly and—stunned and unprepared—left him sprawling over the stones as he landed on his knees.

"And what good would you have done her, Gideon?" Dominic asked, ignoring Finley's warning glance. "Poured ale down her throat and fucked her where anyone could see?"

"At least I made her smile," Gideon said, eyes narrowing on him. "Do you know how I found her after you were through with her? Shivering on the stone floor. Still crying too, even in her sleep."

After he was through with her, after she was through with him…

"Was it really such a blow to your pride to have her remind you that you were human once?" Finley asked him, pushing himself up from the ground. "Is it so difficult for you to remember that at one time you would have *hated* yourself for hurting that boy?"

"Do you think I don't?" Dominic snapped. His skin was hot, throat tight, stomach turning and turning and turning again like a wagon wheel consistently battered against pits in the road.

"You've got no room to talk to him," Gideon said to Finley. "You walked out on her without a word."

"She was safer with you," Finley said.

"She could have had us both," Gideon said, shrugging. "Easily. But that's not what you did. *You left her.* You let her trust you and then you took off."

Finley was sheet white, the bruise Gideon had gifted him with was standing out, a vivid purple around his eye.

"I- I didn't think—"

"No, that much is clear," Gideon muttered, turning his back on the healer. His eyes stopped at Dominic's boots and Dominic braced himself for the worst. "I know we've ruined women before. Taken their reputations under bedsheets. But this was…" His gaze raised to Dominic's eyes red and burning with unshed tears. "This was the worst one, Dominic."

For a moment, Dominic thought he was safe. "She ruined us too."

Gideon's face went taut in a snarl, the sound emitting from his throat a quieter version than the cry on the battlefield. Dominic took one step back and then Gideon was barreling forward, hands fisted in his coat, slamming him back against the brick stone of the house. Dominic hissed as his skull cracked against rock, vision splitting for a moment.

"She *remade* us," Gideon whispered. "Tried to wash all the blood and shit off of us. Let us be men again instead of just the same fucking blades in this war we've been playing day in and out for decades."

"Shut yer Sol-burnt mouths. You all did this."

Gideon's grip slackened and Dominic winced and sighed as he was scratched down the surface of the wall, feet landing on the ground again. Colin was in the doorway, watching them with a solemn expression, as if he were bored or already knew how the whole argument, the whole disaster, would play out.

"Lady ain't a witch or a spirit and she weren't saving your damned souls," Colin said, eyes narrowed as he stared at them. "She just wanted to last long enough for you to leave. And you didn't and that's your fault. So she left first. An' I hope she gets peace for it, though I don't know she will."

"What do you mean?" Dominic could almost stand the thought of her safe and away and with her people, although every battle he fought he would wonder if it was the mile that would take him closer to where she was.

Colin's eyebrows raised at him. "It's alright if she gets there an' no one knows who she is. But Oshain'll know it was her you were stayin' with and they won't do her favors if they do."

Gideon's breath huffed and Dominic didn't even flinch as the thick fist landed with a crunch against the stone by his face. Finley covered his mouth with his hand, the gray tone of his skin turning to green.

"Can you find out?" Dominic asked the boy. "Can you… can you cross and get word of her?"

"I was going to whether you asked or not," Colin said, glaring up at him. "But if she's safe and she can be happy, you lot have to swear that'll be the end of it. You leave her alone."

Finley was already nodding but Dominic had to swallow down the burning refusal that surged up inside of him like a wave of bile. He nodded, once, and wondered what a promise like that would cost him. It felt as if everything inside of him had died and decayed when he'd heard she was missing. Would the rot fester the longer he was without her?

Gideon was shifting faintly in front of Dominic, muscles moving in a restless pattern beneath his skin. Dominic wondered if he wouldn't have to keep Gideon from lunging at the boy for the order. Instead Gideon lowered himself into a crouch until his face was level with Colin's, voice calmer than Dominic expected.

"If you find her, and she doesn't need me, I'll stay away," Gideon said.

SHE'D THOUGHT THEY WERE STILL IN STALOR TERRITORY THE night before, but it was only an hour into their walk the next afternoon that Lumen saw the tents, Oshain's silver and green flag raised above.

"There's a village just another couple miles in. We'll get a ride into the city from there," Oliver said.

"I won't stay at the village?" Lumen asked.

Oliver's head twitched in her direction. He'd been avoiding eye contact with her ever since the night before when she'd refused to share the bed. If his honor was wounded, Lumen was sorry for it, but she didn't regret napping in the hard little chair by the fire. Her neck was sore and her legs were dead weights when she first woke, but she was warm and dry when they left the cabin and feeling solid in her own skin again.

"The village has as many as they can manage already," Oliver said. "And enough newcomers. You'll be safer in the city anyway. No one expects the border to hold much longer."

"Do you think Stalor will make it to the capitol?" Lumen asked.

"Truthfully, Lady Fenn, I think they'll take Oshain entirely," Oliver whispered. "I only hope it takes another lifetime to do it."

Then what was she running from, she wanted to ask. What good was it to move north if the army would only follow?

"If that's true I wish it'd been done already," Lumen said.

Oliver spun and stared at her, shock and anger on his face. "How can you say that?"

"There might have been more souls left alive if the war had ended a decade ago."

"Maybe on their side, Lady Fenn. Not on ours."

Lumen eyed the camp of soldiers up ahead. They were walking near enough to be seen, but farther west. "Will they stop us?"

"Most of the company knows me," Oliver said. "If they see me, they won't stop us. If they stop us it won't take long to sort out."

He was right. There were soldiers not far away, by the edge of the camp, cooking some kind of winter animal over a fire. They watched Lumen and Oliver cross out of the field and onto the road, one of them raising a hand in greeting. Oliver answered it and that was the end of their interest. So simple.

She was on the other side of the line. The realization hit her in the stomach like a fist. A battlefield separated her from Westbrook now. From the Manor and Gideon and Colin too. If Dominic came for her, she would hear the violence coming first. She could run north, or hide in the masses. Maybe she could even find her way to the Convent.

"Would you take me to the Lunar Convent?" Lumen asked as they walked.

Oliver's steps slowed, shoulders twisting in her direction, and then he was marching again, his strides longer than hers, keeping her jogging to catch up. "The capitol first, Lumen."

"Of course. You shouldn't have to bother," she said. He would want to get back. Keep Widow Ramsey and her children safe. "I will find my own way when we get to the city."

Oliver stopped and waited for her to reach his side. His hand reached out, wrapping around her arm and he waited for her to look up into his face before speaking, blue eyes aching. "I will do what I can for you, Lady Fenn."

She stepped to the side and his hand dropped. "You've done enough now, Mr. Spragg and I thank you."

FINLEY SAT down on the bed in the little attic room, pressing his palm to the mattress where he'd last touched Lumen, as if there might still be a bit of her warmth there, weeks later.

Weeks. Weeks without a word, without an explanation. Gideon's voice chorused in his head. *You let her trust you and then you left her.*

Finley understood it a little better now. He thought he was protecting himself. Waiting for the moment she looked at him and realized he was not what she wanted. He'd thought that moment was the morning before he left. Now he couldn't decide if leaving had hurt her or protected her from him in the long run. Maybe he would have left later at Dominic's bidding. Or with the army. Was his will that weak to let Dominic make the decision for him?

He imagined what might have happened if he'd gone to her, told her of the offer to join Meades' ranks for a spell. It felt like pretending to picture it going any other way than her cold relief and his injured pride.

You fucked off and broke her heart, Gideon bellowed in his head.

Had he held so much of her?

THE CAPITOL WAS another night's ride away. Lumen spent it curled up in the back of a cart, wedged against a crate of candles. Oliver sat across from her, his eyes watching the dark scenery pass. She was drowsy and aching, cringing every time the wheel beneath her hit a pit in the road, too tired to stay awake and watch their progress and too bruised and cold to fall asleep.

Morning came and Lumen's eyes were dry and dusty from the road, body stiff from being cramped at the back of the wagon. The capitol of Oshain grew slowly around her, homes packed tightly together at the edge of the city, little logged structures, steepled, shingled roofs patterned with thin layers of snow. Brick and stone buildings grew higher and wider, roads filling up with traffic the deeper in they travelled.

"How far in do we go?" Lumen asked, words scratching her dry throat as she glanced at Oliver.

They'd stopped at a tavern in the village the night before and Lumen realized she had no money as Oliver reached into his bag and paid for a meal shared between the two of them and two pints of watered down cider. It only reminded her that her escape from the Manor was poorly planned. Oliver had been right, she should have left weeks ago. Now she would be stranded in the capitol without coins to buy her a bed or any way of getting herself to the Convent.

If she was lucky there would be a Lunar temple in the city willing to take her on or at least find her transportation. Or she could beg.

"Near the center," Oliver answered. "There's a... process for those crossing back into Oshain territory. They may be able to do something for you, as Lady Fenn."

She didn't think her family had any property outside of the Manor and the estate, but if Oliver was right it would be worth knowing. It might even save her.

They passed a Solar temple on their way, the goldenrod paint peeling from the wooden beams, some of the windows broken in their panes. Lumen stared, waiting for some sign of life, a bit of candlelight or movement.

"Sol's fallen out of favor since Stalor's invasion," Oliver said, watching her study the building. "If He still has disciples in Oshain, they keep their devotion quiet."

"Do you really think Stalor fights for Sol?" Lumen asked, frowning as the hollow temple disappeared around a curve in the road.

"They fly his colors on their flag," Oliver said with a shrug.

Lumen chewed at her lip. "Do you think Sol wants them to fight us?"

"Sol asks for blood and land. I don't think he cares whether it's offered at his bidding or not."

If Sol's devotion was conquering and Lune's was sacrifice, was the war only a manner of prayer between the two faiths?

They reached the heart of the capitol when the sun was high overhead. It was cold but the maze of streets was too dense for wind to come whipping, and the roads busy with traffic and bodies. The city was loud and lively, voices calling out to one another. There were hungry faces, same as there had been at the Manor, but they didn't wear the same haggard exhaustion that Lumen knew drew lines around her mouth and circles under her eyes.

A Lunar temple on a corner built out of glossy pale stone, twinkling light spilling from faceted blue windows that covered the walls like stars. Lumen almost jumped out of the cart then, but remembered Oliver's promise that there may be something of her name left to salvage. She traced the route they took through the streets, determined to find her way back to the temple again.

The cart stopped in a market and Oliver leapt out over his side, stretching and handing coin to the driver. If there was any money left to her family name she would repay Oliver. Maybe even send as much as she could spare back for the tenants. Sarah Blythe and Widow Ramsey and the children.

Oliver waited for her at the foot of the cart, hand raised to help her down, steadying her as she groaned. Her body felt dull and useless. Too much time walking followed by too much time folded up in a knot. And almost no sleep at all.

"That building there," he said, nodding at an enormous stone hall.

"I don't have anything to prove who I am," she said.

"I'll vouch for you," Oliver said, nudging her out of the main market and onto a raised walkway in front of the buildings. "They know me here, Lady Fenn. It will be alright. Just an interview and a little time."

Lumen frowned, shying away as two men passed close on the walkway, eyes glancing at her. They looked away again as if they hadn't really seen her and continued talking of imports from the north and whether they would start early this spring or if the ice would hold. The archway of the building ahead loomed, dark but for a lamp making a weak attempt at transforming a gloomy hollow into an inviting entrance. Oliver jogged ahead of her, pushing the door open and jerking his head for her to follow.

THE BELLS TINKLED around his wrist as he brushed his horse's back. Gideon had stolen from Dominic's secret stash of Lumen's silver—crated and stored under the bed in Dominic's rooms where none of the soldiers would dare to break in. They were the charms Lumen defended from Danvers, nearly turning the man bald before taking the wind out of Gideon's chest with a surprisingly fierce strength.

He loved her.

His mother had said loved burned through you—enough and it would warm your blood on the coldest night, too much and it would leave you a dry and hollow husk after it passed.

That wasn't how his little spirit made him feel and he hadn't known what to call the sensation of all the buzzing under his skin, and how the noisy clatter in his head went quiet when she set her hand on his skin. If he'd realized earlier maybe he would have scooped her up on that sunny day at the gazebo and taken her somewhere safe.

Colin appeared in the barn doorway, kicking a rock ahead of him, head hung at a sullen angle.

"Keep that out of the horses way," Gideon said, glancing at the large stone.

"You mad at her?" The brush in Gideon's hand went still, bells silent on his wrist. "At my Lady," Colin said as if he'd left any question.

"No," Gideon said shaking his head. "I don't blame her."

"I know it's your lot's fault and all," Colin muttered, picking up the rock and chucking it out the other open end of the barn into a snow drift. "I'm still a bit mad. She coulda told me. I'da gone with her. I'm as good as that Spragg fellow."

Gideon tasted the copper on his tongue before he realized

he'd bit down too hard on the inside of his mouth. He moved away from his horse before he spooked the creature, grabbing onto the stall to steady himself, the old wood soft under his fingers. How hard would he have to squeeze before it crumbled? He sagged, arms crossing over the stall wall as breath puffed out his nose, foggy in the cold.

"You're likely better'n the Spragg fellow," Gideon muttered.

"You think she's not safe?" Colin asked, brow furrowing, hands twisting the hem of his shirt.

"If she were with us, I would know she was safe," Gideon said.

"What if she don't want to be with you?"

Gideon swallowed the stone growing in his throat. "She say so?"

Colin squinted, eyeing the boards of the stall as if judging how likely they were to keep him safe if he said something Gideon didn't like to hear. Then he huffed and shrugged, arms flapping at his side.

"No. I s'pose she liked you enough."

It was foolish to let the faintest praise give him the greatest relief but he couldn't help it. If he had been wrong in her affection, and greedily soaked her touch up without reserve, it would make him as bad as... Dominic, he supposed.

"If she doesn't want me then I'll have to leave her be," Gideon said, hating the words but meaning every one. "Which'll mean you'll have to be enough. Anyone teach you sword fighting yet?"

Colin groaned and started shuffling his way out of the barn. "I'm better with a bow. I'm the best with a slingshot."

"Come on," Gideon said, letting himself out of the horse stall and following the boy. "A bit of training won't kill you."

"Against you it might," Colin muttered under his breath.

Gideon grinned but it stretched strangely on his face. It was wrong to smile without her.

LUMEN KNEW AS SOON as she saw the uniforms, gray and green with copper buttons down the front, that this interview was more than just helpful. There were one or two officials who looked as if they might have more interest in welfare than warfare—a woman in a dour black ensemble with hair drawn up high on her head, and a man in a healer's long gray coat.

But the man at the center of the table was unmistakably military, right down to his perfectly squared beard, just the faintest glimpse of red tucked beneath the gray.

"And what date was it, Miss Fenn, that General Westbrook and his men arrived at your estate?"

Lumen wet her lips with her tongue. The room they'd brought her into was inviting, brightly lit and warmly furnished, a high fire burning at her back. She was a dusty muddy little thing amongst the finery, wool and velvet and silver gilding the room, but she wanted to remind them that, shabby or not, she was Lady Fenn, not Miss.

"I don't know the date. Before the final harvest," Lumen said and when they stared at her she pushed herself to think. "After the equinox."

"As much as three months," said the man in the middle, General Cannary, thick eyebrows raising over eyes that reminded her too much of Finley.

"Yes."

"And in those three months what service did you provide the Stalor army?" he asked.

Lumen ignored the warmth in her cheeks and refused to look away. "I... my mother was an herbalist. I continued to provide remedies to my tenants as well as soldiers in the army. I stitched some wounds."

"You were their healer?" the healer at the far right end of the table asked.

"They had a healer," Lumen said. "But I provided some... help, I suppose."

"Were you intimate with members of the Stalor army?"

She couldn't feel her tongue in her mouth and while her head screamed that it wasn't the full moon and she didn't owe these people her answer, the word came out anyway. "Yes."

"How many?"

Her heart was frenzied in her chest, beating wildly, sometimes so fast she thought it even stopped. "Three."

"Were you forced?"

Five faces stared back at her as tears welled in her eyes. How could she explain the argument with herself that first night? That forced was not persuaded, but persuaded was not quite willing.

"No," she said, because it would be hard to say the full truth and that it had not taken long before being forced was far from the issue. She'd craved those men.

"And it was only the three?" the woman asked. "The usual three? Westbrook, Jones, and Brink, yes?"

There was a bitter flavor on her tongue. She was not the first or even likely the third woman to come and deliver this news at this table.

"Yes," she said, grateful when the tears refused to spill, only remained floating in her eyes and obscuring her view of the people sitting across from her.

"And in the course of your intimate relationship with the Stalor army what information did you learn?" General Cannary stared at her with a clinical study that bordered on boredom. As if he'd seen enough of her kind and could have conducted the remainder of the interview on his own.

Lumen shook her head. "I don't understand. What information?"

"Military information," one of the other men said, smirk curling over full lips, blue eyes flicking over her skin. He reminded her of Westbrook, although they looked nothing alike. Only that expression as he eyed her with vague interest.

"I- why would I..." her voice trailed off as she stared at the table. She swallowed and searched through conversations, teasing, and overheard words. What could she offer them to buy herself safety? "The healer, B-Brink went to General Meades."

"They're without their healer?" Cannary asked and Lumen

nodded. He twitched his head and down the table a pencil began to scratch against paper. "What else?"

"Sir, I wasn't privy to any meeting between Westbrook and his men," Lumen said. "My information was limited to their injuries."

"You shared your Manor with them, yes?" asked the woman.

"They *took* my Manor."

"Were their conversations really so private you couldn't hear words through a door?"

"You mean… spy on them?"

"Did you not have access to papers, correspondence?"

The papers pressed beneath her palms as Dominic took her atop his desk, her lips urging him on and silencing his words.

Lumen looked down at her palms in her lap. "My only goal was to hold the Manor intact, to protect its tenants, until the army moved on."

The younger, smirking man shifted in his seat. "Why did you leave, Miss Fenn? If your goal was to preserve your home and your physical relationships weren't being *forced*."

Lumen choked, head shaking, words from her own tongue wrapping themselves around her throat to strangle her voice. "Everything was sold. My people were leaving. The… the chapel was ransacked," she finished at a whisper, tears spilling over and refreshing themselves just as quickly.

"You didn't want revenge?"

"I wanted freedom," Lumen said, voice thick and watery.

"Your brother, Brandon, refused to serve in the Oshain army, is that correct?"

Lumen's head whipped up, salt sliding between her lips, eyes wide on Cannary's face. "I had *five* other brothers, sir, who *did. And* my father."

"Were you close with your brother Brandon?" the young man asked.

"I don't know anything!" Lumen shouted, hands clenching at her skirts. She moved to rise and guards twitched, lined up along the walls. She froze in her seat, searching the face of the officials at the table, searching for one glimpse of understanding.

Not even sympathy, but simple, reasonable *sense*. "I only wanted to have my home returned to me. I'm not a *spy*."

"Unfortunately, Miss Fenn, there's nothing to prove that to us," the woman said.

Lumen's heart froze, lips parted as she stared back. "You think... you think I came here *for* them?"

"Three months is a very long time. The longest we've heard of yet. If there was affection or—"

"No, no, please," Lumen cried, sobs squeezing her throat, head shaking and hands clenching around the seat of the chair. "Please. I left to be away from them. I only want to- to go to the Lunar Convent. *Please*. I just want this whole nightmare to end."

"It's more than likely you overheard something you wouldn't remember right away," Cannary said, standing from his chair.

Lumen's head tossed in refusal. There was nothing. She *knew* there was nothing. She tried to keep the war off her skin, and out of her head, even as it surrounded her in her home.

"We'll give you some time, Miss Fenn." There was no comfort in the words and Lumen was gasping before the guards closed in at her sides, hands reaching out and grabbing her arms in their grip.

"If I knew anything, I would say," she rushed out, lifted from the chair by firm hands. "I would say if only to be let free. Please, please I know *nothing*."

"Take your time to think," Cannary said with a grim smile. "You'll be undisturbed until we are able to spare time to speak to you again."

"Please!"

She was lifted up, toes barely able to scratch at the soft carpeting over the floor, body trying to twist and hang and fall away. Oliver stood outside of the room in the hall, his jacket fisted in his grip, mouth downturned.

"Oliver! *Please*. They won't listen!"

He didn't answer, only watched as she was carried deeper into the building to a set of stairs that led down. Guards marched at her back, like she might be enough of a threat to require six armed men to throw her into a cell. She caught a last glimpse of Oliver as they reached the stairs, her neck craned painfully, eyes clear of tears as anger grew. He knew. He'd known from the beginning of the journey what waited for her here. Did he know she'd have nothing to offer to protect herself, no knowledge to share. The stairwell enveloped her, as she was dragged down the gullet and into the belly of the building.

THE CELL THEY PUT HER IN HAD ONE NARROW, BARRED, OPEN window at the top of the high wall which faced a courtyard inside the building. The floor slanted down at an uneven angle, making Lumen feel crooked as she paced the small rectangle of space. The walls were packed earth over brick or stone and the floor was pitted with previous inmates boredom, cryptic patterns and shallow dents carved into the dusty surface. There was a hole in the corner meant for relieving herself and a pile of hay covered by a thin blanket in the other.

The guards let her keep Oliver's sweater and jacket after an invasive but professional search of clothes and body. She sat alone, but for the faint scratching of a mouse somewhere nearby, in the cell for a full day. One meal of dry bread that hurt her teeth to chew, and a bland, lumpy gruel, was delivered. In spite of everything—the burn of anger and the ache of hopelessness— she slept through the night on the makeshift bed as if she were at home in her own room again. She was alone at least, the faint moans and occasional growling shouts of the other occupants of the jail buried beneath the shelter of Oliver's coat.

He came to see her on the third evening, her window letting in the sounds of guards' laughter and the food at the market teasing its way down to her nose. She had her eyes closed, face tipped up to the window, imagining she could taste the sugar and pastry on her tongue, the sound of the mouse scratching replaced by the memory of fat frying and bubbling.

A throat cleared. "I hate to see you here."

Lumen kept her eyes shut, took deep breaths to push down the sudden spike of lightning quick fury that rushed through her, calling her to leap at the locked gate of bars where Oliver Spragg stood.

"You brought me here," she said after releasing a long breath. The sound of Oliver's shoes scratching on the dry floor echoed too loud in her head and she pressed one ear to her shoulder, glancing at his feet out of the corner of her eye.

"Why didn't you tell them anything?" he asked.

"Because I never knew anything," she said.

"You were with them for three months."

"I haven't forgotten, you know."

Oliver huffed and Lumen winced as she shifted. The cell was cold and open and she had tired of pacing the same little circle on the floor hours ago. She pushed herself to standing and watched as Oliver backed away the closer she stepped.

"Are you protecting them?" he asked, eyes narrowed.

"No." *They didn't need her to.*

"There must be something, Lumen."

"There is nothing." There was something, one thing, but it was useless and would soon be irrelevant. She knew why Westbrook's army hadn't moved for three months. Now that she was gone perhaps the war would progress again.

She didn't care if Stalor took the capitol now. She would be locked down here either way, unless Cannary and his table of peers decided she wasn't worth the expense. More than likely she would be forgotten.

"Why didn't you leave with me?" Oliver asked, and Lumen raised her gaze to his face, brow tangled, mouth frowning. It wasn't apology or sorrow there that she read, it was frustration and bitter resentment. "You let them ruin you for three months and it never occurred to you to take something in return? Something that might *help* your people?"

"I was trying to help my people by *staying*," Lumen said.

His eyes narrowed and his voice hardened. "You should have come to me. You should have accepted *my* protection."

He was handsome, hair shining, eyes bright, shoulders broad and warm. She'd seen all of that and more, months ago. Now she was sick of him.

"Would it really have been so different than Westbrook's?" she asked, watching his breath catch, his step fall back. "What would you have done, Oliver Spragg, if I had laid down next to you in that cabin? Offered your *protection?*"

Oliver turned away, stared down the long hall of cells, jaw grinding.

"I have been a prisoner in my own home for months," Lumen said, tongue snapping around the words. "I will adjust to being a prisoner here."

"I think you are right, Lady Fenn. And now I should return to the estate," Oliver bit back, crossing down the hall.

Lumen's fists wrapped around the bars of the cell, a scream coiling in her chest, holding tight until her fingers ached. She breathed through the anger, forehead pressing to the bars, a guard passing her without a glance, until the feeling was settled to a dull scratch in her head.

METAL CRASHED AGAINST METAL, the vibration bruising through Dominic straight down to the bone. He pushed the man at his front into a clashing set of swords and spun, bring the hilt of sword down on the enemy at his back, a shoulder crunching beneath the force.

There was blood in one eye, a twist in his knee. He could hear every concussive strike around him, every bellow of pain, every crunch of bone and the wet slide of ice and mud beneath their feet until it all bled together into a white silence in his head. Gideon was roaring, chasing a retreating Oshain soldier, his face painted in lines of blood and dirt, sword bleeding down to his knuckles.

"They're retreating!" Gideon shouted.

"Take what you can, Stalor!"

Dominic dove into the turning wave of the battle, hungry

for... for more of this. The violence. The distraction. It skidded through his head, a flash of a round, pale face, and his boot was sucked into mud. He nearly fell into the ground until a fist caught in the armor of his back and drew him upright again. Finley, eyes bloodshot and fixed over Dominic's shoulder.

"Colin," Finley said, although Dominic could only read the name on his lips, the roar of blood pumping too loud in his head.

The boy was running fearlessly onto the field, out of the tree line of the nearby woods, dodging swords and grappling men.

Lumen will kill me if he gets hurt, Dominic thought. Behind Colin came a nervous, weedy young man in Oshain colors, white flag raised tremulously over his head.

"Negotiations?" Finley asked.

"Enough!" Dominic barked at his men. Gideon kept charging, along with few others but they would stop after their last cutting swings and the fighting would end before the negotiations were strictly settled.

His eyes flicked back to Colin and he tensed. He should deal with Oshain's runner first but...

No, he was the General today. He *would* deal with the runner first.

"Hold Colin until I'm done," he said to Finley, waiting until he nodded in agreement before marching forward.

He hated this part, when the fighting had ended and the world was more than flashes of red and black and grey and gold. When his body remembered that there was a cost to fighting and the view of the ground beneath him made his innards do strange dances in their cage. When he was a boy at war he'd waited until the fighting was ended and his master was tended before going into the trees and leaving bitter sick in the leaves. Every time.

It still happened some days, when they pushed harder.

"What do they want?" Dominic asked the runner, a pimply scrawny youth who would be in armor soon if the sprinkling of pale hair on his chin was anything to guess by.

"Two weeks of ceasefire," the runner said, eyes wide and staring at Dominic chest and sword, painted red.

"How much are they prepared to part with?"

"Five miles."

Dominic laughed, genuinely laughed. Two weeks of idleness after victory for *a mile?* "We gained half that in the fighting alone."

He shook a twinge out of his arm and the runner nearly leapt into the air at the twitch of his sword. Dominic resisted a grin and raised his eyebrows.

"They said no more'n ten miles!" the runner bleated.

Then demand twenty, said a voice in his head. Ten miles and they would decamp from Fenn Manor. Twenty and there would be no reason to turn back.

"Ten miles and a week of ceasefire," Dominic said. When the runner's eyes slid to the side, weighing the likely response from Oshain, Dominic added, "Whether your Generals see fit to agree or not. Now get off Stalor land."

The youth took off back into the woods, white flag whipping behind him. When Dominic turned, Gideon was already running back down the field to where Finley waited with Colin, his legs leaping awkwardly over a body laying face down in the mud. Dominic hurried back before Gideon could shake the news out of the boy.

"Did you find her?" he asked.

Colin shook his head as Gideon's steps stuttered and slowed, Dominic's heart dropping down to his feet.

"Spragg took her through the usual village but I think he caught them a ride into the capitol," Colin said.

Gideon growled, stabbing the end of his sword too deep into the ground and Finley sighed, covering his mouth with his hand and closing his eyes.

Gideon on a rage or not, it would be months before they made it to the capitol, and it would take four times as many men to breach the city. She would be long gone by then.

"She left with nothing," Gideon muttered. "How safe can she be there? I need to know, Dominic."

"You can't get into Oshain," Finley said, shaking his head. "Not so far. You're too recognizable. You're too..."

Gideon was too *Gideon* to get to Lumen without getting himself caught or causing a mess in the process.

"Stalor's not going to let us just go and- and check on a woman," Finley said. "She's gone. She's with her countrymen. We should leave it at that."

Dominic scanned the field, hunting out Danvers and Charlie.

"You can't send them," Colin hissed. "They'll just take the coin and use it on ale and come back to tell you she's fine or dead or whatever they feel like spinning."

Gideon's gaze met Dominic's over Colin's head. That was interesting news and would require further investigation. If Danvers and Charlie weren't taking their orders seriously what else was at stake? Their loyalty?

Perhaps it was better that Colin's belonged to Lumen. At least Dominic could rely on his priorities, even if they weren't to the Stalor army.

"I should go," Colin said.

All three men stared down at the boy. They were an ugly, violent set—covered in filth and gore—and Colin only looked back at them, mild and certain. He had twice the courage of Oshain's runner. Or maybe he knew what Dominic knew—he was precious to Lumen and therefore valuable to them.

"Don't be ridiculous," Finley said shaking his head.

"Could you make it?" Gideon asked.

"Of course I could," Colin said.

"Could you find her?" Dominic asked, forehead creasing and skin stretching strangely with the grit of the battle drying in the cold air.

"I know where the fancy folk you've chased away have gone before to get their money and the like," Colin said, shrugging.

Dominic's eyes narrowed. Shit. Did he know where they went? "Where?"

"There's a grand building, where officials meet and with a prison underground," Colin said. "Oliver would've taken Lady there. I can find it easy enough on my way. I can ask the right questions to the right folks too. I'll find her."

"Will you come back?" Gideon growled.

"Maybe," Colin said, tipping his chin up.

"You'll come back if she needs us," Dominic said and the boy glanced at him with eyes wide.

He'd be a fool to give up a spy like Colin, especially if Danvers and Charlie were turning out to be anything less than reliable. But if a woman like Lumen had found him as a boy...

How young would he have needed to be to turn out any way but the way he was? And what else could he offer Lumen at this point than the boy? Silver.

"Or if she needs what I hid," he added, lower so that they were the only four who heard the words.

Colin nodded solemnly. "I'll come back, sir."

"Decamp with us and then leave when the men are settled. No one needs to know your errand."

"'M not stupid," Colin muttered and he huffed away.

"Are you trying to get news of her, or apologize?" Finley asked, staring at him.

"Leave it," Gideon snapped. "The boy'd make her happy at least."

There was resignation in the words. Dominic hadn't thought anything would make Gideon give up his hunt for Lumen. And if Gideon wouldn't give up that might mean he didn't have to either—from a distance, but still in the same pursuit. To try and return some of what he'd stolen and still hold the pieces he now found it impossible to exist without.

"AND HOW MANY men were in residence in your home?"

Lumen tried to wet her lips but even her tongue was dry. She stared through the bars into the dark hall at General Cannary and his flanking assistants.

"Twenty four at first," she said, voice scratched and throat swollen from too many nights in the cold. "Then twice that many. Then twice again. I don't know by the end. Men up to the rafters and out in the yard too."

"Of those hundred or more men, you were intimate with how many?"

She stared at the waiting pencil. They asked this question every time, waiting for the number to change. "Three."

"And those three were?"

She repeated the names, hating the sound of them in her own ears.

"And was this altogether or at separate times?"

"Is this relevant to your army's strategy?" Lumen asked. "Are your men planning on seducing Stalor's finest?"

Cannary blinked at her and Lumen understood. Not his men. But he had women he thought might do the trick.

"Separately," she bit out.

All three men stared at her in varying expressions of surprise, one cocking his head like a dog. "Every time?" Cannary asked.

Lumen nearly shouted at the man but she remembered what Finley had said. Westbrook had shared his women. She was an exception, and even then lines had been blurred. Finley walking in on her and Dominic. Gideon easing her need during Finley's game.

"Every time," she insisted.

"And after those intimacies what did you speak of?"

Lumen snorted. "Generally they just went to sleep."

Her lips wanted to smile. Jennie would have found that funny, would have laughed with her. Cannary did not.

"And on those occasions which were not general, Miss Fenn."

"Once I spoke of my brothers and Westbrook told me how he joined the army. Sometimes Brink would discuss a remedy. Gideon only asked after me. I think he offered to help me escape once."

"Gideon?"

Lumen's heart sank and reminded of where she was again. "Jones."

"And how would he have assisted you in escape?"

She blinked. "I don't think he would have planned it. It was just something he said."

One of the men on the other side of the bars scoffed.

"And you never read anything of any value?" Cannary asked.

"I read my fathers books until they were sold off."

General Cannary's eyes squinted just a fraction and Lumen knew the interview was nearing its end. "Anything that might have been of value to the Oshain army, Miss Fenn."

"No, I did not," Lumen said.

"We'll leave you to your thoughts and perhaps the next time we visit you may have remembered something more useful," Cannary said.

Lumen watched their backs turn to retreat with a sense of panic at being left alone for days at a time again only to listen to the world go by without her, and other inmates go mad in these cold little cells.

"Why do you insist I must know something useful, General?" she asked.

Cannary paused and turned, staring down a long crooked nose at her. "Because all the other women did, Miss Fenn. Their homes were occupied, same as yours. Their virtues stolen, I might guess a hair more thoroughly than yours. Their fortunes sold off, just as yours was. And they crossed back into the safe hold of their country, armed with information against their enemy."

Lumen's heart raced in her chest. Had she really made such a mistake? She'd made the preservation of the chapel her entire goal, as if by setting her expectations so low she was ensuring the safety of being overlooked. Instead she'd let everything be stolen out from under her.

"Think, Miss Fenn," Cannary said, gentle and quiet, his footsteps padding away down the hall and leaving her to this empty, gutted feeling.

IT SNOWED IN THE CITY, HEAVY ENOUGH EVEN IN THE COURTYARD to raise drifts against the building, blocking any light from Lumen's window. The cell grew stale without the cold air and soon damp, as snow began to melt slowly down the window and over the wall.

Lumen gathered up her bedding and tried to shift it across the cell, closer to the bars, when a small gray mouse skittered out of a nest she revealed. It stopped in the center of her cell, Lumen's back pressed to the wall and heart racing as they stared at one another. Her knees wobbled, shock and too little movement in the past weeks of imprisonment, and she sank down to the floor. The mouse trembled in place, watching her in return.

"I've upset your home, haven't I?" Lumen whispered and the mouse made a quick circle on the floor in front of her.

Her nearly cleaned plate of food was waiting by the bars of the cell and Lumen moved at a glacial pace until it was under her fingers and sliding across the floor. The mouse twitched in the direction of the plate.

"Least I can do," Lumen said. It was a tiny thing with thin, translucent ears and paws so small Lumen wondered how they could be real. She smiled as it dashed over the bowl, climbing in and hunting down the smallest scraps of food left.

Footsteps echoed down the hall, a chorus of complaints rising from the cells in the wake of the latest visitor. Lumen watched her mouse and tried to ignore the way her heart leapt into her throat as the steps stopped in front of her.

"Unapproved visitor?"

Healer Graham was her least favorite of the small collection of officials who came to her cell to quiz her. He asked questions about her mother's studies of plants and her own vague training in healing. Which plants could heal and which could harm. How often did she administer remedies to the Stalor army, in what dosages, and was she monitored while she prepared her medicines?

She understood the direction of the questions. How many opportunities had she missed to poison Westbrook and his men? She even started a list in her mind.

She could have put poison in the onion broth she made the night of their arrival, quick and deadly and final. In the vinegar she prepared as a tonic she might have added something slow with symptoms that came on gradually and undetectable. She might have misjudged the Gensen she gave to the men who grew sick and Finley would've considered it an accident. She brought Westbrook and Gideon a dozen ales and not one left them on their knees gasping for breath.

The only time Lumen really thought of taking the life of any of the army was the very first night after Westbrook was done with her. It had been less of a *choice* not to go through with the act and more an understanding that such a thing was impossible for her.

"I think they were here first," Lumen answered, watching the mouse scurry around the bowl, aware of being observed by the predator through the bars and unable to escape its gaze. Lumen reached out and tipped the bowl, lip touching the floor, and the mouse took off into the shadows. "What do you need?" she asked Graham. ·

"It's time for an examination," Graham said.

Lumen's fingers dug into the blanket and hay beneath her. "An examination?"

"To see if you are with child."

"I'm not." Graham snorted and Lumen forced herself to

breathe through her nose, resisted the urge to press her hand over her heart to feel it pound and rattle. "I'm not. I had my courses before I left. I'll have them again before the new moon."

"You can't be sure of that."

"I can be *very* sure of that," Lumen said. She'd taken the tea with a better devotion than she paid her own goddess and no one had touched her since she'd left the Manor, not in that way.

Graham's lips pursed and he glanced down the hall back to the stairs, weighing her words.

"Why would you care?" Lumen asked.

"If there's any argument that it might be Westbrook's child you may be more useful than you've currently led us to believe," Graham said.

Lumen relaxed and pressed her back to the wall, draping the coat across her shoulders and over herself like a blanket. "He wouldn't care."

"Maybe not in the past," Graham said. "Westbrook was a very predictable man in his habits outside the battlefield before he arrived at your home."

Lumen swallowed and ignored the announcement, listening to the sound of the mouse in the corner, scratching at its demolished nest.

"Has anyone told you yet? Stalor gained its first ground in months after you arrived here."

Lumen turned her head and looked up at Graham from her place on the floor. "Let me leave. Let me go to the Lunar Convent."

"Perhaps," Graham said. "We'll see after the new moon."

Graham left her, stopping at another cell, voices low as he continued a new interrogation. Lumen waited for tears to rise in her eyes and then sighed with relief when they didn't. She'd shed enough of those by now and it only left her tired and with a headache.

Her head was full of lists. Times she could have killed Westbrook or his army. Moments she might have left the Manor sooner. And the choices that were not hers to make. Times when Westbrook might have been different. Not demanded she sleep with him. Not sold her family possessions to fund his army. Not tossed her aside for disobeying him, trying to protect Colin. Anger at Finley too for leaving.

It piled up inside of her until sometimes her stomach was so sour and tangled she thought she might be sick if only to release the feeling.

Movement flashed out of the corner of her eye and there was her little friend again, running across the floor to the bowl, rising to his hind legs and climbing back in to feast on the contents. Lumen let the little creature be the sole focus of her attention, curling up on the poor pretense of a bed and folding her arms to hold her head.

THERE WAS RUSTLING, the sound of slush hitting the floor, and she woke up slowly. Cold air slid down from the high window, biting at Lumen's fingertips and nose. She sat up and squinted, watching as another wet clump of snow fell through the grate, revealing the dark sky overhead. The dead of night seemed like an odd time for snow to be melting.

Lumen pulled herself up and her breath caught in her chest. Cut through with the wire of the grate was the full face of Lune, pure and shining, staring down at her. A moment later it was obscured by the dark outline of a messy head of hair.

"Lady?"

Time and hunger and exhaustion gave her a brief reprieve in that moment.

"Colin?"

He hushed her softly, her voice too bright in its surprise.

"How are you- Colin, you can't be here, it's not safe!" she hissed.

He made a soft sound of impolite rebuttal and all the pain of the last two weeks, last months, returned at once, bringing with it fondness for the boy above her blocking the moonlight with his head.

"I'm safe for now, Lady," he said. "Guards won't be back again for a few minutes."

Lumen wanted to rush at the wall and jump, reach through the grate to touch his hair, his cheek. But she held still just so she could stare at his silhouette and know he was *there*, with her again in some way.

"Are you alright?" he asked. She knew by the sound of his voice, smaller and more timid than usual, that he'd already decided the answer to the question.

"I'm alright," she said, nodding a little.

Damn, the tears had returned. She blinked them away.

"I'm going to bring Westbrook, Jones, and Brink to you," Colin whispered, and she saw his fingers wrap through the holes in the grate.

She shook her head. "Don't Colin. Don't bother."

"You can't stay here, Lady. Look at where they've put you."

There was a wobble in his words so she lifted her chin and tried to smile. "I'm alright. Really. It's not so different, here or there. I wasn't free at the Manor."

Colin was quiet above her and Lumen knew she would have to make him leave in a moment, and she would have to keep herself from calling out to him when he turned away.

"Maybe you weren't. But it don't have bars on the windows, do it?"

Her head was too heavy to keep lifted, heart sinking in her chest like a perfect parallel. Colin shifted overhead and moonlight spilled in, crowning her dirty hair.

"I wouldn't bring them, but I don't know who else," Colin whispered.

Lumen looked up and winced at the light, caught a brief glimpse of Colin's face—just the little upturn of his nose, filling the rest in for herself. "Colin I want you to go back. Take the Manor, it's yours. I don't- just be safe for me?"

"I'll be back with the others soon, Lady," Colin whispered. "I have to go now."

She folded her lips inside her teeth before she could call to stop him, just to have the company.

"Oh!" He reappeared, face pressed to the grate and Lumen held her breath. "He didn't sell the silver. He shoulda told you he was hidin' it from the others. But it ain't gone. Just secret."

And then the boy was gone, leaving her with the moon. Lune looked full in the sky but it had been so long since Lumen had seen a glimpse and she'd lost track of days passing when the snow drifted over.

The silver wasn't sold.

She waited for anger and when that didn't come she waited for regret. The cell was cold again but at least the air coming through the window was clean. Lumen closed her eyes, the blue shadow image of the moon bright behind her eyelids. She wished she hadn't told Colin to take the Manor, it would be a weight around his neck just like it was around hers.

Lumen had spent years trying to preserve a house, keep it in a time of peace that she didn't even remember. The war had snatched up her father when she was barely old enough to remember sitting on his knee and then her brothers one by one. Why hadn't her mother decamped Fenn Manor sooner and why had Lumen followed in her footsteps?

Fenn Manor or this prison cell, she didn't care now. If she couldn't go to the Convent she would be one of its disciples where she was. She stepped forward and lowered herself to her knees, icy water seeping through her dress to nip at her skin. Lumen tipped her face back, slowing her breaths and emptying her thoughts, opening herself to Mother Lune's light.

THE ARMY DECAMPED from the Manor on a clear morning, leaving it to Gideon's pick of whores. It looked strange and bare as they emptied it of their supplies and cots. The only furniture left behind after Westbrook's sales were the beds and the less ornate tables. It didn't look like a home at all, Finley thought. Fenn Manor had never made a right kind of sense to him since arriving, with its open courtyard and circling halls left to face rough winters.

He stood in the center of the courtyard and stared down the thin, dark hall to Lumen's chapel, out the blue window that faced the pond. And when he turned his head in the exact opposite direction there was another hall, wider and leading to a large open room they'd filled with cots. The sunrise burned through an enormous set of windows, turning the room red and golden, black tile shining on the floor. Sol's colors.

Not a home, and yet there was regret at the thought of leaving. Finley wanted some promise he would see this place again, spend another night in the courtyard, study another day in Lumen's workshop upstairs.

The men at least seemed glad to be moving on. The army was back at war and their time in this strange stone-walled sanctuary was at its end.

Gideon met him at the front doors, a bundle of cloth tucked under his arm.

"What is that?"

"Some of her clothes," Gideon said. "She didn't take anything with her."

Finley considered running upstairs and grabbing more of the contents of the workroom, but he'd already collected enough as it was.

"What if she doesn't come back? What if Colin stays with her?" Finley asked.

Gideon frowned and his shoulder twitched in a faint shrug. "Then she won't miss them."

Keeping a dress hardly seemed like consolation for losing the woman herself. Except then Finley remembered the hollow ache in his chest the day his sweater no longer smelled of her, so perhaps there was something to Gideon's logic.

Finley hauled himself up into his saddle and started out to the road, passing one of the soldiers who stood, arms wrapped around a sobbing girl.

"Will you wait for me?" he asked.

"We can't just wait here, Phil," she whimpered. "There's no *work* here."

Finley ignored the sound of coin passing between them. If

the man wanted to spend his savings on her, what business was it of Finley's?

"Just wait," Phil whispered. "I'll send more soon as I can."

If Lumen *wasn't* returning, Finley wondered how hard it would be to convince Dominic to give her silver to those women. She'd liked them, befriended them, had the sense to respect them. Gideon and Dominic wanted to believe she would return to them but Finley wanted to believe she had the sense to see herself safely away.

They rode through the morning until the sun was high in the sky and the cold was so sharp that the soldiers were already starting to look behind them, back to Fenn Manor. It would be better once the tents were up and fires were built.

They made it to the last scene of battle, a new layer of snow covering the evidence and Oshain having long since carried away their dead and wounded. Waiting for them, a small cart of supplies hitched to the back of his mule, was Colin. It'd been a week since Dominic let the boy head for the capitol on his own and he looked no worse for the wear.

It made Finley's heart sink to see him. Something was wrong. Or he hadn't found her.

Colin jumped out of the cart, face wrapped in a thick scarf and a blanket twisted around him like a cape. Finley rode up to Dominic's side.

"Get the camp organized," Dominic said to Danvers and Charlie and then he and Finley and Gideon trotted after the boy to the tree line.

Colin was spitting words out as fast as he could, but none of them came through his scarf clearly.

"Slow down," Gideon urged him when they were out of earshot of the army. "And get the wool out of your mouth."

One hand, mittened in the blanket, reached up and pulled the scarf down. "They threw her in a cell to rot."

Dominic's horse jerked and whinnied at the sudden tug of its reins and then Dominic was jumping down, followed by Gideon and Finley.

"They what?" Dominic snarled, dropping to his knees and clasping Colin's shoulders in his hands.

The boy didn't flinch. "It took a bit to hear the right conversations before I found her. They got her in that building with a jail in the basement. Folks that cross the border hafta go and get questioned before they can get safe haven.

"I had to play beggar on the steps for two days and then I heard a couple men with medals talking bout her. Followed 'em to the pub. They're callin' her a traitor and they don't plan on letting her out. They think she's your spy or she's got information she just won't give."

Finley thought he might be sick.

"*Her* people are doin' this?" Gideon asked, a dangerous sound clawing up through his throat.

Colin's nose wrinkled. "I don't think Lady's got people. Not ones who care proper like us."

Finley opened his mouth and then shut it again. The boy was right. Her tenants would care, the old woman and the widowed mother but…

"Spragg did this," Finley said.

Colin nodded. "I got news about him too. Saw it on the way back here when I passed the Oshain army. They conscripted him again."

"He's got one arm," Finley said.

"That's one'll hold a sword," Colin said with a shrug. "They need all they can get."

"She's in a cell," Dominic pressed, his fingers looked tight around Colin's arms but the boy didn't seem to mind.

"Bars on the inside facin' a hall. Tiny window open to the air. She don't look well, sir," he said.

Dominic released him and stood, fingers pressed and pulling down his face, the scar on his left cheek stark and shining.

"I thought I could try an' get her out myself," Colin continued. "But the guard shifts are too close and I never got down into the jail. Just in the courtyard so I could see a glimpse of her."

"We have to go to her," Gideon said and Finley could see him out of the corner of his eye, body shifting in place, ready to run to Oshain's capitol that moment.

"Our army can't take that city," Finley said, before Dominic could get carried away. "We don't stand a chance."

"No," Dominic agreed, but his gaze was out at the horizon looking north. "No. But we can take another fifteen miles tomorrow. Colin, the village just over the border, what's it like?"

"Nearly empty since you won the last battle. Oshain's got themselves parked there for now."

"We take the village," Dominic said. "Do as much harm to their ranks as we can. Give them the two weeks ceasefire they'll ask for. Then we go in for her ourselves."

Finley's heart raced at the thought. He was a healer. He wasn't even a proper soldier but Dominic let him serve his own purpose. He certainly wasn't a spy.

But the picture of her in a cold, cramped cell, left to wither… it made Finley want to find his horse and ride through the night. How long would she last underground in the winter?

"I'll write south today, call for reinforcements," Dominic said. "It'll give us a reason not to move."

"Do you trust Danvers and Charlie to keep their mouths shut?" Gideon asked.

"No and I don't plan on telling them what we're doing," Dominic said. He turned back to Colin. "Will you keep an eye on them while we go and fetch your lady?"

Colin's eyes narrowed and his jaw worked in a way that reminded Finley eerily of Dominic himself. "I'd rather see her safe myself. But I don't trust them neither, so I suppose." He pointed his finger up at his General. "You bring her back safe to me. Don't say nothing stupid and don't do nothing cruel."

Dominic sucked in a breath and Finley waited for the man to snarl back. Instead he went down on one knee, eye level with Colin who looked less cowed than Finley would have in that moment. "You have my word," Dominic said. "We'll need every detail of the city and the building you can give us."

"I can draw if you give me something to write with," Colin said.

Dominic stood and lead Colin back to camp and Finley stopped Gideon before he could follow.

"We'll never get her out. We'll get ourselves killed and her too if we aren't careful," he said.

Gideon pursed his lips and narrowed his eyes and Finley was reminded for the hundredth time that he was yet to be forgiven for leaving. "Two'll be less conspicuous than three if you'd rather stay here," Gideon said, raising an eyebrow.

"Not if those two are *you*," Finley hissed. "You and Dom are the most recognizable figures in the entire Stalor army and you want to walk into the Oshain capitol?"

Gideon blinked and cocked his head, seeming to think the idea over. Then he shrugged. "Not in uniform. Like I said, Brink. You don't have to come. Sounds like you've got a day to think it over."

Finley watched Gideon's back as he left. The entire idea was suicide and yet he was certain he was going. If they made it, he would see her again. He would apologize. He would make sure she was healthy and safe.

She'll die if you don't go, he told himself. He might die first, but that had been a long time coming given his habits in life.

GIDEON ALWAYS LOOKED FORWARD TO BATTLE. IT TOOK MORE effort for him to remain idle and the only calm he'd found so far in life was his arms wrapped around Lumen. He wasn't fond of killing, there were other ways to stop an enemy and send them packing, but if it came to his life or the life of one of the men standing next to him, so be it.

Swords clashed around him, a clumsy affair of grappling bodies appearing in front of him as Charlie tried to toss an Oshain soldier off his back.

"Shields up!" Dominic shouted from Gideon's left. "Cavalry push!"

Gideon didn't fight with a shield—instead he barreled into the soldier ahead of him, shouldering him above his own head as a flurry of arrows cascaded down from the skies. He heard the grunt of the man he carried, the wet *snick* of an arrow biting into flesh.

For the first time, he was looking forward to the battle's end, sending Oshain back to nurse their wounds and sliding past them in the cover of night and the coming snow. It would take them the night to travel to the capitol. Reaching Lumen safely was complicated. Escaping with his little spirit in tow was even more so.

Finley called it suicide but Gideon refused the notion. He was less concerned for his own life than he was for hers. Lumen needed him. Finding her and returning her safely home was the only resolution Gideon accepted. The sooner the better.

When the rain of arrows finished Gideon tossed his shield, the man, back to the ground and pushed forward into the rush of bodies.

Gain the fifteen miles. Move the camp. Cross the line and ride to the capitol. Scoop Lumen up into his arms again.

He'd leave the steps in between up to Dominic.

"Gid!"

Gideon locked arms with the soldier in front of him, grinning at the man, catching the full white of his wide eyes open in terror, and twisted the arm around the other man's back and popped it out of place. He pushed him aside and turned to Dominic who was locked in a sword fight.

"Spragg," Dominic called out, sweat and blood running down his neck. "Ahead and to your right."

Gideon's body found rare stillness in that moment, the battle frantic around him as he froze, eyes hunting through the crowd for his prey.

There he was, Oliver Spragg, hair soaked with snow and one arm swinging a blade. His face was streaked with blood, mouth torn open in a snarl and eyes wild. He was a good fighter, Gideon would give him that much. Strong and better with one arm than some of Gideon's trainees were with two.

But he was a dead man walking and *this* was a kill Gideon could relish.

He shoved away the soldier that tried to rush him while his attention was focused on Spragg, grabbing the man by his front plates of armor and dragging him through the snow to push aside a fighting pair. Spragg caught sight of him while Gideon was sorting his way through the crowd. He didn't turn and run —his eyes were black with the energy of the battle—but there was a grim set to his mouth and he raised his sword to guard himself.

"Who cut your arm off?" Gideon asked, the words muted by the activity that surrounded him. He hoped it'd been him, that he'd done the honors even if he didn't remember the battle.

"A doctor," Spragg said, glowering back at him. Gideon snorted and Spragg lifted his chin. "Are you planning on taking the one I have now?"

"No," Gideon answered, lips pursed and shoulders relaxed. "I don't plan on wasting time with your limbs. I'll see you dead outright for what you put her through."

"What *I* put her through? What about you lot?"

"If Lumen wants revenge from me I'll hold her hand steady while she sticks the sword in." Gideon leapt then, sword slashing. Spragg bellowed as he blocked the blow, knuckles white around his weapon, body trembling as he held his ground.

"I can tell you...where she is," Spragg said through gritted teeth. It was cold and his hair was frozen, sweat slicked through and iced over.

"I know where she is. Where you left her." Gideon tried to pull the man's sword loose from his hand in his withdraw but Spragg was ready, twisting his hand with a wild grimace as he jumped back. Gideon struck again and Spragg was barely fast enough to block the next blow.

"I could get her out again," Spragg hissed, bowing backwards as Gideon pushed..

"Are you bargaining for her life or yours?" Gideon growled. He punched from below, catching Spragg between the ribs and watching with a grin as the man's breath puffed out in a white billow of steam.

"You ruined her life," Spragg wheezed.

"And what did you do with it?" Gideon growled.

He pushed and Spragg stumbled backwards, one foot slipping in the thin coat of snow and blood and ice beneath him, knee twisting before he caught himself from falling.

"Please," Spragg gasped. "I have information. I could—"

"You can have one favor," Gideon said. "I'll make it swift."

It took two more blows. One, Spragg blocked. The next, he didn't.

The edge of Gideon's sword aimed high, and quick, forcing its way through flesh, Spragg's head jerking as Gideon hit bone. He pulled the blade free and watched red soak the collar of his enemy's uniform while sunlight glinted yellow off of armor, as if the blood changed his allegiance in that moment. Sol's colors.

It wasn't satisfaction, nothing could be satisfaction while Lumen wasn't near. But it was done at least. And soon the battle would be too. Gideon went back to work, diving into the tangle of bodies and hunting victory for Stalor.

ALL NIGHT IN THE CELL, the sound of ragged coughs and wheezing breaths echoed against the floor. Lumen lay curled on her small bed, throat burning and lungs sore as her body strained against the spasms. The illness squatting like a toad in her chest kept her awake at all hours and there were moments where she thought the next breath might not come.

No one came to question her again, not even as the new moon neared—which she tracked through the grate now that Colin had cleared the view—and her courses returned. The meals seemed to stretch farther apart and Lumen wondered if there would be a day when they would not come at all or if this acidic sludge in her lungs would have extinguished her by then.

There was one loyal visitor, the little gray mouse, who came and begged scraps and seemed content to sit with Lumen as she meditated, and even stayed when the peace of meditation gave way to tears or anxious pacing.

On the night of the new moon Lumen spread the thin blanket over the damp floor of the cell and lay face down, ignoring the sounds of other inmates, of the guards in the court-yard muttering about the weak pay.

This will likely be my last new moon. I'll pay the right observances tonight, at least.

She lay in a peaceful kind of silence, her lungs itching but giving her a brief reprieve from the worst of their complaining. Stillness and a beautiful clean emptiness filled her in the dark until a faint sound broke its way through, picking at awareness like a nail against a scab.

There was a scratching in the far corner of the cell to the left of the grate. Her little friend, she assumed, until the scratching was a rustling, too dense to be one small creature. Lumen's forehead pressed to the coarse weave of the blanket, brow creasing as the sound grew larger, and then froze as heavy fabric brushed against her skirt.

It was the sound of the pond in summer, barely touched by a breeze, and her mother's thick velvet skirts echoing down the hall, and the wind whistling through a crack of stone in the Manor walls. Lumen's left side was kissed by a strange sensation, something like frost lacing her skin and something like sliding into a warm bath.

She opened her eyes and saw a hint of movement at her left, shrouded in black. She held her breath and for the first time in weeks her chest didn't itch or ache. Lumen turned her head and found a woman at her side, prostate on the floor in a mirror position of her own, draped in black cloth that was somehow sheer and dizzyingly dense, like looking up at the night sky. The woman's head turned and Lumen saw the muzzle of a wolf's mouth pressing against the shroud.

A white hand, fingers delicate and lined with wrinkles creased in black ink, slid across the floor and covered Lumen's hand. The touch was smooth and cold and hard, like bone, and it guided Lumen's fingers to the shroud, lifting it up over the face.

Lumen gasped.

There was no wolf nor any sign of fur, although Mother Lune did have thick hair that ran over her shoulders like oil, black or blue or silver, the color changing as Lumen flinched and pushed up from the floor. The goddess followed, body mimicking Lumen perfectly in reverse. Her eyes were silver coins, so familiar Lumen imagined she might have picked them up from the altar of a temple nearby. Her lips were nearly as pale as her skin, stitched shut with fine embroidery that mimicked white stars across her mouth. Her cheeks were hollow, skin smooth with youth but lined with cracks like ancient porcelain.

Lumen's lips were parted, eyes drinking in her goddess, heart pounding. She wanted to speak, to beg for mercy or forgiveness or to thank Lune for not leaving her alone just as she had not left her alone all the nights prior while Lumen slept under her light.

Lune's other hand linked with Lumen's, this one warmer and softer and tucked beneath the dark of the shroud, belonging to a different phase of the goddess.

Lumen took a breath, released a sigh, and felt the ease of the action again, lungs filling with warm dry air.

Questions clawed their way up to her tongue. Had she been wrong? Bad in her devotion? Or had every loss and every surrender been a step to this moment? Was Stalor winning the war because Sol was stronger or did the gods keep themselves out of the affairs of the humans?

But it was the new moon and it called for silence and Lune's lips were sealed with stars.

The goddess took her face in two hands, one bone white and cold, the other shrouded and warm, and tipped Lumen's head back, rising and growing above her. Lune's face lowered to hers and with it came tears in Lumen's eyes that blurred the goddess, shifting her from young to old, from brilliant to shadowed. When their foreheads touched Lumen released a shaky exhale. Her mother was with her, her grandmother, a long, strong line of women whose blood ran in her veins and sang up to Lune's embrace. And mixed in all that familiar strength was the faintest brush of heat, a gentle reflection of Sol's light, reminding Lumen of men she tried to forget.

It didn't burn or ache or make her regret. Not here with Lune. There were only faint flutters of pleasure, a devotion she now understood honored both Lune *and* Sol, and a delicate memory of sweetness and affection. The bad, the wrong, the painful, was there too, but for one brief night the two sat side by side instead of the awful burying the wonderful.

Lune stayed with Lumen until the sun rose, light filtering through the goddess in gradual measures. Lumen lost track of the hours—one minute she was seated on the floor, face kissed by Lune's, and the next she was back in her bed of hay, blanket tucked up around her. She slept through the day, eyes barely opening at any disturbance, and woke late in the night as her cough finally returned.

"HIDE YOUR DAMN SCAR," Finley hissed.

Dominic twitched the hood of his cloak forward again as they slid out of one alleyway—crossing the quiet street to the capitol jail—and then into another where Colin promised them a narrow alcove in the brick where they could hide until the evening shift of guards left out the back door.

"Faster," Dominic whispered as voices filtered through the glass of the doorway.

The space was there, tucked behind the waste bins, and Dominic grimaced as he saw it. Large enough for a boy like Colin to hide himself without a chance of being seen. But for him, Finley, and *Gideon*? He jumped in after the others and screwed his jaw shut as Gideon wrapped an arm around his shoulder, squeezing him in so tight Dominic had trouble catching a breath. Perhaps that was for the best, the bins were fragrant and he and the others weren't faring much better after their journey.

Dominic's face was mashed to Gideon's chest, Finley's to the brick wall, and they held as still as stone as the alley door opened, a trail of men exiting.

Gideon's head twitched to take a glance, eyes counting the men that left the building. The door snapped shut and Gideon waited in silence. A moment later it opened again, the last man huffing his way to the street.

"Go," Gideon whispered, releasing Dominic, steadying him as he wormed his way out from behind the bins.

The new shift was already inside. Colin said they met on the northern end of the building, changed into their uniforms, and relieved the shift before theirs. They would still be spreading out to their positions but the south side was the last to be filled.

Finley moved ahead, Dominic's iron lock picks lifted from his coat pocket as he crouched in front of the door. Dominic would have been faster with the picks, but Finley was the worst at hand-to-hand. They were better off keeping Dominic and Gideon's hands free and ready to fight. Dominic resisted the urge to order him to hurry, biting on his lips and keeping his eyes focused on the opening of the alleyway for any sign of life. He was not the General on this mission and Finley knew the urgency as well as he did.

Tumblers turned and Finley slid inside, hand beckoning them to follow after a moment.

The building was silent inside, lamps dimmed to conserve oil, and it took him a moment for Dominic to see the weave of staircases and halls around the entrance and match it to Colin's scribbles in his head. Deeper inside of the building footsteps and voices echoed.

"To the right," he whispered, nodding at a staircase leading upstairs and praying that the boy wasn't guiding them into a trap of their own making.

She was down, underground, but these were Colin's instructions.

Up to the second story, cross north by the eastern hallway, the guards will be in the east and west wings off of the first floor long enough that you might make it down to the cells if you're fast and quiet enough.

And then if they were fast and quiet enough, they could incapacitate the guards on duty there.

It wasn't a particularly good plan so Dominic decided not to think about it, his steps careful and light. Gideon was doing his best impression of a cat with all the effort he was putting into muffling his usually thunderous stride.

The second story was silent. A long stretch of office rooms lined up in dark halls.

"Stay back from the windows. We don't need to be spotted by any men in the courtyard or downstairs." Dominic whispered.

No battle had ever felt so tense. Dominic longed for the roar of men and the lightning sharp clash of metal. The hush of sneaking through a dark building made his heart pound so loud in his ears he almost thought it was the sound of footsteps following them. He waited for the charge of guards running up to meet them, shouts alerting each other to the intrusion. It would be better to fight than to wait and fear being discovered.

"Finley, follow Gideon. I'll keep an eye behind us and help Gideon take care of the guards downstairs. Finley—"

"I'll get her out," he said, nodding, fingers wrapped tight around the lock picks in his hand.

"Quiet every step of the way," Gideon recited with his own nod.

Dominic wondered if Gideon had ever kept his voice lowered while fighting before. Not that he could remember. They rushed down the stairs, fast and silent, and Dominic spotted the shadows of guards coming from around the corner as he headed down the next flight, deep into the building where the cells were.

Gideon was halfway to the ground when the guard at the base of the steps began to turn in his direction. Gideon leapt into the air and onto the man's back and Dominic followed suit as soon as he saw Gideon's arm wrap around the neck of the guard. They landed in a heap on the floor, the guard's neck snapping beneath Gideon just as Dominic caught the second man, smothering his shout and knocking him unconscious with the blunt end of his dagger.

"Guards at either end," Finley whispered, which was useless because there was no chance Gideon's acrobatics hadn't been spotted.

"We'll take care of them, you just find her," Dominic said, he and Gideon running in opposite directions.

They were bellowing at either end of the hall, calling for others and Dominic prayed that their back up was upstairs and out of earshot or the whole damn trip might end up a waste. He saw a flash of pale hair out of the corner of his eye, peeking out of a bundle of cloth on the floor.

"Fin! Here!"

He kept running even as his heart lagged behind, ducking below the swinging sword aimed at his head and knocking the guard flat to his back. Dominic's shoulder jarred at the impact of bone against armor. He caught the hand holding the sword in one of his fists, pinning it to the ground, and then quickly swung with the other. His knuckles screamed as he hit the guard, but he ignored the pain, breath puffing and arm rearing back to land another blow.

Too time consuming, he thought and then he grabbed the guard's head with both hands and slammed it against the ground before he could use the sword. It was not Gideon's satisfying crunch, but it bought him time as the guard's head lolled and allowed Dominic to steal the sword from his hand. He hit the prone man with the blunt end against his temple.

"I have her," Finley said, just as Gideon called out, "They're coming!"

Dominic hauled himself up off the floor, breath catching in his chest, blood pumping and head spinning with the rush of fighting. Then he turned and his heart stopped.

Finley had Lumen up in his arms, her head propped against his shoulder, body hanging limp and thin in his hold. Her eyes were open but they looked glazed over and Dominic winced as she began to cough, the sound like a knife scratching at glass as it shuddered and wheezed out of her.

"Get her to the inn," Dominic said. "We'll clear the way for you, but—"

Lumen seized in Finley's arms and Dominic could read the terror on his face as her back bowed and she shook with uncontrollable, wracking coughs.

"Get her out."

Gideon, whose gaze was fixed on Lumen's head from where he stood on the other side of Finley, turned with a threatening resolution sliding onto his face and charged up the stairs, the sound of swords clashing. Dominic ran to join him. He would lead the way for Finley to the doorway and then he and Gideon would make sure no one followed.

L UMEN SHIVERED IN HIS ARMS AS F INLEY DASHED ACROSS THE
street and back into the alley. He didn't care if they were seen.
He was going to keep running until he got back to the inn they'd
rented the night before and then...

It stacked up in his head. Get her warm and dry. Broth. A
bath. Did he bring enough medicine? The *right* medicine?

She's dying.

It made his feet skid on the icy brick beneath him just to
think the words. They'd starved her, left her to freeze and to
wither and to rot her lungs with mold and wet cold.

He could try every trick he knew and it might not be enough,
not with the way her breath sounded in his ear, rattling and
breaking until sometimes he thought she stopped altogether.
Not with how thin she'd become in the weeks since he'd
seen her.

She shivered again, or maybe it was just a spasm of a cough
and she was too weak to release it now. He had to get her back,
in front of a fire, and put something warm in her belly.

The inn was four blocks away from the jail and for a moment
Finley wondered if that wasn't too close, if he shouldn't keep
going and find somewhere else. But then Gideon and Dominic
wouldn't find them—if they even made it out.

He took Lumen in the back entrance, pressed to his chest
until she was nothing more than a tangle of rags, taking care to
keep out of the hostess' eye as he dashed up the stairs and prayed

the woman hadn't tried to share their room when they'd gone out for the night. They'd paid for it, but that was no promise in some places. A man tottered at the top of the stairs and Finley's heart raced as he leaned forward, eyes narrowing down to slits and brow tangling. And then the man exhaled and Finley realized he was *drunk* not suspicious, and squeezed his way past him.

He pulled the key from his pocket—shifting Lumen in his hold, her legs dangling above the floor—unlocking the door and sighing. It was clean, the hostess had built them a fire, and all their things were just where'd they'd left them.

"Fin?"

It was barely a word, he might have imagined it, but Finley turned his head and found Lumen frowning up at him. Her eyes were bloodshot, their color paler than usual, and there was a wince in her expression that spoke of the pain of *seeing*. It was a feeling he was familiar with, striking him on those old mornings as he came down from the previous night's high.

"It's- it's alright," he answered, watching her head shake. And then she was balled up in his arms hacking and gasping for air.

He pushed inside and locked the door behind them, lowering Lumen to the threadbare rug in front of the fire and quickly peeling her out of the sodden coat she was wrapped in. There was a sweater, frozen and dirty and rank, as well as her ruined dress and shift. Thank Sol *and* Lune for Gideon thinking of stealing that dress of hers so she'd have something to wear that wasn't coated in a month of living in a jail cell.

Lumen collapsed onto the rug, bare skin broken out in goosebumps and covered in dirt and filth, and for a moment it was Finley who couldn't breathe. Dominic and Gideon had said she'd started to waste away after he'd left and the food had become too scarce, but this was...

Heartbreak was closer to the feeling of dying than most people realized. Finley had nearly died one night before his roommate had taken him in hand, and it had been as if his entire being was filling up, growing and swelling, only to collapse in on itself all at once, until it was tighter than a fist and more painful than being stabbed and the thought of the ending was a relief.

Seeing Lumen, her skin so pale and cold it was tinged with blue, her ribs popping out like a giant's fingers wrapped around her chest, the ridges of her spine a set of teeth, it felt like laying in his dormitory bed and knowing that there was relief in an ending if his roommate would just *leave him be*.

There was a pitcher of water on the narrow dresser by the fireplace and it was warmer than the touch of Lumen's skin. Finley set to washing her, her eyes blinking in drowsy acknowledgement as he worked. Halfway through he sat her up, propping her against his chest, and tipped her chin up and lips parted, slowly pouring in clean mouthfuls until she was swallowing on her own.

Lumen turned her head away, twisting in front of him, and Finley grabbed the quilt off the nearest bed, wrapping it around her. She wavered, head tipped back and stared at him in silence for a long stretch.

"What are you doing here?" Her voice was strained and a struggling gasp followed the brief question.

"We're going to take you home," Finley said. "We'll get you well again and then back home."

Her head shook and turned away from him, trembling hands reaching for the water. He helped her drink until he knew it might be too much for her to take so soon, and then finished washing her. Lumen's eyes watched the fire, occasionally falling shut, body swaying with sleep. He finished dressing her—the dark blue, velvet dress nearly sliding off her shoulders even after he'd laced it as tight as it could be—and wrapped her in the quilt, tucked beneath another layer of blankets.

Finley stood and made his way to the door to fetch broth and hot water to steep herbs that might help fight the infection in her lungs, when it opened. Gideon barreled into the small room, head bleeding but otherwise fine, and Finley sighed so deeply he bent straight over with relief. Dominic remained in the doorway, eyes fixed to where Lumen slept, Gideon sitting at her side and making the bed creak.

"What do you need?" Dominic asked.

"Broth, not too rich. A hot kettle. And she's going to need more warm clothes, better layers, if we're going to travel with her soon."

How soon? he wanted to ask. He needed time. *Lumen* needed time.

"They didn't get a chance to raise the alarm at the jail but we should leave before the next shift arrives."

Before the sun rose then. Finley glanced at Lumen on the bed, watched as Gideon reached out to touch her before spotting the blood on his own hands and drawing back.

"It may risk her life if we move her too soon," Finley said.

Dominic paled and turned his face away, staring at the fire for a moment. "It may risk hers and ours if we don't."

FENUGREEK AND PEPPERMINT.

She remembered the flavor from childhood when a cold would strike the Manor and her mother would brew tea pot after tea pot, steeped with so many herbs it made the whole round wing of the house smell like the woods.

Thin fingers held her chin, spooning warm tea between her lips. There was warmth at her back, heavy and shifting with breaths, arms crossed around her stomach. Lumen breathed in and the scent of the stables wrapped around her until the breath caught in her lungs and a coughing fit hit.

"Gid," she rasped.

"Shh, little spirit," he soothed, one arm moving until a hot palm rubbed circles on her back and then to her front to cover her breastbone that rattled with each exhale. "It's alright."

She lost time, coughs turning to gasps until she was too dizzy and lightheaded to breathe and she fell into sleep. When she woke again the tea was replaced with broth, salty and hot, tickling her ragged throat and dulling some of the pain.

It was a nightmarish cycle of its own. The heat surrounding her, the constant interruption of sleep as Finley's voice coaxed her to drink more, one foggy instance of having too many men trying all at once to help her relieve herself.

"How much time do we have?" Finley asked.

Lumen wanted to beg him to leave her be.

"An hour, no more than two." She knew that voice. *Dominic.* She turned on the bed, still wrapped up in Gideon's scorching hold, and tried to thrash in his direction but the movement was too much effort.

"Get more of that broth in something we can carry. We'll let her sleep for now."

GIDEON'S HORSE crunched through the underbrush, breaths puffing clouds ahead of them. Lumen was silent against his chest, cocooned inside the quilt stolen from the inn. The coughing fits stopped before they were out of the city and only her breaths, warming the skin over his heart, reassured him that she was still with them.

His poor sweet spirit, down to bones, hair thin and loose on her head, eyes barely seeing when she could keep them open.

Stalor used many arguments to justify their war. Oshain had the best crop lands and the closest port to the peak countries and they taxed exports too high. The country was run by aristocracy rather than by its people. A country unwilling to conquer was willing to be conquered.

Gideon fought Stalor's battles because he was good at it and because he was trained for it and because he enjoyed himself. He had Dominic and Finley at his side and there were always women and the army paid for the ale. Until Lumen was locked in an Oshain cell he'd never really hated the country, its leaders, their people. He hated them now and he wanted to take the woman pressed against him far, far away from the country and its border, to somewhere she would be safe.

"We're nearly to the line," Dominic said, voice lowered. "Keep your eye out for scouts. Gideon, you ride like hell if they spot us."

"Just a little further," Gideon whispered, the bundle of woman and blanket tucked against him. "We'll get to the village, have you well again soon."

And then?

She left you, he reminded himself. That was alright though. He blamed Dominic for her leaving.

Would she want to return home to her Manor or leave with him for somewhere new? Maybe they could go south to his old haunts. Or maybe down past the desert lands to the farthest port. He met a man once who said there were ships sailing out to explore for new lands. If Lumen wanted to forget this place they could take her silver and search for an adventure together.

She tensed against his chest and Gideon fisted the reins in one hand, wrapping his arm around to brace her for the coughs preparing to tear out of her chest. Finley trotted his horse closer, passing the flask of broth to Gideon. He tipped Lumen back in his arms, finding her silver eyes open and staring widely up at him, startled and still.

Gideon smiled at the sight of those eyes. "Drink a bit of this, little spirit," he coaxed, tipping the lip of the flask to her mouth.

She took a sip and Gideon lowered his head to press a kiss to her hair, pausing as she flinched and jerked in his hold.

She didn't want his touch. He would've jumped off the horse in that moment if he thought she could have held herself upright to ride. All his daydreams of travel dimmed as Lumen turned her head away.

Dominic froze ahead of them and then kicked his horse into motion. "They've spotted us. Gid, go!"

Gideon covered the flask, squeezing his legs around his horse's ribs and his arm tight around Lumen. He tucked the flask between them and caught the reins before they slid away, hunching forward as his ride picked up speed.

"Hold tight," he murmured in Lumen's ear, thoughts narrowing through the woods ahead of them as Dominic and Finley turned away to give him time to escape.

Lumen's fists curled into his shirt, breaths hitching unevenly against his skin.

He would get her across the line, back to the village, and everything that happened after that would be up to her.

Lumen squeezed her eyes shut, face pressed to Gideon's chest, body jarring painfully in the saddle as they galloped through the woods.

Dominic was shouting but his voice was distant, quiet beneath the pound of Gideon's heart, the crash of hooves against twigs and snow and leaves, the rush of wind passing.

"Almost there," Gideon grunted and there was a clutter of voices at their back, too many to make out who was who.

"Stop," Lumen whispered but her words were only air, voice buried beneath sickness.

She squeezed and tugged at Gideon's shirt and he answered by holding her closer. He thought she was scared. Was she?

No.

It didn't matter. Here or there.

She'd spent her life in the Manor trying to pretend the war didn't exist even as it ate up one family member after another. Fenn Manor wasn't her home now, it was only a matter of time before Stalor came to eat it up too.

Gideon whooped and the horse jumped before settling, still racing through the woods.

"We're over the line, little spirit. You're safe now."

Lumen sighed and let Gideon nuzzle against the top of her head. She wasn't safe and it didn't matter. Here or there, it didn't matter.

Lumen startled at the sound of a door creaking open as it interrupted her dreaming of the cell in Oshain, boarded up and sealed around her. She forced her eyes open to the foggy vision of a tall, narrow shadow crossing a small stretch of space to a fireplace. Steam spit and clouded as the man poured water into the iron pot hanging over the flames. Lumen reached her hand up to rub the grit from her eyes and the figure spun to face her.

"You're awake."

Finley.

She flinched, wanting to roll away, but feeling her entire body protest weakly at the thought. Finley rushed to her as she released a small moan, his hands grasping at her shoulders and helping pull her upright.

"I went back to the Manor and grabbed some of your mother's notebooks," Finley said, charging into the words as if he was continuing a conversation already started. "Found everything she'd written on lung ailments. I thought dry air would help but she says damp and warm is better. This is the least drafty room we could find in the village and I've been keeping it humid…"

His words trailed off as her eyes widened, raising one of her hands and setting it to his lips to still their rattling.

The room was small and there was a window on the far side, a small table and two chairs waiting there. There was a building visible out the window, across the road, high peaked roofs trimmed in crumbling curls of wood. She was in the old village she and Oliver had passed on their way. She looked back to Finley and found his gaze scanning her. When she pulled her hand away, he caught it with his.

"Why?" she asked.

Finley's eyes darkened, shoulders hunching up around his ears, his fingers gripping tight around hers.

"You were right," he said and her brow furrowed. "I didn't know what I would do if Dominic told me to give you up because I hadn't let myself believe you were really mine. But I *do* now, Lumen—"

"Not that," she said and he made a small choking noise, swallowing a speech he'd been brewing and staring back at her. "Why did you drag me back here?"

Finley's jaw dropped and he drew back, releasing her hand and letting it fall to the mattress. He swallowed twice before speaking. "Colin told us about the cell. That you were ill."

Lumen turned to stare at the wall in front of her, trying to sort through her feelings. Except there were none. Her body was weak, her head was as heavy as a brick, her lungs burnt, but anything else, any emotion, was smothered.

"I'm not yours," she said. "Or Dominic's. Or Gideon's."

"I know."

"You should have left me there."

The war waged in her veins, in her chest, the scales tipping back and forth in a dance of whether or not she would heal, would be well again, would live. She didn't care. No, that was a lie. There had been peace that night with her goddess. She was ready to die. Living was a painful mess that she'd thought she rid herself of.

Finley pushed himself away from her with the same urgency that he'd rushed to her side. "I'll send Gideon up with some tea."

Lumen waited for Gideon, expected him to come and try to coax and tease and cajole her back to life.

He came in gently, tea steaming in a beer mug, cupped between his hands like it was something precious. There was a cut stitched shut along his jaw and a bandage wrapped around one hand like a mitten. Concern sparked at the back of her head but the rest remained buried under exhaustion and a low simmer of resentment. Memories of Gideon tangled in with the others, polluting his sweetness. He was the best of the lot. Of all of them, she thought he would be the hardest to convince to let her go, his focus so determined on keeping her.

Gideon perched on the edge of the bed, leaving room between them in a way Finley hadn't bothered. He passed the mug into her hands on her lap, waiting until her hold was steady.

"Would you like me to stay or go?" he asked and even his usual rumble was softened.

She didn't know the answer so she nodded at his jaw. "When did that happen?"

His mouth flicked with an attempt at a smile and then he winced and relaxed again. Was the injury the reason he seemed subdued?

"Two days ago, on the battlefield."

"There's been fighting? How long have I been asleep?"

"About a week. You've been in and out with a fever," he said. He leaned forward and then drew himself back again, looking down at his lap. "It's good to see you yourse- well, a bit better."

"Are you angry with me for leaving?"

"No, Lumen," he said with a heavy sigh, his fingers twitching with an urge to reach out. "I understand it. Do you regret leaving?"

She thought of Oliver, and of General Cannary, and the jail cell, and nearly dying. "I'm just here again," she said, tears welling up in her eyes at the thought. She had left and for what? "It was for nothing."

It was probably Gideon who moved first but he wasn't alone, Lumen tucking her face into the warm skin of his neck as his hands soothed down her back, bandages and all. "Let Fin fix you up, little spirit, for all the trouble he's caused. And then whatever choice you make next, whatever you need, I'll do everything I can to help."

He *was* good. She believed that about Gideon, maybe even more than she believed of herself. There wasn't enough of her left to really cry, everything drained out. Gideon seemed to realize that, tucking her back into the bed and putting the mug of tea down on the floor within her reach. He hummed as he pulled the blankets up to her chin, and it was a funny tuneless song as if he weren't really listening to himself, just trying to offer care.

36

There was a knock on the small bedroom door and then it opened immediately. Weeks had passed since she first woke up after being snatched back from Oshain. No one waited for Lumen to answer a knock now because she never answered them.

"I brought you something different this time, Lady."

Lumen sighed, turning away from the small window that looked onto the village street, forcing a smile onto her face. It was always Colin who brought her meals. He was the only one she couldn't bear to refuse and as soon as Finley realized, they'd made him the primary force in her recovery.

"General got oranges sent up from the south," he said, bringing her a long tray and setting it on the table in front of her before helping himself to the open seat.

There was a bowl of thin soup, vegetables, orange peel, and meat floating, and a roll still steaming from the oven, as well as the orange, its wedges opened like a flower. Colin's eyes were fixed on the food, tongue peeking out at the corner of his mouth. It must have smelled wonderful, but something had happened during her recovery and she rarely caught a whiff of anything. Most food tasted dull on her tongue now too.

"Have one," Lumen said, nodding to the orange wedges.

"If you do," Colin answered back so quick she narrowed her eyes, wondering if he'd planned the exchange.

She pulled one up to her lips, watching and waiting for him to mirror her, lightness blooming in her chest. She bit as he did and her eyes widened. The fruit *did* taste good, bright and sharp, scorching down her still raw throat, lingering sweetly on her tongue. Colin hummed and closed his eyes, smile sliding up the corner of his lips.

"Have more," Lumen said, pushing the tray in his direction.

Colin snorted. "There's more downstairs so I'll have my fill later. This one is yours."

Lumen tore the roll open, watching the steam escape like a ghost and then dipped a portion into the soup. The mush in the jail cells and the illness had taken their toll on her teeth and sometimes it hurt to chew. She was waiting for the day the whole mess fell loose at once but Finley had taken a trip back to the Manor, collecting her mother's notes and was busy researching every single remedy for each of her ailments.

"Lady," Colin said, the timid tenor of his name for her drawing her eyes back from the window. "You don't have to go back to the Manor, you know? If you don't want to."

She grabbed another orange slice, picking at the white thread of rind on the inside and peeling it away. "Am I just supposed to stay here instead?" she asked. "What about when the army moves on again?"

Colin shrugged and then his hand darted out, grabbing another slice and popping it in his mouth. He grinned at her, teeth replaced by orange and chomped away at his trick as she laughed.

"You don't have to," he said. "I don't- I just know you can't go back to those people and get put in the cell again."

He looked up from his lap and met her eyes, his gaze watery and full. All of the anger and heartache and choking sadness that vanished in the Oshain prison cell after her night with Mother Lune came crawling back up her throat, strangling her and stinging at her eyes. She turned her head to the narrow open room, the small fire burning, the bed pressed snug between three walls, and waited for her emotions to settle again, back beneath the serene shroud of emptiness that often covered her.

"I won't," she said and Colin relaxed in his chair.

"I'll understand if you can't stay with me, Lady, but please live."

She squeezed her eyes shut but not before a tear escaped. Colin rose from his chair, circling the table, and she was ready for him, snatching him up in her arms and holding him so close it made her muscles burn. He squeezed back just as tight until her ribs ached, the pain a welcome distraction.

THE BACKROOM of the village bar seemed as good a place as any to serve as Dominic's new office. It wasn't well lit, it stank of spilled ale, and he was fairly certain there were rats. But it had a door on it to keep the general populace of his soldiers from badgering him, and there was its relative location to another particular room in the tavern. He could hear Lumen as she moved around in the room above him.

Even at that moment he was half-listening to Gideon's report of Stalor's fresh batch of soldiers who'd arrived in the weeks prior, and half-attending to the sound of the floorboards creaking overhead.

"They're green and they're lively and if they aren't careful they'll get themselves killed, but they're adding some energy to the ranks and with a little more training they'll cut through Oshain," Gideon said.

She was leaving her room, out into the hall, and her descent down the stairs creaked along the left wall. Finley's ear was tipped in that direction too, hands white-knuckled around the arms of his chair. Dominic hadn't seen or spoken to Lumen since bringing her back over the border, but he heard the whispers between Gideon and Finley. She was sick, not just in body, but in spirit, and had prepared herself to die in that cell.

His heart felt like a bird in his chest when he thought too long about it, caged and panicking, determined to break free of his ribs. *She must live.*

He was too deep in his own thoughts—imagining if they'd

been late in making it to Oshain—he lost track of the sound of her steps until the knob of the door was turning. Dominic and Finley stood at the faint rattling sound, chair legs screeching against the stone floor, but it was Gideon who made it there first with two loping steps, his arm extended for Lumen to steady herself as she stepped inside.

She was still too thin, the circles too dark under her eyes. She looked as if someone had wrung her out. But when her eyes flicked up in his direction he felt that same shock running through him, a silver needle pricking on his skin with her stare.

"You're up." Of course she was up, she was standing in front of him.

"Has the- are you—" Finley swallowed. "Are you feeling better?"

"I am breathing easier," Lumen said with a glance at Finley that appeared to pain the man.

"Come sit, little spirit," Gideon said and Dominic ignored the hot spike of jealousy that burnt through him as Gideon's head ducked close to Lumen's and she didn't pull away.

"I've had enough rest for now," she said to him, her free hand briefly brushing over his knuckles. Her chin lifted and Dominic almost smiled, so familiar with the gesture. "I've made a decision."

The air in the room seemed to still, all three men bracing themselves for the coming blow. Dominic wasn't fooling himself. He wasn't getting invited back into this woman's life. Not after everything he'd done.

"We will assist in any way we can," he said, every word feeling like the drag of a knife along his tongue.

Finley was bracing his hands at the back of his chair and before a single word had been spoken from her lips Gideon already looked as if he'd heard the worst news of his life.

"I want you to take me to the Lunar Convent," Lumen said.

The air was pulled from his lungs.

"The silver's not all gone," Gideon whispered.

Lumen shrugged, head shaking faintly. "It isn't about that. Give the silver to Colin, or Inda, Rosie, and Jennie."

Yes, just give the silver to the whores, a nasty part of his head sniped and he pushed the thought away.

"Don't go back to them, little spirit," Gideon whispered.

Lumen's shoulders sagged and she turned to him. "The Convent provides sanctuary. I'll be safe and I'll... I'll live in Her faith."

Dominic brought his knuckles up to his mouth to cover his grimace. He liked religion less than ever, partly because Lumen was right. The Convent would protect her far better than he could. Stalor fought under Sol's colors but there were active Lunar temples even in the south. If the war continued north there might be a demand on their silver, but not on the devotees.

"It's in the east, at the base of the mountain range along the coast," she said.

"You might not be ready to travel," Finley said but Dominic knew he was scrambling for an excuse, his voice too tight, eyes wide.

"I will be," she said.

That same part of him, the one he wished he could bury in her presence, wanted to reach out and shake her shoulders for being so calm. So impossibly still, all her expression and feeling hidden too deep for him to read.

"We'll need to buy time so that we can leave with you," Dominic said, ignoring the expressions of betrayal on his friend's faces.

"Someone else could take me," she said, a crease appearing between her eyebrows.

"No," they all said at once.

"No, I don't trust anyone else not to just hoof you over the line again," Dominic continued, staring down at the table in front of him. "We'll be on the battlefield in two days. We can buy a ceasefire to cover our travels then," he said.

Lumen nodded. Already she was drooping, a weary lean into Gideon's side. Finley would have to use every trick in her mother's books before they left again, but Dominic believed she'd make it to the Convent. And they would care for her there, he was certain of that much. He may not know all of the Lunars' secrets but Lumen was made in their Mother's image. If he could see that, so would the priestesses.

"Walk me up," she murmured to Gideon.

They turned together to the door, Gideon so careful not to rush or bump her it looked as if he was escorting a queen. Finley moved the front of his chair and collapsed into the seat as the door shut behind them.

"I should never have left."

Dominic's teeth ground together and that nasty voice in his head agreed with Finley. Except he was learning to ignore that voice altogether. "We both know that's not where the problems began."

"What are we going to be once she's gone?" Finley asked, face pale as he stared at Dominic.

"An army."

Finley frowned, gaze turning dark. "Just as before then."

Dominic sighed, all the resolve he'd offered Lumen disintegrating as he sat down, body too heavy to hold upright. "I don't know, Finley. But we owe her this at least."

GIDEON SHUFFLED in the doorway as Lumen lowered herself back onto the bed. She was sick of being weary and worn out. Always too tired to get up and *do something* with herself but never tired enough to sleep deeply.

"I should let you rest," he mumbled, forehead creased with worry.

"Ask me, Gid," she said.

He looked up, dark eyes full of pleading, and crossed to her side, kneeling on the floor in front of her. "We could leave here, Lumen. I'd keep you safe and we'd go… somewhere else. Be new people. It doesn't have to be a choice of Stalor or Oshain if you're sick of 'em both."

The words lightened his face and she could see the excitement written there. Gideon, who had known war for so many years, would give it up for the unknown with her. It was a promise in his voice. Things would be different and different would be better.

Except there was nothing inside of her, no echo of his excitement or happiness. She tried to picture the adventure he imagined and she came up blank.

"Let me be yours, little spirit," he whispered, hands taking hers in a gentle, warm grip.

The only answer was a weak crack in her chest. "I can't," she said. She pulled a hand free, reaching up to to his falling expression. "I'm so tired, Gideon. I'm tired and I'm angry."

"I know." He nodded, sitting on his heels, eyes landing on her knees.

"Yes. But not at you. At myself. And… and them. I don't want to *be* anyone. And if I'm not a person then I can't belong to anyone, and no one can belong to me." She smoothed her fingertips over his forehead. "If I go to the Convent I will be a vessel for Lune and that suits me."

Gideon huffed, a watery, teary sound. He lifted her hand to kiss her palm and she missed the memory of the way that kiss would stir in her belly and make her blood pump faster.

"Then that's where we'll take you," he said, nodding weakly.

LUMEN WAS a little startled by the sight of the full street, soldiers and women waiting outside of the tavern with the horses. She paused in the doorway, Gideon's hand steadying her at her back as she scanned the faces. It reminded her of the day the army arrived at Fenn Manor, men staring at her as she stood alone in her doorway.

There was no laughter, no sly eyes, no sorrow or apology. Dominic brushed against her shoulder, ignoring the crowd and heading to his horse and even then the stares didn't turn from her. Lumen let Gideon nudge her back into motion, smiling at Inda who was curled against her lovers chest, and realized what those looks meant. It was acceptance. Somewhere in the months of the Manor, of her rescue and recovery, Lumen had become part of a strange kind of community. The men came to bid her farewell in a wordless, but kind way.

Colin met her at Gideon's enormous horse and Lumen's heart was in her throat, squeezing tears up to her eyes. His face was upturned, already broader than it had been that first conversation in the kitchen, his shoulders inches higher.

"Will you ride with us?" Lumen forced out. And when they arrived to the Convent, could she ferret him inside to stay with her?

"Someone better stay and keep an eye on this lot," Colin said with a jerky nod back at the crowd.

Lumen's laugh was watery as she crouched down, the change in height leaving her smiling up at him. Was she making the right choice in leaving? It was hard to tell as she tried to memorize his face, wishing she could be present to watch it change and grow.

"You go and be well and happy, Lady," Colin said, voice hoarse, eyes shining.

Happy sounded like an impossible word.

"Will you try and take care of yourself the way I would care for you?" she asked in a whisper.

Colin blinked rapidly but Lumen let the tears fall from her own eyes. He stepped forward and wrapped thin arms around her shoulder, pressing his face into her hair.

"No one could do that so well as you," he answered, a little whine in the words breaking her heart over and over again. "Will you come back if they don't care for you as I would?"

"Yes," she answered, holding him tight and suspecting that she might be lying.

Colin nodded, kissing her cheek fierce and swiftly, and then pulled himself away. Gideon was there at her side, helping her rise as she reached for him, brushing his own scarf over her cheeks before lifting her up into his saddle. Colin stepped back and Lumen was both relieved and jealous to see Jennie bundle him closer and let him hide his red eyes against her hip. Gideon followed her up onto the horse, body framing hers with immediate warmth.

"We'll be back before the reprieve is up," Dominic announced to his army before clucking at his horse and setting into motion.

Lumen took one of Gideon's arms and wrapped it around her middle to keep herself from jumping down as they rode away from the village.

SHE DIDN'T REMEMBER MUCH of the escape out of Oshain, but she was certain their return was less chaotic. Long hours of riding in front of Gideon in silence, the moods of the men who escorted her heavy and solemn. They crossed the new line without her realizing, keeping east and out of either army's eyes.

Winter was taking an early pause and the snow was melting in patches, the woods and fields they travelled through muddy and barren. The mountains were draped in fog so thick they'd already passed the road that lead to the Convent before rounding a curve and spotting it behind them.

It was an odd sort of building, built of the gray quartz stone mined from the mountains, angles in every direction and rooms stacked on top of one another to a round peaked tower. A river ran in front of the Convent, still warm from bubbling up out of the underground spring, the bridge crossing over was wide and open. The windows glittered from inside, blue and silver panes showing the changing faces of Lune around the tower, burning candles turning into the light of stars.

"Have you been before?" Gideon asked in her ear.

She shook her head. "My mother spent many years here as a girl before deciding to return home and marry. She told me about the priestesses and their work pulling silver from the mountains."

Dominic's head whipped in her direction. "That's where the silver comes from? Here? The Convent?"

"The holy silver. Men mine it for sale farther north," she said.

A bell rang from inside the cluster of buildings. "Will you tell your army?"

"No," Dominic said, eyes wide. "I brought you here for your safety, Lady Fenn. I'm not about to do anything to risk that promise."

She locked eyes with him and found some of his surly fight missing. He was a version of himself similar to the one she knew from her nights in bed with him, but there was more openness in his gaze.

The front door opened as they finished crossing the bridge, revealing a young woman dressed in soft novice blue. "What are *you* doing here?" she asked, green eyes fixed in horror on Dominic.

It was Imogen Mallen, the last lady before Lumen to have received Dominic's particular brand of attention. Lumen almost could have laughed at the twist of queasy shock on every man's expression.

A priestess in soft dove gray appeared behind Imogen. "Inside please, sister."

Imogen hesitated, head turning between Dominic and the priestess, eyes landing briefly on Lumen and narrowing in vague recognition. The priestess nudged the younger woman inside and then clasped her hands over her stomach, peaceful and yet a clear obstruction to the men stepping inside.

"This young woman needs sanctuary," Dominic said.

The priestess pursed her lips, eyes flicking over the men instead, focused in suspicion. She was a tall woman, broad shouldered and strong bodied. She had smooth, ageless skin, features as pale as Lumen's own.

"I am Alana Fenn's daughter," Lumen said, taking the woman's attention. "Lumen Fenn."

Her eyes lit up. "Come here, sister Fenn."

Lumen felt the first bright moment of relief in months at the endearment. She slid down from Gideon's saddle with his help, ignoring the way he followed close at her back as if the priestess might strike out and he was ready to protect her. She passed between Dominic and Finley's horses, felt their eyes on her face, and then put them behind her.

The priestess raised a hand up to Lumen's chin, calloused fingers gentle along her jaw, storm cloud eyes studying her in a slow, thorough, stare. "She has touched you," the priestess said, face relaxing in open awe.

Lumen couldn't speak, her throat tied up, eyes blurring as they filled. She nodded instead.

"Yes, she is one of the Mother's children. She'll be safe here," the priestess said to Dominic.

Gideon's fingers clutched at the back of her coat and then loosened as she turned to him. His eyes were filled and shining too but he forced a wobbling grin on his face for her.

"Be well, little spirit."

Lumen rose to her toes, cupping his face in her hand, and pressed a soft brief kiss to his cheek. "No stitches," she whispered, smiling at his answering puff of laughter.

Gideon's hands clenched harder around her waist as she made to step away and Lumen thought, *this is it, he'll never let me go, just like he said.*

The stubble of his cheek brushed through her hair and a pair of warm lips pressed to her ear. "You ever change your mind, just send word. You're my heartbeat, Lumen."

Lumen closed her eyes against a flood of feeling, the sparkling heat that cascaded against the scars on her cheek, the swell of sweetness in her chest. Because right behind the wave of coaxing emotion came the bruising memories that pushed at her from every side until her lungs were frozen and her heart was near collapse.

A tear hit her cheek—hers or Gideon's, she didn't know—and she forced the feelings down, taking the priestess' outstretched hand that waited behind her.

This was the right place for her. This was the *last* place she had left to turn to. There was no use in wishing Gideon could follow her.

Dominic and Finley sat on their horses, staring at her. Her heart thumped in her chest and she turned away before it could remember how it used to beat for them. Better to forget the whole affair than remember the sweetest parts and try to ignore the worst.

There was no goodbye, just the enveloping warmth as she followed the priestess into the Convent.

EPILOGUE

"High Priestess." Priestess Ellery dipped in a curtsey as her superior joined her at the back of the small meditation chapel.

"Is that the new novice?" High Priestess Wren asked, nodding her head in the direction of the small figure kneeling in front of the statue of Lune in her dark shroud.

"Sister Fenn, she is here every morning and night," Priestess Ellery said. She looked at the High Priestess, watched her cheeks suck with thought as she stared at the young woman, her eyes narrowing. Ellery's heart thrummed in her chest and she whispered, almost afraid to give her own strange thoughts voice. "Do you see it?"

"A shadow hangs around her," the High Priestess said, head tipping.

Ellery sighed, both relieved to be proved right and a little disappointed that the vision wasn't hers alone. "I saw it the day she arrived. It's as if..." Could she say it? Would it be blasphemous?

"As if she wears the Mother's shroud."

Ellery nodded, hands clutched tight over her stomach. She waited, hoping the High Priestess would continue, hoping she would say the thing that Ellery felt certain must be true for the weeks since Lumen Fenn appeared, escorted by the Stone General of all men.

"It's been many years since we have had a New Moon Priestess," the High Priestess mused.

Ellery gasped, even though it was exactly what she guessed herself. "Do we tell the others?"

"Not yet, Priestess," the older woman said, smiling and taking Ellery by the elbow, drawing her back to the door to leave Sister Fenn in the peace of her devotion. "She has only just arrived and is still healing."

Ellery stared over her shoulder as she was lead away, watching that strange shadow shift with every one of the young woman's breaths. She'd never seen anything like it in all her decades of serving Lune. It was as if the Mother wrapped herself around the girl, shrouding and protecting her.

"We will keep our eye on her, Priestess Ellery," the High Priestess said, coaxing her attention away. "She may be good for some of the other novices. A reminder of our Mother's grace."

"It is curious that Westbrook brought her himself," Ellery mused.

High Priestess hummed and frowned. "Yes, and speaking of the man, those two spies of his are back sniffing at the door, looking for the Mallen women."

"Will you let them in?" Ellery asked. She didn't like the Mallen family or the influence they held over some of the recent novices. Their anger polluted Mother Lune's light.

"I'm afraid I must," High Priestess said and a heavy sigh followed. "If it were not our duty to protect women in need, I would find somewhere else to send the lot of them."

Ellery's eyebrows rose high on her face. Those were dark words for the High Priestess. And worse, she was inclined to agree with them.

TO BE CONTINUED...

ALSO BY KATHRYN MOON

COMPLETE READS

The Librarian's Coven Series
Written - Book 1
Warriors - Book 2
Scrivens - Book 3
Ancients - Book 4

Standalones
Good Deeds
Command The Moon
Say Your Prayers - co-write with Crystal Ash

The Sweetverse
Baby + the Late Night Howlers
Lola & the Millionaires - Part One
Lola & the Millionaires - Part Two
Bad Alpha

Sol & Lune
Book 1
Book 2

Inheritance of Hunger Trilogy
The Queen's Line
The Princess's Chosen
The Kingdom's Crown

SERIES IN PROGRESS

ACKNOWLEDGMENTS

I have the most amazing and enormous support team and I genuinely consider myself the luckiest person to know each and every one of these people.

My parents who have supported me in every possible way through this journey. Lindsay, who is essentially family in every way that matters.

My incredible Moongazers, thank you for taking a chance on this book and giving me the time and support to write it, even when I probably should have gone to Summerland!

The A-team: Alicia, who I knew would take this book safely into her heart and who deserves all the best words. Margaret who is a powerhouse of support, and has the best kind of humor. Chloe, who I am going to consistently rely on to show me where I can do better for a story.

Beta babes: Katie, the Jessicas, Sue, HarleyQuinn, and keen-eyed Kristina!

Research and Development - Rachel Lovely Lady Seaman

Miss Meg West, my magical unicorn and kick ass PA for taking me onto your Team Awesome! I still have a book nerd crush on you.

My editor and good friend Sara who took care of this story and who knows my writing probably better even than I do.

Lana Kole, who Alpha'd, brainstormed, listened to me moaning, held my hand, and made me the most beautiful cover for a book I said I wasn't even going to write. I love you lady and I'm so lucky we found each other.

My writing crews, a network that has grown and developed so much recently and left me feeling buoyed and hopeful about all of our futures.

Emma, Waffles, remember that this started as a joke and that you pointed out when it became a real story. Remember that I love you to all the moons and back. You're my fishwife and my hero.

I really appreciate you all for reading this story!

ABOUT THE AUTHOR

Kathryn Moon is a country mouse who has been trying to write reverse harem since The Backstreet Boys had their first album. When her hands aren't busy typing they're probably knitting sweaters or crimping pie crust. She definitely believes in magic.

You can reach her on Facebook, hang out in Kathryn's Moongazers, and contact her at ohkathrynmoon@gmail.com!

www.ingramcontent.com/pod-product-compliance
Lightning Source LLC
Chambersburg PA
CBHW032112310726
48972CB00001B/194